# FIRE MUSIC

*Also by Julia Gray*

**ICE MAGE**

# FIRE
# MUSIC

JULIA GRAY

ORBIT

An *Orbit* Book

First published in Great Britain by Orbit 1999

A CIP catalogue record for this book
is available from the British Library.

ISBN 1 85723 735 8

Typeset by Solidus (Bristol) Ltd, Bristol
Printed and bound in Great Britain by
Mackays of Chatham plc, Chatham, Kent

Orbit
A Division of
Little, Brown and Company (UK)
Brettenham House
Lancaster Place
London WC2E 7EN

*This book is dedicated, with much love,
to Christine and Clive Watts, with many thanks
for their years of friendship and support.
Are there enough battles?*

PART ONE

# Shadows Dreaming

# CHAPTER ONE

'Why won't you talk to me?'

The anguish in Vargo Shaimian's heart made his voice sound cracked and harsh. And yet, of all the various on-lookers, only one truly shared his pain. The villagers had grown accustomed to their guest's eccentric ways and, although they treated him with due reverence, most of them privately referred to him as 'the madman' – and not even Vargo himself would have argued with that description. At that moment, however, he wasn't even aware that anyone was watching him.

'You talked to Andrin once,' he said, his tone caught between despair and accusation. 'And Ysanne – and she hadn't even been born then. Why won't you talk to *me*?'

Vargo wasn't speaking to the villagers but to the clutch of dragon eggs that surrounded him. He moved among them, placing a hand on each in turn, still hoping for a response.

'What do you want of me? You've already taken my music. I don't have anything else to give!'

He sat down abruptly then, his back against one of the massive eggs. Closing his eyes, he leant back until his head rested on the smooth black shell. But even then he felt nothing. The last remnants of a mighty race lay still – cold, hard and utterly impassive.

There were eleven eggs in all, lying within a few paces of each other. They lay near the centre of what had previously been the market square of Corazoncillo, the larger of two villages that shared the small, remote valley in the mountains of northern Tiguafaya. The story of how the eggs had come to be there was already the stuff of legends, but two and a half years had passed since their arrival – and nothing more had happened. Each of the eggs was the size of a wine barrel, and so heavy that it was impossible to move them. Their shells were incredibly strong, and impervious to harm. On one occasion a stranger, who had been driven insane by grief at the loss of his family, had seized a heavy sledgehammer and attacked one of the eggs. The iron head had rebounded from the first blow with such force that the man had staggered away, his arms ringing with pain, and the villagers had dragged him from the square before he had the chance to strike again. The shiny surface of the dragon egg had not even been scratched.

None of this mattered to Vargo now. His disordered thoughts had moved on and he was dreaming, lost in joy and wonder, madness and grief. As always when he was in such a disturbed state of mind, he began to talk to Famara, only occasionally remembering that his old friend was dead.

*I don't know what to do.*

*It's not over yet.*

*I know.* The knowledge weighed heavily upon Vargo's shoulders.

*You're the only one who will be able to understand it all,* his mentor's voice went on.

*Angel knew before I did,* he replied. *We just wouldn't listen. And now everyone knows the truth.*

*But you must be the one to follow the path.*

*I've tried!* he responded bitterly. Then he added aloud, 'I don't know where else to go.'

The onlookers, who had begun to lose interest during the long silence, grew attentive again now, whispering among themselves. Several villagers glanced at the madman's companion, who stood with them but a little apart, her pretty face a mask of concern. Vargo, lost among his ghosts, knew nothing of this.

*Everywhere's the same in the mirror,* Famara quoted.

Vargo was vaguely aware that his memory was playing tricks on him. Those had been his own words, not hers, and if she was trying to tell him something, then he had no idea what it was.

*What does that mean?*

Famara did not reply and, for once, he could not imagine what her answer would have been. Vargo's melancholy deepened. There were times when he wished Famara had left him trapped within the mirror lake. Compared to his present torment, this gnawing sense of futility, the power-lessness of that timeless imprisonment appeared a seductive alternative. There might have been peace in true madness. The only other way to such peace would be in death – and that too was denied him.

Music had once been the core of Vargo's existence, and although that had been taken from him, he did not begrudge the price he had had to pay in order to follow his destined path. His art had been replaced by a new purpose, one that was much more important. The problem was that, no matter how hard he tried, he had been unable to come any closer to realizing that purpose. Unless he did, his willing sacrifice would ultimately have been in vain. So would Famara's – and she had given her *life.* Fate seemed to be mocking him, but he had no choice but to go on, to keep trying.

*You have to help me, Famara. I can't do this alone.*

*Nothing is ever that simple, Vargo*, she replied tetchily. *You can't give up. Too much depends on you.*

*I'm sorry*, he said, ashamed of his weakness.

He saw her smile then, her pale grey eyes bright as they had always been, even at the end.

*Never stop dreaming, Vargo. Never. Dreamers are the only true realists.*

She faded from his mind then, and Vargo let her go. Her advice had left him none the wiser but, as always, her presence had helped calm his mental turmoil. He opened his eyes, and looked around at the clutch of giant eggs. The embryonic creatures inside those impregnable shells were sleeping still, their dreams a mystery he could not solve. Ysanne had been the first to glimpse those dreams, when she too was still unborn. But Ico's daughter had eventually arrived in the world, while the dragons continued to wait, all life concealed within the black shields. No one had any idea when they were due to hatch.

They danced once, Vargo thought, remembering. But there's no music any more.

And then his mind went spinning off in another direction. As always, thinking of Ico filled him with a rush of conflicting emotions, emotions he could never even hope to analyze fully. She haunted him. But, unlike Famara, Ico was very much alive. Her eyes . . .

Vargo forced himself to push the thought aside, and stared once more at the dark shapes around him.

*I've touched the bones of your ancestors*, he told them silently. *Their* spirits talked to me. Why won't you?

It had been in that dusty crater two and a half years ago that so much had become agonizingly clear; the lies of history, the corruption those lies had spawned, and what needed to be done to redeem the future. It had been there that Vargo had taken the first faltering steps along the path that now seemed to be leading nowhere.

Twisting round, he deliberately placed both hands flat on the surface of the egg and willed himself to see inside, to dream. He was met by an implacable wall of silence, a darkness so vast it had no boundaries. Beside this inert blankness the lofty disdain that he had sensed from the long-dead bones would have seemed a positively vibrant response. Here there was nothing. Nothing at all.

He persevered until his hands grew cold and his bones ached, but still there was not even a hint of acknowledgement. Eventually he withdrew, feeling cramped, breathless and sick, having achieved nothing. He swore under his breath as he massaged his fingers back to life, cursing the eggs, their intransigence, his own impotence and the injustices of life in general. His failure was disheartening, and yet he could not bring himself to believe either that his self-appointed task was really hopeless – or that the dragon eggs were actually dead. That possibility had been raised many times, but Vargo refused to accept that such an ancient race could pass into extinction in so inglorious a manner. Why would the spirits have helped Andrin and Ico rescue the eggs from the eruption at Tisaloya if they were never going to hatch? It made no sense. But then, very little in Vargo's life seemed to make sense any more.

In answer to an unspoken summons, he glanced around then and found himself looking at the only part of his existence that *did* make sense. Cat was still waiting for him.

The day was fading towards dusk, the sky the rich colour of lapis lazuli. Vargo had not realized until now just how long he had been lost to the real world. Although the villagers had lost interest in his silent vigil and had gone about their business, Cat was still there, as she always was, the most faithful of companions. Their eyes met and she smiled at him, though he could see the concern on her face. She did not have to ask how he had fared – the weariness in his expression told her all she needed to know.

'Come and get something to eat!' she called. 'You've done enough for today.'

Vargo nodded, but did not move.

'Do you need help?' she asked, walking forward a few paces.

'No.' He knew that Cat, like most people, was reluctant to approach the eggs too closely. She would come to his side if necessary, would even risk touching one of the shells if he asked her to, but there was no need. Get up! he ordered his own limbs, and they responded slowly and painfully, each muscle feeling knotted and sore. As he began to hobble away from the eggs, Cat came towards him, her hands out-stretched in welcome. Then a rapid fluttering of wings announced the arrival of another of Vargo's companions, and Ero came dipping and dancing towards them like an enormous, exotic butterfly, swooping down to his link with a cry of greeting.

The hoopoe alighted on top of one of the eggs, then tried in vain to get his balance, his short legs slipping and sliding as his talons failed to gain any purchase on the glass-like surface. After a few moments of this comic dance, the bird exploded back into the air with a scream of indignation. Landing on secure ground near by, he ruffled his feathers, folded his black and white striped wings and bobbed his tail. Then he fanned his crest proudly, as if to reassure himself – and anyone who might be watching – that he was still beautiful.

Vargo and Cat watched this performance with a mixture of amusement and genuine fondness. It was hard to remain in low spirits when Ero was around.

The hoopoe glanced disdainfully at the eggs, then raised his curved bill and looked directly at Vargo, who burst out laughing.

'What did he say?' Cat asked. Unlike many of their friends, she had not been chosen by one of the birds, and envied Vargo his telepathic link with Ero.

'He says it's no wonder these eggs aren't hatching,' Vargo reported, still smiling. 'No one could ever sit on them long enough to keep them warm.'

# CHAPTER TWO

As soon as Ico opened her mouth she knew that arranging this meeting had been a mistake.

'Ambassador Kudrak, welcome.'

She smiled warmly as her guest was ushered into the room.

'Thank you, Madam President.'

Kudrak bowed stiffly, but his expression remained carefully neutral and his eyes were as cold as a winter's sky. More telling still was the slight stress he had placed on the first part of Ico's title. The ambassador was obviously not used to dealing with a woman in a position of power.

He's not alone in that, Ico thought ruefully. A few years ago the people of Tiguafaya would never have believed that a woman might become their President. Since her election over two years ago, one of her major challenges had been to try to overcome old prejudices.

'May I offer you some refreshment?'

'No. Thank you.'

'I trust your accommodations are satisfactory,' she went on, as they took their seats.

'Perfectly,' the ambassador replied with a touch of impatience.

So much for politeness and hospitality, Ico thought. It was obvious by now that Kudrak was not going to make this easy for her. The imperial envoy probably believed that it was ridiculous, possibly even insulting, for a woman – any woman – to lead an entire nation. In spite of the annoyance provoked by such an attitude, Ico found that she could sympathize with him in some ways. In his eyes not only was she the wrong sex but, at barely twenty-one years old, she was considerably less than half his age. Those who knew her well acknowledged that she was wise beyond her years, but all the ambassador had to judge her by was her admittedly outlandish reputation.

The transition from rebel leader to head of state had been made many times during the course of the world's history, but rarely had it happened with such speed. On top of that, several well-known facts contributed to the President's notoriety. Ico's daughter had been born before she had married the child's father; she had refused to accept more than a pittance as her presidential salary; and she espoused magic as an essential part of her people's heritage. In short, there was hardly a convention she had not flouted. In addition, if even half the tales about her involvement in the dramatic events that had engulfed Tiguafaya two and a half years ago were true, then an outsider might very well conclude that she was either dangerous or quite mad. In fact, the storytellers' fanciful embellishments had been a constant source of embarrassment to Ico. The truth had been remarkable enough.

'May I speak plainly, Ambassador?' she asked, hoping that her misgivings were unfounded.

'There would be no point to this meeting if we were to do otherwise,' Kudrak replied evenly.

Ico ignored the irony of such a statement coming from the lips of a career diplomat, and tried to get the measure of the man. He was of slight build but carried himself confidently, with an air of knowing his own worth. His clothes were of excellent quality without being ostentatious, and his hair and beard were neatly trimmed. The night before, at the formal banquet that had welcomed his party to Teguise, Tiguafaya's capital, he had presented himself with a quiet dignity, eating and drinking sparingly. He had said little, and had held himself aloof from what had been a generally enjoyable evening. Ico had hoped that he would lose some of his reserve once he was no longer on public display, but if anything his manner was even cooler now than it had been in the grandiose surroundings of the great marble hall.

'The Emperor's suggestion that he send his envoy to Teguise came at a welcome time,' Ico began carefully. 'I have long believed that the restoration of cordial relations between our two peoples was overdue.'

Kudrak nodded in acknowledgement but said nothing.

'Don't you agree?' Ico pressed gently, wanting to establish some common ground at the start of their exchange.

'In an ideal world, that would be desirable, yes,' he conceded eventually.

Who lives in an ideal world? Ico thought, trying not to let her rising dismay show on her face. If they couldn't agree on this simple objective, what hope was there for anything more significant?

'Then we must work towards that end,' she said determinedly. 'Are you prepared to help me in that?'

The ambassador regarded her steadily, his elegant hands folded in his lap.

'I think you may be under some misapprehension about the purpose of my visit.'

'Then perhaps you can enlighten me,' Ico responded, more sharply than she had intended.

'My instructions, which come directly from the Imperial Council at the High Court, are to ascertain the truth concerning various rumours emanating from Tiguafaya, and then to pass on to your government a message from the Emperor himself.'

'I see. May I know what the Emperor's message is?'

'Its contents will depend upon my discoveries,' Kudrak answered coolly.

Ico fought to keep her rising anger under control. Since she had become the first Tiguafayan president to be elected by representatives of all the country's people – and not just the privileged few – her temper had proved to be one of her biggest disadvantages. She had never suffered fools gladly, but the huge weight of responsibility had made her even more exacting in her judgement of those around her. In the upheaval that had followed the revolutionary change of government, many people's lives had been disrupted and her popularity had fallen in some quarters. Although that in itself did not concern her, there were times when she had wondered whether their land would ever emerge from chaos. The inevitable compromises she had been forced to accept – realism overruling idealism – had troubled both her and some of her closest allies. Sweeping away the widespread corruption of the previous regime had been a painful and laborious process, but it had been absolutely necessary. Similarly, the army had had to be persuaded to change allegiance. By and large, the military had been loyal to Ico's predecessor, Tias Kantrowe, and because he had been her deadly enemy, many conflicts had arisen, even after he had fled into exile.

Eventually, through hard work and determination, Tiguafaya had begun to claw its way back to peace and prosperity. Even so, one challenge – the greatest of them all – still had to be met, and it was about this that Ico had hoped to speak to the ambassador. However, Kudrak evidently had a very different agenda and she altered her plans accordingly.

'Then I will do my best to answer all your questions fully,' she said, still striving to be polite. 'Giving too much credence to rumours can be dangerous, and I hope I can set your mind at rest. What do you want to know?'

Kudrak smiled then, for the first time – but it was a token effort, and did not reach his eyes.

'I am forgetting my manners, Madam President. I am your guest, and you obviously have your own reasons for arranging this meeting. I would prefer to hear what *you* have to say, before embarking on my own enquiries. Ladies first, as they say.'

'I would rather you granted me such a courtesy because of my position, rather than my sex,' Ico commented mildly. 'I *am* President of Tiguafaya, after all. Please disregard the fact that I am also a woman.'

'That will be difficult.'

Ico fought back a sigh.

'May I ask why?'

'I have never before had occasion to discuss matters of state with such an attractive counterpart.'

You condescending old crab, Ico thought venomously. Am I supposed to be delighted by such flattery? She was not about to be drawn into a discussion either of the role of women in society or of her own position in particular. There were more important matters at hand. The ambassador's obtuse approach had surprised her, but he had asked her to speak, for whatever reason, and now he would have to listen to what she had to say. Doing her best to hide her irritation, Ico began the speech she had mentally rehearsed so many times.

'First and foremost, I want to ask for your help.'

If Kudrak was surprised by this blunt statement, it did not show on his face.

'As I'm sure you're aware,' Ico went on, 'the mountains of Tiguafaya are becoming restless.'

A spark of interest glowed deep within the envoy's eyes, but when he spoke his voice was as calm as ever.

'Surely that is simply a fact of nature. Your people chose to live among the volcanoes, after all.'

Ico nodded in agreement, although she would have put it slightly differently. When, centuries earlier, the first settlers had travelled south from the Empire to the unexplored wilderness that was later to be named Tiguafaya, they had been fleeing from religious persecution. Their choice had been one of necessity. The fact that the awesome landscape of the firelands had not discouraged them was testament to their determination.

'That's true,' Ico conceded. 'We accepted the perils of our home and adapted to them, but not all of nature's ways are known to us. One of them was discovered only recently – because it was failing. If we can revive it, we have a chance to restore the balance to this land, and that's why I'm asking for the Empire's help.'

'And what aspect of nature does this concern?'

'Fireworms.'

For the first time the ambassador's expression revealed a flicker of true emotion, but it vanished so quickly that Ico could not tell whether it had reflected anger, surprise or revulsion.

'The creatures known as dragon-spawn?' he asked.

'That's a misnomer,' Ico replied. 'There is, or rather there *was*, a link between the fireworms and the dragons, but they were two quite different species.'

'What link?' Kudrak asked sceptically.

'The fireworms were the dragons' servants. They used to—'

'How do you know this?' he cut in, growing quite animated now.

Ico hesitated. This was always going to be the most difficult part of the explanation.

'There are no dragons alive in Tiguafaya at present, but their spirits survive. Two people have spoken to them, on separate occasions, and each learned the same thing.'

'One of these people was Vargo Shaimian?'

'Yes,' Ico replied, shocked that the rumours that had reached the Empire were so detailed.

'It is said that he is mad. Can you trust the word of such a man?'

'He's not mad,' she protested, with more conviction than she actually felt. 'And even if he were, he wouldn't lie about such a thing.'

Kudrak brushed this argument aside with a sweep of his hand.

'Who is the other person?'

Ico stared at him levelly before replying.

'Me.'

For a moment the ambassador became very still, his earlier agitation disappearing. In the silence, Ico found herself remembering her unnerving encounter with the unseen spirits. She had been standing on the tiny island rock known as Elva, the oracle that was lost to them all now, and the dragons' initial indifference to the fate of mankind had been chilling. That they had eventually changed their minds and helped her was due to the actions of others, but in the process she had learnt the truth. *The fireworms are your servants?* she had guessed. *They were once*, had been the ominous reply.

Seeing what she took to be Kudrak's confusion, she hurried to explain.

'For centuries the work the fireworms did went unseen, but when the dragons were no longer there to guide them, things began to go wrong. In the minds of men the dragons became objects of fear—'

'They are the messengers of the gods,' the ambassador said. 'It is right that they should inspire fear.' His voice was quiet but intense.

'But fear is often based on ignorance, and that can so easily turn to hate,' Ico countered. 'It was that which corrupted—'

'This is of no concern to me,' Kudrak cut in sharply.

'It will be, because the Empire might be in danger too.'

'What?' he exploded, rising to his feet. 'Are you threatening us?' He sounded incredulous and outraged at the same time.

'No, not at all. The threat comes from elsewhere – and I am offering co-operation so that we may work together to avert it.' Ico stayed in her seat, forcing herself to remain calm.

'Explain,' Kudrak demanded.

'The fireworms—' she began.

'Fireworms?' he interrupted again. 'Are you telling me that these creatures pose a threat to the Empire?'

'Not directly, no,' she replied. 'Sit down, Ambassador, and I'll explain.'

Kudrak glared at her as if he were about to respond angrily, but she met his gaze impassively and in the end, with a nod of his head that told of the reluctant beginnings of respect, he did as she asked.

'The fireworms lived underground, in the boiling mud and lava streams,' Ico began again. 'They did their masters' bidding by absorbing and releasing heat, thus controlling the pressures in the volcanic fields and making the whole place more stable. By preventing catastrophic eruptions and diverting certain lava flows, they made life more convenient for the dragons – and, coincidentally, safer for us. But after the last dragons died out the worms were left direction-less. They performed their duties instinctively for a time but eventually, as people began to think of the dragons as evil, the sickness spread to the worms. They changed then, learning to fly above ground, and became the murderous creatures we know. We were forced to fight them, and we managed to kill all but a few. What we hadn't realized was that this has left the firelands unprotected. During the last few years earthquakes and eruptions have become more frequent, and it's our belief that, unless we do some-thing about it, there will soon be an explosion so great that all Tiguafaya may be destroyed.'

'Even if what you say is true,' the ambassador said, cool again now, 'why should this concern the Empire?'

Ico found the doubt in his voice even more discouraging than his callous disregard for the fate of her country.

'Such a series of eruptions would inevitably release vast amounts of debris into the air,' she told him. 'If the winds were in the wrong direction, half the Empire would find itself in darkness for months, its homes and crops smothered by dust and ash. And who's to say that the eruptions might not spread? Your southern border is only a few miles from the nearest volcanoes, after all.'

She saw from his expression that such a possibility had already occurred to him, and took the opportunity to make her point while the image of such devastation was fresh in his mind.

'We've been searching for untainted fireworms for more than two years now, but all those we've found were already corrupted. We must look further afield. Which is where you—'

'You have seen these creatures with your own eyes?' he cut in.

'I have.' And I've seen what they can do, Ico thought,

remembering the twisted, scorched bodies, the tattered, un-recognizable remains of those who had died in agony, devoured from within by the hate-filled worms. She was about to describe what she had witnessed when the ambassador spoke again, shocking her into silence.

'You're lying,' he stated flatly. 'These worms could not influence the elemental forces of the earth. Such things are the province of the gods.'

'You can't be sure of that,' Ico said desperately. 'And if we can find worms that have not been corrupted—'

'There are no such creatures within the Empire.'

'How can you *know* that?'

'Because we are a devout, god-fearing nation. We—'

He broke off abruptly as the door to the chamber opened, and – to Ico's consternation – Ysanne tottered into the room. Both Ico and Kudrak rose to their feet.

'What's the meaning of this?' the envoy demanded in outrage.

'My daughter,' Ico explained, silently cursing the child's timing.

'Mama. I can't find Tas,' Ysanne declared.

Although she was only two years old, Ysanne was precociously articulate, forthright and often stubborn – qualities she had inherited from her mother. She also had her mother's beauty, her lustrous dark hair and huge brown eyes, as well as her guile and intelligence. Her strength and agility came from her father, Andrin Zonzomas – and her fiery temper was a legacy from both parents. But there were also times when she displayed a stillness, a calm curiosity that was all her own.

'She's not here, little one,' Ico told her. Tas was the tiny firecrest with whom Ysanne was already linked. 'And neither should you be. Mama's busy.'

The child regarded her mother solemnly for a few

moments, obviously feeling that this argument carried little weight. Then the door opened wider and Andrin hurried in. He scooped Ysanne up and, as the child giggled happily, he smiled apologetically at his wife.

'I'm sorry for the intrusion,' he muttered, then nodded to the ambassador and turned to leave.

Kudrak glared at him with contempt, an expression that did not change when the door had closed behind them again.

'Do you have children, Ambassador?' Ico asked, hoping to deflect his obvious rage.

'I do. They are at home with my wife, as is proper,' he responded icily, and Ico knew that she and Andrin had both fallen another notch in the ambassador's regard. He was obviously a man who held an inflexible view of the world. She was trying to think of a way of returning to their earlier discussion without antagonizing him further when he pre-empted her efforts.

'I had hoped this meeting could have been conducted in a professional manner. Clearly that was my mistake. I see no point in prolonging this charade.' All pretence of cordiality was gone now, and to her dismay Ico found that she had no idea how to remedy the situation. It was true that allowing Ysanne to interrupt them had done little for her presidential credibility, but the talks had been turning sour even before that.

'We mustn't lose sight of what's important here,' she ventured.

Kudrak snorted derisively.

'I agree,' he growled. 'Let me see if I have the *important* facts straight. You support the use of magic, do you not?'

'Yes,' Ico replied, taken aback by this new line of argument. 'Universal magic is part of our heritage. It's—'

'And you claim not only to have spoken to dragons but to have flown in the shape of one?'

'I did, but only—'

'Then you are condemned by your own words,' the envoy declared, his voice rising until he was almost shouting. 'You mock the gods! Tiguafaya was founded by heretics and I see that nothing has changed.'

Ico was about to protest her innocence, but there was no stopping Kudrak now. He had reached his own unshakeable conclusions.

'You've told me all I need to know,' he went on. 'Whatever ills are plaguing Tiguafaya are the result of your own blasphemies – and yet you concoct this absurd fantasy in a futile attempt to gain outside help. These so-called fireworms are obviously a punishment from the gods and, unless you mend your ways, worse will soon follow.'

'You don't know what you're talking about!' Ico exploded, losing her temper at last in the face of such bigotry.

'It might be better if Tiguafaya *did* disappear under a sea of lava,' Kudrak added. 'It would at least cleanse the land of your vileness. But I tell you this – if the earth's unrest reaches out to harm the Empire because of your wicked heresies, then the Emperor will not stand idly by.'

'And what do you mean by that?' Ico demanded.

'You must return to the paths of righteousness. Abandon magic and all its evils. If you do not do so voluntarily, the Empire will enforce the gods' will.'

'And how do you propose to do that?' Ico asked, furious now, but dreading the answer she knew must come.

'With a holy war,' the ambassador replied, then turned on his heel and strode from the room.

# CHAPTER THREE

'He's asleep,' Cat said, sounding like a mother whose unruly child had finally succumbed to exhaustion. 'Now we can talk.'

'You look pretty tired yourself,' Nino replied as she sank gratefully onto a seat. 'Wouldn't you rather get some rest?'

'Not yet.' She glanced at her visitor and smiled wearily. Although Nino Delgado was several years older than she, he was only a little taller. He was thin and wiry, carrying himself with the poise of a natural athlete, and she knew from personal experience that he was stronger than he looked and could move fast when he needed to. His dark eyes mirrored those of his linked bird, a magnificent peregrine falcon named Eya. A flash of grey and yellow, sewn onto the shoulder of Nino's shirt, denoted this particular allegiance. Under the old government, when magic of any kind had been frowned upon, such a public display would have been unwise, to say the least, but now it had become a sign of pride once more.

Cat sighed wistfully.

'It's been a long time.'

Nino nodded in agreement.

'We've been busy.' They both smiled at this under-statement.

They had seen little of each other during the aftermath of the dramatic events that had changed their country – and their lives – for ever. But then, Cat thought, I haven't seen much of *anybody*, except Vargo, during the last two years. This was one of the reasons why she had been so glad to see Nino when he had arrived in Corazoncillo. Although she did not regret one moment of the time spent with Vargo, she was always grateful for news from the outside world.

Together with Vargo, she and Nino had been members of the Firebrands, the small group of young rebels, led by Andrin and Ico, who had been instrumental in Tiguafaya's revolution. Even then she had not known Nino very well because he lived in the interior, among the volcanoes, while she and most of the rest were based in Teguise. It was not until the Firebrands' temporary exile that they had spent much time together. Now, however, she regarded him as an old friend – and the chance to look back for once, instead of forward, was welcome. Ironically, now that she had the chance, she felt very tired, and did not seem able to form any of the questions that would have begun the conversation.

For his part, Nino was happy to wait. He had arrived in the village that evening, trudging purposefully down the trail from the eastern end of the valley in the deepening twilight. He had joined Vargo and Cat in the guest hall that had been built on the outskirts of the village, and in whose central room he and Cat now rested. The hall was unusually large, and had been built to cope with all the visitors who came to Corazoncillo to see the dragon eggs. For a time the village had become a place of pilgrimage, and although the number of visitors had fallen away as the months went by, Nino was still surprised that no one else was in residence.

He himself had visited the valley only once before, more than a year ago, and now experienced the same feelings of reverence, awe, and even a little fear as he had stopped to gaze at the eggs. Nino had kept his distance, as did most people, before going on to find lodgings. He had been delighted to discover that Vargo and his companion were still there. He too needed to talk.

'Why are you called Cat?' he asked eventually, realizing that neither of them were ready to face more serious matters yet. He knew that her real name was Allegra Meo, but wasn't sure how she had earned her nickname. Although she had matured a good deal since he had first met her, Cat retained the fluid grace that had always marked her movements. She was small and pretty, and her green eyes, although hooded now by tiredness, had a certain feline quality.

'When I was little, my friends thought Allegra was much too grand a name for a fisherman's daughter,' she explained, 'so it got shortened to Allie. That became Alley Cat, then just Cat.'

'It suits you.'

She shrugged.

'I've never really thought about it.'

A noise came from the adjoining room, where Vargo was sleeping, and she glanced round, instantly concerned. Then all was quiet again and she relaxed, but it had been a telling moment.

'He has terrible dreams sometimes,' she said gravely.

'Are you two . . . ?' Nino began, then didn't know how to finish the sentence.

Cat did not respond for so long that Nino became embarrassed by his own tactlessness.

'I'm sorry. It's none of my business.'

'It's all right,' she said quietly. 'I just don't know how to answer. Sometimes I think . . . Sometimes we're like an old married couple, kept together by convenience and habit, all passion gone. Not that there's ever been any real ... passion.'

Nino felt sorry for her. Was it really possible that Vargo did not know how much Cat loved him? He would have to be blind. Or mad. Nino had seen the way she'd gazed at him, at the tangle of brown hair lying on his pillow, his usually expressive face relaxed in deep sleep.

'Then at times he can be so wonderful, so ...' She faltered again. 'And sometimes he looks at me as if I'm a stranger.'

'It sounds as if he's confused too,' Nino commented.

'At least he's got an excuse,' Cat replied, with a rueful smile. 'He's often not in the same world as the rest of us.'

'So you have no idea how he feels about you?'

'He takes me for granted sometimes, in a nice way. And he's my friend.'

'But if he wanted it to be more than that, I take it you wouldn't object?'

It was Allegra's turn to be embarrassed now, and she was grateful for the dim lamplight that allowed her to hide her blushes.

'I wouldn't object,' she confirmed, 'but you must promise not to breathe a word of this to Vargo.'

'I promise. I'm sorry I've been so nosy.'

'Don't apologize. Everyone assumes ... just because we've been together all this time. At least you were honest enough to talk about it openly.'

Which is more than I can do, even now, she thought. There was one vital fact about her relationship with Vargo that she had not mentioned – the fact that he was still in love with someone else.

'Have you tried talking to *him* about it?' Nino asked.

'Not really.'

'Why not?'

'It's hard enough having a sensible conversation with him about anything except our work. I wouldn't want to find out that he didn't feel . . . And I don't want to distract him.'

Nino couldn't help wondering whether this was perhaps just the kind of distraction Vargo might need, but he had already trespassed enough on private ground. He was about to change the subject when Cat surprised him with a further admission.

'He's very protective towards me,' she said. 'That's a sign that he cares, isn't it?'

'Of course,' Nino replied, recognizing her need for reassurance.

'He once attacked two White Guards who were threatening me, even though they had swords and he was unarmed.'

'That sounds pretty much like love to me,' Nino commented.

Cat smiled gratefully, but then tears came to her eyes and she began to cry. Nino moved over beside her, and put his arm around her shoulders. It was a comforting gesture, almost fatherly, and she laid her head against him gratefully. He said nothing, but stayed where he was until the tears subsided and Cat wiped her face.

'I'm sorry,' she mumbled, and moved away.

'You've nothing to apologize for. I shouldn't have—'

'I'm glad you did,' she interrupted. 'You might as well know the rest now.' After almost three years as Vargo's constant companion, she was desperate to share her feelings with someone, and Nino's easy manner and ready sympathy invited confidences.

'Only if you're sure.'

Allegra was silent for a few moments.

'I don't think Vargo will ever love me as I love him,' she said eventually.

'Why not? He's very preoccupied at the moment, and he's never been the easiest person to deal with at the best of times.'

'That's true enough,' she agreed, 'but there are some things even he can't hide.'

'Such as?'

'He's in love with someone else.'

Nino's expression did not change.

'Do you know who it is?'

Cat nodded.

'Ico.'

Her companion did not seem particularly surprised.

'He told you this?'

'He doesn't need to. I can see it in his eyes every time we meet her, every time he even talks about her. Oh, he pretends it's all a joke, that they're playing an elaborate game, but that's just his way of hiding his feelings from her. How can I hope to compete with Ico? She's so beautiful, and she's done so much.'

'Don't underestimate yourself,' Nino told her firmly. 'Besides, you have one very big advantage over Ico. She's married to Andrin and, unless I'm very much mistaken, nothing short of death will ever separate those two.'

'That's what makes it so frustrating!' Cat exclaimed passionately. 'She's unavailable, like a dream, so she remains perfect, the ideal I can't match. I'm all too real, having to deal with every mundane, practical detail of our lives. How can it be as romantic when I'm with him all the time?'

'Surely that's another advantage?'

'Possession is nine tenths of the law, you mean? Not when it comes to someone's heart, it isn't. I'm not sure I even have *one* tenth of that.'

'That can change.'

Cat shrugged helplessly.

'I don't see how. Vargo's fragile in so many ways, and this has been a very hard time for him. I keep thinking he's gradually gaining some sort of stability, and then something happens and he falls back again. And the pattern keeps repeating itself.' She traced a slow rise, then a sudden descent, with her finger in the air. 'Like a sawtooth. It doesn't even have to be anything big that knocks him down. His life is complicated enough, and he gets so depressed sometimes. I can't risk being the cause of another fall.'

'Are you worried about him now?'

Allegra nodded.

'He can't communicate with the dragons, and he's taken it very hard. That's why he exhausted himself today. We've been here five days now, and that's the longest we've stayed anywhere during the last two years, but he's getting nowhere. At least the other setbacks were beyond his control.'

'Maybe this is too.'

'Try telling *him* that,' she replied with a touch of bitterness.

'What were the other setbacks?'

She sighed.

'I suppose the loss of his music was the first.'

'I still don't understand how that happened,' Nino admitted. 'Surely talent can't simply disappear?'

'I don't think anyone really understands it,' Cat replied, 'least of all me. But I've had to accept it. Vargo says that when he played for the dragons, so that they'd help Ico and Andrin, it took everything he had. It's all gone.'

'For good?' Nino asked, disbelieving.

'According to him, yes. It didn't seem to bother him until he had to go to the Musicians' Guild and resign. He'd worked so hard for so long, and he'd have been a full member by now. Giving that up brought home to him just how much he'd lost. Lots of people have tried to help, including the best musicians in Teguise, as well as some of Famara's other pupils, but it's made no difference. Even Ero and Lao don't try any more.'

Uniquely among those chosen, Vargo was linked to not one but two different birds, both migratory visitors to Tiguafaya. In summer the hoopoe was his companion, but in winter Ero was replaced by Lao, a sandpiper curlew, whose dignified bearing and soft chirruping song contrasted with his counterpart's flamboyant appearance and comical attitudes. Vargo's erratic moods tended to be governed, to some extent, by the presence of one or other of the birds. In summer he dressed in brighter colours, acted even more unpredictably than usual and generally saw the funny side of things. The colder months saw his garb change to the hues of earth and stone and a sad look come to his eyes. In the past, both birds had shared his music, Ero dancing to the lively tunes from his master's lute and Lao singing the melancholy songs of Vargo's winter viol. Now all that was silent, to the mystification of both. Cat had often seen the hoopoe practise a few tentative steps, then glance hopefully at Vargo, only to be disappointed yet again. The confusion in the bird's eyes made her sad, but Vargo never seemed to notice.

'And then I suppose it was Ico's wedding,' Allegra went on. Her eyes were bright with tears again now. 'No, Ysanne's birth came first, didn't it. He put a brave face on both, of course, but afterwards he was utterly dejected. There was the time last year when Lao left before Ero had arrived, and he was completely lost for a while. And then it was when we found a small nesting site for the fireworms. It had taken us ages to track them down, only to find that they were already tainted. Vargo was almost killed then, and he actually told me later that he wished he had been. His hopes had been so high that when they were dashed it was devastating.'

'You're not the only ones looking for the worms,' Nino pointed out.

'I know, but Vargo seems to think he has to do it all on his own. He keeps talking about the path he has to follow.'

'And it led you here?'

'To the eggs,' Allegra confirmed. 'Which is why his lack of progress with them worries me. It's just the sort of thing to unbalance him again.'

They sat in silence for a while, and Nino tried to think of something encouraging to say. He'd learnt a lot about this strange partnership, and his respect for Cat's loyalty had risen even higher.

'I wish Famara was still alive,' Allegra said eventually. 'She might have been able to help him sort himself out.'

'I never met her,' Nino said.

'She was a wonderful old lady – the closest thing Vargo had to a mother, as well as being his mentor.' Cat's eyes glowed at the memory of the wizard she had known only too briefly.

'He never knew his real parents, did he?' Nino said.

'No. They abandoned him when he was a baby. Everyone's always assumed they were travelling entertainers,' Allegra explained. 'For a long time Ico and Andrin – and Famara – were the closest thing to a family he's ever had. Now she's dead and he hardly ever sees the other two. I suppose I'm all he's got left.'

Nino looked at her, measuring the young woman's words and her worth.

'He's lucky to have you,' he said.

# CHAPTER FOUR

Early the next morning Cat and Nino emerged from their bedrooms almost simultaneously. They nodded in greeting, then turned their attention to the food that had been brought in by one of the villagers. Like most mountain communities, Corazoncillo still honoured the ancient laws of hospitality, even though this had put a considerable strain on their resources at the height of the interest in the dragon eggs. Bread, fruit and water had been left on the table, and the two travellers breakfasted in an amiable if slightly strained silence. They both felt a little awkward about the nature of their discussion of the previous evening and, by tacit agreement, the subject of Cat's relationship with Vargo was not raised again. When they did speak it was in a much more businesslike manner.

'Why did you come here, Nino?' Allegra did not need to add that it was unlikely to have been to discuss her love life.

'Several reasons,' he replied. 'I'd heard you two were headed this way, and it's been a long time since anyone in Teguise had a report of your progress.'

'Or lack of it,' Cat said disgustedly. 'What else?'

'I wanted to have another look at the dragon eggs for myself.'

'Why?'

'Curiosity.'

Allegra rubbed her eyes, which were still a little sore from crying, and then gave her companion a quizzical look. She could not believe his reasons were that simple, but Nino chose not to elaborate.

'This valley's important in other ways too,' he went on. 'It's a sort of focus.'

'A focus for what?'

'Energy. You know about the work I've been doing?'

'Not really.' She had heard rumours, but nothing she could rely on. 'Something to do with the nets?'

'That's right, but on a much bigger scale.'

'How big?'

'If it works, it would cover the whole of Tiguafaya.'

Cat stared at him as if he were insane.

'In one net?' she exclaimed incredulously. She found herself remembering a scene from what now seemed to be the distant past, almost another life. Famara had been linked to the leader of a clan of sparrows, and on one memorable occasion Cat and Vargo had watched mesmerized as, under their mistress's guidance, the tiny, boisterous birds had woven a filigree of magical light in the air. That had been the first indication that linked birds could work together in what became known as 'nets', shaping magical power to greater effect than could be managed by any individual. The idea that this principle could be applied on such a vast scale had never occurred to Allegra, but Nino's enthusiasm and determination were obvious from the gleam in his eyes.

'That's the idea,' he said eagerly. 'It's nowhere near complete, of course, but the results so far have been encouraging. If we can ever co-ordinate the entire network, it would be like an invisible spider's web of magic covering the entire country.'

'That's incredible,' Cat breathed, astonished at the scope of his vision – which made her own concerns seem almost mundane by comparison.

'Not really,' Nino went on, getting into his stride now. 'The birds have always been central to Tiguafaya's magic. It's the one aspect we've never lost, no matter how hard people tried to suppress it. Where else would we look for a project this big?'

'Can all the species work together?' she asked.

'It's not easy,' he replied wryly. 'But with the help of their links, I think they can.'

Allegra was silent for a few moments, thinking about this amazing concept. Now more than ever before she wished that she was linked, and could be part of this great undertaking. But that was something over which she had no control – and, she told herself, her own role was important too.

'Famara used to say that half of magic was focusing the power of the mind,' she said.

Nino nodded.

'And the other half is shaping the power of external sources and making it do what we want,' he added. 'Well, we've plenty of outside sources now. What we need is a mind big enough to use them all.'

'What do you mean?'

'It's not something that's easy to put into words,' he told her, 'but I've glimpsed it when I've been involved in the net, with Eya. We're close to something so vast, so powerful, that there'd be nothing we couldn't do.'

'You're beginning to scare me.'

'I know. It seems as if we'd be trespassing on the domain of the gods, but it's not like that. The birds have their own laws and beliefs. They won't let this power be abused. Besides, if it works, we're going to use it for strictly practical purposes, to help people.'

'What purposes?' Cat asked.

'The potential is limitless,' he replied. 'For instance, the net would naturally be sensitive to the location of fire-worms.' He'd chosen an example he knew would be close to Allegra's heart. 'It could help in the search. And it could revolutionize communications. Think of it – messages could be passed telepathically between almost anywhere in Tiguafaya, instantly! And it could act as an early warning system for eruptions. Think how many lives it would save.'

'You really think that's all possible?'

'I *know* it's possible,' he said fervently. 'Whether we'll be able to work out how to do it in time is another matter.'

Before the volcanoes destroy everything, Cat realized soberly, her wonder replaced by an all too familiar dread. Nino was also quiet for a while, his enthusiasm dampened by the same thoughts.

'And you think this place is important?' Cat asked eventually, returning to something Nino had said earlier. 'Because the dragon eggs are here?' She was aware that the birds claimed a common heritage with the dragons – they were all winged creatures, after all – and presumed that they too must be drawn to the last remnants of their distant cousins.

'I think the valley was special before the eggs were brought here,' Nino replied. 'In fact, it might have been *why* the dragons wanted them to come here.'

'But Ico flew here because she needed to save Maciot and our allies from the worms,' Cat objected.

'I know,' he conceded. 'Maybe the dragon spirits had foreseen that.'

'This is getting too complicated for me,' she muttered.

'There are other things that mark this place out,' Nino added. 'For a start, do you realize that *no one* who lives in the valley is linked? In villages the size of Corazoncillo and Quemada you'd normally expect two or three to have been chosen, but there's not a single one.'

The ability to communicate telepathically with a specific bird was granted to only a very small percentage of the population, and those involved had no control over the selection process, but almost every settlement of any size boasted at least one linked individual.

'If it's a focus,' Cat argued, 'then surely there'd be more, not less.'

'I don't understand it either,' Nino admitted. 'But that's not all. Even with all the recent activity, no eruption of any size has taken place within thirty miles of here – and yet this area should be no more stable than anywhere else in the firelands. There haven't even been any tremors here.'

'Some sort of natural protection?' Allegra guessed.

'Perhaps. But I believe this is the heart of the spider's web. I'm sure of it. We've begun to see patterns within the nets we've already formed, and it can't be a coincidence that so many of the lines point here. Understanding this place might be the key to success.'

'Vargo thinks so too, but that's because the dragons are here.'

'*You* don't sound so sure,' Nino remarked, picking up on the scepticism in her voice.

'The eggs make me feel ill,' she replied. 'Vargo too, thought he won't admit it.'

Nino looked puzzled, but Cat did not elaborate. Instead she posed the question that had been on everyone's mind since Andrin's discovery of the eggs.

'Do you think they'll ever hatch?'

'I hope so.' Dragons had lived in Tiguafaya for a long

time before the coming of man and, to Nino, the idea that they could die out completely was somehow unthinkable. 'Let's go and take a look at them.'

Cat grimaced, but stood up.

'All right. Just let me check on Vargo first.'

She was only in Vargo's chamber for a few moments, but during that time Nino heard a soft call, hoo–poo–hoo, and realized that Allegra was not the only one keeping watch.

'He's still fast asleep,' she reported on her return. 'After all his efforts yesterday, I wouldn't be surprised if he slept till noon. In any case, Ero will come and fetch me if I'm needed.'

'Let's go then.'

As soon as they got outside Nino looked up at the sky. It was another cloudless day, and instinct guided him to the only fleck of darkness in the azure expanse. He smiled, without knowing he did so, and watched as the tiny speck grew larger and took shape.

Eya's approach was breathtaking, a steep dive that seemed reckless in its speed, but as the peregrine neared his link, his broad wings spread and he swooped round in a graceful arc before circling lazily over the village. As always, Nino was filled with love – and with a sense of pride that such a magnificent creature had chosen *him* to be his partner. Beside him, Allegra, who had followed the line of his gaze and witnessed the bird's spectacular arrival, gasped in wordless admiration.

*Did you find any other links?* Nino asked silently.

*Only the hoopoe,* Eya replied, and his tone made it clear what he thought of that particular bird. *It's too cold here,* he added cryptically.

*What do you mean?* The morning sun was already warm on Nino's skin.

*There are shadows,* the peregrine replied.

It was clear that Eya was not talking about shade cast by any physical object, but of something beyond human senses.

*Because of the dragons?* Nino guessed.

*I don't know*, Eya answered irritably. *And the hunting's bad too.*

*I'll find some meat for you*, Nino said solicitously. He had often contemplated the irony of an inlander like himself being linked to a bird whose natural habitat was the cliffs and crags of the shoreline, where fish and other prey were plentiful. In Tiguafaya, unlike other lands, no bird hunted others of their kind, and in some remote parts of the mountains – such as the Corazoncillo valley – even the peregrine's peerless eyesight and deadly talons could find little sustenance. Eya had grown used to occasionally having to rely on his human companion for food, but admitting his hunger still stung the falcon's pride. With a raucous cry, *aak-aak-aak*, he flew off to see if he could remedy the situation himself.

'What did he say?' Cat had been aware of their conversation, even though she could hear none of it.

'Nothing much,' Nino replied, deciding not to tell her about the bird's references to cold or shadows. She already had enough on her mind. 'He's hungry, that's all.'

They set off for the centre of the village, which was already bustling with activity. Several people nodded in greeting, and a few children stared at them, but no one tried to engage them in conversation. Like most small communities – and in spite of the interest caused by the dragon eggs – Corazoncillo minded its own business and let others do the same.

By comparison, the area around the square where the eggs lay was quiet and still. Nino thought the air was cooler there too, but told himself he was imagining things. The black shells looked like extrusions from the rock beneath them, as if they had lain there since the beginnings of the earth, but both onlookers knew how false that impression was. A mere two and a half years earlier the eggs had been secreted in a cave deep within a volcano called Tisaloya. Andrin, together with two companions, had found them there, just before the mountain had utterly destroyed itself in a massive eruption. The only reason that they – and the eggs – had escaped was because in the final moments, and with the help of the dragon spirits, Andrin had at last found his own, long-denied magical talent, and had encased them all in an unbreakable shield of ice. Even then they had needed Ico, in her guise as a dragon, to pluck them from the lava flow and carry them to safety in the valley where the eggs now lay. Although Nino and Cat both knew this story by heart, they had witnessed only small portions of the drama for themselves.

'I wish I'd seen them arrive,' Nino said quietly. 'It must have been quite a sight.'

'It was, apparently,' Cat told him. 'Just ask anyone here. They all saw it – and the tales get more exaggerated every time they're told. Not that they need much exaggeration.'

They had come to a halt some distance from the clutch of eggs, and tried to imagine the scene.

'Vargo and I were stuck in the middle of nowhere,' Allegra said. 'We saw the eruption and the snow, but we were too far away to see any details. At least you got to see Ico.'

'Even though I didn't know it was her at the time,' Nino replied, recalling his strange lack of fear as the massive dragon had swooped down, its black scales glittering, and fixed him with a burning yellow glare. Their conversation had been brief and to the point, and the giant creature had flown off again almost immediately, but the memory of that encounter would remain with Nino for ever. Unless one of the eggs actually hatched, it was the closest he would ever come to seeing a real dragon.

'Vargo told me what had happened,' Cat went on. ' He'd seen it all in his dreaming, but it was a long time before I got the chance to talk to anyone else and heard the whole truth. We began our search for the fireworms then, and we seem to have been looking for them ever since.'

She wounded weary, and Nino felt sorry for her. Allegra was still very young – nineteen or so, he would have guessed – but her life had already taken her down some strange and arduous pathways.

'If you want to get any closer,' Cat told him, 'you're on your own. I don't like it here.'

'Why not?'

She shrugged.

'I just don't.' After a pause, she added, 'We taught ourselves to hate the dragons. Do you think they could have done the same?'

Nino thought for a moment.

'If that was the case, why did they help Ico and Andrin?'

Allegra did not reply. In fact, she gave no indication of even hearing his question.

'Vargo told me the dragons never hated mankind, but I'm not so sure,' she said. 'He said they just regarded us as insignificant, the way we regard ants.'

'Not very flattering,' Nino commented.

'No,' she agreed. 'Especially when you think about what we do to ants when they annoy us.'

Shortly after midday, Cat and Nino were back in the guest house. Nino had spent some time studying the eggs, and had even plucked up enough courage to touch one of them, but he hadn't felt anything. Although he had made no progress, he still believed that Corazoncillo was important somehow. Then he had talked to some locals, ensured that Eya was fed, and returned to his lodgings.

As Allegra had predicted, Vargo was still dead to
the world and showed no sign of waking, so Nino decided
to try to get some of the answers he was seeking from Cat.
In truth he was not unhappy about this. In the depths
of his eccentric mind Vargo might well know more than
anyone else about Tiguafaya's problems and their possible
solutions, but his speech was so confusing at times – almost
unintelligible – that his responses often raised more
questions than they answered. At least Allegra could be
relied upon to be consistently rational.

The search to find a new breed of fireworms had been
going on for some time now, moving further and
further afield as it met with no success. The few small
swarms that had been detected had all been tainted, useless
for the purposes Vargo had glimpsed, and instantly
hostile towards humans. It was only because the Firebrands had developed techniques for controlling the
vile creatures – by using magically created waves of
cold – that there had not been many casualties among
the searchers. Almost all the central and eastern areas
of the country had been covered, with Jurado Madri –
among others – using his knowledge of the fireland's
cave systems to help the hunt continue underground,
and they were running out of options now. Nothing in
Vargo and Cat's recent journeyings had brought any
progress.

'I'm beginning to think it's hopeless,' Allegra concluded.
'We'll never find them.'

'Don't say that,' Nino responded. 'We've come too far to
give up now.'

'Even if we *do* find new worms, who's to say they won't
become corrupted too?'

'They won't if we stop hating them.'

She sighed.

'That's easier said than done.'

'But if we don't, then the whole search is pointless,' he told her earnestly. '*We* were the ones who corrupted them in the first place, but now we know the truth and surely that makes a difference.'

'Knowing the truth isn't everything,' Cat replied. 'You can't just expect hatred to disappear like that. Too many people suffered because of the worms. They saw the dreadful things they did – and they can't forget that, no matter how often the theory is explained to them.'

'That's the problem, isn't it,' Nino said thoughtfully. 'It's just theory to most people. Vargo's the only one who *knows* what the dragons told him.'

'You do believe him, don't you?' Cat demanded, defensive now, her own uncertainties pushed aside.

'I do, and so do Ico and Andrin and any of us who know him personally. But there are people in my village, and everywhere else, who find it hard to accept. And let's face it, even if we make contact with untainted worms, it's going to be hard to look at them and not feel revulsion – and we know the truth, we know we have to accept our collective responsibility. So what chance is there for those we haven't convinced yet?'

Nino and Allegra both knew that there were two things that most people might find difficult to believe. The first was that the fireworms had actually helped control volcanic activity once, and the second was that it was human attitudes that had changed the worms – for the worse. Vargo was utterly convinced of this – and his conviction was persuasive – but he took it for granted that everyone else already accepted his findings. Although he had many allies, many more people remained uncertain, even though his explanation did seem to fit the facts.

'A lot of people are questioning the resources allocated to

the search,' Nino went on, adding to Cat's unease. 'They think they could be put to better uses.'

'Like what?'

'Like using our own magic to help control the lava flows.'

'I can't see us having enough talents or power to do that. Magic is exhausting, especially when it has to affect the physical world. Besides, even if we tried that, we can only react to eruptions *when* they happen. The worms used to *prevent* them.'

'True enough,' Nino agreed. 'Perhaps that's why Vargo is so sure the dragons' help is vital. If they wanted to, they could keep the worms healthy.'

'Gods, this is depressing,' Allegra groaned. 'I was hoping your being here might cheer me up.'

'I'm sorry,' he replied, with a wry grin. 'Looking on the bright side, we don't know how long it takes for healthy worms to become tainted. Even if we can't completely control how we feel about them, there might be some leeway.'

Cat shook her head.

'That's no good. We need to find a long-term solution or the volcanoes will kill us all eventually.'

'Now who's being depressing?' Nino asked, smiling ruefully.

They looked at each other in silence for a few moments.

'So what now?' Allegra asked eventually.

'We do the best we can, in our various ways,' Nino replied. 'That's all we can do.'

'So we just go on looking, I suppose,' she said resignedly. 'There are still some remote areas to the west and south that haven't even been touched yet.'

'Perhaps we'll have to go further afield,' Nino suggested. 'Into the Empire even. With any luck Ico will have seen their envoy by now, and got their permission.'

# CHAPTER FIVE

'I spend more time looking after Ysanne than anything else,'
Andrin declared grimly. 'And I can't even do that properly.'
He was referring to his daughter's unfortunate interruption
of Ico's meeting.

'You're a wonderful father,' Ico told him, pushing aside
her own anger. 'And her coming in didn't really have
any effect on the meeting. It was a disaster from the start.
Kudrak never had any intention of taking me seriously.'

They were strolling around one of the inner courtyards
of the Presidential Palace, taking advantage of a few rare
moments of free time together.

'At least he didn't look at you with utter contempt,' Andrin
remarked. He knew that the ambassador had regarded him as
nothing more than a nursemaid – an unworthy occupation for
any man. Implicit in Kudrak's glare had been the message
that a man who let his wife take the leading role in their lives
was no man at all. 'The worst of it is,' he added, 'I'm not
sure I don't agree with him.'

Ico was instantly dismayed.

'But that's absurd!'

'Don't tell me what's absurd,' Andrin snapped back.

'Kudrak's the worst kind of chauvinist,' she persisted. 'Don't compare yourself to him.'

'That doesn't stop me feeling about as useful as a third shoe.'

'I couldn't do any of this without you,' Ico protested. 'You know that.'

'Couldn't you? You spend more time with Maciot than you do with me.'

Stung by this accusation, Ico fought to keep a tight rein on her own volatile temper.

'You knew that the Presidency would be a huge responsibility,' she said. 'I can't back away from it now, and Maciot is my chief advisor.'

As soon as the words were spoken she wished she could take them back, but it was too late.

'And I'm just your husband,' Andrin said bitterly, 'so my advice counts for nothing.'

'You're not stupid, my love. Why do you pretend to be?'

'Because I *feel* stupid. Stupid and useless.'

'That's—' She caught herself in time. '*You* could have run for President, you know. They'd have elected you even faster than me, but you didn't want it.'

'I still don't,' he stated flatly. 'But I didn't want you to be President either.'

'We've been over this,' Ico argued patiently. 'It was our duty. We couldn't just smash everything that had gone before, then step back and let someone else pick up the pieces. We *had* to take the responsibility.'

Andrin stared at her, and saw the fire burning deep within those deceptively soft brown eyes. His wife was so beautiful she made his heart ache sometimes, and he still did not really know what he had done to deserve her love. But he knew, beyond any shadow of a doubt, that she did love him.

They had been lovers for several years now. When they had first met he had been a dock-rat, the son of a crippled ex-stevedore and a drunken mother, while Ico's family had been moderately wealthy and widely respected. Her father, Diano Maravedis, was a merchant jeweller of some standing who had passed on his mastery of the craft to his daughter. Indeed, Andrin and Ico's paths might never have crossed if magic had not brought them together. They had each been chosen to be linked at an early age. Andrin's bird, a magnificent white eagle named Ayo, had given him a certain status, strangely out of kilter with his station in life, while Soo, Ico's sparrowhawk, was as sleek and as single-minded as her mistress. Together with other like-minded young people they had formed the Firebrands – and had known from the beginning that they were destined to be together. Even so, their relationship had never been one to run smooth, and was marked by periodic explosions of volcanic emotion. The extra stresses and strains of public office had only exacerbated this tendency. On this occasion, however, Andrin decided not to fight fire with fire.

'You were the better candidate,' he said quietly. 'You're the diplomat.'

'You wouldn't think so if you'd seen me with Kudrak this morning,' Ico replied, her voice thick with self-disgust.

'I'd probably have killed him,' Andrin countered.

It was Ico's turn to stare. She knew he was serious, but in the end she couldn't help grinning. The contrast between the envoy and her husband was marked. Andrin was tall and well built, with short, white-blonde hair that sometimes made him look as if he were giving off sparks. At twenty-two years of age, his piercing green eyes were as full of contradictions as they had been when they'd first met and she had felt them gazing into her soul. Wondering now if her husband would ever really grow up, Ico found herself hoping that he would not.

Eventually he smiled back at her.

'Well, all right,' he conceded. 'I'd probably just have beaten him up.'

'I'd've done that myself if I'd been quick enough,' Ico said. 'Pompous little halfwit.'

'Either way, it wouldn't have been very diplomatic, would it?' Andrin sighed. 'I sometimes wonder what we're doing here.'

Ico had wondered the same thing on many occasions, but she was not about to admit that now. The cloistered silence of the palace drew in around them as she led him to a stone bench and they sat down.

'I meant it when I said I couldn't do anything without you,' she said. 'Look at everything we've achieved.'

'*You've* achieved,' he persisted obstinately.

'We've overseen the rebuilding of Teguise,' Ico went on, undeterred. 'We have a viable navy again. Trade is increasing all the time. The mines, the farms and vineyards, the merchant halls – they're all prospering more than they've done in decades, in spite of the upheavals. And we've made a start on bringing education to everyone.' This was one of the policies closest to Ico's heart. Her association with the Firebrands, many of whom had been unable to read or write, had made her realize just how privileged her own upbringing had been. 'Those are no mean achievements. *And* we've set up the Magicians' Guild, so they have a voice alongside all the other trades. We've freed the archives so that anyone can read about the lore that's so important to our whole way of life. And before you say anything,' she added quickly, forestalling his intended interruption, 'you're part of all those things and a lot more besides. I just took the credit.'

'And the criticism.'

'That goes with the job. We're never going to persuade everyone to approve of everything we need to do. If it hadn't been for your work behind the scenes, there'd have been far more problems than there were.'

For once Andrin did not bother to argue. They both knew that without his tireless efforts at mediation, relations between the Firebrands and their former adversaries could easily have been unworkable, and might even have turned to widespread violence. Ico and Andrin had tried to include all the former rebels in their plans for the future, but even among their friends there had been some dissatisfaction. A few had even claimed that Ico had become what they had been fighting against – although this was something she vehemently denied, pointing to the very real differences between her administration and that of her predecessor. Nevertheless, some of the Firebrands had found it difficult to come to terms with the fact that they were now approved of by officialdom, that they were part of the establishment. In the same way, many of those who had previously been influential – even if they had taken a neutral position during the actual conflict – resented the way in which Ico and her equally youthful colleagues had become so powerful so quickly. Balancing the various factions of Tiguafayan politics was a tricky business, and Andrin's role had been significant, relying on his supposedly non-existent diplomatic skills and the force of his personality to bring about the desired results.

He had also been one of the driving forces behind the formation of the Magicians' Guild, speaking eloquently to the newly elected Senate about the need to re-establish their links with the neglected secrets of the past. His words had been heeded, not least because everyone knew of his part in recent events. If he had not become the Ice Mage, the outcome would have been very different.

Less publicly, Andrin had also helped organize the systematic search for the fireworms – a task Vargo could never have faced alone – and, through Ayo, he had enlisted the help of almost all the avian clans in furthering Nino's plans.

'I'm still just a nursemaid half the time,' he said, pretending to be grumpy still.

'You love spending time with Ysanne,' Ico accused him.

Andrin smiled, admitting his guilt.

'Everything is simple when I'm with her,' he said. 'She knows exactly what she wants.'

'And usually gets it,' Ico added.

The bond between Andrin and his daughter was the strongest Ico had ever witnessed. She knew that this was partly because Andrin's own family background had been far from happy and he was determined that Ysanne would not suffer as he had. Andrin's father and brother were dead and only his mother, Belda, remained. Sober now but still frail and ineffectual, she was a permanent guest at Ico's father's house. Diano, who had been a widower for more than a decade, had given her refuge during the revolution, and both seemed quite content with the new arrangement. Andrin never spoke of his father, who had been cruel and spiteful, but he still grieved for Mendo, his brother, who had been only fourteen when he'd been killed by fireworms.

'Do you think Kudrak meant what he said?' Andrin asked softly, serious again now. 'About a holy war, I mean.'

'I hope not,' Ico replied. 'It felt like it at the time, though.'

'What do the Empire think it would achieve?'

'Who knows?'

'Did you believe all that stuff about heresy?'

'Kudrak sounded as if *he* believed it,' she said, 'but it's been a long time since religious considerations have counted for that much in the Empire. It's possible it's just an excuse. Or a bluff. I—'

Their conversation was interrupted then by Soo's arrival. The sparrowhawk glided across the quadrangle, and landed lightly on a low wall that surrounded a stone fountain. Her expression was as alert as ever, but there was a slight flare of madness in her eyes and her plumage was streaked with black in places, giving her an oddly dishevelled appearance. All this was the legacy of her encounter with the dragon spirits, and Ico was aware that she would never know her link as well as she had done. Although this would once have made her very sad, Soo's mere presence was now a reason for thankfulness. Ico had thought she had lost her link for ever, believing her to be dead, and had held the sparrowhawk's lifeless body in her hands. But although life had been miraculously restored, Soo had never been quite the same. In her own words, she had 'flown with the dragons to the heavens and back'.

*Do you need to talk?* Ico asked. Soo had been less talkative since her change, and her remarks were sometimes as cryptic as Vargo's. However, her insights were still extremely valuable, and Ico respected her too much not to make time to listen.

*The dreaming begins*, Soo replied.

*Whose dreaming?* Ico asked, intrigued.

*The sky's.* The sparrowhawk cocked her head to one side and closed her eyes, a sign that Ico had come to recognize as meaning she wanted to be left alone.

'Is she asleep?' Andrin asked curiously.

'I'm not sure. Dreaming, maybe. Or thinking.' Ico could not help wondering what was going on inside that fierce predatory brain.

'At least she still comes to see you,' Andrin commented.

'I hardly ever see Ayo these days. He's so preoccupied with his fledglings he's no time for anything else.'

'A bit like you, really,' Ico teased. 'You don't begrudge him his happiness, do you?'

'Of course not.' He was about to go on when he realized that Ico was no longer paying any attention to him. Soo had woken up too, and was twitching wildly. 'What is it? What's the matter?'

Ico did not answer. A frightened voice was sounding shrilly inside her head, and it did not belong to Soo.

# CHAPTER SIX

Ysanne had spoken to Ico only once from the womb. In that time of crisis she had been able to talk to 'the dragon babies' – the eggs – and had relayed their thoughts to her mother. Since her birth, the little girl had displayed other telepathic abilities, linking with Tas when she was only a year old. And before she could even talk aloud, there had been evidence of a continuing link with Ico. Although this was erratic and sometimes confusing, it went beyond the normal intuitive bond between a mother and her child. Ysanne's fluency was far greater in thought than in speech – although her tongue was catching up fast – but on this occasion, her cry had been little more than an instinctive wail of terror.

Ico ran, her heart pounding with fear, and Andrin was close on her heels. Unable to follow them inside, Soo had soared into the air, chattering wildly. The link between Ysanne and Ico confused and frightened the bird, and there were times when Ico thought the sparrowhawk might even be jealous – but none of that was in her mind now.

When Andrin wrenched open the double doors to the nursery, he and Ico were hit by a blast of unnaturally cold air, but the bizarre and horrifying scene before them soon claimed all their attention. Angel was sitting on the floor, his back half turned towards them, holding a wide-eyed and struggling Ysanne tightly in his arms. Above them Tas hovered fretfully, a fluttering burst of colour, uttering her sharp piercing cry of alarm. And the reason for their alarm was immediately obvious. Floating in the air, no more than two paces in front of them, was a fireworm.

It was fully grown, as long as Andrin's forearm and as thick as his wrist, a featureless, grey tube of malice. The onlookers needed no special insight to realize that it was already tainted. The thick miasma of hatred that surrounded it was unmistakable. The fact that the fireworms were eyeless and did not react to light or sound, and the inexplicable way they were able to fly without wings, made them all the more terrifying. They usually 'swam' through the air, with a rapid snake-like action, but this one was static, though it undulated slowly. For a few terrible moments Ico and Andrin were frozen to the spot. Even Ysanne stopped wriggling and screaming.

Andrin was the first to realize what was happening.

'More cold, Angel!' he yelled. 'Now!'

The other man whimpered and shivered, but the temperature in the room dropped even further. As Andrin grabbed a sturdy wooden chest from the floor, he saw that the fireworm was moving even more sluggishly, the cold counteracting its need to attack human foes. It gradually sank towards the floor.

'Colder!' Ico urged, wanting to snatch her daughter into her arms, but not daring to risk interrupting Angel's concentration.

As another freezing gust of air blew across the nursery, the worm became almost motionless. When it finally touched the ground, Andrin pounced, smashing the heavy chest down upon the creature. The fireworms' leathery skin was impervious to sharp blades or spikes and could not be cut – but they could be crushed, especially when they were cold, away from their natural habitat of lava or boiling mud. The chest shattered on contact, but it had done its work. The fireworm had split open and now lay dying, oozing a sticky grey mush onto the floorboards.

Uttering a strangled gasp of relief, Ico leapt forwards and took her now sobbing daughter from Angel's arms. Relieved of his double burden, he fell back, exhausted, and the temperature in the room began to rise slowly.

'Where did that thing come from?' Andrin asked of no one in particular. 'And how the hell did it get in here?'

'It's all right, little one,' Ico whispered in Ysanne's ear. 'It's all right now.' She felt a feather-like touch as Tas alighted on her shoulder, calling softly, and she was glad of the bird's presence. The child was quiet now, her tiny fingers holding on to the comfort of her mother's neck, and Ico turned her attention to Angel.

'All you all right, Tre?' she asked anxiously.

Angel, whose real name was Tre Fiorindo, opened one of his mismatched eyes and glanced at her miserably. To anyone who did not know him, his gargoyle-like appearance would have seemed repulsive. A terrible disease from his seafaring days had left him with a twisted face – with one side of his mouth lower than the other, bulbous growths on his nose, and hair that grew in irregular clumps. His limbs were crooked and he moved in a peculiar, disjointed manner. However, what he lacked in bodily beauty, Angel made up for in mind and spirit.

For many years he had lived like a hermit, wandering in the firelands and exploring its caves. Most people who caught a glimpse of him believed him to be mad, but he had eventually gained a reputation for being able to drive away evil, and the up!and villagers began to welcome him into their homes. Midwives in particular sought his presence at confinements – and no birth he had attended had ever gone badly. At Ico's request he had been there when Ysanne made her entry into the world, and his presence then had been an undoubted comfort.

Angel's mind was remarkable too. He was a natural weather mage, requiring none of the learning and diligent practice that others needed to assimilate even the most basic rudiments of magic. He could instinctively conjure heat, cold, wind and rain, and even thunder and lightning from the air – and his quick reactions had saved Ysanne and himself from the fireworm. The creature's death, however, had given him no pleasure. Until their original purpose had been discovered by Vargo, Angel had been the only one who had known of it. Their mass destruction after the eruption at Tisaloya had been – in part – his doing, but it had cost him untold agonies.

'I'm sorry,' he muttered now.

'What for?' Ico asked.

'I frightened her,' he replied, meaning Ysanne.

'You *saved* her,' Ico replied, shuddering at the thought of what might have happened if Angel had not been there. 'Thank you.'

During the last few months, Angel had been a frequent visitor to the palace. After Ysanne's natural uncertainty had been overcome and her understandable curiosity about his outlandish appearance satisfied, the little girl had happily accepted him as a friend and playmate.

'Tas says the dreaming's beginning,' Ysanne piped up, sounding none the worse for her ordeal. 'What's that mean?'

'I'm not sure, sweetheart,' Ico replied.

Andrin was still staring malevolently at the mutilated fireworm, which had just given a final twitch and expired.

'Gods,' he breathed. 'These are the things we're supposed to *like*?'

'And that's when he stormed out,' Ico said, concluding her report on the meeting with Kudrak to her chief advisor.

Alegranze Maciot, who was both a senator and the head of the Travellers' Guild, sat quietly, thinking about what he had been told. He had been one of the Firebrands' few friends in high places when Tias Kantrowe had been in power, and Ico and Andrin owed him a great deal from that time – as well as more recently, when his advice and knowledge of the ways of the world had proved invaluable.

Ico watched him now, looking for any signs of disappointment.

'Perhaps it would have been better if you'd been there too,' she suggested.

'I doubt it,' Maciot responded. 'It sounds to me as if Kudrak was determined on a confrontation. If the truth is unacceptable to the Empire, then I don't see what else you could have done.'

I could have lied, Ico thought. Made up some version of events that would have been less controversial. But she said nothing. She was glad that Maciot did not seem to blame her for the fiasco.

'Kudrak and his entourage left on the first tide,' he went on. 'I didn't see any point in trying to delay their departure. It would probably only have made things worse.'

'You could hardly have blockaded them in, anyway,' Ico remarked. 'Then they really would have an excuse to declare war.'

'However, I did arrange for a few friends to talk to some of the ambassador's crewmen before they sailed. And what they learned was quite intriguing.'

'Really?' Ico had supposed that the delegation would be

in Teguise for some time, and was relieved that someone had taken the initiative to gather intelligence before their hasty departure. 'What?'

Before Maciot could answer, Andrin came into the room, looking harassed and weary. The two men nodded to each other and Andrin sat down beside his wife. She had no need to ask what he had been doing or how he had fared. His investigation into where the fireworm could have come from, how it had entered the palace and, more importantly, how it had reached the nursery without being detected, had clearly been fruitless. Frustration was written into the set of his jaw and the angry look in his eyes. Ico briefly covered one of his hands with her own, before signalling Maciot to go on.

'As far as I can gather, there's a new faction within the Empire which is gaining in influence. They call themselves the Kundahari – "heaven's messengers" – and they claim divine guidance in their efforts to restore people's religious beliefs.'

'Hence their antagonism to magic,' Ico commented. 'Is Kudrak one of them?'

'He may be a genuine convert, or he may just find such allegiance politically convenient. We can't be sure. What *does* seem certain is that there's someone in the High Court at Zepharinn who has the ear of Emperor Madar. He's still a young man, and inexperienced, so it's possible he's being manipulated.'

'Do we know who this person is?' Andrin asked.

'No. I don't think he's a member of the Imperial Council, though, which means he may be one of Madar's personal friends.'

'Which could make him all the more dangerous,' Ico added. 'The Council might at least act as a calming influence.'

'Not if it's more expedient for them to be reckless, they won't,' Andrin commented cynically.

'So you think we should take the threat of a holy war seriously?' Ico asked.

'I think we should take the prospect of war seriously, holy or otherwise,' Maciot replied. 'The fact that Kudrak even mentioned the possibility means it's been discussed in Zepharinn, and if the Empire's politics are really that volatile, then who knows what they might do.'

'But you believe their objection to magic might just be a smokescreen?' Ico persisted hopefully. She had no intention of abandoning the search for wizardry.

'It's perfectly possible,' Maciot admitted.

'Let's hope so,' Andrin put in. 'If they're hostile to magic, just think how they'd react if they found out what Nino's trying to do.'

'Why else would the Empire want to invade us?' Ico said, not wanting to dwell on that alarming thought. 'It's true that we're wealthier than we've been in a long time, but it's nothing compared to the riches of the Empire.'

'Tiguafaya may have become more important strategically,' Maciot replied. 'As you know, we've been getting reports that the Empire is trading with lands far to the east, and they've probably been exploring further south too.'

'You think they may be set on expansion?' Andrin asked. 'And we're just a stepping stone?'

Maciot shrugged.

'Who knows? Their borders have been static for about two hundred years. Perhaps Madar has it in mind to become a conquering hero, make his mark on history. He wouldn't be the first to be ruled by such motivation.'

'And a holy war would be the perfect excuse,' Ico commented wryly.

'You don't think this might be some *unholy* alliance?'

Andrin wondered. 'Between the Empire and someone of Maghdim's persuasion?'

Ico and Maciot both glanced at him in some dismay. Although such an idea had evidently not occurred to either of them, now that it had the prospect was appalling. Maghdim had been hired by Kantrowe to help him fight the Firebrands' magic, and to advance his own grandiose schemes. The self-styled anti-mage – who had come from an unknown land far to the east, on the other side of the Inner Seas – had harboured a fanatical hatred of magic.

'Gods, I hope not,' Ico whispered. When Maghdim had been killed, she had hoped never to see his like again.

After a long, uncomfortable pause, it was Ico who brought them back to more practical considerations.

'We need information,' she stated. 'We're groping in the dark here.'

'Agreed.' Maciot was businesslike again now. 'Do you think an official envoy would be received?'

'I don't know. All we can do is try.'

'We should also try to alert our contacts overseas. Someone's got to know what's going on.'

'Do that,' Ico concurred, knowing that in his position as leader of the Travellers' Guild, Maciot had access to a whole network of merchants, couriers and seafarers.

Andrin made no further contribution to this part of the discussion. He was lost in his own thoughts now, and it was only when Maciot rose to take his leave that his reverie was disturbed.

'It's a pity your contacts with the pirates have faded away,' the senator commented. 'If the Empire's connections to the east and south are growing in importance, the brethren of the isles would be among the first to know.'

'That friendship was never going to last long,' Ico replied. She had spent some time as a prisoner aboard one of the pirate fleets that roamed the Inner Seas, and although she had eventually won their approval and loyalty, many of them had subsequently been killed – and in the process she had made deadly enemies among the other buccaneers. For years, pirates had ravaged Tiguafaya's eastern coastline, but in recent times they had presented no threat and the loss of her remaining contacts had therefore seemed unimportant. 'In any case,' she added, 'I don't think the brethren would part with that sort of information easily, even to me. They'd be much more likely to think up some way of using it for their own benefit.'

# CHAPTER SEVEN

For the first time in his life, Galan Zarzuelo knew that he was out of his depth. He could not betray his uncertainty to his deputies, of course. Such a sign of weakness would have been unthinkable. So he said nothing and, to give himself time to think, looked away from the woman to the two robed attendants who flanked her, keeping his expression carefully neutral. Behind him Yawl and Chavez were also silent.

The woman had spoken in a language the pirates could not even begin to comprehend, and which seemed to consist merely of a succession of clicks, whistles and sighs. One of her companions was evidently acting as her interpreter and, after nodding briefly to her, he turned to fix a steady gaze upon Zarzuelo.

'The Emissary wishes to know your views on magic.'

'I don't like it,' the pirate replied instantly, sure that here at least he was on safe ground. 'It's not natural.'

The translator, whose face had seemed to have been carved from stone, now gave a slight smile. When he repeated the pirate leader's words in her own language – a process that seemed to take an inordinately long time for such a straightforward statement – the woman also revealed muted signs of pleasure. She spoke again.

'Then we can do business,' her companion explained.

Zarzuelo had been in his 'palace' when news of the strangers' arrival had first been brought to him. Ever since the deaths of his two main rivals, he had been the undisputed leader of the brethren of the isles and, as such, had had the choice of many islands on which to build a new home. However, he had decided to remain at his original base. This was a broken circle of islands, surrounding a calm lagoon, which had been formed by a volcanic eruption more than a thousand years earlier. The largest of these islands was crescent-shaped, with its inner coastline buttressed by a small cliff. Because it supported not only his residence but also a sizeable town, vineyards, farms and plantations, and – most important of all – an excellent supply of fresh water, it had been an obvious choice.

The palace itself was a sprawling construction which had been added to piecemeal over the years, so that it now contained almost a hundred rooms of all shapes and sizes. These included Zarzuelo's treasure house, accommodation for his harem, a feasting hall, a five-storey lookout tower, and numerous stores and cellars. It had been the scene of many wild celebrations, endless drinking contests, debauchery and occasional outbursts of violence, but more often than not it was a quiet place. The buccaneers always regained their thirst for adventure quickly, and sailed away again, leaving the palace in the care of their women. Although Zarzuelo and his men had accumulated considerable riches, which enabled them to indulge in almost any pleasure they desired, these all paled beside the joys of battle and the thrill of the chase. It was the life Zarzuelo had been born to. His father, also called Galan, had been the leading pirate of his day – and had been guaranteed immortal fame when he had led the fleet that had smashed the Tiguafayan navy, commanded by the infamous Admiral Jurado Madri. That had been more than thirty years ago, and nothing any of the buccaneers had achieved since then had been remotely as memorable.

Zarzuelo still dreamed of the day when his own deeds might eclipse his father's, but in his honest moments he knew that that day was a long way off – and indeed might never come. His forebear's real triumph had been to unite all the pirate fleets into one truly formidable force for the battle, but that success had been only temporary. Once victory at sea had been achieved, the various factions had squabbled over the spoils and, as a result, they had failed to occupy Tiguafaya and had returned to their petty internecine wars. The present situation, in which Zarzuelo had no serious rivals, was the closest the brethren had come to unity since then. However, alliances among the pirates tended to be fragile at best, and Zarzuelo was only ever really confident of his own fleet – which numbered twenty-seven ships and almost two thousand free men.

In a strange way, he missed his former rivals. Vicent Agnadi, who had been known as 'The Lawyer', and The Barber – whose real name no one had ever known – were both dead, their fleets divided into smaller bands, each led by men with ambitions of their own. Some had seen sense and agreed to join Zarzuelo, but others had chosen to exercise their nominal independence. Although none of them was capable of being more than a nuisance to him, such nuisances were somehow more unsettling than the earlier open rivalries had been. The Lawyer, in particular, had been a worthy opponent and, on one fateful occasion, partner. The leaders of the two largest pirate fleets had combined forces to assist Tias Kantrowe, while the enigmatic Barber, with his own inexplicable logic, had sided with the Tiguafayan rebels, and Ico Maravedis in particular.

The conflict that had followed – which involved witch-craft as well as a clash of arms – had claimed many ships and men, almost half the Barber's fleet and most of the Lawyer's. Zarzuelo himself had sustained relatively few casualties, and as a result had gained the nickname he had sought for so long. 'The Survivor' was not the epithet he would have chosen, but he was stuck with it now. However, Kantrowe's defeat on land had meant that he was unable to fulfil his promises, and the pirates' weakened position had left them unable to exploit Tiguafaya's confusion. Nor had they been able to prevent the new government from eventually equipping a modern navy. Some of the Barber's men had even allied themselves to the new regime in Teguise, claiming to have been saved from even greater catastrophe by Ico's sorcery and by the actions of some birds she controlled. Predictably, that alliance had not lasted long, and the pirates had returned to their old ways. Nevertheless, Zarzuelo could not bring himself to trust them now.

The first messenger had arrived as he was finishing his midday meal, and brought news that an unknown ship was approaching the atoll.

'A single ship?' Zarzuelo asked.

The messenger nodded.

'Heading straight for us.'

The pirate leader glanced at his dining companions, who included his deputy commanders, Earless Yawl and Chavez, then shrugged.

'Let them come,' he decided. 'We've nothing to fear from one vessel. Just make sure the duty crews are on watch.'

The messenger hurried away to do his bidding, returning a short while later with a second report. And this time the pirate leader's curiosity was aroused.

'Its sails are black and so's the hull. There's not a scrap of colour anywhere, except the flag.'

Zarzuelo frowned. The only black-sailed vessel he had ever known was his own flagship, the *Night Wolf*, and so the visitor's appearance could be seen as a veiled insult.

'What flag?' Yawl asked.

'A single plain yellow triangle, like a pennant. I asked around, but no one knows what it means. But that's not the strangest part,' the messenger went on. 'There are five mollymarks flying with them.'

'Five?' Zarzuelo exclaimed in disbelief. 'Are you sure?'

'I saw them with my own eyes.'

This was the most unsettling news of all. Mollymarks – or albatrosses, as they were called by landsmen – were usually solitary birds. Seeing two together was unusual, and five was unheard of. Because seafarers believed them to be singularly ill-omened creatures, the appearance of so many was doubly portentous.

'Are they in the lagoon?'

'They will be by now. They were just entering Goat Channel when I left the viewpoint.'

'I think we'd better see this for ourselves,' Zarzuelo decreed, and led the way to the cliffs that overlooked the shallow, shark-infested waters.

Half an hour later, they were still none the wiser about the visitors' intentions. The ship had dropped anchor in the lagoon, some distance from any other vessel, and her sails had been furled. The huge birds still circled lazily overhead, to the consternation of many onlookers.

The newcomers clearly had no aggressive intent, but by the same token they showed no concern about being attacked themselves, the crew going about their business in an unhurried, professional manner. That in itself spoke of un-reasonable confidence. The captain of any ship who dared sail into the middle of a pirate stronghold, alone and without permission, was either very foolish or immune to fear. The buccaneers had been happy to let them enter the lagoon, knowing that if they proved to be valuable friends they could simply be made welcome; if not, they could easily be overwhelmed, the crew killed or enslaved and the ship and its cargo commandeered. Even so, Zarzuelo's men were not used to such bravado, and the presence of the mollymarks was unnerving too. Everyone was waiting to see what their leader would do.

When it was clear that no one on board the strange vessel was going to make a move, Zarzuelo ordered a small skiff to approach and hail them. After a series of terse exchanges, it emerged that the ship's most important passenger was some sort of envoy, although from which land was not specified. Moreover, this envoy refused to come ashore, but wished to meet with the pirates' leader. Such arrogance annoyed Zarzuelo initially, but his curiosity eventually got the better of him and he agreed to a meeting aboard the *Night Wolf*. He made his way to his flagship, then watched as a boat was lowered from the black vessel and three foreigners, all dressed in long flowing robes, were rowed across by a crew of six oarsmen. It was only when the delegation had come aboard that Zarzuelo realized one of them was a woman.

He had invited the visitors to join him and his deputies in his cabin, a venue that he knew intimidated most guests. It was a large room by seafaring standards, decorated in gaudy colours, with silk drapes and gilt ornamentation. But there were also two human skulls nailed to one of the walls and even now, when its master had not been to sea for several days, it retained a fetid quality, an animal stench overlaid with a decaying sweetness. In one corner stood a birdcage, containing a sleeping parrot whose brilliant red and green plumage was frayed with age.

Zarzuelo had also made sure that his own appearance

was as imposing as possible. He was a large man, deeply
tanned by sun and wind, who wore his hair long. Heavy
gold jewellery glittered at his neck and on his hands, and a
jewelled dagger hung from his belt. However, this seemed to
make no impression on the visitors, none of whom had yet
spoken a word. The men's faces were unreadable masks, and
the woman's eyes seemed dead, like those of a baked fish.
They were all dark-skinned, but with an underlying
pallor that spoke of lives spent indoors. They appeared to be
carrying no weapons, although these might have been
concealed by their robes. Zarzuelo looked for signs of any
thin blades secreted in their sleeves or wire garrottes in the
hems of their garments, but he could detect nothing, and he
sensed no violent intentions.

The visitors stood quite still, the woman a little behind
the others. They were offered refreshments, but these were
refused with a simple shake of the head. Zarzuelo then
waved them to chairs at the table. Although they chose to
remain standing, the pirate leader sat down anyway, angered
by their rejection of his hospitality and determined to assert
his sovereignty. Inside he was feeling far from confident.

'My name is Galan Zarzuelo. In the name of all the
brethren of the islands, I welcome you here. What do you
wish to discuss with me?'

At this point both men looked round, obviously deferring
to the woman. Until that moment the pirate leader had
assumed her to be a servant, but now he was forced to revise
this assumption, and his sense of unease deepened. After a
few moments' wordless consultation the silence was broken,
and it had been then that the interpreter had asked for
Zarzuelo's opinion of magic.

After that the conversation had proceeded as fast as the
process of translation would allow. The Emissary grew

animated, listening closely to everything Zarzuelo said, even though it was clear she understood none of his words. For his part, the pirate leader could make neither head nor tail of her bizarre language. But although he felt happier talking to her translator, there was no way he could pretend to be ignorant of where the real authority lay.

'We come seeking information and, perhaps, your help,' she told him via the interpreter.

'The brethren of the isles are the only true free men,' he replied. It was the creed he had believed in all his life – as his father had done before him. 'Our knowledge is our own.'

'But may it not be shared if mutual advantage is thus gained?' the visitors replied, the words sounding stilted and oddly accented.

'Perhaps,' Zarzuelo agreed carefully. 'If you can tell me why we should help you.'

This was followed by a lengthy exchange in the clicking tongue.

'The Emissary believes that it would perhaps be better for us to explain the purpose of our mission. Then you may decide on your own course, depending upon the aspects of your own stars.'

Zarzuelo shrugged, trying to appear indifferent.

'Go ahead.'

'We follow in the footsteps of the Martyr,' the interpreter declared. 'We have vowed to avenge his death, and to rid the world of the evil that claimed his life.'

'And this evil is?'

'Magic.' He spat the word, and his face revealed the depths of his revulsion and contempt. At the same time the other man let out an angry series of clicks, but when the woman glanced at him sharply he reverted to his habitual, stone-faced silence.

'Vile sorcery is rising again in Tiguafaya, and unless it is crushed it will destroy us all.'

'I hardly think—' Zarzuelo began, but the translator interrupted him.

'The fires below are reaching up. Even here, in the midst of the ocean, no one will be safe.'

'The volcanoes?' The pirates had noted some slight tremors on the islands during recent months, and had also observed some unusual currents and large waves they could not explain.

'The flames of retribution,' the foreigner confirmed.

Zarzuelo sat silently for a while, trying to digest this idea.

'How are you going to oppose magic?' he asked eventually.

This time it was the Emissary who answered, even though his question had not been translated for her. Her un-intelligible reply went on for some time, and the pirates were forced to wait until the interpreter turned back to them.

'We use our minds to counteract the unnatural forces that the usurpers of nature's elemental powers use for their own ends. But that is only in a direct confrontation. We will do all we can to prevent sorcery from being used in the first place, if necessary by killing the wizards and all their acolytes.'

'Good luck to you,' Zarzuelo said. 'But I still don't see how this concerns us.'

'Two of those we wish to kill are Ico Maravedis and Andrin Zonzomas, and we believe you bear a grudge against them. Do you know where we might find them?'

'Yes. Of course,' the pirate leader replied, then allowed his sometimes sluggish thought processes to catch up with his tongue. 'But if you know who they are, surely you know *where* they are. They're not exactly hard to locate.'

'We believe them to reside in Teguise,' the interpreter admitted, 'but that city is unknown to us. Your guidance would be welcome.'

'And my swordsmen?'

The man bowed his head in acknowledgement.

'Those too, perhaps.'

'It's true I have no love for these wizards or their magic, but why should I risk my fleet simply for revenge? There's little adventure or profit in assassination.'

There was a slight delay before he received the Emissary's answer.

'We can make it worth your while. Our resources are considerable – and of course there is the possibility of plunder once Teguise is in turmoil.'

'These resources, are any of them on your ship?'

'Some of them.'

'Then what's to stop me simply taking them for myself? You are considerably outnumbered, after all.'

'That would not be wise. We can defend ourselves.'

'I've seen no weapons,' Zarzuelo pointed out.

'We have all the weapons we need in our speed and in our minds. Shall we demonstrate?'

The silent man moved then, becoming a ghostlike blur, and at the same time all three pirates felt a paralyzing uncertainty invade their own thoughts. A moment later time began to flow again, but the foreigner was now behind Zarzuelo's chair, one hand resting lightly on the back of the pirate leader's neck. Had he held a knife and been inclined to murder, the Survivor's nickname would no longer have been appropriate. However, the visitor merely returned to his former place and stood quite still once more. By then both Yawl and Chavez had drawn their weapons, but Zarzuelo motioned for them to remain calm as the Emissary spoke again.

'The gods protect us on this voyage,' her colleague translated. 'We have read the omens among the stars. We wish only to be your friends.'

'You've a funny way of showing it,' Zarzuelo muttered, still shaken by the encounter. He was no longer surprised by the fearless way they had sailed into the lagoon. 'Tell me, what is the difference between magic and what you do? Both seem unnatural to me.'

It was an honest but tactless question, and the Emissary's fanatical eyes stared at him with disdain when it was relayed to her. Even so her answer was civil enough.

'Some of us are born with minds like swords, which we use to cut away the foul growths of magic. This is a sacred duty, to punish and prevent these crimes against nature and the stars.'

Zarzuelo was not sure he understood the distinction, but it was clear he would get nothing more out of them on that topic.

'We have said enough for now,' the interpreter stated. 'The Emissary will leave you so that you may discuss your response.'

'Does the Emissary have a name?' the pirate asked quickly, not wanting the meeting to end as if he were being dismissed.

'I have taken the name Lamia,' came the reply.

'And this Martyr, the one you're following,' Zarzuelo went on. 'Does *he* have a name?'

Once again he waited for the translation of the envoy's reply.

'His name was Maghdim. He was my father.'

Some time later, after a confused and fruitless discussion with his deputies, Zarzuelo was alone in his cabin once more. Although part of him wanted to have nothing more to do with the dangerous lunatics, another part insisted that refusing to help them might be even more perilous. Nothing about the events of the afternoon had given him much comfort. His one hope was that the Emissary really did need his aid, and that their proposed alliance might therefore be genuine. In such a way revenge might be combined with profit – a heady mix indeed.

Doubts continued to assail him as he turned to look at the parrot.

'Olivina?'

The bird stirred, ruffled its mangy feathers, and regarded its master with a malicious gleam in its eyes.

'Did you understand what the woman said?' Zarzuelo knew that the parrot had only been feigning sleep, as usual. The bird's perfect memory had proved invaluable to him on many occasions.

'Some of it,' Olivina replied.

'Did the interpreter translate all she said accurately?'

'Most of it.'

'But not all?' He had suspected treachery all along.

'No.'

'What else did she say?'

'That this cabin smelt worse than a camel trainer's dung-heap,' Olivina replied, then squawked with laughter.

# CHAPTER EIGHT

Vargo finally woke late in the afternoon. In spite of Allegra's fears, he did not seem downhearted about his failure to communicate with the dragon eggs, and now that his long sleep had banished the fatigue of his vigil, he appeared strangely invigorated.

Although she was glad he had not succumbed to depression, Cat was still wary. She had seen him this way before – and at such times he had often been at his most reckless. There was little danger while they remained in Corazoncillo, but in his present state Vargo was likely to be contemplating new adventures. He was quite capable of setting off without giving any thought to the consequences of his actions, leaving Cat to deal as best she could with practical matters such as food, water and somewhere to sleep. As a result she was glad that on this occasion Nino was there, and might provide some distraction.

Vargo was delighted to see his old friend, and the two men spent several hours together in animated conversation. The idea that the valley might be some kind of focus clearly fascinated Vargo, and he was enthusiastic about Nino's progress towards creating a bird-linked web – demanding to be told about everything that had been achieved so far, and about Nino's plans for the future. It was only when they came to discuss his own progress and the futile search for untainted fireworms that Vargo became less optimistic. Even so, he remained lucid, and Nino began to wonder whether his reputation for incomprehensibility was really deserved.

Very little of what they spoke about was new to Allegra and, once she had satisfied herself that Vargo was all right, she left them to it. Finding herself suddenly restless, she decided to walk to Quemada, following the well-worn trail that wound between the plantations of fig trees and the rows of lava-lined pits that sheltered vines. It was dusk by the time she returned and – hearing the murmur of conversation still coming from inside the guest house and not wanting to interrupt – she sat on the step outside and let the gentle, constant breeze dry her perspiration. Even though her walk had been nothing more than a short stroll compared to some of the journeys she had made with Vargo, Allegra was nonetheless glad to rest her legs. A few days in one place and you're already going soft, she told herself disapprovingly. She wondered when they'd be setting off again and found, in spite of her general weariness, that she was hoping it would be soon. She would have Vargo to herself again then, no matter how preoccupied he was.

Leaning back, she deliberately cleared her mind of all such speculation, knowing that it was not her choice to make, and contented herself with watching the sky. Sunset was painting the heavens in bands of pink and gold, outlined by some thin high clouds that had blown in from the western ocean. It was achingly beautiful but doomed to fade and, for reasons she did not fully understand, Cat found herself on the verge of tears. Gold dulled to orange and pink to purple as the evening drew on, and it was then that she realized she was being watched.

Turning her head to look at the building opposite, she saw Eya perched on the edge of its roof. The falcon was perfectly motionless, his head hunched into powerful shoulders. In such a position he seemed far too solid to be capable of the glorious freedom and speed he displayed when he flew, but the eyes that glittered in the failing light were as alert as ever. Allegra shivered at the thought that had she been a mouse, that feral glint would probably have been the last thing she ever saw.

As she was wondering how long the falcon had been there, and whether he ever slept, her attention was diverted by the arrival of another, much more familiar bird. Ero landed on the ground in front of her, raising a small cloud of dust that seemed to cause him some confusion. As it settled, he called softly, bobbed his tail and then fanned his crest as if to confirm that the dirt had not spoiled its delicate colouring. Apparently satisfied, he then waddled over towards Cat and hopped up onto the step beside her.

'Hello, Ero,' she said quietly. 'Where have you been?'

The bird cocked his head on one side, as if considering his answer, then moved even closer and gently laid his head against her thigh, one black eye gazing up at her hopefully. It was such an unexpectedly intimate gesture that Allegra was taken by surprise and, for the second time in a few minutes, found herself close to tears. Ero had never touched her like this before, and she did not know how to react. She felt that he was trying to tell her something – if only she could have heard what it was – but even if it was simply a sign of affection she was grateful.

She reached out a tentative hand, meaning to stroke the hoopoe's smooth breast, but something made her glance upwards and she saw Eya watching Ero's performance with lofty disdain. A moment later the falcon swooped away into the gathering gloom, and Ero spied something to eat and went off hunting. His probing bill soon captured the grub and he swallowed it happily. The moment had passed; Ero was his normal exuberant self once more and Cat was alone with her thoughts again. She sighed – and that was when the music began.

It was one of Vargo's winter songs, a bittersweet lament that had been one of the few things he had written during the Firebrands' exile in the wilderness. For one heart-stopping moment, Allegra thought that his gift had returned, but then she realized that the faint sounds were coming from her right, towards the centre of the village, and not from behind her. Further listening confirmed these first impressions. Whoever was playing the viol did not have Vargo's deft touch and the voice, while perfectly pitched and full toned, missed many of the nuances of the composer's own singing.

Curiosity warred with fear in Allegra's heart. Who was the musician? And how had he come to know this particular song? Although she wanted to know, she was also worried about the effect it might have on Vargo. Would he be reminded of all he had lost, of the cruel price the dragons had forced him to pay? Would he even recognize his own creation? Concern won out over curiosity and she stood up, then hesitated, deciding whether to open the door and let the music in. When she realized that the windows were un-shuttered anyway, she went in and found the two men still deep in conversation. They fell silent and looked up as she entered, and the music drifted gently in with her.

At first Vargo's expression was unreadable, but then he smiled.

'Cabria said there was going to be a dance tonight,' he remarked, sounding not at all put out. 'Is it that late already?'

'The sun's just setting,' Cat replied.

Vargo listened for a few more moments.

'It sounds quite good,' he commented.

'It should do,' Nino began. 'After all, you—'

He broke off then, and glanced quickly at Allegra.

'Shall I close the shutters?' she asked.

'No. I'd like to listen.'

The song's melancholy coda faded into silence a few moments later, and was replaced by the sturdier rhythms of a traditional dance tune. Other musicians joined in with the violist now, and if it had not been for the tension inside the guest house, Cat's spirits would have been lifted by the gaiety of their playing.

'One day we'll dance again, under skies of fire,' Vargo said, evidently quoting from something only he could remember. His pale grey eyes seemed to look far into the distance, but then he stood up and glanced at Cat and his eyes were bright, with a fire she had not seen in a long time. 'Shall we go and dance, Allegra?' he asked quietly.

'Are you sure?' she replied, her own uncertainty obvious.

'Of course! You too, Nino. And Ero will be delighted.' He spent a moment in silent communication and was answered by a jubilant call from outside. 'Come on.'

Nino and Cat exchanged glances and then followed him onto the street, where they were joined by the hoopoe – who was fluttering in the air in a state of high excitement. Above them the sky was almost black, but the sudden nightfall was illuminated by streaks of red, as if there were rivers of lava flowing between the stars.

The dancing was already well under way when they arrived at the small square where the band were playing. Although the presence of the visitors caused some sidelong glances and whispered comments, they were soon absorbed into the merriment. Vargo took Cat's hands and whirled her off into the throng, and before long Nino had been approached by one of the village girls and was dancing too, while above them all Ero cavorted in an ecstatic celebration of his own.

Allegra still did not quite understand Vargo's mood, but she was delighted to see that he was genuinely enjoying himself, throwing his whole body into the music. She felt a small pang of sadness that his movements were clumsy and merely wholehearted when once they had been elegant and wonderfully expressive – but nevertheless this was surely progress. She dared not hope that it might be his first, faltering step back towards rediscovering his own music, and decided just to enjoy the moment for its own sake. She had forgotten that such simple joys existed.

Vargo was tireless, and was still dancing long after both Cat and Nino had been forced to sit and watch, drinking thirstily from cups of celona. Vargo's enthusiasm had soon dispelled any reticence the villagers might have felt towards him and, once the ice had been broken, there was a procession of women who were more than willing to partner 'the madman'.

'It looks as if he might be getting over the loss of his music,' Nino commented.

'I hope so,' Cat replied, but wasn't sure whether she meant this or not. Getting over his loss might mean that he had given up any hope of recovering his gift.

'You'd better watch out,' Nino teased. 'Half the female population of Corazoncillo is flirting with him now.' His grin removed any serious import his words might have had, and Cat smiled back.

'I don't care. Just as long as he's happy.'

There was only one potentially awkward moment, much later in the evening, when one of the musicians asked Vargo if he would care to play or sing with them. Vargo replied, good-naturedly, that he had no talent for such things and refused politely. If any of the onlookers knew of his previous reputation, they had enough sense not to mention it and, much to Allegra's relief, the incident passed without further comment.

On the other hand, Ero – who had never been able to pass up an opportunity to show off – was more than happy to play his part in the evening's entertainment. The comical way in which he strutted across the stage before exploding into flight, and the aerial ballet that followed, were greeted by a roar of approval from everyone present. He danced and sang in the air in perfect time, and Cat found herself helpless with laughter. As Ero milked the applause shamelessly, she turned to see tears running down Vargo's face and her joy instantly turned to concern.

'What's the matter?'

It was a few moments before he replied.

'It's been so long,' he told her sadly.

Allegra waited for him to go on, but he said nothing, his eyes fixed on the hoopoe's antics.

'For Ero?' she guessed.

'I had no right . . .' Vargo whispered. 'Look at him. He was born for this.'

A cheer went up as the music ended with a flourish – and Ero matched it with a flamboyant swooping turn before alighting, with exquisite timing, on the band leader's hat. The laughter and applause continued, but Cat did not hear it.

'Don't be sad,' she begged.

'I'm not.' Vargo grinned suddenly through his tears. 'I chose my path. Ero didn't, any more than you did, my sweet Cat. Don't ever let me forget that again. Just because I'm in the mirror all the time, it doesn't mean I have to drag the rest of you in too.'

'What do you mean?'

'Never mind,' he replied, as the music started up again. 'Come on, Cat. Dance with me.'

He took her in his arms then and, together, they too took wing.

# CHAPTER NINE

The febrile energy that had suffused Vargo drained away again the next day, and he slept on well into the morning. Allegra and Nino met at breakfast, and smiled at each other as they recalled the events of the previous night.

'I remember my grandparents dancing,' Nino remarked. 'It was a much more stately affair in those days, though, even when they danced by lava light.'

'Did people really do that?' Cat asked. She had heard such stories often enough, but had always thought them to be apocryphal.

'Oh, yes! The last big eruption went on for so long, and the lava flows were so constant, people just got used to them. It was a matter of honour to see who would dance closest, and Lechuza and Ama nearly always won.'

'How is Lechuza?'

'He died last year.'

'Oh. I'm sorry.'

'I think it's what he wanted,' Nino said. 'He'd outlived Ama by five years, and when he decided he was too old to go prospecting any more it was as if there was nothing left for him to do. I still miss him, though.'

Allegra did not know how to respond to that. Her own grandparents had all died before she had been born.

'We had some grand times together,' Nino went on nostalgically.

'Do you miss the prospecting?' Cat asked.

'Sometimes. Life was a lot simpler then.'

'Tell me what it's like, being a prospector.'

Nino's reaction made it clear that he was glad to be talking about something uncomplicated for once, something he understood completely.

'There's something majestic about the deep firelands, where there aren't even any paths or camel tracks,' he began eagerly. 'It's like a new world, untouched, with the lichens just beginning to bring life back to the land. Other than that it's just rock and sky and the wind.'

He went on to describe how, under Lechuza's tutelage, he had learnt to read the hidden messages in the different kinds of lava – from the dusty stretches of black sand to the brittle coils where the molten flows had solidified into smooth waves, rope-like tangles or razor-sharp edges. He painted oral pictures of the surprising variations in the colour of the rock – reds, oranges, yellows and browns – which more superstitious folk believed to be the trails left either by fireworms or by the breath of dragons, and of the telltale signs that led a prospector to the treasure he sought, the crystals known as dragon's tears.

Much of what Nino described was already familiar to Cat from her own travelling, but she had always come to the wild places as an intruder. He came as a native, and to hear him talk was to understand the true nature of the firelands. She too had crawled into lava tubes, explored the pointed caves that were called 'dragon's horns', and had experienced the astonishing power of the hot spots – where the temperature rose dramatically only a few hand spans below the surface – and yet Nino made it all sound fresh and full of wonder, granting her a new appetite for voyaging into these potentially dangerous and strangely beautiful realms.

One thing Nino did not need to describe was the object of the prospectors' searches. Dragon's tears were familiar to most people in Tiguafaya, and to everyone associated with the Firebrands. Indeed, they had become the most important tool in the re-establishment of magic. These transculent green crystals were uniquely potent. Ancient lore stated that they had been formed when certain types of lava had cooled rapidly in water, its heat dissipating as steam, and it had been known for centuries that if the crystals were destroyed, then this process was reversed – the gemstones absorbing vast amounts of heat from their immediate surroundings. This was very dangerous, especially because it had originally been believed that the process was not only irreversible but also impossible to control. Anyone caught near by was liable to become frost-bitten, or even to freeze to death. As the end result also reduced a valuable jewel to worthless green powder, great care had always been taken to avoid damaging the essential structure of the crystals.

After months of painstaking research, Ico had discovered that the destructive reaction within the stones could be set off using telepathic signals corresponding to each crystal's unique resonance – and her revelation had led to the cold being used first to kill the fireworms and later to control them. Techniques had been evolved to slow down the disintegration and to shape the cold, thus making the dragon's tears even more effective.

'Of course there were times when we didn't find anything for days on end,' Nino concluded. 'Now I'm not sure I could even remember how. Ca was the best spotter I've ever known. It sometimes seemed as if he could see the crystals through layers of solid rock.' Ca had been Lechuza's linked magpie. 'Eya can fly further and faster, and his eyesight's better, but there'll never be a bird with instincts like Ca's.'

'Well, you've got a different job now,' Cat said.

Nino nodded, then sighed. 'And I suppose I should be getting on with it, moving on.' He paused, then added, 'I keep feeling there's something else I'm supposed to do here, but I don't know what it is.'

'Like Vargo.'

'Not really. He has a specific object in mind. Even if he fails, at least he can leave knowing that he tried.'

'I want us to go,' Allegra admitted. 'Being here's doing him no good.'

'Even after last night?' Nino asked. 'He looked pretty happy to me.'

'I don't think that'll last.'

Nino wanted to coax his friend out of her pessimism, but realized that she knew Vargo and his volatile moods far better than he did. In the event Cat changed the subject herself.

'How is your family?' she asked. 'They can't have seen much of you lately.'

Since the revolution two and a half years earlier, Nino had married and had a son.

'Not nearly enough,' he admitted ruefully. 'I haven't been home for more than a month.'

'Then that's where you should go now,' Allegra stated. 'Definitely. Corazoncillo will still be here when you—'

The sudden noise that choked off her words and propelled her to her feet in panic came from Vargo's room, but it did not sound even vaguely human. It was a screech of pain, a grating metallic howl that hurt her ears and shredded her nerves. Although it had stopped by the time she reached the doorway, her fears did not subside. Vargo was sitting bolt upright in bed, his eyes wide open but sightless, one fist clenched tightly in front of his chest. Cat called out his name and hurried to his bedside, but he did not seem to be aware of her, even when she reached out to touch his arm. There was a look of absolute horror on his face.

'Vargo? Vargo! What's the matter?'

He did not respond. His mouth moved but no words came out, only a small rattling sound that left flecks of spittle on his lips. Cat saw that blood was dripping slowly from his hand, and she tried in vain to prise his fingers apart. They were rigid and immovable, as if carved from stone.

'I'm here, Vargo. It's Cat. You're all right, you're safe now. Wake up.' She spoke softly, fighting to keep her voice calm. He had had dreadful nightmares before, but she had never seen him react as badly as this. 'It's all right, my love. I'm here. You were only dreaming.'

Vargo's eyes were still staring at things only he could see and, for once, Allegra was glad she did not share his visions.

'Can I do anything?' Nino asked quietly. He had come as far as the door but was reluctant to trespass further, and felt awkward watching what seemed to him to be a very private scene. The sudden noise and commotion had startled him badly, and his admiration and sympathy for Cat had risen another notch. Seeing someone you loved so much in such agony, and not being able to do anything about it, was the worst form of torture he could imagine.

'Fetch some water and a cloth,' Allegra replied, without turning round. It might not do much good, but she knew Nino would feel better doing something.

'The ravine,' Vargo whispered. His voice was hoarse and sounded far away. 'The ravine. *In* the ravine.'

'What's in the ravine?' Cat asked.

'Shadows. Dreaming,' he replied, even though he still did not look at her. 'Shadows dreaming. And the sea. Underneath. *Underneath* us!'

His words were perfectly clear, even if they made no sense. Nino reappeared, carrying a bowl, but before Cat could begin to mop Vargo's forehead he blinked and his eyes came back into focus. He glanced around, and the expression of utter relief on his face when he saw her kneeling next to him made Allegra's heart swell.

'It's all right,' she said softly. 'It's over.'

'Over?' he replied, in something like his normal voice. He was still obviously puzzled as he looked down at his hand and slowly unclenched his fist. He was holding his talisman, a silver, ring-shaped brooch set with clear brown stones with swirls of gold – like tiny ferns – inside them. He had been holding it so tightly he had made dark indentations in his fingers and palm. The clasp had been open, and the pin had pierced the skin at the base of his thumb.

'Ouch,' he said faintly, staring at his own blood.

Cat took the brooch and set it on the bedside table. She knew that it was very old and that Vargo treasured it, not least because it had been a gift from Famara, but she was more concerned with his injured hand. She wiped it with the damp cloth Nino had brought, then pressed her own thumb over the puncture until the bleeding stopped. Vargo watched her in silence, still looking vaguely surprised.

'There,' Cat said. 'I don't think you'll come to too much harm. Do you want to talk about it?'

'About what?'

'The dream. You had another nightmare.'

Vargo did not answer immediately, and seemed slightly bewildered.

'We have to leave here,' he stated eventually.

With a sense of timing that Allegra could not believe was wholly coincidental, a messenger arrived in Corazoncillo later that same morning. He brought news of unconfirmed reports of a previously unknown colony of fireworms, far to the west and, naturally enough, Vargo took this as a sign. Cat began to make arrangements for their departure.

At first light the next day, Vargo, Cat and Nino left the valley by the western trail, climbing at a steady pace, each carrying a heavy pack. At the rim Nino said his farewells and turned south, towards his own village. The other two continued westward, heading for the distant ocean.

Three days later they stood on the edge of a vast canyon, staring into its depths. Cat could not help wondering if this was the ravine Vargo had glimpsed. They were well into their journey now, in a region that was quite unfamiliar. Any settlements were few and far between here, and Cat had already begun to ration their supplies, not knowing when they would next be replenished.

Vargo had remained sure of his purpose, striding eagerly into the wilderness. But Allegra felt uneasy. She had not liked the Corazoncillo valley, but the further away from it they travelled the stronger her conviction grew that something was wrong.

# CHAPTER TEN

Ambassador Kudrak was not used to being treated in such a cavalier manner – and nor was he accustomed to doing business in establishments like the one he found himself in now. However, the summons had been couched in unequivocal terms, and was unquestionably genuine. Although Kudrak had no idea what Prince Tzarno was doing in this seedy dockside tavern, the courier who had brought the sealed letter had known the appropriate imperial passwords – and his escort of competent-looking soldiers had given the message a further weight of authority.

The guards remained at the bottom of the staircase as Kudrak followed the courier to a private chamber above. Tzarno was there, attended by two young women who were dismissed as soon as the envoy was ushered in. The courier left too, closing the door behind him.

'Welcome back to the Empire, Kudrak,' the prince said, waving the newcomer to a chair. 'I would say welcome back to civilization, but I daresay you don't believe Uga Stai deserves such an appellation.'

'It is always good to return to one's homeland, Your

Highness,' the ambassador replied smoothly, 'wherever one makes landfall.'

Uga Stai was the largest of the ports on the coastline of the Inner Seas, and had the best road connection to the capital, Zepharinn, but it was not a cultural centre of any distinction. Its inhabitants enjoyed their reputation for being as ruthless in business as they were in fighting. When they were not engaged in these pursuits, they took their pleasures seriously – as evidenced by some of the sounds that were filtering up from the ground floor.

'You look surprised to find me here,' Tzarno remarked, smiling affably.

'It's not for me to dictate the movements of a prince,' the envoy replied, 'yet I had thought to see you in Zepharinn.'

'In more salubrious surroundings, perhaps?'

Kudrak knew that he was being mocked, albeit gently, but he was a diplomat, and knew when to say nothing.

'I can't always be at my brother's side,' Tzarno explained, 'and visiting places like this helps me keep in touch with our people.'

'An admirable objective, Your Highness.'

Tzarno smiled.

'Do I detect an element of sarcasm, Ambassador?'

'Not at all,' Kudrak replied, straight-faced.

'Tell me, did President Maravedis admit the error of her people's ways?'

The abrupt change of subject caused the envoy no more than a moment's confusion. Although the prince was younger than his brother, and Madar had therefore ascended the imperial throne on the death of their father, there were many in the capital who felt that Tzarno had the sharper mind of the two. As Commander General of the Imperial Army he had already proven his worth in battle, but his wit and ready tongue also made him a formidable opponent in any debate. By now, Kudrak had realized that the prince's real purpose in summoning him was to get the news from Tiguafaya before anyone in Zepharinn.

'She confirmed our suspicions of heresy,' he replied. 'Indeed, she seemed to be rather proud of it.'

Tzarno grinned again, displaying his famously sharpened teeth, which had given him the nickname 'the Emperor's Wolf'. It was a fashion Kudrak found repulsive, but he knew that others – women especially – found the prince extremely attractive. He was tall and slim, built for speed rather than power, and his lean, bony face was clean-shaven. His hair was the colour of pale straw, cropped short, and his eyes were a brilliant blue-green.

'You pointed out the error of her ways, no doubt,' the prince commented.

'I passed on the Emperor's message, yes.'

'And she did not back down, even then?'

'No,' Kudrak replied, ignoring the fact that he had given Ico no time to respond to his ultimatum.

'I think I should like to meet this woman.'

'She is dangerous,' the ambassador opined.

'I would hope so,' Tzarno said, laughing. 'Better that than completely docile, like most of the women at Court. I don't envy my brother having to choose which one of *them* to marry.'

Kudrak chose to ignore the slight upon the women of Zepharinn.

'Maravedis is a sorceress,' he pointed out. 'And, we must assume, a politician of some skill – although I saw little evidence of it. The fact that she is also a woman only makes it more likely that she is duplicitous.'

'I would have thought duplicity a necessary qualification for any president,' Tzarno remarked. He was aware of the ambassador's prejudices, and enjoyed needling him from time to time. When Kudrak did not rise to the bait, he added, 'She's married now, isn't she?'

The envoy nodded.

'To a ruffian whose lack of breeding is immediately obvious.'

'She's no respecter of convention, is she? And beautiful too, I hear.'

'In a barbaric way,' Kudrak conceded reluctantly.

'It's no wonder you don't like her,' the prince said mildly.

'It's her mind and her ideas I don't like,' the ambassador responded, allowing his annoyance at being teased to show for once. 'Blasphemy is a crime that can never be condoned.'

'The Kundahari certainly wouldn't like it.'

'Nor would any god-fearing citizen.'

'Do you really believe that?' the prince asked.

'Of course,' the envoy replied, though he sounded less certain of his ground now.

'I've always felt that the gods help those who help themselves,' Tzarno said.

'The needs of pragmatism and religion have to be carefully balanced,' Kudrak agreed cautiously.

The prince nodded approvingly.

'And fanaticism has its uses,' he added. 'Tell me everything that happened with the Maravedis woman.'

The ambassador found himself in a difficult position. Having been sent on his mission by the Emperor himself, he should have reported directly to Madar before speaking to anyone else. On the other hand, there was no way he could disobey a direct command from an imperial prince. Tzarno evidently recognized the envoy's predicament, and sought to reassure him.

'I only ask because, if the army should be needed – and it certainly seems that it might be – I want to be prepared. I'm sure my brother would approve. Besides, it seems foolish that such vital intelligence must travel all the way to Zepharinn and then back to me here in the south, don't you agree?'

'It does,' Kudrak admitted hesitantly. 'However, I trust you won't take any action based upon my report until the Emperor and his council have had time to consider it.'

'Don't worry. I'll make sure anything I do is seen as a result of my own perspicacity rather than any indiscretion on your part.' Tzarno smiled, accepting the ambassador's need to protect himself, while secretly despising the hidebound ways in which imperial bureaucracy functioned.

Although Kudrak was still uneasy about having been put in such an awkward situation, he did as he had been asked and gave a full account of the meeting in Teguise – including the interruption by the president's daughter. To Kudrak's irritation, this seemed to amuse Tzarno.

'Perhaps she was trying to distract you,' the prince suggested.

'It would take more than the appearance of her brat to do that!' the envoy protested indignantly.

'So now that you've met Maravedis, how do you think she'll respond to our threats?'

'I prefer the term demands.'

'As you wish,' the prince said mildly. 'Do you think she'll set her dragons on us?'

Kudrak's expression made it clear that he found this suggestion distasteful.

'I do not care to speculate on the actions of such a person,' he said coldly. 'There is no way that Tiguafaya can match our military strength, however, so—'

'So magic is their greatest asset?'

'If such a godless pursuit can be called an asset,' the ambassador acknowledged grudgingly.

'It's odd that they should have asked for our help, don't you think?'

'I assume it's a measure of their desperation. Their evil is catching up with them, and they're clutching at straws.'

'Interesting,' Tzarno concluded. 'Thank you, Ambassador. I won't delay your return to Zepharinn any longer.'

Recognizing his dismissal, Kudrak rose to his feet, but before he left he could not resist one last question.

'Tell me, Your Highness, how did you know when and where I would return?'

'I didn't,' Tzarno replied simply. 'I came to Uga Stai to meet someone else. Your arrival was just a happy coincidence. And as any old soldier will tell you, you don't question good luck, you take advantage of it.'

As the ambassador bowed before taking his leave, he could not decide whether the prince was telling him the truth. Tzarno's motivations were complex, and a wise man often chose not to examine them too closely. Kudrak would have liked to ask him who he *was* planning to meet, but knew that if Tzarno had had any intention of telling him he would have done so already.

'May good fortune continue to follow you, Your Highness.'

'Safe journeying, Ambassador,' Tzarno replied.

When the door had closed behind the envoy and his footsteps had retreated down the stairs, the prince spoke to the empty room.

'He's gone.'

Behind him, another door – one whose existence was concealed amid the wooden panelling – opened silently and a man stepped out. He had the face of a corpse and his skin was the colour and consistency of tallow. It was stretched so tightly over his skull that there seemed to be almost no flesh upon his bones. His sunken eyes were pale too, but they were lit from within by a spectral fire. Few men could look into those eyes and not feel fear, but Tzarno had grown used to his companion's unnerving appearance.

'Well, Prophet, what did you make of that?' Although Tzarno imbued the title with a hint of mockery, the other man remained impassive.

'It went much as I expected,' he replied. His voice was thin and reedy. 'Kudrak was a fortuitous choice. I can't imagine anyone more likely to infuriate Ico – or to be infuriated by her.'

The use of the Maravedis woman's first name intrigued Tzarno.

'You speak as if you know her personally.'

'I feel as if I do.'

And you have a score to settle, Tzarno added silently. Aloud, he said, 'She won't back down?'

'No.'

'Then it seems we may have a war on our hands soon.' The idea clearly appealed to the prince, and he stood up abruptly and strode over to the window as if he could keep still no longer. Outside was the bustle of a busy port, but Tzarno's eyes were drawn to something in the distance.

'Come and look at this.'

The other man joined him at the window, and a slow smile spread over his cadaverous features.

The ship that had just entered the harbour was completely black, down to the last scrap of rigging.

'Our guests are arriving, Your Highness,' the Prophet said.

# CHAPTER ELEVEN

'We think you're the ideal man for the job,' Maciot persisted.

Jurado Madri looked at him in disbelief.

'Me? An envoy? To the Empire? Which one of you thought up this brilliant idea?'

'Actually, it was Andrin,' Ico replied.

'Then he's as crazy as you are.'

'We thought so too at first,' she admitted.

'Either crazy or inspired,' Maciot added. 'We eventually decided it was the latter.'

'Why?' Madri asked, obviously bewildered. 'I've been out of public life for decades. I'm not even officially part of your government.'

'So much the better,' Ico said. 'We need someone who can be seen as impartial.'

'You had a reputation as being above politics when you were an admiral,' Maciot went on.

Madri laughed sourly. 'The only part of my *reputation* that's likely to be remembered in the Empire – if they remember anything at all – will be the fact that I lost an entire fleet to the pirates and set my country on the road to ruin.

That's hardly likely to command much respect, is it?'

The battle he was referring to had been against the forces led by the elder Galan Zarzuelo, and it had indeed been a devastating blow to Tiguafaya's security. Madri had shouldered the blame for the disaster and had been forced into exile, living as a hermit in the caves of the firelands. His wife had been killed and he had been quite friendless – except for the sporadic company of Tre Fiorindo, his former first officer – until the Firebrands drew him back into the world.

'That wasn't your fault,' Ico said. 'Everyone knows that now.'

'Do they?' Madri responded sceptically. 'I'm not sure I do. Every commander faces the possibility of treachery from within his own ranks. I should have seen it coming.' He spoke quietly, without any great heat. In the last few years any remaining bitterness had been replaced by the melancholy that Ico sometimes saw in his eyes. He had changed physically too, filling out from the scarecrow-like wraith the Firebrands had found in the caves to the sturdy figure that belied his advancing years.

'I don't agree,' Maciot replied. 'In any case, that was a long time ago. What's important now is that we have faith in you, you've had personal experience with the fireworms, and you've got the right combination of tact and directness that might just appeal to Madar.'

'And you don't share my notorious habit of changing into a dragon,' Ico added with a grin.

Madri smiled back. He had been with Nino when she had spoken to him in the guise of the massive beast.

'If Kudrak's reaction is anything to go by, magic is a sensitive subject in the Empire,' Maciot went on. 'You'll have to approach it with great care.'

'You're assuming that I'm going,' the older man pointed out.

'Will you?' Ico asked hopefully.

There was a long pause before Madri replied.

'On one condition.'

'Anything,' Ico agreed readily. 'What do you want?'

'Tre comes with me.'

'I'll talk to him.'

'No,' he said quickly. 'I'll do it. You and your daughter can twist him round your little fingers. No one's going to put any pressure on him. It'll be his own decision – and if he decides he doesn't want to go, then neither do I.'

Ico accepted this admonishment meekly for once. She had wanted to deny that she would have brought any pressure to bear on Angel, but it would have been a lie. And Madri knew her too well.

'Fair enough,' Maciot agreed.

'I assume I won't be the only one trying to get information from the Empire.'

'No, but you'll be our official representative,' the senator replied. 'The others are working independently.'

Madri nodded thoughtfully.

'And you've had no news since Kudrak left?' He'd already been given a full briefing on the envoy's visit, and knew that he was probably back in his homeland by now.

'It's too early yet,' Maciot said. 'I'll let you know if we hear anything before you leave.'

The ex-admiral stood up.

'I'll go and talk to Tre.'

'Thank you,' Ico said. 'This isn't going to be an easy job, after the mess I made of things.'

'Thank me when I do any better,' Madri replied bluntly.

Ico was relieved when Angel agreed to accompany his former commander, and preparations for their departure were put in hand. The only person who objected was

Ysanne, who had taken the appropriation of her playmate as a personal affront.

The last few days in Teguise had otherwise been relatively quiet. Ico had had no news from either Vargo or Nino for some time and, having sent messengers to try to find them and let them know of the latest developments, there was little for her to do except wonder about their progress.

It seemed that the Empire already knew about Vargo and his work, and it was only a matter of time before Nino's efforts became common knowledge too. His project was just too big to remain secret for long. In consultation with Andrin and Maciot, Ico had decided to address that problem only when they needed to. In the meantime, she had done all she could to warn Nino and his colleagues, sending couriers to both the Corazoncillo Valley and his home village. Ico hoped he would be able to proceed with discretion, and hoped that his plans did not become the spark that ignited the Empire's desire for war – at least before Madri had the chance to remedy the situation. And surely Madar *had* to see reason, even if Kudrak would not.

Finding herself for once at something of a loose end, Ico decided to take advantage of the situation. When she reached the nursery, she found Ysanne in the company of Yaisa, one of the maids, rather than Andrin as she had expected. The little girl was explaining in great detail exactly how her father had crushed the fireworm, complete with all the relevant actions and expressive sound effects. In the few days since the still unexplained incident, Ysanne had not tired of the story, and had told it dozens of times to anyone who would listen.

'He squished it dead!' she concluded dramatically, then looked up as Ico came in and reached up with her arms, squealing with delight. 'Mama! Mama!'

Ico picked her up and swung her round and round until Ysanne was breathless from laughter. As always she took great pleasure in her daughter's demonstrative love, revelling in the closeness of physical contact that seemed suddenly all too rare.

'More. More!' Ysanne demanded as their spinning stopped.

'You're getting too heavy,' Ico complained. 'How would you like to go and see Grandad instead?'

'Yes!' her daughter cried, easily diverted by this beguiling prospect.

'Do you know where Andrin is, Yaisa?'

'He said he had business at the docks, my lady.'

Ico winced inwardly at the way the maid addressed her. Although being President and living in a palace made it inevitable that she would have a large staff, she often felt awkward about the deference shown to her by the servants, and tried to maintain friendly relationships with them. None of them felt comfortable calling her by name, however, and 'ma'am' or 'Madam President' were horrible, so as a compromise 'my lady' was the best she could hope for.

'Did he say what?'

'No, my lady.'

Probably something to do with Madri's trip, Ico surmised. Or one of the new ships that were being built. It was disappointing, but she could hardly expect him to be at her beck and call all the time.

'If he returns before I do, please tell him I've taken Ysanne to see my father. Come on, little one.'

Andrin had gone to the docks, but in truth he had no business there. He just needed to be alone for a while. He was aware of most of his faults, and brooding was one of them.

Sitting on one of the jetties, he stared at the comings and goings of the harbour without really seeing them, thinking about how so much had changed – and in so short a time. He had gone from being a penniless dock-rat to a man of influence, someone who received respectful greetings on any street in Teguise. He was married and a father, had lost one family and gained another. His old home had been completely destroyed by pirates, and visiting Diano's house still never felt quite right. He hardly recognized the frail, sober creature that Belda had become as his own mother and – even though it made him feel guilty – rarely made the effort to see her. He had discovered, almost too late, that he had a latent talent for magic, but even that now seemed improbable, like the last remnants of a fading dream.

Of necessity, even his relationship with Ico had changed. That they loved each other was not – and never would be – in doubt, but the duties of her position, the prolonged aftermath of the revolution and Ysanne's arrival had made it inevitable that they had had to make personal sacrifices. Although Andrin knew it was selfish of him, he sometimes thought he had been better off when he'd earned a meagre but honest living in these very dockyards, when he had still been astonished at the miracle of finding Ico, when he had known who his friends were – and where to find them. He missed Vargo. They had been best friends from childhood, ever since Vargo had made his escape from the orphanage, and yet now Andrin did not even know when he would see him next – or whether Vargo would be sane enough to recognize him when he did.

The Firebrands and their fight against complacency and injustice had given him a cause he believed in. Now their enemies were different – and so remote that sometimes they hardly seemed real. And, above all, there didn't seem much he could actually *do* to oppose them. For all Ico's reassuring words, Andrin still thought of himself as a passive spectator. He needed to act, to face a new and definable challenge.

His reverie was interrupted by the skirling, melancholy cry of a seagull as it wheeled in the air above him, and he was filled with envy. Wings meant freedom.

Andrin would have liked to talk to Ayo then, but he knew that the eagle was nowhere near, their link stretched way beyond its limits. He was probably too far to the south, with his mate and the two fledglings who had brought him so much joy. Andrin had only seen the young birds once, mottled grey creatures who could not match their sire's fierce beauty, and he had never met the female who had given them life. For reasons Andrin did not really understand, Ayo was very protective of his mate. Pride had forced him to bring his offspring north to the city, to show them to his link, but their mother had stayed behind. Ayo was reluctant to talk about her, and had not even told Andrin her name. It was as though he feared that revealing her to his link might lead to a conflict between the two, or possibly in his own loyalties. Andrin found this hard to understand – family was one thing, their link something else, after all – but he respected the eagle's wishes. However, at times like this he missed Ayo's presence. Instinct would bring him back to Teguise if it were really necessary – and that fact only reinforced Andrin's feeling that he was currently redundant.

'Looking for a job, Andrin? Or has palace life made you too soft?'

Andrin glanced up to see a burly stevedore, known as Click, with whom he had often worked in his previous life. He returned the other man's grin.

'Be careful who you're calling soft, old man. One word from me and the guards'll throw you in jail.'

Click looked unimpressed.

'That's fighting talk, boyo.'

'Truce, then,' Andrin replied. 'I only came here to think.'

'Too much of that is bad for any man,' the docker remarked sagely. 'What you need is some action.'

How right you are, Andrin thought wryly, but he said nothing.

The relative peace of her old home was slowly seeping into Ico's heart and head. Here, in her father's workshop, surrounded by the tools of her trade – the neatly labelled drawers containing gemstones, silver wire, beads and tiny pots of paint and glue – she was in her element. It was quiet, hidden away from the world, and she could free her mind of political concerns and concentrate on the simple task of creation.

Ysanne was ensconced with her beloved grandfather, being fussed over not only by Diano but also by Belda, her paternal grandmother, and Atchen, the housekeeper. The household had been delighted by the unannounced visit, and Ico knew she could safely indulge herself for an hour or more before her daughter became restless. Although Belda had been disappointed that her son was not with them, she had accepted his absence resignedly, and was now doing her best to help entertain Ysanne. Atchen had immediately protested that she did not have enough food in the house, and Ico had been forced to reassure the matronly cook that they were both well fed.

Soon after her election as President, Ico had offered all three of them living quarters within the palace, but Diano had refused on their behalf, and she had been glad that he had. She needed to know that this house, this home, still existed outside her political life, a haven to which she could always return.

Now she turned her attention to the job in hand, to the

pendant that was taking shape under the delicate movements of her fingers. It consisted of a single large gem, a
translucent red stone known as dragon's blood, enclosed
within a filigree of silver and attached to a simple cord. It
was almost finished, and Ico already knew that it was
destined to become her new talisman. Her old one, which
had been a much more ornate piece – a silver necklace set
with seven of the deep red stones – now lay at the bottom of
the ocean near Elva. It had been one of the first major pieces
Ico had ever made, and its loss still hurt. The only other
talisman she had ever used also lay on the sea bed, but there
was no regret attached to its loss. It had been a map, drawn
on human skin, and Ico was very glad that she would never
see it again. However, a new focus for her magic was long
overdue, and the jewel her father had shown her was perfect.
In fact it had virtually chosen itself. It felt right.

Dragon's blood stones were formed when sap from old
cauldron trees leaked out and solidified in the air. They were
beautiful and valuable, and were also held to have great
healing powers, which was why Ico had chosen them in the
first place. She twisted the last piece of metal into place,
polished it again, then took the pendant over to the lamp to
examine it more closely. Then she slipped it over her head.
It lay just below her neck, heavy and comforting against her
skin. All that remained now was the pilgrimage back to the
ancient tree, whence the stone had originally come, to ask
for its blessing. Only then would Ico feel fully content to call
the talisman hers, to use it as she saw fit.

A timid knock at the workshop door brought her musings
to an end, and she wondered how long she had been closeted
alone.

'Come in.'

Atchen's plump face peered round the door, her expression apologetic.

'I'm sorry to interrupt you, dear, but there's a man outside who wants to see you.'

'A messenger?' Ico asked, wondering why the house-keeper hadn't invited the man in.

'No, dear. He says he wants to sing to you.'

'Sing?' Ico laughed at the absurdity of this development. 'Who is it?'

'I've no idea, I'm sure,' Atchen replied, obviously torn between disapproval and curiosity. 'He says it would be better if you listened from your old bedroom. He looks harmless enough,' she added doubtfully.

'All right. This I have to see.'

It was only when she was halfway up the stairs that Ico realized she had not even considered the possibility that it might be Vargo. The thought saddened her, reflecting the fact that she had accepted the loss of her friend's music. Don't be silly, she told herself. He's probably miles away – and besides, Atchen would have recognized him.

Nostalgia tugged at her as she entered her old room. Nothing had changed – except that it seemed unnaturally tidy – and she fought the temptation to curl up on the bed and sleep like the child she had once been.

Music brought her back to the present, the gentle melody of a well-known song filtering through the closed shutters. She walked over to the window and opened them, and saw the man who had apparently come to serenade her in the square below. He was standing with his back to her, conducting the four musicians who were playing so beautifully. Then he turned round and looked up – and Ico froze in horror.

It was the jongleur, the leader of the chivaree, whose barbaric, angry 'music' had once terrified Ico and the rest of her household as it shook the walls with the force of a minor earthquake. His smile faded as he saw her reaction,

but before she could slam the shutters closed again, he
began to sing – sweetly this time where once he had mocked,
his eyes imploring her to listen. The tune had not changed,
but the words were his own:

'Forgive me, Ico,
If I offend,
I only desire
To be your friend.

I maligned you once,
In dance and song,
And this day I seek
To right that wrong.

If you—'

'Enough!' Ico called, holding out her hands to emphasize
her point. The jongleur and his musicians fell silent almost
instantly, and Ico became aware of other sounds from the
ground floor of the house. Ysanne had been giggling with
delight and the others, who obviously did not recognize
the leader of the chivaree, murmured their surprise at her
sudden interruption.

'Tell me why I should listen to any more of this?' Ico
demanded.

'Because I am sincere,' he replied. 'And true music heals
many wounds. I want to offer my services to you, to help you.'

'As you *helped* me before?' she asked harshly. It was hard
to disassociate this figure from her past, and from the
torment she had endured then.

'I am truly sorry for your suffering. I was just doing what
I was paid for,' he explained. 'Like the White Guards – and
you forgave them when they swore allegiance to you.'

It was a reasonable point, one which gave Ico pause for thought. Below her, Ysanne piped up.

'Sing,' she instructed imperiously. 'Sing!'

'Your daughter is convinced, at least,' the jongleur said, smiling hopefully.

'How did you know I was here?' Ico asked, still suspicious.

'You're too famous to move unnoticed through the city,' he told her. 'Which is why someone like me can be of use to you.'

'What do you mean?'

The jongleur paused, and gestured with his hands.

'Could we discuss this more privately?'

Conflicting emotions warred within Ico but, in the end, curiosity won out.

'Let him in, Father!' she called down.

She became aware that those below had fallen silent, presumably awaiting her decision. There was movement now, and the sound of Ysanne protesting about the lack of music. Ico waited to see the jongleur dismiss the musicians, then hurried down the stairs to the hallway where her father was waiting to confront her. Belda, who was carrying a now fretful Ysanne, was already retreating towards the kitchen.

'Is that who I think it is?' Diano asked, having belatedly caught on to the implications of the song and the subsequent exchange.

'Yes.'

'Are you sure you want to let him in?'

'Yes.' She had made up her mind now, and was determined to see this through.

Diano nodded to Atchen, who unlatched the door. The jongleur came in, a picture of humility.

'In here,' Ico said shortly, indicating her father's small study. 'Father, would you and Atchen go and help Belda with Ysanne?'

'Don't you want me to . . . ?' Diano began, then fell silent, accepting that his daughter's willpower far outstripped his own.

'I don't think I have anything to fear,' Ico told him, then followed her visitor into the study. 'Well?'

'My friends and I can be your eyes and ears in Teguise,' the jongleur told her.

'I have plenty of eyes and ears to call upon. Why should I need yours?'

'Because not all your enemies are beyond the city walls,' he replied.

# CHAPTER TWELVE

*We can hear them, can't we?* Ysanne asked.

*They're all singing different bits*, Tas replied, sounding half indignant, half confused.

*But they're all singing. It's fun!*

The little girl and the firecrest were alone in Ysanne's bedroom, and should have been asleep long ago. Because of this, even though their words were private and could not be heard by anyone else, their telepathic conversation was conducted in the mental equivalent of secretive whispers. Even so, Ysanne could not stop herself from giggling aloud, whereupon she clamped both hands over her mouth, her eyes wide in alarm. Seeing this, Tas uttered a single piercing call – *tseet* – and glanced around nervously. However, it soon became clear that no one had heard them, and they relaxed again.

*What are they singing about?*

*It's all different*, Tas repeated, *and there are some bits missing.*

*That's because Uncle Nino hasn't told them all yet*, Ysanne explained, trying to sound very grown-up.

The firecrest was puzzled. Her memory was far from perfect – especially when it came to trying to remember the names of all the humans she had met. Which one was Unclenino, she wondered, and why couldn't they have simple names, like the birds did? Ysanne did not notice her link's confusion.

*I'm hot*, she announced. *I wish we could open the shutters.*

*Your Mama says not to*, Tas warned, sounding worried. *Because of the worm things.*

*Oh, phoo!* Ysanne responded in disgust, but she made no move to get out of bed or go towards the window. Instead she stretched out a hand, and Tas hopped from the top of the bedpost onto her forefinger. Ysanne studied the tiny bird, thinking how neat her feathers were. Even in the dim moonlight that filtered down from the glass-covered skylight, she could see the firecrest's characteristic stripes of brilliant colour – black, white and red on her head, yellow on her throat. *Mama says we're as beautiful as each other*, she told her link thoughtfully. *Do you think I'm beautiful?*

*No. You're huge and fat and lumpy*, Tas replied without hesitation. *Not like me at all. And you can't fly*, she added, as if this proved her case.

*I'm not lumpy!* Ysanne retorted, but she did not sound in the least put out. *And one day I'll fly like Mama did, you wait and see.*

A little while later Tas asked, *Do you think we should sing too?*

Ysanne thought about this for a few moments.

*If we did*, she asked eventually, *would we be able to do magic?*

*Do you trust this man?* Tao asked.

*I'm not sure*, Maciot replied. *Ico believed him – and she has more reason than most to distrust his motives.*

The senator had been told of the President's meeting with the jongleur, but although the import of what he'd had to say was alarming in some ways, Maciot was not one to jump to conclusions. Now, as day turned to night, he was glad that he and Tao had the large, comfortably furnished house to themselves and could concentrate on their discussion. Maciot lived alone, and his servants only entered his home by day. During the hours of darkness he preferred complete privacy – except for Tao, the one companion with whom he was always at ease.

*But chivaree are like mercenaries,* Tao persisted, *willing to work for the highest bidder. Even if the jongleur is being honest today, what's to stop him betraying us later if he gets a better offer?*

*There are no guarantees,* Maciot admitted, *but Ico thought he was genuine, and she's usually a good judge of character.*

*As she judged Kudrak?* Tao enquired pointedly.

*That's unfair. Kudrak never had any intention of giving her a fair hearing, but she still had to try. The real point is that if there's a possibility the chivaree can give us information we might otherwise miss, we'd be foolish not to take the chance.*

Tao dipped his head several times, as if in agreement, but his next words showed that he was still suspicious.

*Did he ask for any money?*

*No. He agreed that any payments were conditional on his giving us some worthwhile intelligence – preferably something we can verify for ourselves.*

*Which is exactly how I would have acted if I was trying to gain someone's trust in order to dupe them later.*

*You're very cynical this evening,* Maciot remarked.

Tao clicked his beak, which usually meant that he was annoyed, and ruffled his iridescent black wing feathers. The mirador chaffinch was an unusually clever bird, and the senator knew that he was lucky to have been chosen by such a link. In his opinion Tao was more intelligent than most humans. The problem was that Tao was of the same opinion, and rarely felt the need to disguise the fact.

*You should learn to tell the difference between cynicism and prudent questioning of one's motives,* he stated huffily.

*Sometimes you just have to take a risk,* Maciot told him.

*Agreed,* the bird replied with exaggerated patience. *All I'm saying is that our faith should not be blind.*

*You know me better than that,* the senator said. *And Ico's no fool. Until the chivaree prove themselves trustworthy, we won't be taking anything at face value.*

*I still don't see why this can't be handled by our own network,* Tao grumbled.

Ah, so that's why he's so irritable, Maciot realized. He's taken it as a personal affront that the chivaree might be able to learn something we can't. He kept the thought to himself.

*My allegiances are well known,* he replied. *They may be able to move in circles where our own allies might not be welcome.*

As head of the Travellers' Guild, Maciot had many contacts throughout Teguise – and indeed all of Tiguafaya and beyond – and, via Tao, had many birds who acted as his informers. In fact birds had always played a vital role in communications within the country, and almost every business enterprise of any importance had several linked people in their employ.

Tao's silence seemed to indicate that he had accepted the point, albeit reluctantly. The bird turned his back on Maciot, and hopped along the edge of the settee on which his link lay sprawled among the embroidered cushions. When he was level with Maciot's feet, he turned round again and fixed him with a jewelled gaze.

*So what has this jongleur promised to discover? Who are these enemies he's going to smoke out? It's hardly world-shattering*

*news that we may face some opposition from within the city.
There will always be people who are dissatisfied with their lot –
and others who'll take advantage of them.*

The mirador's unflattering view of the ways of humankind were very clear, but Maciot saw no reason to argue with
him. Instead he answered the earlier question in as straightforward a manner as possible.

*He mentioned two factions who are apparently growing in
strength. The first are those who still believe magic is responsible
for all our troubles and want to ban it altogether.*

Tao clicked his beak again, angered as always by human
stupidity, but he said nothing.

*There's nothing new in that, of course,* the senator went on.
*Just because Kantrowe's been discredited, it doesn't mean all his
followers are going to abandon their beliefs. We may know that
magic is as natural as sunlight,* he added, anticipating his
link's response, *but it's still alien to a lot of people, in spite
of everything that's happened – and in spite of where we'd be
without it.*

The mirador bobbed his head again, but remained silent.
It had been Tao who had guided Ico – when she was flying as
a dragon – so that she had been able to bring the others to
the Corazoncillo Valley and eventually save the people who
had been trapped there. He had experienced the impact of
magic at its most potent, had seen its capacity for good, and
his faith in the ancient lore was as unshakeable as ever.

*The second group is much more interesting,* Maciot continued. *There's apparently a new cult grown up around the
fireworms.*

*A cult?* Tao asked curiously. *In what sense?*

*Apparently, its followers believe that fireworms are earthly
manifestations of the gods' emotions – their anger mostly, as far
as I can understand – and as such they should be worshipped and
revered.*

*Even the corrupted swarms?* Tao exclaimed, his tone betraying his incredulity.

*Even them*, Maciot confirmed grimly, knowing what his link's reaction would be.

*The depths to which your species is capable of sinking when it comes to self-deception never fails to astonish me*, the bird commented, but he sounded sad rather than angry. *So what do these cultists propose to do? Offer themselves up for sacrifice to the worms?*

He had not meant it as a serious question, but Maciot chose to answer it as one. Human sacrifices – to appease the dragons – had been an accepted ritual in Tiguafayan society long ago, and the repugnant practice had been revived – for a thankfully brief period – during Kantrowe's reign of terror. In spite of such recent horrors, Maciot found that he could imagine history repeating itself all too easily.

*I doubt they'd choose from among their own numbers if it came to sacrifices*, he said. *Easier to offer up some non-believers.*

*You can't be serious!*

*It's all speculation at this point*, the senator admitted, *but if there's anything to it, I'd rather we knew about it sooner rather than later.*

For once Tao seemed to be at a loss for words. Maciot knew that his link had difficulty dealing with anything to do with fireworms. The mirador believed that all winged creatures shared a common heritage, and that all birds were thus related to the dragons – albeit distantly. Even though they were able to fly, fireworms were emphatically excluded from this ancestry and, like most birds, Tao had hated the unnatural creatures. The discovery that the worms actually *had* been linked to the dragons, admittedly in a way no one had expected, had been hard for the mirador to take and, even now, he harboured mixed feelings about Vargo's search for an untainted swarm.

The bird fluttered his wings briefly, and twitched for a while before growing calm again.

*Did the jongleur have any evidence of the existence of this cult?* he asked with typical incisiveness.

Maciot smiled. Nothing threw Tao off his stride for long.

*It's all just rumours at the moment, but even they have to start somewhere. We can make some enquiries of our own, of course . . .*

*But the chivaree have a better chance of infiltrating such a depraved organization,* Tao completed for him. *Unless of course it's all a figment of their overheated imaginations.*

*Let's hope it is,* Maciot replied. *We'll find out soon enough. Are any of the chivaree linked?*

*I don't know,* the senator answered, silently berating himself for not having thought of this earlier.

*I think we should find out, don't you?* Tao muttered.

*Definitely,* his link agreed, knowing that the mirador would take on the task without further encouragement.

*Do you believe this might have something to do with the worm in Ysanne's nursery?* the bird asked.

*We've been wondering about that,* Maciot responded. News of the incident had spread rapidly but, as yet, no one had been able to come up with an explanation. *But we've no proof either way. All the palace staff are on guard now, though.*

*Including the birds?*

*Soo and Tas definitely. I'm not sure about the rest. With Ayo away, Andrin may not have been able to contact them all.*

Tao cocked his head to one side and chirruped softly, indicating that he was in something of a quandary. He was reluctant to denigrate any of his own kind, but honesty compelled him to go on.

*Ayo's been away a great deal recently. It seems that the responsibility of fledglings weighs more heavily than others for him and Andrin.*

Although the bird's tone was mildly disapproving, Maciot did not believe that Tao was blaming either the eagle or Andrin for their recent preoccupations. Like the senator, Tao had never taken a mate. In fact, to Maciot's knowledge, Tao had not even indulged in the passing entanglements that had comprised his own love life to date. Nor had the bird seen fit to comment upon those short-lived affairs, presumably knowing that they were unlikely to last, and confident of the stability of the relationship between himself and his link. In that Tao had been proved right, because no woman had ever come close to capturing Maciot's heart – although many had tried – to the point where he wondered if any ever would. He hoped that if either he or his link ever did fall in love, that they would wish each other well. However, neither of them spent much time dwelling on the prospect.

*The point is,* Tao went on now, *that Tas is too young to be of much use and Soo isn't exactly reliable at the moment, so we can hardly leave the security of the palace to them.*

*Sounds like another job for you,* the senator commented dryly.

*While you lie around drinking yourself into a stupor, no doubt,* Tao replied acidly.

Maciot knew better than to try to defend himself while the mirador was in this mood, so he just grinned and reached for the goblet of wine which stood on a nearby table.

*Is there anything else you wish me to do?* Tao enquired.

*Actually, there is.* The mention of the other birds had jogged Maciot's memory. *Soo said something recently that Ico couldn't make sense of.*

*That's hardly unexpected. After what she's been through . . .* The bird gave the mental equivalent of a shrug.

*This was a bit more obscure than most, and apparently Tas said something similar to Ysanne.*

*Well?* Tao cut in impatiently. *What did they say?*

*Something about the beginning of a dreaming. In the sky. Does that mean anything to you?*

The mirador chirruped again, and would not meet Maciot's eyes. His link's reaction surprised the Senator, because it was clear that Tao did indeed know something about this mystery but was reluctant to talk about it.

*Tao?* he prompted gently.

*You wouldn't understand*, the bird replied uneasily.

*Try to help me.*

*The sky's dreaming was the beginning of all things*, Tao replied after a short pause.

*The birth of the world?*

*And of all the creatures in it*, the mirador confirmed. *The transforming of the shapes that were waiting into living things. But it's more than that.*

*What do you mean?*

*If the oracles are right*, Tao replied hesitantly, *then the sky's dreaming will also be the end of all things.*

# CHAPTER THIRTEEN

Ayo felt as though he were being pulled apart. This had nothing to do with the wind that had awoken with the dawn and which was now gusting strongly above the southern firelands. His massive wings – which were so broad that one less poetic observer had once described him as looking like a flying door – rode the air currents with their customary ease. From below, had there been anyone to see him, he would have appeared the picture of supreme confidence – of arrogance even – as he circled on the updraughts, a pure white emperor of the skies. The reality was rather different, even though the conflict was all within the eagle's mind.

For all his physical prowess, Ayo was troubled. Fate had not always been kind to him, and the timing of his linking with Andrin had robbed him of his first love. He had never been able to explain to Iva about the siren call that had taken him away from her, and the memory of her pain haunted him still. He had never seen her again. Later he had obeyed the commands of his kind, regardless of his own circum-stances, and had played his part in the great events that shaped Tiguafaya's recent history. It had seemed that he'd won his freedom then, and had been granted his reward. He had long ago given up any thought of ever finding a mate, but when he received another unexpected summons to Pajarito – the mountain that was the most hallowed place in the avian world – he had found that he was not alone. A female eagle had been waiting for him – and from the moment they first set eyes upon each other, then locked talons to dance together in the sky, he had known that his mate had been chosen for him. She was not Iva, and Ayo knew that he could never duplicate his feelings for her, but he had fallen deeply in love with Ara anyway. She had also been delighted by their arranged pairing, enjoying all the customs of their long courtship before joining him in building a nest. Their mating had produced two fine fledglings, whose strength and beauty – even in the awkward early days of adolescence – had been a joy to both parents.

In all, Ayo's life had been a strange journey, with many unexpected twists and turns along the way, but he had always known instinctively which path to follow. Until now.

Although his decisions in the past had often been painful, he had always been sure in his heart that they were right. He had been aware of forces greater than anything he could comprehend shaping his destiny, and had accepted this, regarding it as a blessing as well as a curse. But now the various demands being made upon his heart and mind were pulling him in different directions, and he had searched in vain for clear guidance. The invisible walls that had once defined his existence were no longer there – and he had no idea who or what had destroyed them. It was up to Ayo to choose his own course, and him alone.

He had sought out the open spaces above the desolate lava fields in the hope that here, alone, he would be able to clear his thoughts and reach a decision. However, the only thing made clear to him so far was that, no matter which of his present options he chose, he would be losing more than he gained. There were three claims upon his soul and, for the moment at least, he could select only one.

The first of these, and the most immediate, was the lure of his own family, of the straightforward, natural process of rearing his young. Teaching them to survive in the rugged terrain of Tiguafaya's southern coastline, showing them how to hunt for fish and the occasional rabbit, passing on his knowledge of the mysteries of the wind, of sea and spray, cliffs and canyons, was a joy to him – especially as he shared it all with Ara. The beguiling simplicity of this way of life was something he thought he had lost many years earlier, and he had been exhilarated by its rediscovery. But the longer he stayed in the south the more he worried about the second aspect of his fate.

He knew that he had been neglecting his link with Andrin for some time and, although he tried to reassure himself with the fact that Andrin had never complained, a deeper, subliminal part of his mind kept nagging away at him. Of course his link had also been preoccupied of late, having produced a fledgling of his own – and for the first few months of life human offspring were even more helpless than birds – so Ayo had not been entirely responsible for their recent sporadic communication. Even so, the eagle knew that great events were still to take place in Tiguafaya and, by rights, he and Andrin should have a part to play in them. The only way they could realistically do that was if they worked together. Much as he would have liked to turn his back on such things, and indulge himself in the pleasures of his partnership with Ara, he knew that his bond with Andrin was older and – in some ways – stronger. He would have to answer its call sooner or later.

The reason he had not answered it yet was the third part of his dilemma. Pajarito, the oracle of all birds, was calling him – or at least he thought it was. In the past its summons had been unequivocal, commands that demanded obedience from every fibre and feather of his being. This time it was simply an instinct that fought for precedence over the other, more strident voices in his head. He had once told Andrin that he only went to Pajarito 'when there is need, or when I am called', but now he was not absolutely sure that either was true. And yet to be called and not answer was unthinkable.

The eagle screamed, venting his frustration in a howl of pain and indecision that was swept away by the wind. In the silence that remained, Ayo made his choice. With a heavy heart he stopped gliding in circles, and his ponderous but immensely powerful wingbeats drove him forward as he set his course. Westward. Towards Pajarito.

Pajarito was among the oldest of the volcanoes that ran in a more or less unbroken line from the tip of the southern peninsula to Tiguafaya's border with the Empire. Further north the line split, spreading out to cover much of the country's interior, but here, where the land's roughly tri-angular shape meant that there was less distance between the Inner Seas and the Great Western Ocean, the mountains rose in haphazard sequence – each isolated from the next, like jewels set in a vast pendant.

Many centuries ago, Pajarito had spewed forth an astonishing volume of molten rock, and the black lava fields that spread for many miles in every direction were testimony to its power. The last great explosion, that which had crafted Pajarito's present, apparently time-less shape, had been different from all that had gone before. The plumes of fire and ash, the rushing clouds of smoke and gas, the hail of burning stone, had all been flung out at an angle so that the crater they eventually produced was deep but lopsided. Not only that but, as the rock cooled, it had set into patterns of colour that contrasted strongly with the darkness that surrounded it, making the mountain even more conspicuous.

Ayo could see his destination clearly even from several miles away. The crater faced east, towards him and the rising sun, its great western rampart more than three times the height of the nearer wall – so that from the eagle's line of approach all but the very bottom of the crater was open to view. From a distance the great tilted bowl appeared a dull, uniform red, but as Ayo drew closer he could make out the intricate underlying patterns within the tumbled stone. Countless small patches and bands of ochre, crimson, rust and coral, each with its own shape and texture, merged into a single gigantic formation. Ayo was aware that staring at it for too long, trying to make sense of the overall design, could make even the most level-headed bird feel dizzy. Yet the conviction persisted that there were messages here, if only they could be deciphered. Pajarito was beautiful, in a stark, uncompromising way, but it was not a place of ease or comfort.

The harshness of its setting meant that men never came here and, from past experience, Ayo knew that all other forms of life also shunned the crater. There were no rabbits or lizards, no insects, within the crooked mountain. No plants grew there, not even the stubborn lichen that had staked a claim in every other barren place. The only creatures who came to Pajarito were the birds – and then only when they were called.

They came because, for them alone, it was the place where the sacred voices of the sky spoke to the earth. They alighted in that forbidding arena, hoping to prove worthy to hear the distant echoes of those voices – and perhaps, if they were very lucky, to have their questions answered by the oracle.

No bird ever dared trouble Pajarito with anything other than the most important problems, and even then the answers they received were unlikely to be couched in straight-forward terms. Like all oracles, its words were often enigmatic or even deliberately obscure. More often than not the meaning would only become clear much later, when the time for revelation had come.

As he began his descent, Ayo found himself recalling the way he had described Pajarito to Andrin many months before. *It is more than a mountain. It is a voice, the past and future, memories and prophecies.* And now he was about to enter this time-honoured sanctuary with no real idea of why he had come there.

Ayo felt the initial stirrings of fear as he flew into the vast red jaws. Although he knew the earth had not moved here for countless years, he could easily imagine himself being swallowed now. He was insignificant, a mere speck of white dust. However, to turn back would be an act of folly as well as cowardice. There was no escape. Pajarito had already measured his intentions. All he could do now was await its judgement.

He landed on the large boulder, near the centre of the depression, which had acted as his perch on all his previous visits, folded his great wings and stood erect in defiance of his inner dread. The crater was usually full of sighs and whispers from the sky, tiny murmurs from the rock itself, but it was utterly silent now. Nothing stirred; even the wind was still, and Ayo's nervousness increased. The whispers normally contained all that any visitor was meant to hear, although Pajarito was also capable of speaking with a voice like thunder, whose echoes could shake the entire crater. But Ayo did not believe that anyone had ever encountered the absolute silence that enveloped him now.

He waited, all his senses attuned to the tiniest signals, any clue that might allow him to make sense of his predicament. But there was nothing; no sound, no movement other than the slow crawling progress of his own shadow as the sun rose behind him.

Unable to stand the tension any longer, he cried out. The eagle's voice was as harsh as the terrain, unsuited to song or the forming of words, and his cry only set up a fading series of unintelligible echoes. At the same time his mind was pleading with the oracle. *Tell me what to do.*

The answer when it came was so clear, so unexpectedly gentle, that at first Ayo thought he must be imagining it.

*There is safety in slumber.*

*What?*

*Take care what forces you awake.*

Ayo was now hopelessly confused. Who was asleep and who awake?

*I don't know what you mean.*

*Broken dreams do not end*, the oracle pronounced. *You are meddling with matters you do not understand.*

Ayo had no difficulty agreeing with that last statement, but he still did not have the answer he needed.

*What should I do?*

*Play your part*, Pajarito replied – and there was fondness in the oracle's tone, as well as a deep sadness. *Do not oppose the inevitable.*

*I should go back to Teguise, to my link?* Ayo asked, hoping for some clarification.

Pajarito's reply did not answer his question, but simply left him with another vague piece of advice.

*Be ready*, the sky voices whispered. *The earth is stirring.*

# CHAPTER FOURTEEN

'I can't see Grandma's house any more,' Malika Guern complained.

'Then you must have your eyes shut, little one,' Lexa replied indulgently.

'I haven't, Mama. I haven't,' the girl insisted, in so plaintive and sincere a tone that Lexa turned to look for herself. What she saw made her blink in disbelief, then stand up, the bowl of peas she had been shelling falling unnoticed to the floor.

The valley in which their farmstead lay was so wide that at its base it formed an almost flat plain to either side of the slow, meandering river. It was a remote place, where there were few roads and only scattered settlements, and where the land was fertile enough to allow self-sufficiency for the hardy, but no more. There was no great wealth here, and it had always been peaceful because no one ever thought it worth fighting over. The seasons came and went, but in the valley little changed from year to year. Until today.

From where she stood on the porch of their home, Lexa should have been able to see her mother's cottage, less than half a mile away, across the fields of beans and maize that her husband, Sohan, tended so carefully. But now the fields rose up in a gentle slope, completely hiding the distant house. Where there had always been flat ground, there was now a small but significant rise.

'Stay here,' she told her daughter.

'You spilled the peas.'

'Well, pick them up then,' Lexa instructed as she hurried away.

'Where are you going?' Malika called after her.

'To find Papa.'

She found Sohan on the other side of the new ridge, staring down at the lower spring. Ordinarily, water ran from the rock in a clear stream, a constant flow that had never failed. Now, however, the water burst out in fits and starts, spitting and hissing loudly. Steam rose into the air.

'I came to take a drink, but it's so hot I almost scalded myself.' Sohan's voice held both wonder and fear.

'That's not all.' Lexa's own foreboding increased as she told him about Malika's discovery. Her husband did not believe her at first, and she had to drag him to the cottage to prove her point. From there they hurried back to their own home, only to be intercepted by Javid – their elder son – who was returning from the river and who also looked perturbed.

'I haven't been able to catch a single fish all morning,' he told them, obviously bewildered. 'And there's a terrible smell of bad eggs down in the meadow. What's going on?'

'I wish I knew,' Sohan replied grimly.

When they returned to the farmstead, they found Malika being comforted by Jena, Javid's pregnant wife. The child had been crying, and glanced at her mother reproachfully.

'Have you seen . . . ?' Jena began, pointing to the fields.

'We've seen,' Sohan cut in.

Javid went to put his arms round his wife, while Sohan scooped up Malika.

'What's happening, Papa?'

'Nothing for you to worry about,' he replied, as confidently as he was able.

Before they could do or say anything else, the family became aware of their neighbour, Kusik Riall, running towards them. This was yet another unsettling sight; Kusik had the reputation as the laziest man in the valley, and no one had ever seen him move so fast before. He was red-faced and breathless when he arrived, and had to wait a few moments before he was able to speak.

'Pigs've gone mad!' he gasped eventually. 'Smashed the gate to kindling and just took off. Two of 'em ran straight into the river and were swept away,' he added, sounding understandably distraught. 'The others came this way. Have you seen 'em?'

Sohan glanced at his family, but they all shook their heads.

'We've not seen any of them.'

'I think it must've been the water,' Kusik said miserably.

'What water?'

'They didn't have any. My well's run dry. Doesn't make any sense. River's as high as usual this time of year.'

'Javid, go and check our well,' Sohan instructed.

His son ran off, and the others soon joined him – but the empty clang as the bucket hit dry rock at the bottom told them all they needed to know. Kusik ran off again, muttering about having to find his pigs, while the Guern family stood silently, each wondering what to say or do. These mysteries were so far beyond their experience that they had no idea how to respond.

'I thought I heard some strange noises last night,' Jena said quietly. 'I didn't think much of it . . .'

'What sort of noises?' Javid asked.

'Creaks and groans. I don't know really.' She sounded embarrassed, and wished she'd kept quiet.

The final member of the Guern family arrived now. At fifteen years of age, Orazio was the younger of Sohan's two sons, and had been despatched to tend their goats, which grazed as best they could to the north of the valley. The land there grew increasingly barren, until the upper slopes were only suitable for the hardiest of animals.

'What are you doing here?' Sohan demanded.

'Appleleaf Tarn has turned red!' Orazio blurted out. He too had been running, and was breathing hard.

'Don't talk nonsense, boy.'

'It's true. I swear it.'

The others considered this latest phenomenon. Although it hardly seemed any more incredible than the other events of that morning, it added another layer to their unease.

'You left your duties to tell us this?' Sohan said, more harshly than he had intended. 'You're supposed to be a goatherd.'

'They won't wander far,' Orazio replied defensively. 'I can easily find them again.'

'Then you'd better do that. Now!'

'But—'

'Sohan?' Lexa said doubtfully.

The farmer shot his wife a look, then turned back to Orazio.

'Go back to the herd, boy.'

'I only wanted—'

'Go!' Sohan repeated angrily.

Orazio turned and fled. No one spoke for a while. The only sound came from the half-stifled sobs of Malika, who had begun crying again.

'Perhaps we should all get away from here,' Javid suggested eventually.

'And abandon our home?' Lexa replied. She understood her son's need to protect his wife and unborn child, but where could they go? She dearly wanted to become a grandmother, and her family's safety was paramount, but she knew that Sohan would never leave the land he had shaped with so much love and hard toil. She looked at her husband, hoping for guidance, but he stood like a statue, staring at nothing.

'We can come back if nothing else happens,' Javid persisted.

'We must pray,' Sohan stated decisively, dismissing his son's words out of hand.

No one moved.

'You heard me.' He glanced at each of them in turn, but only his wife would meet his gaze. 'The prophets said we'd be punished if we didn't honour the gods.'

'Those fanatics?' Lexa exclaimed. 'Surely you didn't take them seriously?'

'Maybe they were right,' he replied obstinately. 'Can *you* explain what's happening here?'

'What do seers and city folk know of us?' she countered.

'Then why are we being punished?' Sohan shouted, the colour rising in his cheeks.

'It may not—' she began.

'We are surrounded by ill omens,' he stated firmly. 'We will pray.'

This time he set off determinedly and the others followed, with varying degrees of reluctance. The family shrine was a small stone altar, set a little way from the house. Like most in the valley it was painted with symbols – meant to signify good luck and rich harvests – which had once been colourful but were now faded and peeling. Sticks bearing prayer flags flanked the stone. None of the people in the valley could claim to be devout in their worship, and few observances were kept – except on major festival days, when the flags were renewed, the farmers' wishes inscribed upon the pennants to be taken up to the gods by the wind. Such things were regarded by all except the oldest residents as a harmless ritual, a prelude to the real point of the holidays – the feasts, drinking and dancing.

At the altar Sohan knelt and the others followed suit, repeating words which until now had meant little to them.

Orazio scrambled up the rocky path, muttering under his breath. When he'd seen that the upland lake had turned red he had been intrigued, but he had been frightened by his father's uncharacteristic anger. Sohan must have been truly worried to react in such a way. The others had seemed afraid too, but as usual no one told him what was going on. They never did, even though he was a man now. He caught his shin on the edge of a boulder, swore violently and almost compounded his error by kicking the rock.

He was just beginning to wonder whether he really could find his herd again as easily as he had boasted when he spotted one of the animals higher up the hill, bounding along at a reckless pace even for so sure-footed a creature. It was true that the goats had been behaving skittishly for the last day or so, but they trusted Orazio, and he didn't think they'd run away. He could hear the distant pealing of the herd leader's bell now, and hurried on, anxious to be sure of his charges.

Stopping to catch his breath some way higher up, he turned back to look down into the valley. Although from this distance everything appeared normal enough, something was wrong. He could feel it. From where he stood he could also see beyond the hills on the other side of the valley, all the way to the foreign mountains far to the south. Those forbidding peaks might as well have been on a different world as far as Orazio was concerned; no one he knew had ever travelled further than the next valley.

Thunder boomed suddenly in his ears and, startled, he looked up to the heavens to see where the unexpected storm was coming from. But the sky was clear, a uniform shade of silvery blue.

The next thing he knew he was sitting down, having fallen to the ground with a bump. And the earth beneath him was shaking.

To the rest of the Guern family, the roll of thunder was so loud they felt it in their chests and stomachs rather than hearing it with their ears. It was instantly terrifying, drowning out all possibility of speech or thought, a gigantic rumbling noise, as if the earth were tearing itself apart. Moments later their eyes confirmed what their other senses had told them. The earth *was* tearing itself apart.

The ground heaved like a living thing, the slight ridge becoming an obscene bulge, with rippling waves spreading outwards as if the soil had turned to liquid. The tremor threw them all to the floor, and in that moment Sohan knew their prayers had gone unanswered.

The bulge swelled into a shifting, shuddering hill, then burst apart in an explosion of such ferocity that it defied belief. Sheets of flame, half a mile high, howled into the sky. At first it was so bright it was like the birth of another sun, but the fire was soon obscured by clouds of smoke, ash and steam, and by the continuous fountain of rock that was being hurled upward only to return as a deadly, suffocating hail.

Sohan and everyone with him were dead long before the mountain, forcing itself into what had once been their peaceful valley, buried them for ever.

From this vantage point, Orazio watched as everything he had ever known was obliterated. The first eruption terrified

him to such a degree that he had been sure he was going to
die. As it went on and he suffered no ill effects – beyond the
fact that the air became hot and was occasionally filled with
choking drifts of smoke – his fear did not lessen, but was
joined by other emotions. By grief and anger.

Coughing and rubbing his stinging, tear-filled eyes, he
watched as a cone-shaped mountain grew, spreading
upwards and outwards as the earth's inner fires gave vent to
their rage. He saw liquid fire inside the crater, boiling and
splashing, but he did not know what it was. He did not know
that rock could melt and flow like red water, or be flung
into the air in orange balls that turned black as they cooled
before hurtling back to the ground. He did not know
that the massive tower that now hung over the valley, like
an enormous grey tree, was not just made of smoke but of
particles of ash and clouds of gas so hot that it could strip
the life from anything it encountered. All he knew was that
his family, his farm and his home were all gone.

Several hours later, in the late afternoon of a day in which
a false dusk had come much earlier than usual, the eruption
seemed to be relenting. The flames were smaller now, no
longer continuous, and the rattle of stones as they fell
had also lessened. The mountain rested. Although it
had devastated the entire middle section of the valley, the
higher regions at the eastern and western ends had been
spared the worst, and Orazio could just make out some signs
of activity. He was not the only one to have survived.

Orazio's clothes and skin were almost white now, covered
with a thin film of the ash that had reached the upper slopes,
but the ground beneath his feet was steady and the
deafening roar of the volcano no longer drowned out every
other sound. He stood up on shaky legs and began to walk
down to what was left of his home territory, only to stop
abruptly after a few paces.

The new mountain gave a great, groaning sigh, then collapsed in on itself, as if its own weight was too great for its foundations to bear. Then the implosion reversed itself, not in flame or flying rocks but in great, silver-grey clouds that travelled at incredible speed outwards from the crater, hugging the contours of the land and covering it in a glowing, opaque blanket. It filled the entire length of the valley, moving so fast that Orazio knew no one could outrun it. The searing torrent scorched everything in its path, flattening plants, houses and trees, reducing wood to charcoal and stone to blackened glass.

After that the volcano seemed to lose interest. The eruption died away still further, until it was no more than a smoking pile of rubble, and the clouds slowly dispersed. In the dim light slanting in under the sky-borne debris, Orazio could see that the fire had done its worst. There was nothing left in the valley, nothing to go back for. The devastation was complete.

Choking with rage and horror, and wiping away useless tears, he turned his back on the blackened, lifeless scene and began to stagger away. He had no idea where he was going or what he was going to do, but one thing was clear in his disordered mind. Someone was going to pay for this. That was the reason his life had been spared. Whoever had brought this catastrophe down upon his people must be punished. He would demand justice, retribution. Someone, somewhere would listen, would help him. After all, he was a citizen of the Empire, the greatest nation in all the world – and that had to count for something.

# CHAPTER FIFTEEN

It had taken Vargo and Cat almost two full days to edge their way down into the ravine. The terrain was so irregular – with turrets of stone rising between crevasses, and steep slopes of tumbled scree – that navigation had been a matter of trial and error. Such paths as there were had obviously been made by animals – they had glimpsed a few long-haired wild goats – and often led nowhere. Many times they had been forced to backtrack to avoid a dead end or a sheer drop. In theory Ero should have been able to help them; from the air, such obstacles should have been obvious. But the hoopoe had little or no conception of what it meant to be tied to the ground, and quickly grew impatient with his companions' inability to follow his suggestions. Because Cat had long since learnt not to rely on him, Ero was in effect free to please himself, flying to and fro, and only offering advice when he was asked a specific question.

They had spent the first night camped on a moss-covered ledge. Although it was wide enough to be completely safe, Allegra still felt exposed, afraid that Vargo might wander off and fall if he woke before she did. As a result she lay awake long after he was soundly asleep. She spent hours listening to the song of the wind as it twined around the rock pinnacles, and rustled the leaves of the bushes and stunted trees that clung to the sides of the canyon.

Their second day in the ravine was coming to an end now, and they had nearly reached the bottom. Cat still could not understand why Vargo had been so insistent on their making the descent. She knew that he followed a path only he could see, but this latest venture made little sense even by his bizarre standards. As far as she could tell there were two things that had led them there – Vargo's dream, which he had not been able to recall in anything other than the vaguest terms, and the report of an untested colony of fireworms in the west. But Cat could not see how these two things were connected. The ravine lay in one of the few areas of Tiguafaya that had never been directly affected by volcanic activity. The rock here was obviously older than even the most ancient of the volcanoes, and it had been shaped not by lava flows and heat but by the slow erosion of water and wind. They had caught glimpses of a wide brown river at the base of the canyon, and the air had become cooler and more humid the lower they had gone. The plentiful vegetation within the ravine made it doubly clear that its climate was quite different from that of the firelands. All of which made it an unlikely place to encounter fireworms.

However, none of this seemed to bother Vargo in the slightest, and he was eager to complete their journey. When they turned the final corner and emerged onto a small flat plain next to the river, he smiled as he looked around.

'Can you hear it?' he asked softly.

'Hear what?' The river here moved sluggishly, in silence, as if weighed down by the silt it was carrying. All Allegra could hear was the gentle sighing of the breeze and the distant twittering of some birds.

'The stone heartbeat,' he whispered. 'Listen.'

Cat's own heart sank. If Vargo was entering one of his unintelligible, 'mad' phases, then their stay within the ravine would be even more difficult than she'd anticipated. Even so, she stood quietly and listened intently. At first she could hear nothing out of the ordinary, but gradually she began to realize what Vargo meant. It was so faint, so faraway, that it was almost indistinguishable from the coursing of her own blood. It was a slow, rhythmic pulse, a rustling that ebbed and flowed like the sound of a distant ocean.

'It sounds like the sea,' she said eventually.

'It does, doesn't it?' Vargo replied happily, then strode forward to the edge of the river bank.

They were standing in a small cove, with cliffs rising to either side. The only way in or out was either the gully they had come down or the river itself. The water was completely opaque, so there was no telling how deep it was, and Cat thought for a moment that Vargo was going to wade straight in.

'We can camp here tonight,' she said quickly, 'and explore further in the morning.'

To her relief Vargo nodded, shrugged off his pack and turned round to face her.

'We're close,' he said.

'Close to what?'

'I don't know,' he admitted, 'but it's important.'

'Oh, that's all right then.'

Vargo was obviously surprised by her unusual flippancy. Then he grinned.

'Why do you put up with me, Cat?'

The obvious answer rose to her lips, but force of habit kept it inside.

'You know why,' she replied instead.

'Do I?'

'Someone has to stop you from getting yourself killed.'

Vargo nodded, and seemed about to say something else when he was distracted by Ero's typically flamboyant arrival – dipping low over the river, then swooping to land near his link. With a familiar mixture of relief and frustration, Allegra left them to their silent conversation and inspected their campsite. Given the circumstances, it was almost ideal. Water was plentiful, even if she would have to strain it first, there was shade and shelter, and there were even some berries on the bushes that grew round the edge of the cove. She was on her way over to see whether they were edible when the first tremor hit.

It was very slight, no more than a vibration, but it was enough to tell them that somewhere a major eruption was in progress. Ero took to the air again as Vargo and Cat looked at each other. The whole canyon seemed to be humming, and in the distance they could hear the horrible slithering sound of a rock fall. They seemed to be in no immediate danger, however. The low cliffs that surrounded them were relatively stable, and after a while Allegra's biggest concern was that the quake might make their journey out of the ravine even more treacherous than the descent had been.

There were several other tremors as they set up their camp, but they were all minor and none lasted more than a minute or two. By the time darkness fell and Cat and Vargo were preparing to sleep, the vibrations had stopped altogether. As night enfolded them, all the tiny sounds of the ravine were magnified. The stone heartbeat, as Vargo called it, was plainly audible now, a measured resonance beneath the chatter of insects and the soughing of the wind. Rock clicked intermittently as it cooled, and the placid river water lapped gently on the shore.

Much later Cat awoke to find that the music that had haunted her dreams was still playing. She sat up, and looked around in wonder. Everything about her was silvered by pale moonlight, or hidden in deepest shadow, and there was no sign of where the music might be coming from. It was entrancingly beautiful but very strange. No human voice or instrument could have produced those liquid notes or the fragmented, rippling melody. It was almost like a kind of bird song, but it was of far too low a pitch and too sustained for that to be the case. It seemed to be coming from no particular direction and from everywhere at once, as if the walls of the cove were capturing the sounds and reflecting them to its visitors. The overall effect was eerie, but not at all frightening. If anything, this was music of welcome, and Cat lay down again and let it soothe her back into her dream.

Beside her, Vargo smiled in his sleep.

Allegra woke later than usual the next day. Whenever they were sleeping in the open she normally rose at first light, but this morning the sky was already pale blue. Whether her long sleep had been because of the deep shadows of this hidden place, or the hypnotic effect of the music, she felt better rested than she had in a long time. Vargo was already up, sitting at the edge of the river, tossing pebbles into its murky depths. Cat unwrapped herself from her blanket, stretched and went to join him.

'Hello, sleepyhead,' he greeted her, looking up.

'You sound like my father,' she said, sitting down beside him.

'You mean I treat you like a child?'

'Sometimes. Did you hear the music?' she asked, wondering why she had not thought to awaken him in the night.

'What music?'

'Never mind,' she replied, knowing she'd never be able to describe it properly. 'It was probably just the wind.'

Vargo nodded, accepting her explanation at face value, and threw another stone. As happened so often, Cat felt that he was on the point of saying something more – but, as usual, he kept his silence.

'Is this the ravine you saw in your dream?' she asked eventually.

'Which dream?' he replied, frowning.

'The one you had in Corazoncillo, where the shadows were dreaming. Isn't that why we came here?'

It was some time before Vargo answered, and when he did he still sounded puzzled.

'I don't know,' he said, looking round as if something in their surroundings would solve the mystery. 'There are plenty of shadows here.'

'We're a long way from the sea, though.'

'What?'

'In your dream the sea was beneath us,' she reminded him.

'Sometimes I think you take me too seriously,' he said with a grin. 'Which is something you could never accuse Ero of.'

The hoopoe came dancing across the water then, calling in greeting, and landed in the small space between the two humans. Allegra felt a small pang of regret at the intrusion. It often seemed that the bird timed his appearances in order to keep their conversations from becoming too revealing. Perhaps he's trying to keep us apart, she thought, only half joking, so he can have Vargo all to himself. However, Ero was such an endearing character that it was impossible to feel annoyed with him for long.

'I asked him to scout along the other bank of the river,' Vargo explained. 'I'll see what he's found.' He turned to his link. *Anything of interest, Ero?*

*Only if you like holes. I found some caterpillars though*, the bird added smugly. If he had had hands instead of wings he would have rubbed his stomach in satisfaction.

*Are they big holes? Big enough for us to go inside?*

*Oh, yes. But they're dark and there are bones.* He gave a little shudder of distaste.

*How far away?*

*Three swoops*, Ero answered doubtfully.

That didn't really tell Vargo very much. One swoop, in Ero's inexact terminology, could be anything from ten to fifty paces and, as the bird couldn't count any higher than three, he used that number for anything larger.

*Upstream or down?*

*Down.*

'Right,' Vargo said aloud.

'What did he say?' Cat asked.

'There are some caves on the far bank some way downstream. With bones near by, apparently.'

'Bones? So we might be walking into a bear's den?'

'We haven't seen any signs of large animals,' Vargo pointed out reasonably.

'On this side of the river,' Cat agreed. 'Perhaps they don't like to swim.'

'Neither do I,' he replied. 'But I will if necessary. There's something down here, Cat. I know it. And I'm not leaving till we find it.'

'All right,' she muttered. 'Let's just hope it doesn't eat us.'

Less than an hour later, they came to the mouth of the first of the caves, which was set into the base of a towering cliff. Having decided to bring all their gear with them, rather than risk leaving it at the campsite, they had forded the river with the help of long sticks to probe the river bed in front of them. Although the water had been bitterly cold, it was no deeper than waist height, so the crossing had been easier than expected. The growing warmth of the day had already dried their clothes, and they'd brushed the silt dust away.

'Well, do we go in here or check on some of the others first?' Allegra asked. From where they stood they could already see several more cave entrances further along the cliff face. 'And where are the bones Ero was talking about?'

'I think he meant those,' Vargo replied, pointing to some pale shapes within the gloom.

'They look more like rocks to me.'

'Let's go and find out.'

They left their packs by the entrance, and Vargo called for Ero to come and guard them.

'He wouldn't put up much of a fight if a bear turned up,' he explained, 'but he might be able to warn us.'

Like all birds, Ero had an instinctive dislike of going underground, and Cat knew there was no way he would go with them into the caves. They left the hoopoe strutting back and forth, his chest puffed out, evidently taking his sentry duties very seriously. Cat could not help smiling.

'It'll only last till he sees something more interesting,' Vargo said fondly. 'Come on.'

Upon inspection, the white shapes turned out to be very intriguing. They were clearly made of rock, but some of them did indeed seem to be shaped like bones – albeit bones that had been broken and then fused together with others.

'What do you make of it?' Allegra asked.

'I haven't a clue,' Vargo replied, 'but I don't think it's the leftovers from a bear's dinner.'

Cat glanced into the darkness ahead of them.

'So do we explore further?'

'Might as well.'

She had already taken their oil lamp from her pack,

and she lit it now with one of their precious sulphur-tipped tapers. Its wavering light revealed a wide passage leading deep into the earth. In her other hand Cat held a piece of chalk, which she used to mark the way they went. The Firebrands had used secret signs, written on kerbstones, to send messages in Teguise, and had adapted the technique for exploring the caves of the firelands during their exile. If she and Vargo were about to venture into yet another unknown world, the least she could do was make sure of finding their way out again.

Although there were no side passages to divert them, their progress was necessarily slow; the floor of the tunnel was uneven, forcing them to scramble on all fours in places, and both ceiling and walls were made hazardous by rocky projections. The cave was dry, although it was clear that water had played some part in its formation, and the air remained fresh and cool. They discovered nothing of real interest, however, and when they stopped for a brief rest Cat was beginning to wonder what the point of the exercise was. With the sound of their echoing footsteps silenced, a new noise became audible. It was the stone heartbeat that they'd heard before, but it was noticeably louder here, as though the whole mountain was breathing in and out.

'What is it?' Cat whispered.

'The sea.'

'But that's miles away!' she protested.

'Listen.'

She did as she was told. It did indeed sound like the continuous swell of the ocean, the rise and fall of waves as they crashed against the shore.

'You think these tunnels reach all the way to the coast?' Cat asked in awe. If it were true, all the other cave systems she had been in were insignificant by comparison.

Vargo shrugged.

'We won't find out standing here.'

'We can't go all that way!' Cat exclaimed.

'I know. Let's just get to the gate.'

'The gate? What gate?'

'Maybe the sea will come to us,' he said as he set off.

Allegra followed, knowing that in his present mood Vargo was quite capable of going on even in total darkness.

After a while they passed the first of several side turnings, but on each occasion Vargo seemed to know where he was going, and Cat knew better than to question him. She continued to signpost their route, making sure her chalk marks were clear. It seemed that the entire mountain-side might be honeycombed with caves and tunnels, and she could not rely on Vargo's sense of direction working in reverse. Their journey already seemed to be lasting for ever.

'We can't go much further,' she warned eventually. 'Or the lamp won't last out for our return.'

'It's very close now,' he replied, excitement filling his voice. 'Look!'

Allegra rounded a corner, and found herself staring across a wide low cavern. The floor was covered with water, and the surface moved gently in a slight breeze. She caught the faint tang of salt in the air.

'Look at the far wall,' Vargo said.

Cat looked, and saw what at first seemed to be a crude picture of a dragon painted upon the stone. Then, as she continued to study it, she realized that it must have been carved from the rock.

'Who could have made that?' she whispered.

'No one made it,' Vargo answered. 'It's a real dragon.'

'But it's too small,' she objected.

'It's one of their young – one that never got the chance to grow up,' he replied sadly. 'It's been dead longer than you can imagine. It's a fossil.'

They stared at the stone-encased skeleton for a while, then Cat put the lamp down on a ledge.

'Is this what you were looking for?'

Vargo nodded.

'Let's see if we can reach it,' she said, kneeling down to test the depth of the underground lake, and shivering as she recalled another, similar place. The water was icy on her fingers. It looked quite shallow, at least near the edge, but she never got the chance to explore further.

Vargo suddenly gave a strangled cry and waved to Cat to move back. She looked up in alarm, and saw the cause of his fear. A small swarm of fireworms was flying across the lake, heading purposefully in their direction. She scrambled back in horror – this was the last place she'd have expected to meet these deadly creatures – and prayed that Vargo would be able to deal with them. It was clear, even to her, that the worms were intent on attacking.

Vargo already had one hand clasped round his talisman, and she felt him draw cold from the surrounding stone and water and hurl it back towards the swarm. The magical shield he created would have been even more effective if he'd had any dragon's tears, but as it was his efforts were good enough. The fireworms hesitated, then fell back, veering away from the deadly chill.

'Let's get out of here,' Cat gasped, but Vargo did not move. She put a hand on his arm. 'Come on!'

He seemed to be in a daze, and did not react. Allegra turned away, intent in retrieving the lamp and dragging him away by force if necessary, when too late she saw one of the fireworms coming back – moving so fast that she did not even have time to throw herself in front of Vargo to protect him.

The worm clamped itself onto Vargo's forearm and began to eat its way into his flesh.

# CHAPTER SIXTEEN

Allegra screamed. Vargo had taken risks before, but never like this! What was worse, he seemed stunned and was not even trying to fight back, to shake the worm loose or freeze it. Moments from now it would be inside him, eating its way towards his heart.

Without conscious thought, Cat pounced. She screamed again – a battle cry this time – and something stirred inside her, her mind tearing loose from its moorings. Words came from unknown depths, from an ancient place within her that she had not known existed. *Help me. Help me, Ero.*

She collided with Vargo as her outstretched hands clutched at the writhing worm, and together they fell to the ground. She grasped the worm as tightly as she could, trying to tear the vile creature away from him but it was stuck fast. *Help me!* Cat felt the repulsive leathery skin squirm in her grip, and hung on desperately as the struggle continued. Her own skin felt as if it were being scalded.

And then something very strange happened. Glancing down at her hands, she saw not fingers but three-toed talons ending in sharp claws. She was too terrified to be astonished, and when she felt a new rush of strength course through her she channelled it all into those alien limbs and squeezed. She knew that the claws, however sharp, could not hurt the worm, but if she could exert sufficient force . . .

Cat howled again, feeding all her fear, all her love and anger, into closing the vice. With a sickening tearing sound, the fireworm split open from end to end, its grey innards spilling out into the frigid air.

Her hands were her own again now and, even though she was trembling violently and felt as weak as a kitten, Allegra pulled the disgusting remnants of the creature away from Vargo and flung them into the lake. There was a round hole in his sleeve, the edges of which were charred, as if they'd been eaten away by acid. The flesh beneath was exposed and bleeding where a circle of skin was gone, but that seemed to be the extent of the damage. Vargo himself was barely conscious, his head lolling back and his eyes unfocused. As Allegra pulled him into her arms, a shudder ran through his body and he gasped for breath, almost choking.

'Vargo. Vargo! Are you all right?' She had to fight to stop herself from shaking him. 'Speak to me.'

'Someone opened the gate,' he mumbled, then began to cough.

That was enough for Cat for the moment. He was alive, and for now little else mattered. Tearing off the sleeve of her own shirt, she wrapped it around his wound as a temporary bandage.

'We have to get out of here,' she told him urgently. It was only a matter of time before the other fireworms returned, and neither of them was in a fit state to offer any resistance. 'Can you stand up?'

His eyes came back into focus briefly as she helped him to his feet.

'Cat? What's happening? What are you doing here?'

'What I always do,' she replied. At least he recognized her. 'Stay here while I get the lamp.'

'The mirror doesn't work for other people,' he said, sounding confused.

'Come on.' Allegra picked up the lamp, then took hold of Vargo's good arm. The most important thing was for them to get out of the caves. Although there had been no further sign of the swarm, that didn't mean there would not be another attack.

The journey back to the open was gruelling, and Allegra's anxieties constantly threatened to overwhelm her. She worried about the fireworms catching up with them, about the oil burning dry and leaving them lost in darkness, about Vargo's ability to keep going – and about her own fast waning strength. In the event their luck held. The swarm did not reappear, the lamp only guttered out when they were in sight of daylight, and their combined reserves of energy were just about equal to the task. The sunshine in the ravine was almost blinding as they staggered to the spot where they had left their packs. Cat would have liked to move further away, in case the worms belatedly renewed their assault, but had neither the strength nor the willpower to go on. They collapsed on the soft ground and tried to catch their breath.

It was only then that Allegra noticed Ero. The hoopoe had moved a little way from his post and was now waddling around in small figures of eight, his crest erect and his head bobbing from side to side. He looked wide eyed and dazed when he finally stopped, and as he glanced at her Cat wondered for the first time just what had happened inside the cave. The more she thought about it, the more incredible it became. Had she been hallucinating? Or had she really been able to use some sort of magic? Had her desperation given her abnormal strength? Or had some outside force crushed the fireworm?

Allegra's knowledge of magic had always been purely theoretical. She had studied, read voraciously when she had the chance, imagined . . . but nothing in all the previously forbidden archives had told her how to recognize her own talent – or lack of it. She did not even know if she had any. But she did know that magic, that uniquely personal fusion of mind and power, was precious, a gift that must never be wasted – even when, like Vargo, you possessed it in abundance.

More questions filled Cat's mind as she watched Ero fall asleep – even though his crest was still raised. Had it been only in her imagination that she had cried out for help? To Ero? That made no sense. The hoopoe was Vargo's link, not hers, and in any case, Ero was not usually much use in a fight. And yet the claws she had seen, the talons that had killed the worm, had surely been giant versions of Ero's feet. How could that be? Even if, in her extremity, she had unleashed some long-dormant magic, why had it taken that form? She wished she could talk to Ero, ask him directly, but the bird was sound asleep now – and if he felt half as tired as Cat did, he was unlikely to wake for some time. She herself was struggling to keep her eyes open. And that, she realized, was consistent with the use of magic. The use of such power always exacted its price. *My own magic?* she thought incredulously. *Could it really be?*

It occurred to her then that she had never *needed* to use magic before. Vargo's had always been more than enough for both of them. That reminded her of the fact that Andrin had only become the Ice Mage when it had been absolutely necessary, when he'd had no other choice. And today she had faced a similar crisis.

Could it really be?

But there were still too many things she did not understand. First and foremost was the question of why the fireworms had been there in the first place. The ravine and its caves were about as far from their normal habitat as could be imagined. Perhaps it had something to do with the fossilized dragon that Vargo seemed to think was so important. Or perhaps these worms were a different strain, and they'd adapted to living in different conditions. Cat rejected this last idea almost immediately. The fireworms had looked just like the ones she already knew, even down to the disappointing fact that they were obviously tainted with hatred. She had sensed their implacable malevolence. One other possibility, even more chilling than the rest, occurred to her now. Could the swarm have been drawn there by Vargo's presence? Had they been following him, waiting for a chance to attack? That too seemed unlikely, given the number of opportunities they would have had for an earlier ambush. So what *was* the truth?

And what had Vargo meant by his ramblings about gates and mirrors? Right now there seemed little chance of getting any explanations from Vargo himself. He had fallen into a deep sleep as soon as he'd lain on the ground, and showed no sign of waking. Looking at him now, Cat saw to her horror that blood had soaked through the makeshift bandage.

They each carried a rudimentary medical kit in their packs and she opened hers, taking out a length of bandage and a small pot of salve which was used to treat burns. She carefully removed the red-stained cloth and inspected Vargo's arm. Although the laceration was not deep, it looked horrible – part burn, part open wound. Blood was still oozing in several places, and there was another, clear liquid visible at the edges of the injury. When she touched it cautiously her own skin began to sting. Being as gentle as she could, Cat washed the wound quickly with clean water, applied the salve and then bound it with the fresh bandage. Vargo did not stir, and she was glad that his unconscious state was at least sparing him what surely must have been a great deal of pain.

And then Cat could manage no more. Exhaustion overtook her and she fell asleep, slumped awkwardly where she was, her head resting against Vargo's shoulder.

When she awoke it was because Vargo had twitched violently in his slumber, knocking her head away. She groaned as soon as she tried to move. Her entire body felt as if it had been pelted with rocks, and her arms and neck were horribly stiff. One of her legs was numb – from where she had been resting on it – and she massaged it roughly, enduring an agony of pins and needles before she could even put any weight on it. As she did so she watched Vargo to see whether he showed any signs of returning consciousness, but he lay still again, only his eyes moving rapidly beneath closed lids. He looked very pale and his skin was sheened with sweat, but at least the wound had apparently stopped bleeding.

Dusk was approaching, the sky already streaked with the colours of a particularly lurid sunset, and Cat went to fetch a blanket to lay over her patient. She heard the rumbling sounds of thunder in the distance, and hoped the storm would not reach them. The nearest shelter was the mouth of the cave, and she had no wish to go in there again.

Having covered Vargo, Allegra renewed her vigil, noticing for the first time – and with a pang of concern – that Ero was nowhere to be seen. Vargo was her main concern, of course, and every slight change in his shallow breathing, every tiny twitch of his facial muscles, made her more anxious. When he finally opened his eyes the movement was so sudden that it made her jump.

'Skies of fire,' he said quite clearly, then mumbled something she couldn't catch.

'Are you all right?' Allegra asked quickly. 'Vargo? Are you all right?'

He gave no sign of having heard her, continuing to gaze, wide eyed, at the sky.

'I could never play as well as you,' he said.

'What? What do you mean?'

'You could play again if only you'd let someone heal your hands. You could do it yourself if you wanted to. Tek knows that too,' he went on. 'Why won't you listen?'

Cat realized what was happening. Vargo was talking to Famara, not to her. Tek had been the old woman's link, the matriarch of a boisterous clan of sparrows.

'It's me, Vargo,' she said. 'It's Cat.'

But his eyes were still fixed on other places, other times.

'Why did you choose me?' he asked. 'Did you think it would make me happy to know you were pregnant?' The mixture of tenderness and pain in his voice now was heart-rending. 'It sent me mad,' he said. 'It was too heavy a burden.'

This time it was all too clear who he was talking to, and the realization made Allegra very uncomfortable. Subconsciously at least she had always regarded Ico as her rival for Vargo's love and attention, and to hear him speaking to the other woman now in such an intimate way made her feel hopelessly outmatched.

'You must have known what you meant to me,' he went on plaintively. 'Andrin too. How was I supposed to cope with that?'

'Vargo, wake up. It's me, Cat.' She shook him gently, unable to stand any more. 'Wake up!'

He closed his eyes for a moment, then opened them again and turned to look directly at her.

'I love you,' he said quietly.

Allegra's heart skipped a beat, then hammered in her chest. She had longed to hear him say those words but how, in the midst of his delirium, could she be sure he meant them? Even if he did, were they meant for her or for Ico? It was all she could do not to burst into tears.

'A camel never forgets,' Vargo added sagely, before she was sufficiently composed to say anything in return.

The incongruous comment only served to underline Cat's uncertainties, but she knew that she had to speak. Even if the conversation disappeared into the impenetrable mists of Vargo's clouded memory, she would have placed her confession in the open. At least she would have heard herself say the words.

'I love you too,' she told him softly.

He smiled then, and for a brief, glorious moment she thought he might have heard and understood her, in spite of his condition. However, her hopes were cruelly dashed by his next statement.

'They can only see from inside,' he exclaimed. 'Inside the mirror. And I'm inside the mirror!'

Cat had no idea what this meant and nor, at that precise moment, did she care – but it clearly excited Vargo.

'Can't tell Cat,' he muttered then, in a much quieter voice. 'Mustn't tell Cat.' He glanced about wildly, as if searching for something – or someone – he couldn't see. 'Don't tell Cat.'

I might as well be invisible, she thought miserably, pierced to the heart by the idea that there were secrets Vargo felt he could not share with her. And this time she could not hold back her tears.

Much later, when it was dark and she had calmed down again, Cat wondered about the possible causes of Vargo's delirious fever. Could the shock and pain of the attack have been enough to cause such mental ferment? Or was it the result of some poison from the fireworm's bite, poison that might even now be coursing through his veins? Perhaps it was because of something she had done, some inexplicable consequence of her own untutored use of magic. That thought made her feel quite sick, but all she could do was wait and see if – when – Vargo recovered. Once she realized that she would get nowhere by dwelling on unanswerable questions, Cat fell into an exhausted and thankfully dreamless sleep.

When she next awoke, the morning sky was thick with dark clouds and it was obvious that rain was on the way. A good deal had already fallen upstream by the look of the river, which was now churned up, white foam flecking the brown waves as they raced over hidden boulders. Cat stared at the new-born rapids as her mind struggled into wakefulness, then froze in horror as the significance of what she was seeing gradually sank in. There was no way in the world they could ford this raging torrent – and the cliffs on this side of the river were much too high and sheer for them to be able to climb out that way. Unless the river abated, or there was another route they had not spotted yet, they were trapped.

What made matters worse was the fact that their food supplies would run out in a few days. Although Allegra had seen plenty of berries and other provender on the other side of the river, this bank was practically barren. She cursed her lack of foresight, and looked up into the darkness of the heavens. As if to reinforce the hideousness of the situation, thunder rolled overhead and it began to rain.

She roused Vargo, gratefully noticing that at least he seemed to be in his right mind after a night's rest – even if he was a little groggy – and between them they moved their gear just inside the entrance to the cave.

After a while, when she hoped that Vargo was fully aware of their predicament, they sat near the pile of 'bones' and stared morosely at the continuing downpour. The river was rising steadily now.

'It can't rain for ever,' Cat said gloomily.

'There is another way out of here, you know,' Vargo said.

Cat looked at him, curiosity turning to horror when she realized what he meant.

'Oh, no! You're not getting me back in there.'

'I've always wanted to see the Great West Ocean,' he replied, unmoved by her vehemence. 'Now's our chance.'

# CHAPTER SEVENTEEN

It wasn't the screaming that woke him, nor the incredible sequence of images that filled his dream. What woke him was the silence, the *emptiness*, that followed the dream's end.

Nino sat up and looked down at the darkly beautiful face of his wife. She was still peacefully asleep, and he wondered how she could remain unaware of what had happened. This had been no ordinary dream. He had glimpsed something incredible, something so vast and so important that it should have shaken the entire country. And now it was gone again. He felt its loss keenly.

It had taken Nino three days to complete the trek from Corazoncillo. He had been anxious and weary when he'd arrived home, but in the two days since then a little of the village's usual tranquillity had begun to rub off on him. Tinajo was near the heart of the central firelands, and most outsiders would have found it impossible to imagine it as a peaceful place; its proximity to several volcanoes seemed unlikely to encourage peace of mind. But the truth was that Tinajo had always been lucky, a fortunate haven surrounded by the ravages of nature. The houses there still stood on old soil, not lava, even though several flows had passed near by. At times of an eruption, people from the neighbouring regions fled *to* Tinajo for protection.

Tavia, Nino's wife of eighteen months, had been overjoyed to see him. They had been sweethearts from childhood, but it had only been the recent upheavals in Tiguafaya that had brought home to them the realization that they were not children any more. They had both known that they wanted to marry – in spite of the fact that Nino would obviously not be able to settle down quietly just yet. Baby Nino had been born within the year, and sealed the already unshakeable bond between them. Nino was shocked to see just how much his son had grown during his most recent absence, and vowed to come home more often. Tavia, more realistically, knew that her husband was engaged in important work, and told him to come home when he could. She would always be waiting. The restless fire in his eyes was a sign that he would soon be off on his travels again, and she was determined – as always – to make the most of the time they had together.

The news that a winemaker's daughter, who lived less than a mile from Tinajo, had recently become linked with a rook had delighted Nino. It was important because rooks are communal creatures, and there was therefore a good chance that others in the rookery would be able to work with the linked bird and thus create a net – which in turn might become a useful strand in Nino's grand design. This meant that he could plan a trip to the vineyard and convince himself that he could continue his work while staying at home – at least for a while.

On his second day in Tinajo Nino was relaxed enough – for the first time in as long as he could remember – to take a siesta during the hottest part of the day. Baby Nino was already asleep, used to resting when the sun was high, and his parents went to their own bed – not that they did much sleeping for the first hour or so. Later, when the cares of the world had receded to a safe distance, they did sleep – and Nino began to dream.

The screaming carried him to a place that was cool and dark. He knew there was water near by, but he couldn't see it. Some sort of battle – a matter of life and death – was going on, but that was also out of his range of vision. All he could see was his own hands, the fingers spread wide.

'Help me!'

Although the voice was familiar, he could not place it. He would have responded to her plea if he had known how, but he didn't know what she wanted, or even where she was.

And then his hands became wings, his fingers feathers. He flew into the great pattern, the welcome of the sky, joining all the others. Although they were invisible he knew they were there – link beyond link beyond link. He sensed their joint power, their purpose. He heard their music.

His hands became claws, predatory talons – and for a moment he saw the interlocking pattern as a whole, as it could be. It was breathtaking, powerful beyond anything he could ever have imagined. No enemy could stand before *this*.

Lines and circles danced before him, fluid yet precise, ever shifting and yet incredibly strong. He saw with Eya's falcon clarity and his eyes were everywhere, catching glimpses of countless places, some familiar, some not. Only the foci, the important intersections, were clear enough to register properly in his mind. The Corazoncillo valley was clearest of all, as he'd known it would be. He looked down on Elva, the lost island-rock that had once been humankind's oracle. He saw several overlapping scenes from Teguise, flying above the city's rooftops while simultaneously resting within the palace. Other visions were of places unknown to him. There was an ancient, river-carved ravine, full of greenery and lined with caves; a vast red volcano with a lop-sided crater; and a dusty place of long-dead bones.

Countless other views, some enclosed and claustrophobic, some open panoramas, flashed before his dreaming eyes, too fast for comprehension. He watched, mesmerized, and was vaguely aware that others – too numerous to even try to name – were watching too.

*Yuck!* Ysanne exclaimed. *They squished it.*

*The singing helped*, Tas replied. *It was all at the same time for once.*

*The claws made it go splat!* Ysanne added, with evident satisfaction.

The firecrest put her tiny head on one side.

*Was it Ero?* she asked, obviously confused.

Ysanne wasn't sure how to answer this question, so she didn't even try.

*He's silly*, she said, giggling. *At least he usually is*, she added thoughtfully.

*Did he do magic?*

*We all did*, Ysanne decided.

To prove it she ran around the room in triumph, her arms spread out like wings, while Tas fluttered overhead.

*That's not really flying*, the bird remarked scornfully.

*I'm practising*, Ysanne replied. *Wheee!*

Ayo was high in the air above Roncador Point when his vision suddenly split and he began to see two different worlds. It was worse than being blind and he flew on only by instinct, crossing the bay to the south of Teguise.

After leaving Pajarito he had gone to see Ara and their fledglings, to bid them farewell – at least for the time being. It had been one of the hardest things he had ever done. Knowing he was right was one thing; convincing Ara was another. Like the vast majority of birds she had never experienced what it was like to be linked, to share your mind with an alien creature, to teach and to learn. And so she could not understand. They had parted in sorrow, and Ayo was not sure she had believed him when he told her he would return. He could only hope that she, unlike Iva, would be waiting for him when he did.

He flew towards Teguise with the oracle's words echoing in his brain. *Play your part*. As soon as he was in range of Andrin's thoughts he would know what to do.

The surge of images, of power and possibility, took him by surprise. Something that had been sleeping had awoken, albeit briefly, and he knew it was a sign of things to come. *There is safety in slumber*. But now there was no safety left.

He felt the cry for help, gave his will over to the general response without conscious thought, sliding into the pattern that united them all. He knew that Ero was involved somehow, but it had not been Vargo who had asked for their help . . .

Alone again, Ayo flew on. It was all he knew how to do.

Soo had seen it all; the fireworm attacking Vargo, Allegra's brave attempt to save him, and the incredible response that her anguished appeal had provoked. But the sparrowhawk's feral gaze had also seen something else, something that drowned out the singing and made the dreaming irrelevant. The image of the stone dragon burned into her half-demented mind, and she knew that she had seen her journey's beginning. And its end.

And then it was over, and the union vanished into the ether whence it had sprung. For a few precious moments the network had been alive, incandescent. It had given its immeasurable support where it was needed, and victory had been won in a small but significant battle. And so the need was gone.

Nino's dream collapsed in upon itself, leaving a void that sucked him into wakefulness – and into the knowledge that he would not be able to rest until he had the chance to dream again.

# CHAPTER EIGHTEEN

When the ambassador's party crested the Argan Ridge, and he was at last able to gaze across the wide plain to the city that he loved, Kudrak smiled with pure pleasure. Zepharinn was not only a place of great beauty – if you ignored some of the less palatable districts on its outskirts – but it was also the epicentre of all life within the Empire, and thus the entire civilized world. The political and financial decisions made there affected millions of people. Every aspect of their society, every field of human endeavour, depended ultimately on what took place in the imperial capital. And it was here that Kudrak was able to indulge his tastes for the finer things in life. Music, theatre, poetry and dance all thrived in Zepharinn. Painters and sculptors and other artists were drawn there from the most far-flung outposts of the Empire and beyond.

Returning home from one of his trips always made the time away seem worthwhile, and Kudrak felt privileged as well as proud to number himself among Zepharinn's most influential citizens. This place was the province of his heart.

It was also where his wife and children resided, but that was a comparatively minor consideration.

As the horses brought them closer to home, the ambassador was able to pick out individual landmarks within the city. At the centre, dominating everything around it, rose the Imperial Fortress, its massive, honey-coloured stone walls a formidable presence looming above the other buildings. It had been constructed on the highest piece of suitable ground in order to achieve this very effect, and two nearby hills of almost equal height had been levelled so that no man could ever look down upon the Emperor's abode.

Although the castle had long since outgrown its original purpose – the city had not needed defending for several centuries – the imposing battlements left no one in any doubt as to the location of the ultimate seat of power. The walls were still manned by a detachment of the Seax Guards, but their presence was more for ceremonial purposes than for any military need. And once inside the walls it soon became clear that the Imperial Fortress was much more than a place of protection. Within its labyrinth of halls and chambers it was possible to find every luxury known to man. Members of the High Court – which was, in effect, a city within the city – lived in a style not to be matched anywhere in the world. Kudrak could hardly wait to rejoin them.

As always, the ambassador enjoyed his entry into the city. Even the poorer residents of Zepharinn were relatively prosperous but Kudrak's bearing, his clothes, his fine mount and his armed escort all marked him as a man of importance, and everyone they met greeted him with due deference. After a generally disagreeable voyage, this was like presenting cool water to a man returning parched from the desert. He drank it in.

After a brief halt to make the necessary oblation at the

Sixth Temple, the party continued on its way to the castle. Kudrak took his devotions seriously and, even though he was anxious to end his journey, he would never dream of offending the gods by passing one of their holy places and not offering thanks. There were seven temples in all, one for each of the nameless major deities, equally spaced in a circle around the fortress. Although Zepharinn housed numerous other smaller sepulchres and shrines to the lesser gods, the Seven were by far the most important. Each month, at the new moon, processions would wind their way around the circle, completing what was known as the 'pilgrim ring'. In recent times, with the rise of the Kundahari, these public reaffirmations of faith had become almost mandatory for any respectable citizen, and the size of the crowds was becoming a problem. Although such fanatical devotion made Kudrak feel a little uneasy, he approved of the general reverence being shown to the gods. If nothing else, the Kundahari had roused many people from indolence or apathy, and that was something the High Priests had not been able to do for many years.

Once they were finally inside the great gates of the fortress, Kudrak dismounted, thanked the commander of his escort for his services, and went to ready himself for an audience with the Emperor. News of his arrival would have already been sent to the court, but he would not be expected to present himself until he had bathed, washing away the dust of his travels, and changed clothes in the guest lodge. Discreet but quietly efficient servants attended to his every need and, by the time he was ready, a page was waiting to convey him to the imperial quarters. He was informed that he was to give his report to the Inner Council, rather than to a full assembly, and this was a relief to Kudrak as well as another boost to his self-esteem. He was always more at ease in the company of a few individuals, rather than in front of a largely anonymous gathering, and the fact that he would shortly be sharing his expertise with the most powerful men in the world only made his anticipation all the keener.

Five men were already seated at the beautifully inlaid conference table when Kudrak was ushered into the chamber. At the head of the table, Madar rose to his feet and came to greet the ambassador, who bowed deeply, gratified by this more than civil display of courtesy by the Emperor. In deference to their master, the other four also stood, but remained where they were, each watching the newcomer.

'Welcome home, Excellency.'

'Thank you, Your Highness. It is always an enormous pleasure to return to Zepharinn.'

'We've been awaiting your news with some eagerness.' Madar shared his brother's lean face and slim figure, but his eyes were a darker blue and his hair was light brown rather than yellow. In Kudrak's humble opinion the Emperor was a good-hearted man, if young and a little naïve for such responsibility. At least he had not done anything to his teeth.

Madar waved the ambassador to a chair, and he and the others resumed their seats.

'You know everyone here, I presume.'

Kudrak nodded. It would be a rare person among the upper echelons of Zepharine society who did not recognize the men in this group. On Madar's right sat First Chamberlain Ruhail, the Emperor's chief advisor and the man who was ultimately responsible for the day-to-day running of the vast machinery of imperial government. He was small and sharp faced, a physically unremarkable character whose intelligence and phenomenal memory were legendary – as was his abstemiousness. A cup of water stood before him, although the others had wine. His political skills were unmatched throughout the Empire. Next to him was Treasurer Meos, a ponderous, heavy-set man, who controlled the imperial purse strings with a devotion that stemmed from his own love of gold and power.

On the other side of the table, Castellan Ty took his time-honoured place at the Emperor's left hand. He commanded the Seax Guards, having inherited an ancient title which now encompassed far more than the security of Madar and his fortress home. His élite regiment had begun life as personal bodyguards who had subsequently taken on the wider duties of manning Zepharinn's castle. But they were now responsible for policing the entire city, gathering intelligence from far and wide and, when necessary, adding their considerable weight to any particularly hazardous military enterprise. Ty himself looked like a caricature – the grizzled veteran with his scarred face and his well-worn uniform – but he was not to be underestimated. His bluff exterior concealed a ruthless mind, as sharp as the edge of his sword, which hung in its scabbard from the back of his chair. The castellan was the only man entitled to bring a weapon into the presence of the Emperor. Although this was now purely symbolic, there was no doubt in anyone's mind that Ty would be able to wield his blade effectively should the need arise.

Last and – in this context – very much least, was Hierophant Nandi, a florid, nervous man who had clearly drunk rather more wine than was good for him. The position of hierophant was taken in turn by each of the high priests of the seven temples, with the ceremonial robes of office being exchanged at the end of the monthly procession. Their temporary elevation to the Inner Council allowed the priests to represent the religious viewpoint on matters of state, and the rotation of the office ensured that all seven major gods were honoured equally. Some of the high priests responded to these extra duties better than others – and Nandi, the High Priest of the Second Temple, was clearly uncomfortable.

'My brother should have been here, of course,' Madar went on, 'but he's been detained in the south and sends his apologies.'

Kudrak was fairly certain that Tzarno had done nothing of the sort, but he was happy to see that Madar felt it necessary to observe the formalities. The ambassador knew that he would eventually have to admit to his meeting with the prince, and chose to get the awkward moment over with as quickly as possible.

'Actually, Your Highness, I did have the chance to exchange a few words with your brother three days ago in Uga Stai. At his command, I told him of the results of my visit to Tiguafaya.'

As he spoke Kudrak kept his gaze fixed upon Madar, but was keenly aware of the varying responses his words had provoked around the table. Ruhail tried hard to conceal his annoyance but only partially succeeded. A slight smile crept over Ty's bearded face, while Meos looked resigned, as if such a breach of protocol was to be expected from Tzarno. Nandi, like the Emperor, betrayed no reaction at all.

'He gave me his assurance that he would not act upon the information until the council had considered my report,' Kudrak added, hoping to appease the chamberlain.

'Then we'd better hear it,' Madar responded mildly.

In essence, the ambassador told them the same story he had told the prince, and when he had finished he sat back without offering any opinion about what he thought should happen next. That was up to the others now.

'Well, gentlemen,' Madar said. 'You've all heard the ambassador's report. He has delivered our ultimatum – and it has been rebuffed.' He looked round the table. 'Your thoughts, please.'

Unusually, it was Meos who was the first to speak.

'They will surely reconsider that decision. Even

Maravedis cannot fail to be aware of the consequences of war. They must relent.'

'Decisions made in haste rarely bear much examination,' Ruhail agreed. 'I expect we shall receive a delegation from Tiguafaya before too long.'

Kudrak did his best to remain nonchalant while these comments – with their implicit criticism – were being made. He had been aware for some time that his abrupt departure from Teguise had been ill advised. He had made his point, in dramatic fashion, but should have waited aboard his ship a little longer before setting sail. Perhaps then his report would have had a different conclusion. As it was, he decided to stick to what he had said to Tzarno – which, after all, had been his honest impression at the time.

'I don't think she'll back down. If we do receive an envoy, I believe it will only be to repeat her earlier assertions.'

'Then she's mad!' Meos declared.

'Her outrageous concoction about these so-called fire-worms is nonsensical,' Ruhail added.

'Perhaps not,' Ty put in. 'Such creatures do exist. My people have sent several reports of flying worms that burn and kill all in their path.'

'Yes, yes, I know that,' the chamberlain said impatiently. 'But they *cannot* affect anything as powerful as a volcanic eruption. It's absurd.'

Ty shrugged, choosing not to argue the point.

'The point is,' Ruhail went on, 'that these worms offer no real threat to the Empire. They are confined to the firelands. Tiguafaya's request for our help in finding more of them is clearly a smoke screen – but to what end?'

'You don't give any credence to the suggestion that volcanic activity might spread beyond their borders?' Madar asked.

The question obviously caused the council some unease, and for a few moments no one spoke.

'I think it highly unlikely,' Meos replied eventually.

'If it ever does, it won't be because of a few worms!' Ruhail added.

'Can we be so sure?' Nandi asked timidly.

The others all turned to look at him, their faces showing varying degrees of surprise.

'I mean,' the hierophant went on, looking down at his manicured hands, 'it seems to me that the problems besetting Tiguafaya are a punishment for their blasphemies.'

'So why should that concern us?' Meos asked.

'It is true that we are a god-fearing people,' Nandi replied. 'For the most part, at least. But volcanoes, like all forces of nature, are not always predictable. The righteous chastisement of these heretics might set off a chain of events that could lead to hardships for the innocent.'

'Poppycock!' the treasurer exclaimed.

'I'm only saying it's a possibility,' the priest said defensively, then fell silent, aware that his views were in the minority.

'We should give some thought to their use of magic,' the castellan said. 'It's simultaneously their most serious crime and their greatest asset. How else could they even hope to defy us?'

'You see it as a real threat?' Madar asked.

'Half the rumours we've heard must be false,' Meos put in.

'But if the other half are true,' Ty countered, 'we should take the threat seriously. Not that it's anything we can't handle, of course,' he added confidently.

'Hierophant, you must have a view on what action we should take with regard to this alleged magic,' Madar prompted.

'I . . . The teachings of the elders tell us it is evil,' Nandi replied, collecting his thoughts, 'and must be crushed.'

'By war?'

'If . . . if necessary.'

'It seems to me,' Ruhail commented, looking pointedly at the priest, 'that if the Kundahari get wind of this we won't have much choice. That prophet of theirs is already stirring up trouble, and they'll soon be demanding action.'

'A full-scale war would be an expensive business,' the treasurer warned. 'Very expensive.'

'But in the end it could pay for itself,' the castellan argued. 'The silver mines in Tiguafaya are more productive than ever. There would be other assets too, not least the fact that it would open up trade routes to the south.'

'But we all know that the firelands are treacherous,' Madar said. 'We could lose the whole army in there and gain nothing.'

'It would have to be carefully planned,' Ty admitted. 'Our attack should come by sea, for the most part.'

'Where they are strongest?' Ruhail queried.

'Their navy may have been rebuilt, but it's still no match for ours. Take Teguise, and the rest of the country falls with it.'

The chamberlain did not looked convinced.

'We must not do anything rash,' Madar decided.

'Might I suggest we dispatch a courier to Uga Stai, to convey our thoughts to your brother?' Ruhail said dryly.

The Emperor nodded his assent.

'The real question is, how long are we prepared to wait for Tiguafaya to back down? I don't want war on such a scale, but if it is the will of the gods I will not hold back. Keep me informed of all developments.'

Madar stood up then, signalling that the meeting was at an end. As the others rose, he turned back to Kudrak.

'One last thing, Ambassador. The formal announcement will be made soon, but you may as well know now. I am to be married within the month.'

'Congratulations, Your Highness.' Kudrak was genuinely delighted by the news. The sooner Madar secured the imperial succession by producing a son and heir, the better it would be for the stability of the Empire. 'May I ask who is to be the lucky bride?'

'Katerin of Acubar.'

Kudrak struggled not to betray his astonishment. Madar had chosen outside the Imperial Court, in defiance of tradition. The ambassador knew of Katerin only by her reputation. She was the only child of the noble family who ruled the Imperial Demesne of Acubar, some one hundred miles west of Zepharinn. Apparently she was also beautiful, strong-willed and sharp-witted. As such she was either a very shrewd choice, or the biggest mistake of Madar's young life. There would certainly be a few noses put out of joint in court circles.

'I'm sure she will make an admirable Empress,' he replied lamely. He could not help thinking of Tzarno's scathing description of the women of Zepharinn, and wondered what the prince would make of this news.

Madar smiled.

'I know she will,' he said.

Could he actually be marrying for love? Kudrak wondered incredulously, trying to gauge the attitudes of the other members of the Inner Council. Their polite but neutral expressions told him nothing.

Further discussion was curtailed by an urgent knocking at the door of the chamber. Madar glanced briefly at Ruhail, then called for the newcomer to come in. The courier who entered seemed flushed and dishevelled – and his expression told them that he was clearly the bearer of bad news.

'Your Highness, My Lords, there has been a terrible disaster. Two days ago, in the south, the earth opened up and drowned an entire valley with fire and ash.'

For several heartbeats no one spoke.

'Well, gentlemen,' the Emperor said at last. 'It seems the Hierophant's fears were justified after all. This is hardly the kind of news that can be suppressed for long. War may come sooner than we thought.'

News of the eruption had reached Tzarno, who was still in Uga Stai, a day earlier. After his encounter with Lamia it had come as no great surprise.

The prince smiled now as he remembered how her ship had caused considerable interest – and a certain amount of alarm – among the hardy citizens of the port, who usually took everything in their stride. The vessel's unusual colouring had been part of it, of course, but it had been the five albatrosses that had provoked the most unease – as they would have done in any seafaring community.

The meeting that had followed had been more than satisfactory. Lamia and her strange entourage had stayed only for a few hours before setting sail again, but during that time Tzarno had become convinced that he had found a potentially useful ally. The foreigners' loathing of magic, and their claims to be able to counteract it, suited Tzarno's purpose perfectly. He had been looking for ways to combat sorcery, and now – unless he was being duped – he had found it. Whether Lamia, her crew and their mysterious 'resources' would be sufficient for the task was another matter. However, there was the possibility of others of her kind joining the crusade from their distant homeland and, in the meantime, the other alliance she brought with her also had many advantages. From what he knew of Galan Zarzuelo, the prince believed that the pirate leader could be persuaded to join the invasion of Tiguafaya. Zarzuelo's dream was evidently to outdo his legendary father, and this would present him with the ideal opportunity. Together the pirates and the easterners would make a formidable force – and a useful ally for the Empire. Having refitted their navy, Tiguafaya was strongest at sea – and it made perfect sense to let someone else fight them there first.

For his part, Tzarno intended to continue his preparations for a land attack. Because of what was generally regarded as impassable terrain in the mountains of northern Tiguafaya, this would be the surprise tactic that would ensure victory – and the glory that went with it. Most of the army was already in a state of readiness, and further reinforcements would be arriving soon. Reconnaissance missions were underway and, as soon as he had heard of the eruption, observers had been dispatched to gather what information they could. Conquering Tiguafaya would be a major undertaking, and Tzarno intended to leave as little as possible to chance.

Until his exchange of information with Lamia, the prince would have regarded the timing and location of the eruption as purely fortuitous. It meant that if the Empire stood by its own ultimatum, then war was certain – and this gave Tzarno cause for grim satisfaction. However, one aspect of his conversation with the Emissary, as she called herself, had been genuinely unsettling. This had been her insistence that the earth was becoming increasingly volatile. He could still recall the interpreter's exact words as he translated her impassioned series of clicks and whistles.

'The fires below are reaching up. Even in the Empire, no one will be safe.'

The easterners had seemed to believe this implicitly and, although Tzarno found it hard to accept that something as nebulous as magic could be the cause of such a massive upheaval, their theory fitted in exactly with the Empire's current thoughts about heresy. This made his case for an invasion, a holy war, all the stronger. When, two days later, the news had come about the eruption, it only served to reinforce the prince's own conviction that he had been right to accept Lamia's claims. However, there were serious implications for his invasion plans.

In parting, Lamia had made another statement that had stayed in Tzarno's mind.

'You must study the aspects of your own stars. Those who ride on flame fly high and fast, but their fall can be all the greater.'

As the translator repeated her message, the Emissary had fixed Tzarno with her dead eyes, measuring him deliberately. The prince had met her gaze. He had found her fascinating, especially as she seemed immune to his charms, but his self-belief was such that he had paid little attention to her elegantly phrased warning. The Prophet, on the other hand, had been less impressed with their visitor. He claimed to have known her father, Maghdim, and while admitting that the man had had certain talents, he was also at pains to point out that he had had his weaknesses too – weaknesses that had eventually led to his death. Even so, he agreed that – together with the pirates – the foreigners were useful allies. If nothing else they would provide an invaluable diversion.

Now it was a question of waiting to see whether recent events had been enough to force Madar's hand. Tzarno grew impatient, reckoning that Kudrak could only have reached Zepharinn that day, and knowing that the Council would probably deliberate for a long time over the ambassador's report – and over the implications of the eruption. So when an imperial courier arrived during the early evening, the prince told himself that it could not possibly be the answer he wanted. It was far too soon. Even so, he could not help hoping.

When he opened the sealed letter, and discovered that it

contained news of an entirely different matter, his disappointment was compounded by other emotions. The
Prophet and several of his senior officers were with him as
he read the message, and it was for their benefit that he forced
a smile onto his lips as he relayed the contents to them.

'Madar is to marry Katerin of Acubar. Within the
month.'

Tzarno continued to smile while his companions offered
their loyal congratulations at the joyous news. Only the
Prophet saw the rage burning deep within the prince's eyes.

# CHAPTER NINETEEN

*Pajarito told me the earth is stirring.*

*I think we've known that for some time,* Andrin replied, before the implication of the eagle's words sank in. *When were you at Pajarito?*

*Two days ago,* Ayo replied. *This will be no ordinary stirring.*

*We don't live in ordinary times,* his link remarked dryly.

*What can we do?*

*We're doing all we can.* But Andrin wondered if this was really true.

*I must play my part,* Ayo said gravely.

*We all must.*

Andrin had begun to feel whole again now that Ayo had returned. Until the eagle's reappearance he had not realized just how much he'd missed his link's company. However, Ayo's unhappiness was all too clear. Although the reason for it was obvious, they had avoided the subject until now. But Andrin had decided that this had to change.

*Are your mate and fledglings well?*

*They are well,* the eagle replied, sounding oddly formal.

*You miss them.* It was a statement rather than a question.

Ayo did not reply, but grew very still.

*We all have to make sacrifices at times like this*, Andrin said, trying to reassure him, then hated himself for spouting platitudes. *At least you had a chance to explain to them. You have told them, haven't you?* he added doubtfully.

*Yes*. Ayo did not elaborate.

Andrin knew he was not being told the whole story. The eagle was a proud creature who never discussed his personal life.

*Do you ever wish we'd never been linked?* Andrin asked quietly.

It took Ayo such a long time to answer that Andrin regretted the question, fearing the worst. When the reply eventually came it was at least partly reassuring.

*No*, Ayo said. *There is no point in opposing the inevitable.*

*I'm glad you're back*, Andrin said fervently. *I think we're going to have some work to do before too long.*

As Ico slipped the newly acknowledged pendant over her head, she was filled with a sense of wellbeing. She had made time to visit the gnarled cauldron tree, whose sap had hardened into the gemstone that now hung round her neck, and her silent homage had been rewarded by a feeling of approval, even joy – just as she remembered from the blessing of her first talisman. It was a good omen, and right now Ico was in need of good omens.

At her own insistence, she had travelled to the tree alone – except for Soo, who was gliding high above – and the peaceful silence of the place made her feel at ease. But even though she knew she had received the tree's blessing, she also knew that it was not yet time to return to Teguise. She still had unfinished business.

'What is it?' she asked, speaking aloud to the ancient tree. 'What do you want me to do?'

When the answer came it was not in words but in the form of a sudden certainty, a kind of childlike excitement. For all the wonders Ico had seen and experienced, she was first and foremost a pragmatist. She regarded magic as a tool, as a means to an end. Furthermore, it could not be used for everything; it was not a cure-all and was not to be wasted, but saved for important matters. Talent and power were precious commodities . . . and yet for some reason this occasion seemed to demand a little frivolity.

Ico glanced around, feeling a twinge of mischievous guilt, and when she had assured herself that she was alone, she began. Taking the pendant in her hand, she felt its readiness. There was enough eager power here for what she wanted, without her having to draw on outside sources. Ico closed her eyes and let her mind roam freely through her memories, before coming to rest upon the image that seemed right. Then she projected her thoughts, giving them shape and substance. When she opened her eyes again to look, the illusion was complete. Ysanne, as she had been as a tiny baby, lay in her cot in the dappled shade of the tree, contentedly asleep. Ico stared at her daughter, her heart aching with love.

A few moments later, Ysanne sat up – something she should not have been able to do at that age – and smiled at her mother. Ico was taken aback, knowing that these images were no longer coming from her memory, but she could not help responding to that glowing smile. If the illusion seemed to have taken on a life of its own, it was still a picture of happiness.

All that changed in the next instant. Ico glimpsed a tiny flutter of wings, a burst of colour, then – to her horror – the writhing shape of a fireworm. Ysanne started to cry as flames licked around the sides of her cot.

'No!' Ico screamed.

She let go of the pendant, and the images vanished as she turned and began to run back towards the city. It was just an illusion, she told herself. A false illusion.

Above her Soo chattered and flew on ahead, covering the ground far more quickly than her link was able to do.

Ysanne and Tas had decided that they would do some magic – because it seemed like fun, and because they wanted to scare Yaisa, who'd been mean to them after they'd spilled milk all over the nursery floor. They were quite sure the magic would work. They had seen other people do it, after all, and they'd heard the singing. It looked easy. But now it had all gone wrong.

When some sixth sense had told Ysanne that her mother was doing some magic – and, what was more, that it somehow concerned *her* – the little girl could wait no longer. By now she and Tas were so used to the singing that they just had to listen, and ask for help. They knew in the next instant that all they had to do now was choose an image. Yaisa came in then, and Ysanne instinctively picked out the memory of the fireworm because that had been the most interesting – and the most scary – thing that had happened recently. She smiled when it appeared, but Yaisa screamed in terror and Tas fluttered up into the air, frightened by their own creation. Neither of them knew where the flames came from. The maid tried to put them out, flapping ineffectually with a blanket, but the fire had not burned anything. Yaisa fainted then, and Ysanne shouted over the singing that she wanted to stop now. Although everything had gone away, she felt tearful and shaky, and she wanted the maid to wake up.

When others arrived, drawn to the commotion, Ysanne was crying – but they assumed that this was because Yaisa had fallen and scared her. When the maid came to, her

frightened babbling made little sense – and Ysanne decided
to say nothing.

A little while later, when some semblance of normality
had returned to the nursery, Soo arrived, cornered a
trembling Tas and fixed the tiny bird with fierce eyes. A
few moments later, after an admonitory glance at the still
nervous girl, the sparrowhawk flew off again.

Ico found it difficult to keep her mind on the council of war
that afternoon, although it had been called at her own request.
When Soo had returned with the news that Ysanne was
unharmed, and that the fireworm and the flames *had* been
false illusions, she had felt weak with relief – then angry, then
curious. When her repentant daughter had told her part
of the story, it was enough to put all the pieces together.
Although Ico decided that Ysanne's fright had been punishment enough, she insisted that her daughter apologize
to Yaisa, and – feeling slightly hypocritical – also lectured her
sternly about the need to treat magic with the respect and care
it demanded. Ysanne had nodded meekly. Whether she had
really learnt her lesson remained to be seen.

Now, after only a short interval in which she had tried to
restore her equilibrium, Ico was forcing herself to consider
some even more unpalatable matters. She hoped and
prayed that Tiguafaya would never have to go to war with
the Empire, but if it did it would be inexcusable for her
country to be caught unawares. To that end she had
called for a meeting between herself, Maciot, Admiral
Dias Cucura and Commander Ardell Kehoe, who had
overall responsibility for their naval and land-based
forces respectively. Both military men had been high
ranking officers during the previous regime, but had sworn
new oaths of allegiance – and had lived up to them. Ico
believed that neither man would have willingly served Tias

Kantrowe if they'd known the truth about his corrupt presidency. Their expertise in their respective fields had never been in any doubt, and Ico felt comfortable with them now. In turn she had earned their respect and loyalty. Whatever their differences in the past, they all knew it was the future that really mattered.

The first part of the meeting had been given over to a review of the current strength of their forces, the numbers and deployment of ships, men, weapons, camels and supplies. They had then turned their attention to contingency plans, and to what they knew of the intentions of their potential enemy – which was, in effect, nothing. The threat of war had come out of the blue. Tiguafaya's forces, both at sea and on land, had been set up to defend the eastern coastline from raiders, not an invasion fleet. But, as Cucura pointed out, that was only a difference of scale.

'If they do come, it'll be by sea,' the admiral said. 'Nothing else would make any sense.'

Kehoe nodded.

'It would be insane for them to even try to come overland,' he said. 'There are no roads, and there aren't even any reliable maps of the area. The volcanoes have made it treacherous, if not impassable, and any army big enough to stand a chance of success would be too unwieldy. The logistics would be a nightmare. Not to mention their problems with supplies. There's not much foraging to be done on lava flows.'

The argument sounded irrefutable, which was why Ico distrusted it. The reputation of the northern firelands had been the main reason for Tiguafaya having been cut off from the rest of the world for so long, and the reason for it becoming largely self-sufficient. But she was not prepared to gamble the future of the entire country on one assumption. Her commanders were continuing to have their say, however.

'And if they do come,' Cucura went on, 'we'll give them a

good run for their money. They'll be weighed down with troops, equipment and stores. Our ships will be lighter, quicker and more manoeuvrable, and we know the coastal waters better. Their fleet may well be bigger, but ours will be the more effective.'

'If any of them do reach land,' Kehoe added, 'we'll be ready to react. They won't find it easy to get ashore. And even if the worst comes to the worst, Teguise will be a hard nut to crack. We could withstand a long siege here if necessary, and the Empire knows that they won't get anywhere unless they take the city.'

'Let's hope it doesn't come to that,' Ico put in, hoping that their display of confidence was more than mere bravado.

'Of course.'

'I just wonder whether we should completely discount the possibility of a land assault,' she went on. 'Prince Tzarno has the reputation of a man who likes to take risks, and he might decide to spring a surprise.'

'I hope he does,' Kehoe responded. 'It'd be suicide.'

'How many lookout posts do we have in the mountains?' she asked, ignoring the comment.

'A few. Any more would be a waste of resources. In that terrain any outpost can only cover a limited area of the border country. The number of men it would take to do the job properly would be unacceptable. We'd have no one left to defend Teguise!'

'What if we gave the sentries a few extra pairs of eyes?'

The commander regarded her curiously.

'Some of my former colleagues in the Firebrands have been looking for a job that suits their talents,' Ico explained. 'Some are linked to birds who can cover huge distances in the air. If we used them, we could patrol the border more effectively, without having to commit any more of your men.'

'If they're willing to take up such posts, my men would

welcome the company. The northern stations aren't the most popular assignments,' Kehoe answered with a wry smile. 'I still think they'll be wasting their time, though.'

'Do it to humour me, then,' Ico said, smiling back.

'With pleasure, ma'am.'

'Good. They'll report to you when they're ready to travel. Anything else?'

'Has there been much pirate activity recently?' Maciot asked.

'No. It's been very quiet,' Cucura replied. 'Zarzuelo's the only leader with much of a fleet, and he seems happy to sit at home most of the time now. The rest are split into small groups, and they're confining themselves to a few raids here and there. They're still capable of making a nuisance of themselves, but the situation is better than it's been for years.'

'Any sightings of Endo or any of his cohorts?'

Endo had been one of the Barber's former followers, and had briefly allied himself with Ico during the aftermath of the battle that had claimed the life of his captain.

'Not that I'm aware of. Why?'

'Do you think it's worth trying to re-establish contact, renew the alliance?' Maciot said. 'The more ships we have the better.'

'I'm not sure I'd want to rely on *pirates*,' the admiral said bluntly, glancing at Ico.

'Me neither,' she agreed, 'but it can't do any harm to ask if they might be interested. I'll give you a personal message for your captains to pass on if the opportunity arises.'

Cucura nodded, although he still looked doubtful.

'What we really need now is intelligence,' Kehoe said. 'We need to know what's going on in the Empire.'

'Agreed,' Maciot replied. 'Madri should reach Uga Stai in three or four days' time, but I'm expecting reports from other sources before that. I'll keep you informed.'

The two commanders left then, leaving Ico and Maciot to discuss other matters.

'Has there been any word from the chivaree yet?' the senator asked.

Ico shook her head.

'It's early days.' It had only been three days since her interview with the jongleur. 'Have you come up with anything?'

'Not much. Tao's been working hard, but if there are spies in Teguise they're well disguised. We can hardly arrest every merchant who comes along.' Maciot had been using his own network of informers to try and trace any infiltrators, on the assumption that Kudrak had not been the only recent visitor from the Empire. Although the ambassador had been the only *official* presence, Maciot knew that if the positions had been reversed, he would certainly have sent others as well. 'However, I do have a new rumour for you.'

'What's that?' she asked wearily, expecting another piece of far-fetched speculation.

'Apparently, someone's been keeping fireworms in captivity, perhaps even breeding them.'

'That's ridiculous,' Ico stated. 'We've no idea *how* they breed.'

'I'm just reporting tales from the street.'

Ico knew that it was theoretically possible to capture worms intact, but all those she had known about had died in confinement.

'It's probably just some nonsense being spread by this new cult,' she guessed.

'They're the most likely source,' Maciot agreed, 'but it could explain how the worm got into Ysanne's nursery.'

Ico had no answer to that.

The next morning, as Ico and Andrin were finishing their breakfast, Maciot came in unannounced.

'I'm sorry to bother you, but I've just had some rather disturbing news.'

What now? Ico thought, her heart sinking.

'One of my agents returned from Uga Stai during the night,' the senator went on. 'Apparently there's a new voice in the Empire, a rising influence within the Kundahari, who is also known to be close to Prince Tzarno. Among his followers he's known as the Prophet, but according to my sources his real name is Kantrowe.'

Ico and Andrin were silent while they absorbed the news that their old enemy had returned to haunt them. Then Andrin swore violently under his breath.

'I should have killed the bastard when I had the chance,' he muttered.

'Too many people died as it was,' Ico said.

'Yes, but he *deserved* to.'

'You're assuming it's really him,' Maciot said.

'What do you mean? Who else could it be?' Andrin asked.

'Another member of his family, perhaps,' the senator suggested. 'Tias wasn't the only one of them to go missing.'

Before the revolution that had deposed him, Tias Kantrowe's family had been immensely powerful, its influence extending into almost every sector of Tiguafayan life. Afterwards only a few had remained; the rest were either dead or scattered to the four winds. No one, not even his wife of more than twenty years, knew what had happened to the man himself, but the Empire would have been the logical place for him to escape to. If he really was the Prophet, then the prospects of war had moved even closer.

'It's him,' Andrin stated with conviction. 'So what are we going to do about it?'

# CHAPTER TWENTY

'All right,' Cat declared. 'If we're going back in there, there are some things you ought to know.'

After a day spent mostly watching the rain teem down and the river rise even higher, she and Vargo had slept – fitfully in her case – in the mouth of the cave. The next day had been dry but still overcast, and the raging torrent that the river had become showed no sign of abating. Cat had insisted that they spend the day trying to find another way out, but the small, relatively level area of ground they were on was completely encircled by the river and the sheer, unscalable cliffs. Now, in the evening, it had begun to rain again and – with their supplies further depleted – she had finally accepted the inevitable.

Although Vargo had not pressed the issue, he still seemed oddly keen to try the caves again, repeating his confident assertion that they would eventually get through the mountain to the ocean on the western side. Now that Allegra was at last beginning to consider the idea, he was prepared to listen to anything she had to say.

'Go ahead.'

'When we were in there before, and the fireworms attacked, something very strange happened.' She faltered, not knowing quite how to go on. Until then she had avoided talking about the incident with Vargo, and had been trying to puzzle it out for herself – with a conspicuous lack of success. She had not wanted to add to his burdens. He had been in considerable pain, the wound on his arm showing no sign of healing in spite of her careful ministrations, and although he was generally rational now, there had been a few worrying moments when the delirium had returned briefly. However, this evening he seemed to be calm and alert.

'Something very strange?' Vargo prompted, after Cat had been silent for a while.

'Yes,' she replied, gathering her resolve. 'One of the worms came back, despite the cold, and fixed onto your arm. You went into some sort of trance.'

He looked down at his bandaged forearm and frowned.

'You didn't try to fight it off or anything, so I grabbed it.' She reached out with her hands, palms down, fingers bent like claws, to demonstrate.

'That's when you burnt yourself,' Vargo said gently. He took her hands in his own and turned them over. The weals and blisters that Cat had barely even noticed at the time were no more than faint red marks now. 'Does it still hurt?'

'No, it's fine.' She was touched by his concern when his own injury was much worse. 'The point is, I couldn't have crushed a fully-grown worm with my bare hands, could I?'

Vargo looked surprised, as if this had not occurred to him before. His next question made Allegra wonder just how much he remembered about the whole affair.

'You killed it?'

'Yes. It split open and I was able to pull it away.'

There was a short pause while he considered this.

'Maybe the cold had weakened it,' he suggested doubtfully.

'Maybe, but I didn't do it on my own. I had help.'

'Who from?'

'Ero.'

Vargo was stunned.

'But—'

'When I looked at my hands I saw claws and talons, just like his. *They're* what killed the worm, and I've no idea where the strength to do that came from.' She had been hoping that Vargo might offer some explanation, but his bewildered expression made it clear that he could not. 'I don't know whether I was hallucinating, or it was some kind of magic, or . . .'

'Ero?' Vargo asked, as if he still could not believe it.

'I think so,' she replied. 'I've been hoping he'd come back so you could ask him about it.' There had been no sign of the hoopoe since they'd fallen into an exhausted sleep a day and a half ago.

'Did you ask him for help?' Vargo asked.

'I think so.'

'If you were in the mirror, he might have heard you.'

'The mirror' was a mystery to Cat, and Vargo had never been able to explain it properly. The best he could do was to say that it was another world, which was in their own but apart from it, a place where the normal rules did not apply.

'But what does it all mean?' she asked.

'I haven't a clue. I'm just glad it worked. I'm not ready to be eaten yet.' He grinned.

'There's something else,' Allegra said gravely.

'What?'

'Afterwards, when you were delirious, you mumbled something about the mirror and then said, "Can't tell Cat. Mustn't tell Cat."'

'Then I'd better not.'

'Vargo?' she said warningly. 'What was it?'

'I've no idea,' he replied, shaking his head and spreading his hands wide, the picture of innocence. 'I don't really remember anything that happened from the time we saw the dragon until we woke up the next morning.'

Allegra couldn't tell whether he was being truthful or not. Either way, she knew she'd get no more out of him. And she knew there would be no point asking him if he remembered telling her he loved her. She wasn't sure whether that thought made her want to laugh or cry.

'Don't ever hide things from me, Vargo,' she said quietly.

'Of course not,' he replied earnestly. 'We're a team, aren't we?'

'Yes, we are, and that means you have to listen to me occasionally. If we're going into those caves again, then you've got to promise me some things.'

'What things?'

'That you'll be on your guard, that you won't go looking for trouble.'

'Me?' he asked, wide-eyed.

'And that you have crystals ready at all times, in case of another attack,' she went on determinedly. 'I don't know how I saved you the first time. We can't rely on my being able to do it again, so dragon's tears are vital.'

'All right,' he agreed. 'I promise. Anything else?'

'We go a different way. I don't want to risk that cavern again.'

Vargo shook his head.

'We have to go that way. All the passages lead to the dragon lake. It's the hub of the entire system. If you want to get through to the other side, there's nowhere else *to* go.'

'How do you know that?' she demanded, even though she realized she was fighting a losing battle.

'I just do,' he replied. 'Besides, I need to see the fossil again, to touch it if possible.'

'Because it's important?' she guessed wearily.

'Exactly.'

'Important enough to get us both killed?'

'We'll be careful.'

Cat let out a humourless chuckle.

'Of course, if we don't find our way out quickly enough, the worms'll be the least of our problems. If we stretch our rations, they should last three days, four at the most – and that's assuming we can replenish our water along the way. Apart from that, we've got just about enough oil to keep the lamp going if we burn it low.' She did not need to spell out the consequences of their being stranded in darkness.

'There may be crystals I can use for light if necessary,' Vargo said.

'I thought about that too,' Cat replied, remembering another, quite different set of caves, 'but we can't rely on it, and I'd rather you saved your magic unless it's absolutely necessary.'

Vargo nodded his agreement.

'That's about it, I think,' Allegra concluded. 'The only other thing we're going to need is luck.'

'And the right instincts to follow the path,' he added.

'That's your department, not mine,' she told him. 'It'll be dark soon. We'd better get some sleep.'

'We could just go now,' he suggested. 'Once we're in there it won't matter whether it's day or night.'

'We need to rest,' Cat replied. 'We won't get anywhere if we're exhausted before we start.'

An hour later Vargo was fast asleep, and she envied him his ability to allow his mind and body to simply let go, to relax completely whatever the circumstances. Her own thoughts refused to become still and she lay there, listening to the thrum of the rain and trying – unsuccessfully – to visualize their triumphant emergence on the other side of the mountain. Any number of different perils could get in their way, and she was certain there'd be others she had not foreseen. Her stomach rumbled, complaining at the scanty nature of their earlier meal, adding another element to her discomfort.

'It was a beautiful yellow, wasn't it?' Vargo remarked.

'What was?'

He shifted and in the faint moonlight she saw, to her surprise, that he was still asleep.

'Ico's wedding dress,' he replied.

Allegra's heart shrivelled a little more. Don't you ever dream about me? she asked silently.

'No more white,' Vargo mumbled. 'No more white.'

That, at least, was something Cat could agree with. White clothes were usually a symbol of sorrow or grief, and there had already been too many funeral processions in her young life. Compared to that, the bright, life-enhancing colour of Ico's dress had indeed been beautiful.

Cat was still wondering bleakly if she would ever get to wear yellow when she finally fell asleep.


'We're almost there. Go carefully now.'

The journey to the entrance of the fossil cavern had been completed in good time. Even though they were now carrying packs, and their lamp gave out only a dull glow, they'd had the chalk marks from their previous visit to guide them, and both travellers remembered where they needed to duck their heads or squeeze past a particular outcrop. However, now that they were approaching the fateful cavern, Cat was feeling nervous. She edged round the final corner and stared across the lake, straining to see the far side. Vargo came up beside her.

The outline of the dragon was barely visible this time, but the air was almost unnaturally still and there was no smell of the sea. The surface of the lake was completely smooth, reflecting a perfect replica of the ceiling. Thankfully, there was no sign of any fireworms.

'Shadows dreaming,' Vargo breathed.

'Did your dreams tell you how deep this is?' Cat asked. 'Can we wade across?' She knelt down, trying to see past the reflection.

'Don't touch the water!' Vargo said sharply, making her jump.

She stood up again carefully and looked at him.

'That's where the worms came from,' he explained.

'From the lake?' she asked incredulously.

'From the mirror. Everywhere's the same in the mirror.'

'This is like the other lake?' Cat asked, remembering the time when she thought she'd lost Vargo for good. 'The one in the firelands?'

'The lakes are all the same,' he said reverently. 'It's another sort of link.'

'But the gate only opens if we touch the water?' Allegra guessed, recalling the icy feel of the liquid on her fingers just before the swarm had appeared. Could that simple contact have been enough to bring on the attack? It was an appalling thought. She took an involuntary step back, away from the lake.

'You didn't know,' Vargo reassured her.

'And you didn't tell me,' she replied angrily.

'I didn't realize it myself until a moment ago.'

Allegra's resentment drained away quickly when she saw his apologetic expression.

'So what do we do now?' she asked, looking round. 'Fly across?'

'We can go around it.'

'Where?'

'That way,' he said, pointing to their right. 'There are enough cracks and holds in the walls to support us, and if we can reach that ledge the rest is simple.'

'I think flying across would be easier,' Cat remarked, peering into the gloom. 'And if the worms come while we're halfway round, we'll be completely helpless.'

'They won't unless we disturb the lake.' He paused, glancing back at her. 'Anyway, what's the alternative?'

'You could freeze the lake with crystals. That way the swarm wouldn't be able to get out and we'd be able to skate across.'

Vargo looked horrified, then shook his head.

'Wouldn't work.'

Cat decided not to argue. Her suggestion had only been half serious.

'We could go back and wait for the river to go down. Of course we'd probably starve, but . . .' She laughed, and the sound echoed hollowly all around. 'Oh, what the hell. Let's do it.'

She went first, feeling with her fingertips and the toes of her boots for every hold. She had tied the lamp to her belt, over her left hip, so that it gave her some illumination, but the shadows wavered and she had to rely almost completely on her sense of touch. The load on her back made balancing all the more precarious, and at one point she was spread-eagled like a fly on the wall, unable to get sufficient purchase to go either forward or back. Panic threatened to paralyze her and, for a moment, she was sure she was going to fall.

'Cat?' Vargo called softly. 'There's another crack a little way above your left foot.' He had recognized her plight, and the concern in his voice gave her new strength.

She edged her foot upwards, hoping she wouldn't dislodge any pieces of rock and, after what seemed like an age, found the foothold he had told her about. Now, with her knee bent, she had the leverage for further movement and was soon on her way again. A few minutes later she reached the ledge and was able to stand freely, turning round to look back at Vargo. He was grinning.

'Well done.'

'Your turn,' she said, trying not to let her own relief appear too obvious. 'I'll turn the lamp up so you have better light.'

'No. It's all right. I was watching you closely. I'll be fine.'

Although he set off confidently enough, Cat still watched anxiously. Vargo was less agile than he'd once been, and his memory was not exactly reliable. Several times she almost called out advice about his next move, only to find that he was making it already, following the route she had pioneered. Before she knew it he was beside her, grinning again.

'Easy,' he said. 'Let's go and talk to the dragon.'

Cat put her arms around him and he responded, but their packs made the embrace awkward and they soon moved apart again. They passed three tunnels as they went on around the lake and, for the first time that day, they both heard the deep rhythmic throbbing of the stone heartbeat. More dark shadows on the other side of the fossil promised even more possible onward routes, and Cat could not help wondering which one they would take. For the time being, however, she knew that Vargo had other things on his mind.

When they reached the dragon she stepped back and let him examine it more closely alone. From where she stood the stone skeleton looked remarkably complete, from the eyeless skull down to the small toes that ended in wickedly curved talons. No matter how the young dragon had met its end, the rock had preserved it almost perfectly, and Allegra was engulfed by an unexpected wave of sadness. She found it hard to imagine the countless centuries that the creature must have slept here, the immensity of history defeating her, and she wondered if she and Vargo were the first visitors in all that time. It was a melancholy thought.

Vargo had put down his pack, then reached up to run his fingers gently over the shapes of the bones. He said nothing at first, and Cat instinctively kept quiet, letting him concentrate. She had seen him like this several times before – most recently with the eggs in Corazoncillo – and knew that he was trying to 'read' the fossil, to absorb its secrets through his fingers and his mind. It was a bizarre and unreliable talent that she could not even begin to understand. Eventually he stepped back, his hands falling limply at his sides.

'It's dead.' He sounded flat, disappointed.

Cat was about to respond that of course it was dead, but she realized in time that this was not what he meant, and remained silent.

'The last time we were here . . .' His words died away and he shrugged. 'I could've learnt so much.' He turned to face Cat. 'We'd better get on.'

While she shared his disappointment, she was also relieved that they could move on now. She had half expected him to want to stay there for hours, time they could ill afford if they were ever to find their way out.

'Which tunnel?'

'I've no idea.' He sounded as if he did not care, and for the first time Cat sensed the depths of his frustration. Coming to this place had evidently meant a great deal to him, and it had ended in disillusionment. But that did not alter the fact that they still needed to escape from the labyrinth.

'Come on then,' she urged. 'Help me choose.'

Eventually, for want of any better criteria, they took the

largest of the tunnels heading westward and made good progress for a time. Cat continued to mark the route with chalk, while hoping fervently that they would not need to backtrack. After a number of twists and turns she began to lose all sense of direction, but Vargo – who seemed to be slowly recovering his spirits – could usually be relied upon to confirm her decision when they were faced with a choice. Eventually, Allegra realized that she had instinctively been following the sound of the stone heartbeat, assuming it came from the sea.

In perpetual darkness, time had long since ceased to have any meaning, but after a while tiredness forced them to stop and they found a level piece of ground on which to sleep.

'I'm going to turn the lamp out to save oil,' Cat told Vargo. 'We've enough tapers to relight it four times.'

'All right.'

'When you're ready to go on, wake me.'

Vargo nodded.

'You do the same.'

She doused the flame, and they were plunged into darkness so complete it was like being blind.

They slept twice more in the caves, listening to the pulse of the mountain – which grew gradually and reassuringly louder as their journey progressed – and to the occasional bursts of slow music that seemed to come from the rock itself. Night and day no longer existed except in the rhythms of their bodies, and their need for food and sleep regulated all they did. Twice during their exploration they had come to a dead end and had been forced to retrace their steps, but they'd found fresh water – an underground stream – and in general they seemed to be making steady progress. Even so, they both knew that they must find a way out soon.

Cat woke first, escaping from a dark, crushing dream to a

reality that was almost worse. She roused Vargo, then felt for the taper and lamp, whose positions she had been careful to memorize. As on previous occasions the sudden flare of light was dazzling, but once the lamp was set to its usual dim glow, they were able to collect their things and continue on their way.

A slight breeze soon brought with it an encouraging tang of the sea, and before long the roar of the waves was unmistakable. They hurried on eagerly, and were rewarded by the longed-for glimpse of daylight ahead of them. The sight that greeted them when they finally emerged, blinking, into a new morning was awe-inspiring. The Great West Ocean stretched out before them, as limitless and grey as the angry sky above. Far below them, gigantic waves surged and crashed upon the rocks with a noise like thunder, hurling plumes of spray hundreds of paces into the air. There was rain in the wind as well, and the dark clouds promised more to come. But compared to the caves it was warm, and just to be in the open again was such a pleasure and relief that Cat and Vargo hardly cared about the weather. They looked at each other and grinned, tasting the salt of the ocean.

'We're not safe yet,' Allegra said, looking around.

They were in a harsh, storm-blasted landscape of cliffs and crags. Such vegetation as there was clung tenaciously to the rock, leaning inland with the prevailing wind. Gulls wheeled and squawked above the tumult of the waves.

'We'll have to find food soon – and shelter for the night. It looks like there are more storms on the way.' In spite of her cautionary words she was feeling unreasonably optimistic. After beating the darkness in the mountain she wasn't going to let anything else stand in their way. 'We can go up there to start with,' she said, pointing.

Vargo did not respond, and when she glanced at him it

was clear he was not even listening.

'There are a lot more caves below the water line,' he said. 'That's where the music comes from. Underneath us. Listen.'

Cat could hear nothing except the roaring of the ocean, but she was happy to accept Vargo's explanation. It made as much sense as most things she'd seen and heard recently.

'It makes me wish . . .' Vargo fell silent without completing the thought, but Cat could see the regret in his grey eyes, and knew this was one of the rare moments when he mourned the loss of his own music.

'Come on,' she said quickly. 'We've some climbing to do.'

They went south, scrambling up and among the rugged slopes of the coastline, until they reached the top of the rise and were able to look inland for the first time. The view was not entirely encouraging. A narrow plain of scrubland promised little in the way of sustenance or shelter, and beyond that the mountain rose, bare and forbidding. The uppermost slopes of grey rock were lost in cloud. Trying to climb over such a huge natural barrier was out of the question.

'We need to get away from here before we head east anyway,' Vargo said, in one of his rare practical moments. 'Otherwise we'll find ourselves back in the ravine.'

'Not to be recommended,' Cat agreed. 'I guess we keep going south until we find a pass.'

They trudged on, their earlier exhilaration gradually evaporating. The landscape around them appeared quite unchanging, populated only by seabirds and the wind. Intermittent thunder competed with the ever-present rumble of the waves, and several heavy showers of warm but stinging rain dampened their spirits further.

As dusk approached they began to look for shelter, and settled upon an overhanging rock that protected them from the worst of the wind. After a very frugal meal, which nevertheless used up half their remaining food, they slept fitfully.

At dawn, feeling cramped and ravenously hungry, Cat woke to the sound of flapping wings, but caught only a glimpse of some large white birds as they retreated. Her thoughts strayed briefly to Ero – wondering where he was and when he would catch up with them – but then she saw something lying on the grass just beyond their shelter and went to investigate. To her astonishment she found three large fishes, one of them still twitching feebly.

By the time Vargo got up she had gathered enough wood to start a small fire, and was roasting the fish over it.

'So you've decided to follow in your father's footsteps,' he remarked.

'Not really,' she replied. 'These were handed to us on a plate. I think some birds brought them.'

Vargo looked at her, wondering if she was joking.

'It's true,' she protested. 'They were lying over there when I woke up.'

'Did you find any magic rings in their stomachs?' he asked.

Cat laughed.

'No, but they should line our own quite well.'

Buoyed up by the food, she began to repack their gear, eager to continue their journey in a new mood of expectation. So far the gods had been on their side. She did not notice Vargo become very still, staring into space.

'They're breeding evil,' he whispered.

'What?' Cat looked round.

Vargo made a throttled, choking sound and she saw that his face was sheened with sweat. Her concern turned to alarm when she noticed that the bandage on his arm was soaked with blood again, and she went quickly to his side, seeing the emptiness of delirium in his eyes. She took his hands in her own. His skin was clammy.

'I'm here, Vargo,' she said, feeling helpless. 'I'm here.'

'They feed,' he breathed hoarsely. 'They watch. Evil feeds on evil. And it grows.'

# CHAPTER TWENTY-ONE

'We are the keepers of the flame.'

The watchers obediently repeated their leader's words.

'We are the keepers of the flame.'

'The flame of life and death will burn until the end of time,' the robed man intoned.

As the onlookers echoed his promise, two of his assistants placed more coals on the fire. The heat in the windowless room was sweltering, the air full of acrid fumes. Although the worst of the smoke escaped through a hole at the apex of the roof, far above, and a little fresh air was drawn in through ducts at ground level, the atmosphere was still stifling.

A stone box that looked like a huge coffin was supported by scorched granite pillars in the centre of the floor, and it was under this box that the fire burned with furnace-like intensity. Bellows operated by more acolytes made sure the temperature of the coals never dropped too far.

In the harsh red glow of the fire, the robed man's face looked demonic, bathed in shining perspiration. He strode around the coffin, heedless of his cape flapping perilously close to the flames, and fixed each of his followers in turn with eyes that shone like black rubies. They were the mad, compelling eyes of a fanatic, infused with equal measures of faith and loathing.

'I am the Seer!' he cried. 'I am the sword of retribution, the purifying essence – and this is my creation.' He pointed dramatically to the stone casket. 'Do you wish to see?'

The response was muted, ragged and uncertain.

'Do you wish to see?' he repeated more forcefully.

'We wish to see,' the onlookers chanted, louder this time.

The Seer motioned to his assistants then, and four of them came forward, attached thick metal chains to hooks embedded near the upper corners of the box, then withdrew. At a further signal came the sound of pulleys being set in motion, the clanking of counter-weighted systems. The chains grew taut, rising up into the darkness of the roof. With a reluctant grating sound, the lid of the coffin began to rise.

The watchers shuffled closer, pressing against the waves of heat that radiated from the stone and, as the gap widened slowly, they peered within. As the interior of the sarcophagus was revealed, they saw that it contained a jumbled pile of rocks, some glowing dully, others giving off a choking, grey smoke so that the atmosphere became even thicker. Then some of the stones shifted and a fireworm wriggled into view, basking in the scalding heat. Murmurs of wonder rose from the watching, sweating faces as they stared with a fascination born of hatred and fear.

'Behold the plague that will cleanse us,' the Seer announced. 'Watch!'

All eyes were riveted on the fireworm as it appeared to swell up, its leathery skin stretching and becoming tight, almost smooth.

'Feel the terror,' the Seer hissed. 'Focus your hatred. Prepare!'

With an ugly ripping noise the worm split open from end

to end, its skin folding back like a grey flower opening its grotesque petals to the sun. The watchers groaned, then fell silent as the real meaning of what they were seeing became clear. Inside the fireworm was not the amorphous mush they had expected but a writhing mass of tiny creatures – miniature versions of the worm that had given them birth, as pale and featureless as monstrous maggots. Slowly, under the mesmerized gaze of the audience, dozens of them crawled away from the carcass, finding their own places amidst the heat and fumes of the rocks and then lying still once more.

'The dragon spawn,' the Seer explained in hushed tones.

When it was empty, the husk of the adult worm began to shrivel and turn black. Then it flared briefly and crumbled into ash. Strands of thick black smoke rose from its pyre and spread throughout the room.

'Breathe deep,' the leader ordered. 'Inhale the essence. Thus will the righteous be saved when the conflagration comes.'

The dark fumes added another, almost narcotic element to the dense atmosphere, but the onlookers drank it in devoutly, gladly.

'These are not the first nor will they be the last,' the robed man declared, returning his rapt attention to the tiny, immature fireworms that were now nestled in their coffin-like nursery. 'They will grow.'

He hesitated as he caught a brief glimpse of a small black shape – probably a bat – darting above the heads of the gathering. It vanished into the gloom among the rafters, flying erratically towards the hole in the roof. No one else seemed to notice the intruder, and the Seer put it from his mind.

'They will grow,' he repeated, as the heavy stone lid was lowered into place. 'And then they will eat!'

Fireworms danced through Ico's dream. Their skins were no longer grey, but all sorts of bright, attractive colours –

and their movements were no longer sinister or frightening but graceful, like an aerial ballet. The music that controlled them came from a shadowed corner and all around, faceless people watched, entranced and unafraid.

Then the music stopped and terror returned with a sickening jolt. People fled in panic as the worms, now grey again, turned upon them – but Ico was frozen to the spot, unable to move. Vargo emerged from the shadows. He was naked, and looked utterly bewildered.

'Where are you going?' he cried to the retreating figures. 'I need your help.' He turned to look directly at Ico, appealing to her.

'Mama, Mama! Where's Papa?'

Ico felt herself being shaken awake by small, determined hands. She groaned as she opened her eyes, trying to cling to the quicksilver remnants of her dream.

'Where's Papa?' Ysanne repeated.

'He's had to go away, sweetheart. Just for a few days. I told you, remember?' Outside it was barely light, and Ico was groggy from her sudden awakening.

'But Papa sleeps here,' Ysanne protested indignantly.

'Of course he does, little one,' Ico replied patiently, as her dream slipped away. 'But he's too far away to come home every night. He'll be back soon.' She pulled back the covers. 'Get into bed with me. We can go to sleep together.'

'I'm not tired,' the child announced brightly, but she climbed up eagerly, slid under the bedclothes and snuggled into her mother's arms.

I am, Ico thought, nonetheless resigned to the fact that she would get no more rest that morning. At least her daughter's presence made the large bed seem less empty.

'Did Ayo go too?'

'Yes.'

'He's big,' Ysanne said admiringly.

'Yes, he is.' Ico smiled as she recalled the last time she had seen Ysanne and Ayo together, a few days earlier. The massive white eagle had seemed ill at ease, but the little girl had giggled with delight when he'd allowed her to touch his feathers and stroke his neck. The sight of Tas – who was hardly bigger than one of the eagle's talons – perched next to him, looking up in awe, was something Ico was unlikely to forget in a hurry.

'He's not scary, though,' Ysanne added. 'Not like Soo.'

Ico was about to protest that Soo was not really scary, but realized this was no longer true. The sparrowhawk had always been an intense personality, and since her unimaginable experience with the dragons there was something about her that even Ico found a little intimidating.

Her thoughts wandered back to the interrupted dream, but most of the details had faded now. She remembered the contrasting emotions, Vargo's music and his nakedness, as well as the incongruous fact that the spectators had all been wearing grey robes. The feeling persisted that it must mean something – she had had prophetic dreams before, after all – but the significance of this one eluded her.

She was about to ask Ysanne why she'd woken up so early when she realized that her daughter was fast asleep.

Although Maciot arrived at the palace before the morning was half over, Ico had already been up for hours.

'Well?' she demanded as soon as he came in. 'Is there any news?'

They had had a tip-off from the jongleur about the fireworm cult, and Maciot had taken personal charge of the operation that followed.

'Well, for a start,' he said, 'we know that the leader of the cult is a man called Giavista Martinoy.'

The name seemed vaguely familiar to Ico, but she could not place it immediately.

'He's a retired spice merchant,' the senator went on, 'and he's apparently been interested in wizardry for a long time.'

Ico had it now.

'He's the one who was arrested because of the books,' she exclaimed.

'Arrested?' Maciot looked puzzled. 'We haven't even found him yet.'

'No, not us,' she explained. 'Kantrowe arrested him, before the revolution. Martinoy owned some books on ancient lore, and they'd been outlawed. He was arrested just after Vargo had gone to take a look at them. I presume he was freed with all the others when the government fell.' She paused, frowning. 'He doesn't seem like the sort of person to turn against us.'

'Maybe being locked up in the Paleton sent him mad,' Maciot suggested. 'He's certainly mixed up in some weird stuff now.'

'Sorry. I got sidetracked. Go on.'

'We've been to his home but, needless to say, he wasn't there. The housekeeper said she hadn't seen him for over a month, and I'm inclined to believe her. The poor woman was beside herself with worry. Other people we've talked to recognize the description – he's taken to wearing a long grey robe even on the hottest days – and—'

'A grey robe?'

'Yes. Is that significant?'

'It might be. Go on.'

'Apparently Martinoy's been moving about quite a lot recently, and he's proving elusive to say the least. We're watching his house, just in case, but he's capable of popping up anywhere. And even when he does, it doesn't help much.'

'What do you mean?'

'He has the reputation of being able to make himself invisible, of slipping through any net.'

'A useful talent,' Ico remarked dryly.

'Then we got wind of a meeting in the artisans' quarter last night,' Maciot went on. 'We knew he'd be there. The trouble is, the chivaree weren't able to get anyone inside the building and nor could we, so we don't know what went on. The place is guarded by a group of blacksmith's labourers who make Andrin look like a mere stripling. Short of using the army to fight our way in, there's not a lot we can do. Not only that, but either Martinoy and the others are all still inside, or they've slipped away without us noticing. Neither option seems very likely to me.'

Ico had a sudden strong desire to have Andrin at her side. This was the sort of thing he excelled at, solving a mystery that required both mental and physical skills. But her husband was many miles away. He had gone north, with the Firebrands and their links who had volunteered to help man the border outposts. Although Andrin apparently wished to supervise the location of the various lookouts – and, at the same time, check on the possibility of fireworm swarms in a previously unexplored area – Ico suspected that this was not his sole reason for going. She knew that he seemed to absorb energy from the volcanoes, and understood his need to walk among them occasionally. Preventing him from doing so would have been like imprisoning a wild bird in a cage. That didn't stop her from missing him, though.

'Are the cult meetings always held in the same place?' she asked, returning to the matter in hand.

'We're not sure.'

'We have to find out what's inside.'

Maciot nodded.

'Tao's been trying, but I haven't heard from him since yesterday afternoon.' The senator sounded worried. 'If anyone's capable of infiltrating their security, it's him.'

'Let me know as soon as he gets back.'

'Of course. Should I make arrangements to storm the place anyway, just in case?'

'Not yet,' Ico decided. 'Keep a close eye on it, but discreetly. And no violence.'

She had just thought of one possible interpretation of her dream. If Vargo really *did* need the cult's help to solve the mystery of the fireworms – unlikely though that seemed – she didn't want to do anything that would harm his chances.

'All right,' Maciot said. 'And we'll keep making enquiries. Sooner or later we have to come across someone who's willing to talk.'

'Was there any other news from the chivaree?' Ico asked.

'No – though they've given us a few names of people who are saying openly that magic will be the death of us all. We'll keep an eye on them, but I don't think it's serious.'

'We can't stop people speaking their minds,' she said. 'If we try, we sink to Kantrowe's level. Speaking of whom, has there been any word from the Empire?'

'Nothing about him,' Maciot replied. 'Madri should have got there a couple of days ago, but we've not heard from him yet. My other sources say that there are quite a large number of troops in the south, most of them to the west of Uga Stai, but they've been there for some time, apparently, so that may not mean much. Other than that, it's all pretty quiet. Has Cucura had any response to your message?'

'Not as far as I'm aware,' she answered. 'I'm not even sure how he intended to pass it on.'

'He's a resourceful man. He'll find a way. It's not in the pirates' nature to hide themselves away for too long.'

'It was a long shot anyway,' Ico said, and was about to go on when they were distracted by the sudden appearance of a dark shape in the open window.

Soo glided into the room, carrying a bedraggled black shape in her talons. Hovering in front of Ico for a moment, she gently dropped her burden into her link's hurriedly outstretched hands.

*He lives, but his singing is weak.*

Ico looked down at the apparently lifeless bird in her hands. It was a mirador chaffinch, and she was in no doubt that it was Tao.

'He's alive,' she said quickly, glancing up at Maciot's stricken face.

'He's not answering me,' the senator replied, as close to panic as she had ever seen him.

As Ico handed the bird over, she saw that her fingers were smeared with what looked like ash. Maciot cradled his link gently.

*Soo, what happened? Where did you find him?*

*On the roof of the fish market. I heard a call, but I don't know how he came to be there. He was asleep when I arrived.*

The market, Ico knew, was at the edge of the artisans' district.

'He's covered in soot, but he doesn't seem burnt,' Maciot said quietly. The mirador's normally bright plumage looked dull, and his eyes were unseeing. 'Did Soo tell you anything?'

Ico relayed the sparrowhawk's information.

'Do you think he got inside the cult meeting?' she added.

'Maybe,' the senator replied. 'Unless he wakes up, we'll never know. His heart's still beating, but he's deeply unconscious, and my thoughts are getting no response at all.'

Ico felt a rush of pity for her friend. She knew from personal experience what it was like to lose a link, and she could only hope that Tao would return to Maciot as Soo had done to her. Not that the sparrowhawk had come back unchanged. The black streaks in her plumage had been signs of some unfathomable alteration from within. At least the dirty marks on Tao were external. If he lived, he'd be able to clean them off.

Let him live, she begged silently. Let him live. Apart from the effect his death would have on her friend and advisor, they needed to know what the mirador had discovered.

Tao twitched in Maciot's hands, but did not wake.

*Tao? Can you hear me?*

The bird did not answer. His beak opened briefly and he made a tiny, weak coughing sound. A small but clearly visible cloud of smoke drifted from his mouth.

# CHAPTER TWENTY-TWO

Galan Zarzuelo was standing in the observation tower that crowned his palace when the final ship sailed into the lagoon and found a mooring space. They had all come, and that in itself was a singular achievement. The last time the brethren of the isles had gathered together had been more than thirty years ago, when Galan's father had led them in the defeat of the Tiguafayan navy. Now, drawn by the Survivor's cunningly worded messages, his rivals had put aside their differences, their appetites whetted by the promise of feasting and – perhaps – a great adventure. Above Zarzuelo's head flew a large square banner, and every ship in the lagoon displayed the same colours on their masts – the plain black flag of truce. For the first time since he had begun this ambitious exercise, Zarzuelo's pride and confidence outweighed his inner nervousness. The rest of the world – friends and foes alike – would soon learn that pirates were men to be reckoned with.

As her ship entered the harbour, Lamia breathed deeply. After many days spent almost entirely at sea, she allowed herself pleasure in the prospect of their imminent return. She relished the dusty, sun-baked smell of home.

All around her the crew went about their business with their usual quiet efficiency, leaving her free to gaze at the seaport where she had lived since she was four years old. Nearly all the buildings were made of a pale amber-coloured stone that glowed in the strong midday sunlight. They spread out over the coastal plain and the low hills beyond, none of them more than two storeys high. Anything taller was forbidden. The jetties and quays of the docks were constructed of the same golden stone and, as always, the harbour was a hive of activity. However, as the Emissary's ship drew closer, most of the people on the shore stopped what they were doing and turned to watch.

The vessel came neatly alongside one of the piers, moving so slowly now that she hardly needed the mooring ropes to bring her to a halt. There was a reception committee already waiting for them on shore, but this did not surprise Lamia in the least. Even though she had not expected to return so soon, she knew that many in the city would have foreseen her arrival in the stars. Among the waiting dignitaries was Vitrahk, the present Master of the Amagiana. That too was only right and proper.

Lamia was the first to disembark, and she went straight to Vitrahk and knelt before him.

'Welcome home, Emissary,' he said, laying a hand lightly on her shoulder.

'Thank you, My Father,' she replied.

Zarzuelo was about to descend the tower's spiral staircase when one of the sentries called out.

'More sails!' he cried, pointing to the north.

Zarzuelo went to the man's side, and gazed in the direction he indicated. It was soon possible to see that there were six vessels in the flotilla, a not inconsiderable force, but not enough to present a genuine threat to the pirates gathered in the lagoon. Zarzuelo's own duty crews were already on alert, so if the newcomers thought they'd be attacking helpless ships at anchor, they would soon realize their mistake.

'They're flying the black,' the lookout reported.

Zarzuelo relaxed then, but only a little. Although no true pirate would violate the truce, there were renegades in all walks of life, and until he knew the identity of these unexpected visitors he would take no chances. By the time the leading vessel was approaching the northern entrance to the atoll, Earless Yawl – so called because a sword fight had reduced his left ear to little more than a hole in the side of his bald head – had come to stand beside his captain.

'I know that ship,' he said. 'It's the *Dawn Song*.'

'Zophres?' Zarzuelo exclaimed. 'What's he doing here?'

'We'll find out soon enough,' his deputy replied. 'They're dropping anchor.'

The pirates had had dealings with Jon Zophres before. He was not really one of the brethren, although his varied career had included spells of piracy, but he was well known to those who plied their trade on or around the Inner Seas. The last time Zarzuelo had met him face to face, Zophres had been acting as an envoy for Tias Kantrowe, trying to enlist the pirates as allies for the former ruler of Tiguafaya. He had switched sides soon after that – apparently for his own amusement – and had helped the Barber sack Teguise. Only the gods knew what he'd been up to since then. He was a mercurial character, as adventurous as he was amoral, and capable of acting upon any whim that took his fancy. But in spite of this he commanded a great deal of respect. This was not because he was rich or charismatic – although he was both – but because of his almost mythical reputation for invincibility. Whatever reckless scheme he turned his hand to, however many battles he waged, Jon Zophres had never received so much as a scratch. His lithe, well-muscled body was not marked with a single scar. He might be un-trustworthy and unpredictable, but luck like that could not be ignored.

'Keep a close watch on those ships,' Zarzuelo ordered, then beckoned Yawl to follow him. 'We've work to do,' he told his deputy. 'I'm not going to let Jon Zophres wreck everything.'

'Do you think he wants to join us?'

'In what? No one except us knows what we're proposing yet.'

'Yes, but he must have got wind of something,' Yawl pointed out. 'And he'd be a useful ally. It'd help to persuade the others, at least.'

'I won't need any help persuading the others,' Zarzuelo stated peevishly. 'And allies like Zophres are a mixed blessing.'

Privately he was worried as well as angry. The interloper was the only man present who might have a chance of challenging his authority as leader of the proposed alliance – and Zarzuelo had no intention of letting anyone stand in the way of his destiny.

The Amagiana was the second largest building in the city, after the royal palace, and it sprawled over a huge area, making it seem like a small town in its own right. There were dormitories, gymnasia, classrooms, libraries and halls, as well as open spaces and accommodations for the tutors and their families. There were quiet rooms of contemplation, repentance pits, and gardens where the students grew food for their own refectory. There was even a small hospital and an astral observatory – and all this was contained within the high walls that had marked the boundaries of Lamia's world for many years.

As she entered the gates a feeling of peace, a sense of belonging, crept over her. It had been an honour to be chosen as the Emissary, but her taste of freedom had not made her hungry for more.

As soon as she had displayed her gift, at the age of four, she had been brought here – as all children of talent were – so that she could be guided and trained. At first she had been lonely and unhappy away from her family, but as her education progressed and she had begun to feel pride in her calling, that had changed. The man who had been her Master then, Maghdim, had become her new father – as he did to all the students – and she had been one of his most dedicated pupils, absorbing his teachings until they were an integral part of her own being. Sorcery, she had learnt, was evil incarnate. Many years before, wizards had created spells of such iniquity that the gods of the earth had been forced to crush them with a series of plagues. The earthquakes had been so severe that all buildings over two storeys high had been ruined, and whole towns had been destroyed. The drought and illnesses that followed had claimed an even greater number of lives, until the entire country had been on the verge of annihilation. Only the intervention of the first anti-mages had saved her people from extinction, killing the wizards and obliterating all traces of their magic. This was Lamia's proud heritage, and one that now extended to hunting down evil wherever it appeared in the world.

When Maghdim had chosen to leave on his mission, she had felt lost without him. When the news of his death had been brought to the city, she had felt sadness and rage but above all a steely determination to avenge her mentor. She vowed that the Martyr's sacrifice would not have been in vain, and that vow drove her still. Her recent travels had given her no pleasure, only a small degree of satisfaction. If it was decreed that she should leave her home again she would go gladly, intent on her single purpose, but a part of her would always long to return.

Although there were many important people seated round the conference table when she gave her report, Lamia spoke to Vitrahk alone, and when she had finished it was he who asked the questions.

'Is Prince Tzarno trustworthy?'

'His motives are impure,' she replied, 'and his ambitions transparent, but he has power and desire. We can use him. The one who calls himself the Prophet concerns me more.'

'Why so?'

'He said little, but saw much.' It was an expression of praise. 'He also claimed to be one of those who had worked with the Martyr.'

Vitrahk looked a little uncomfortable at the mention of his predecessor. Maghdim's decision to go to Tiguafaya himself, rather than appointing an emissary, had been controversial. Because of this, some regarded him as a hero, others as a fool. Worse still, his failure had devalued the prestige of the Amagiana in the eyes of many.

'Does this prophet have influence?' the Master asked.

'Some,' Lamia replied. 'But the Empire is larger than any one man. Once set on its course, its momentum will be unstoppable.'

Vitrahk nodded, looking thoughtful, and she realized that although he might want to pursue the topic of the Prophet further, he would not do so until they were alone.

'And what is your opinion of the pirates?' he asked instead. 'Can we work with them honourably?'

'They're superstitious barbarians, and are easily read,' Lamia said. 'They're driven by greed, pride and lust, but their dislike of magic seems genuine enough.'

'Can Zarzuelo unite them into a viable force?'

'I think so,' she replied. 'It may not last long, but it should be sufficient for our purposes.'

Zarzuelo's feasting hall was bursting at the seams. As well as a prudent number of his own followers, every captain and first mate of the ships currently moored in the lagoon were there – well over a hundred men in all. The food had lasted most of the afternoon, but there was little more than scraps left now. That did not matter. Everyone had eaten their fill and, in any case, they had now gone on to more serious pursuits – singing and drinking. Various contests had already rendered several members of the gathering insensible, while others simply became drunk and rowdy. There had been a number of fist fights, but nothing had got out of hand. It was all part of the entertainment.

Most of those present had forgotten that Zarzuelo's summons had a purpose other than revelry, but a few held themselves a little aloof from the general merriment, waiting to see what the Survivor had to say. Of these, three in particular had caught the attention of their host. If they voted with him, success would be assured. If they opposed him, there would undoubtedly be trouble. Zarzuelo surreptitiously studied each of them in turn, trying to gauge their moods.

Endo had once been the Barber's deputy aboard the *Revenge*, and had been one of the few to survive her sinking in the battle at the Dragon's Throat, a notoriously treacherous inlet on the coast of Tiguafaya. He now commanded his own ship, and led a fleet of seven more – one of the largest apart from Zarzuelo's own. He had entered into a short-lived pact with Ico Maravedis, and this had made him a figure of some suspicion for many of the other buccaneers. Endo had seemed preoccupied and watchful throughout the feast, and his host could not help wondering why that was. Did he suspect treachery? Or had he somehow discovered what Zarzuelo was about to propose? Turning against his former ally would surely present Endo with no real problem – unless there had been more to their parting than met the eye.

The privateer called Snake had been part of the Barber's fleet when it had attacked Teguise, but that partnership had ended as soon as the adventure was over and the booty divided. He now led a force of only five ships – whose crews nonetheless had a reputation for being the most ruthless and battle-hardened on the Inner Seas. Their co-operation would be important, not least because Snake himself was something of an icon – his missing right hand having been replaced by a brass hook which, according to rumour, he had used to disembowel at least a dozen enemies.

The third possible problem – and the most enigmatic – was Zophres. His arrival had caused some unrest, which he had overcome through a combination of his own ready tongue and confident charm. He had claimed member-ship of the brethren, based on past exploits, and no one had wanted to be the first to argue with him. No man in his right mind picked a fight with Jon Zophres. Although he seemed relaxed, having drunk a good deal of wine, Zarzuelo was not fooled. Zophres was still the only man the pirate leader feared and, if it came to a direct challenge, the stakes would be very high. Lose and, one way or another, his life would be over. On the other hand, any man who triumphed over the reputedly invincible renegade would assume an almost godlike status.

Choosing his moment, the Survivor stood and shouted over the noise for quiet. When he had got his wish – and the sleeping drunks had been roused by the simple expedient of having cold water sloshed over their heads – he looked around slowly. Secure in the knowledge that he had their full attention now, he could afford to take his time. A dramatic performance was required, and he was determined to give them nothing less.

'My brethren!' he cried. 'Fate has presented us with the chance for the greatest adventure of our lives!'

'You've done well, Lamia,' Vitrahk said.

The two of them were alone now, walking in the Master's private gardens. The sight and scents of the beautiful flowers there had gladdened Lamia's heart, but not as much as those few words of praise. She would rather they had come from Maghdim, the master who had shaped her life and mind, but she accepted Vitrahk as her father now, and that was enough. Lamia hung her head so that he would not see her smile and think her guilty of undue pride.

'The assembly are debating our course of action,' the Master went on.

'Should you not be there to guide them?' she asked.

'The decision has already been taken,' he replied, 'and the rest is a formality. The fleet will sail in due course. With you at its head.'

'Surely—' she began.

'I wish I could go myself,' he added, cutting off her protest, 'but the stars have chosen your path. And chosen well. You are the Emissary now.'

'I am honoured,' she whispered humbly.

'Your faith honours us all,' he replied. 'Great deeds lie ahead.'

The discussion in the feasting hall had continued well into the evening. Although Zarzuelo's enthusiastic presentation had at first met with an equally positive response, several of the captains had later decided that they had questions they wanted answering. It came as no surprise to the Survivor that the most disruptive of these came from the three men he had been studying earlier. Snake had been the first to raise a potentially difficult point.

'What do they need us for?'

'What do you mean?'

'If they're so powerful, with their secret weapons and all, why do they need us?'

'Because they are few and we are many,' Zarzuelo replied. 'They are foreigners, and we know the waters off Teguise. Their concern is sorcery, not swords,' he added impatiently.

'So they want us to do their fighting for them?'

'Yes. And what's more they're not concerned with the spoils.'

'We only have their word for that,' someone pointed out.

'And do you think we'd let them betray us?' Zarzuelo retorted. 'We have a way of dealing with traitors, and I never met a mage yet who could do much with a blade in his throat.' His indignation hid his own private doubts on this score. 'This is our chance of great deeds. Riches beyond anything we've known before. Would you spurn such a chance?'

There was a good deal of shouting then, as the argument broke into several separate confrontations, but finally Zophres caught the gathering's attention.

'Do you have any details of the alliance between the Emissary and the Empire?'

'Yes, of course,' Zarzuelo lied. He knew only what Lamia had told him, but he couldn't admit to that.

'It seems to me that such details are important,' Zophres stated bluntly. 'If we're to take on the Tiguafayan navy, what's to stop Tzarno and his army from claiming all the spoils? We could end up doing all the work and getting none of the reward.'

This provoked more heated exchanges. Eventually

Zarzuelo was able to make his voice heard again.

'The Empire is only interested in two things,' he argued, hoping this was true. 'The first is the long-term exploitation of Tiguafaya's resources by absorbing the land into their territory. Plunder isn't their objective – that's *our* concern – and we have the power and speed at sea to take it, no matter what they do. The second is the same as the Emissary's – they want to bring an end to magic.'

'You really believe magic causes eruptions?' another captain said.

'You've all felt the tremors,' the Survivor replied. 'It's as good an explanation as any I've heard. And even if it's not true, it makes no difference to our prizes. Wealth and revenge. We'd be mad to turn it down!'

Although that was received well by the majority of his audience, Endo chose to drop his bombshell then, revealing the reason for his earlier preoccupation.

'There is another possibility!' he shouted, waving his arms to gain their attention. 'Two days ago I received a message.' He held up a rolled parchment for all to see. 'It's from Ico Maravedis.'

When the noise that greeted this announcement died away, Endo went on.

'It offers us a different alliance. With Tiguafaya, against the Empire.'

'How do you know it's genuine?' Zarzuelo demanded.

'Because it carries the presidential seal, and because I know her hand,' Endo replied calmly.

'And this just dropped out of the sky onto your ship, I suppose?' the pirate leader remarked sarcastically.

'I found it nailed to a well-head, on an island we some-times use for overnight mooring.'

Zarzuelo was unsettled by this unexpected development, but he recovered quickly enough.

'Even if it's genuine, which I doubt,' he said forcefully, 'we'd be mad to make such an alliance.'

'Not necessarily,' Endo responded. 'Joining up with the Tiguafayans would make us a match for the Imperial navy. With their sea power destroyed, think of the possibilities for raiding their southern coast. There are richer pickings there than in the whole of Tiguafaya.'

'You broke your alliance with Maravedis before,' Zarzuelo pointed out. 'Why?'

Endo shrugged.

'Frankly, it was dull,' he said, to the amusement of many of his colleagues. 'I don't think it would be this time.'

'But then we'd be making enemies of the Emissary and her people as well as the Empire,' Snake pointed out.

'True,' Endo agreed. He did not sound very concerned about this.

'The Empire's navy is bound to be weakened, one way or another,' Zarzuelo claimed, seeing his opportunity. 'When we've dealt with Tiguafaya, there'll be nothing to stop us turning our attentions to their coastline.'

He paused, sweeping the gathering with his gaze and daring them to defy him.

'So, do we vote?' he demanded.

Lamia slept that night in her old bed, and dreamt of great white birds.

When she awoke her thoughts turned to the unknown creatures who had persisted in shadowing her vessel until it was almost home again. Neither Lamia nor any of her crew could understand why they had done so or what it might mean. The stars had revealed nothing about their presence.

Shaking off such inconsequential musings, Lamia performed her morning exercises for body and mind, and felt invigorated as always. She gave thanks for the fact that her talent – which could so easily have turned bad if she had been left to her own devices – had been converted to truth and purpose, a counterbalance to evil. In a sense, she and her fellow adepts had been trained as soldiers, whose greatest weapons were their minds.

She went to the refectory to break her fast, aware of the curious, sometimes envious glances her presence provoked. Vitrahk found her there, and his news was conveyed in a voice that turned the message into an announcement, to be heard by all the others who were there.

'The rituals are complete and the stars have spoken,' he told her. 'The black fleet will sail at your command, Emissary.'

Most of the pirates who gathered the next morning were suffering from the over-indulgences of the previous day, and the debate was therefore much more subdued. Although there was still some disagreement, the pirates eventually resolved to settle the matter once and for all. The vote the night before had been inconclusive. Zarzuelo had claimed victory, but many of those present had been uncertain as to what exactly they had been voting for, and even the Survivor's most vociferous supporters had become confused. He had eventually decided to try again when their brains and blood were less sodden with alcohol.

He took his chance during a lull in the arguments, before tempers began to fray even more.

'I vote we accept the Emissary's offer and join the invasion of Tiguafaya,' he stated emphatically. 'Who's with me?'

A large majority of those present raised their hands, including – to Zarzuelo's relief – all three possible dissidents. There were several abstentions, but it was already clear that the motion would be passed.

No one voted against.

# CHAPTER TWENTY-THREE

Eleven days after leaving Teguise, Jurado Madri finally arrived in the imperial capital of Zepharinn.

The first part of the journey – aboard the *Goshawk*, the fastest merchant craft available – had been uneventful. They had been escorted by three naval vessels for a while, but after three days at sea they had been left to continue alone. Although the crew were trained to defend themselves against pirates, it would have been Angel, in his capacity as a weather mage, who would have been their main protection. However, no one had challenged them, and the voyage to Uga Stai had been completed without mishap. Madri had been sorely tempted to ask Angel to use his powers to get up some wind and speed them on their way, but resisted the inclination, knowing that magic should never be abused for mere convenience. But as soon as he was on land again, he became impatient to complete his mission.

Almost before the *Goshawk* had completed docking, Madri had taken his leave of her captain, and had gone ashore to investigate the possibilities for the onward journey. Because he had no idea when he would be able to return, he arranged for the ship to wait for him in Uga Stai twelve days later – which he reckoned was the earliest she might be needed. If he was unable to make the rendezvous, he would send a message with further arrangements.

The party that went ashore consisted of six men – Madri himself, Angel, and a four-man escort – soldiers who had discarded their uniforms for civilian clothes. Rather than proclaim his ambassadorial status, Madri had decided to travel as if he were a merchant. He would be able to ask questions more freely, and his escort would be taken as guards hired to protect his goods. The letter to the Emperor and his own accreditation – which both carried Ico's presidential seal – were carefully hidden away in his luggage, and would stay there until needed.

In Uga Stai Madri had hired horses to carry men and luggage. For appearances' sake he haggled over the price, even though he resented the time this took. Evening had been drawing in when his transactions were finally completed, and he and his companions had been forced to stay in the port overnight. Telling himself that fretting over lost time would do no good, he had made the best use of the delay he could, listening to gossip in the tavern where they were staying. Amid the merchants' talk and general banter, he had heard a rumour that the Emperor was planning to wed a country girl. This was apparently something that divided the citizens of Uga Stai. Some treated the possibility with righteous indignation, while others were obviously amused, making ribald comments about the origins of the young lady in question. Madri had also learnt that Prince Tzarno was still in the south, and heard several mentions of an intriguing character called the Prophet, about whom he was determined to learn more.

The next morning they had joined a merchants' convoy which was setting off north. It had taken them five days to reach Zepharinn, which – although it was longer than Madri had hoped for – was still fairly good progress. During that time no one had questioned his reasons for travelling, and the only curiosity displayed by his fellow wayfarers was about Angel. Tre's grotesque appearance drew many sidelong glances, and a few horrified stares. Madri explained his companion's presence by saying that he was both a good luck charm and a reader of omens – which was not so far from the truth.

During the journey Madri had tried to learn all he could about the situation in the Empire, seeking out the most garrulous of the merchants. He discovered that the Prophet was a foreigner who had become a close associate of Tzarno, and who was also popular among the Kundahari. However, he was apparently regarded as a potential troublemaker by the business community, because of his penchant for rabble-rousing. This especially concerned the merchants at the moment because the Emperor's forthcoming wedding would mean great opportunities for trade, and none of them wanted to see the celebrations disrupted.

When Madri had carefully directed the conversation towards imperial attitudes to Tiguafaya, his informant had been dismissive.

'Same old story. All sorts of ridiculous rumours. Some people think we ought to go in there and teach them a lesson, but I think the volcanoes'll probably do it for us. There was another big eruption a few days ago. Not far from the border, from what I hear.'

That had come as unwelcome news to Madri, but there was nothing he could do about it – and the merchant made it clear that he did not want to talk about Tiguafaya, preferring to concentrate on the opportunities ahead of them in Zepharinn. Madri had not pressed him. If his indifference was typical, it would be hard for Madar to gain popular support for war – but nor would he face any real opposition.

Now, as they entered the city at last, and the convoy split up into its various parties, Madri was able to set speculation aside and concentrate on his own immediate objectives. He could see no point in any delay, and went straight to the Imperial Fortress. There he presented his credentials and requested a meeting with the Emperor. He encountered a solid wall of bureaucracy, and was passed from one official to another until – after repeating his story for the umpteenth time – he began to get angry. Judging by the number of whispered conversations and messages being sent to and fro, it became clear that a delegation from Tiguafaya had been expected, but it was also clear that their unannounced arrival had caused some consternation.

He was eventually ushered into the presence of yet another functionary, who introduced himself as the First Secretary to the Castellan of the Imperial Fortress. After carefully reading the letter confirming Madri's status, the secretary looked up and treated his visitor to a moment's silent scrutiny.

'Well?' Madri demanded, having exhausted his supply of politeness.

'Your request is being dealt with.'

'And when will I see the Emperor?'

'I can't say. His appointments—'

'How long?' Madri cut in.

'Two days perhaps,' the secretary replied, pursing his lips in disapproval.

'That is not acceptable. I am—'

'The official ambassador of a sovereign nation,' the official completed for him, not bothering to conceal his disdain. 'I know. Nevertheless, Emperor Madar is a very busy man, especially at this time. Of course, if you have any letters for his Highness, I would be happy to pass them on for you.'

'I'd prefer to do that in person,' Madri replied coldly.

'Very well. I suggest you go to the guest lodgings that have been arranged for you and your party, and I will inform you when a time for your audience has been agreed.'

The ambassador retraced his footsteps to the gatehouse, where he had left Angel and the soldiers, and they went to their lodgings together. Although these were luxurious by any standards, they did nothing to alleviate his feelings of anger and frustration. In fact he grew steadily more enraged as time dragged by – until he realized that this was almost certainly a deliberate tactic on the part of the Empire. It was a simple way of demonstrating his low standing in their order of priorities, a subtle indication of contempt. If he allowed his indignation to get the better of him, and was not thinking straight when the meeting finally took place, he would be at an immediate disadvantage. So, after a brief period when he ranted and raved in his empty room, he forced himself to calm down. He still cursed himself for having accepted the mission in the first place, but he was damned if he would fail before he'd even begun. He went to join Tre, hoping his friend would be able to help him pass the time.

'I could make it rain on the castle until they grant you an audience,' Angel suggested as Madri came into the room. He had evidently overheard the envoy's bout of exasperation.

'They'd only use it as another excuse for delay,' Madri replied, but he smiled, appreciating Angel's attempt to lighten the mood.

'How about hailstones the size of apples?' Tre added, with a lopsided grin. 'That should get their attention.'

'I don't think they'd move any faster even if we burnt the place down,' Madri replied, but he was already feeling better.

\*

As the First Secretary had predicted, the meeting with the Emperor and his inner council took place two days later. Ambassador Kudrak was also present. Madar himself made the necessary introductions and, although the expressions around the table were grave, Madri sensed no great feeling of antagonism. In fact, the general mood seemed to be one of expectation. They believe we're going to capitulate, he thought. To give in to all their demands. This was going to make what had always been a delicate task even more difficult.

'You will have to forgive me, Ambassador, if I seem a little preoccupied,' Madar added. 'My bride arrives in Zepharinn tomorrow.'

'Please accept my congratulations, Your Highness. I wish you and the Empress every happiness.'

'Thank you. Please proceed.'

Madri had rehearsed this moment in his thoughts many times, imagining a number of different approaches. He had to balance honesty with the need to avoid antagonizing the council. He remembered Maciot's words – 'You've got the right combination of tact and directness that might just appeal to Madar' – and hoped the senator had been right. He decided on the simplest approach.

'I bring a message from President Maravedis,' he began, taking the letter from his large document pouch and passing it down to the Emperor, who was sitting at the far end of the table. During the time it took Madar to glance at the seal, break it, and then read the contents, the envoy took the opportunity to study the others at the table. To his right were Hierophant Nandi, Kudrak and Castellan Ty. Opposite them were Treasurer Meos and Chamberlain Ruhail. Although Madri knew a little of their reputations, he had never met any of them before.

Madar finished reading, and passed the letter to Ruhail

before looking up at the ambassador. He was about to speak when the door burst open – and Madri turned round with the others to see a man who could only be Prince Tzarno stride into the room.

'My apologies, brother. I have only just arrived, but I did not want to miss this meeting.' He sat down next to Meos and nodded to the others, turning last to Madri. 'It has long been an ambition of mine to meet you, Admiral.'

'I'm no longer an admiral, merely an envoy.'

'Nonetheless, you must have tales to tell, the ones the historians have chosen to forget. I've often wondered—'

'Is this historical discourse really necessary?' Ruhail enquired pointedly.

Tzarno grinned, and sat back in his chair.

He annoys them on purpose, Madri thought. And he knows just how to do it. The prince had added a dangerous and unpredictable factor to the meeting.

'Your president is eloquent,' Madar said now. 'I too desire peace, but not at any price.'

Madri took this as his cue to outline the situation in Tiguafaya, as Ico had tried to do in her meeting with Kudrak. However, he was only part of the way through his explanation about the volcanoes and the fireworms when he was interrupted by Ruhail.

'Ambassador, I see little point in rehashing Kudrak's meeting with President Maravedis. He made our position clear to her then, and we stand by that. Do you have anything *new* to say?'

'I ask you only to look at the evidence without prejudice,' Madri said.

'Do you agree to renounce magic?' Nandi asked. He was two days away from the end of his term as hierophant, and had hoped that this discussion could be delayed until the responsibility was another's. But now he was anxious to play his predetermined role, to justify his presence to the rest of the council.

'We can't do that,' Madri replied.

'Then you condemn yourselves,' Meos said.

'It is heresy,' Nandi confirmed.

'Magic is fundamental to my people,' the ambassador argued. 'Without it we would have been destroyed long ago.'

'That is self-serving nonsense,' Ruhail responded. 'If you persist in this insanity, magic will be the *cause* of your doom.'

'You wouldn't say that if you'd seen what I've seen.'

'Let me guess,' Ty remarked sarcastically. 'A dragon?'

'I saw the woman who is now our president fly as a dragon,' Madri confirmed.

'Blasphemy!' The hierophant was outraged.

'No. Don't you see?' the envoy pleaded. 'The dragon spirits *allowed* her to assume their shape. Her actions were blessed by the dragons, by the messengers of the gods.'

'You can't be serious?' Ruhail exclaimed.

'The gods *approved* her actions,' Madri persisted. 'Why else did she succeed? If you accept that, it follows that what the dragons told her about the fireworms is also true. We need the untainted creatures to save Tiguafaya, perhaps to save the whole world.' His vehemence and evident conviction silenced them for a few moments, but then the chamberlain returned to the fray, his antagonism undiminished.

'You cannot use sorcery as your own defence. Illusions are not blessed by the gods. And even if we were to accept this farrago of lies, you can't seriously expect us to believe that these so-called fireworms really affect the earth's fires.'

For answer Madri reached down, took a cloth bag out of his pouch, and emptied its contents onto the table. The fireworm landed heavily, with a dull thud, but lay still. Ty was on his feet in an instant, his hand on the grip of his sword, while the others drew back instinctively.

'It's dead,' Madri informed them. 'It can't harm you.'

'This is an outrage,' Ruhail spluttered.

'These are remarkable creatures,' the envoy went on evenly. 'They have no wings, yet they can fly. They have no eyes, no ears or nostrils, yet they can sense and locate their prey with deadly accuracy. They can live in molten lava, in temperatures that would be instantly fatal to all other forms of life. Their skins are impervious to any blade, no matter how sharp. Test it if you like, Castellan. The only thing that can defeat them is cold. This one froze to death. When the worms are cool enough, it's possible to crush them. I've seen them burn houses, melt solid rock and devour people from within. They can absorb and radiate huge amounts of heat.' He paused to let his words sink in, noting that everyone was staring at the worm in horror. 'Who is to say,' he went on, 'that if there were enough of them, working in concert, they could not divert the course of fires below the ground? Before they became corrupted, that is just what they did. And that is what we need them to do again. For that we need your help.'

The ensuing silence lasted for a few heartbeats, then Tzarno, who – like his brother – had not yet contributed to the debate, began clapping.

'A wonderful speech, Ambassador,' he said, laughing. 'You almost convinced me for a moment there.'

Madri knew in that instant that he had failed – and also knew that he must keep on trying.

'The problem is,' Tzarno went on, 'that even if we believe this fairy tale, surely it's the *magic* that corrupted the worms. Either way you must stop. Or we'll make sure you have no choice in the matter.'

'No. Listen. You don't understand—'

'No, *you* listen,' the prince snarled. 'Eleven days ago a new volcano destroyed an entire valley, a whole community.

Only this time it was in the Empire, not Tiguafaya.'

Madri did his best to hide his dismay, but it was clear that his efforts had been doomed from the start. Madar now entered the conversation for the first time.

'You see the position this puts me in, Ambassador? I cannot allow my own subjects to be put at risk.'

'Surely that's all the more reason to help us find a solution,' Madri argued.

'Efforts such as those being made by Nino Delgado?' Tzarno asked mildly.

The envoy pretended not to understand. He saw by the blank expressions around the table that this was news to the others.

'I've been hearing some very interesting stories about him,' the prince added, revelling in his superior knowledge. 'Did you know they're calling him the bird-man?'

'This is irrelevant,' Ruhail cut in, before Madri had a chance to respond. 'Ambassador, nothing you've said has changed anything. I had hoped that when President Maravedis had had some time for reflection she would have reconsidered her position. I see now that is not the case. Ambassador Kudrak was correct in his assessment. This is a matter that will have to go before the full council, but you really don't leave us much choice.'

'If it comes to war, there can be no victors, only losers,' Madri claimed, playing his last card. 'It would be a war you cannot win.'

'With the gods' blessing any cause may be won,' Nandi responded piously.

'The terrain of my country is not easily conquered,' the envoy persisted. 'You may ruin us, but you'll gain nothing and will lose a great deal. And in the end the volcanoes may have the last word. All because of your foolishness.'

'Enough!' Madar decided. 'Return to your quarters,

Ambassador – and take that *thing* with you. We will inform you when our deliberations are complete.'

Madri stood up, realizing he had gone too far.

'If you're still here in two days' time,' Kudrak told him, with ill-disguised malice, 'you will see how a genuinely god-fearing people honour the deities.' He had not spoken during the meeting, and was now feeling a quiet satisfaction at the outcome. He had been completely vindicated – as Chamberlain Ruhail had seen fit to acknowledge – and his self-esteem had risen accordingly.

'This audience is over,' Madar decreed, rising to his feet.

The last thing Madri saw before leaving the chamber was Tzarno's wolf-like smile.

Later that same day, Madar and his brother were in private conference, something the Emperor had insisted upon in spite of Ruhail's objections.

'I suppose it'll take the council days to come to the obvious conclusion,' the prince said.

'These are not decisions to be taken lightly, brother,' Madar replied, and ignored Tzarno's exclamation of disgust. 'What's the situation in the south?'

'We're ready.' It was an exaggeration, but the prince was in no mood to admit that.

'What exactly are you ready for?'

'We've been preparing for war,' Tzarno replied angrily. 'Making alliances, gathering intelligence, planning strategies. You know, all the things we humble soldiers do.'

'Tell me about these alliances,' the Emperor said mildly.

Tzarno saw his mistake and did his best to remedy the situation. He had meant to break the news of his negotiations with Lamia at a time of his own choosing, but now he was forced to explain as best he could.

'Allies about whom you know so little could be dangerous,'

Madar concluded, once he had heard his brother's tale.

'They share our objectives,' Tzarno said, 'but none of our ambitions.'

'Ambitions?'

'To expand the Empire,' the prince explained irritably. 'They also bring extra forces with them.'

'*More* allies? Who?'

'Galan Zarzuelo.'

'Pirates!' Madar exploded. 'You made an alliance with *pirates*?'

'It makes sense,' Tzarno answered defensively, his own anger growing.

'Have you forgotten they raid our shores as well as Tiguafaya's? Are you mad?'

'They'll fight the Tiguafayan navy,' the prince retorted. 'With any luck they'll cripple each other, leaving us with the easy task of invasion. That's what *I've* been doing! What about you? This would all have been settled by now if you hadn't been dragging your feet – and weren't so distracted by the thought of your pretty little country maid.'

Madar opened his mouth to reply, then bit back the furious words and spoke quietly, with a disconcerting, icy calm.

'Remember who I am, brother. No one, not even a prince, is above my judgement. If you ever speak about Katerin in that way again, I will have you publicly flogged. Do you understand?'

Tzarno had grown quite still, every muscle in his body rigid, and he did not reply.

'Do you understand?' the Emperor repeated more forcefully.

'I understand,' the prince replied, his voice devoid of any emotion.

'Good,' Madar said, turning his back. 'Now get out of my sight.'

# CHAPTER TWENTY-FOUR

Allegra woke in the middle of the night, feeling an emptiness that began in her stomach and extended to her heart. The desperation that followed was becoming all too familiar, but where once she would have chastised herself for such a negative attitude, now it only made her want to cry. It had been five days since their last good meal – the fish that had appeared as if by a miracle – and although they had eked out their remaining provisions with a few roots and berries they'd found along the way, it had not been enough to sustain them. Cat felt weak and sick all the time now, while Vargo was present in body only, his mind and spirit wandering somewhere she could not follow. The only bright spot had been the plentiful supply of water. Intermittent rain and the nature of that part of the country meant that they had been able to refill their canteens as often as they needed. However, even that was dying out now; after first heading south, they had been travelling east for the last two days, and were entering the firelands again.

During all that time they had seen no settlements, no people – no sign that anyone ever came to this remote region.

Cat was fairly sure of her bearings, but the geography of the area was unknown to her, and the only village she was reasonably certain of locating was still several days' walk away. Unless they found food soon, they would never make it.

Above her the old moon was only a thin crescent and although the stars were bright, there was not enough light to guide them through the lava-strewn terrain – even if they had had the strength for it. The wound on Vargo's arm was still refusing to heal and bled every so often, in spite of her care and attention. During the days he stumbled along, often needing help, while at night he fell into a slumber so deep it was sometimes difficult to rouse him the next morning. At one point Allegra had even considered leaving him behind, and trying to go on at a quicker pace in the hope of returning with help. But she had rejected this drastic idea instinctively. Even if she could make him understand what she was planning to do, there was always the chance that he'd wander off somewhere and she wouldn't be able to find him again. The idea of his dying alone, if she were unable to get back in time, was unbearable. The only thing she could do was carry on, and pray.

Cat had never been particularly religious. The gods, if they existed, had always seemed impossibly remote, with no real relevance to her life. But she prayed now, silently and fervently, looking up at the cold stars and hoping that someone – something – might hear her.

She could not keep that up for long, however, and after a while her thoughts returned to the all too familiar litany of her own failings. Her only purpose in life had been to help and protect Vargo. He was important – perhaps the most important person in Tiguafaya's future – and she was supposed to keep him alive so that he could fulfil his destiny. That had not seemed much to ask, and yet she was on the brink of abject failure. Her own fate seemed trivial by comparison, but even there she had made a mess of things. Here she was, lying next to the man she loved with all her heart, and she had not even been able to tell him, let alone act upon her feelings. Unless something happened soon, she never would.

Cat finally fell asleep again, trying to reassure herself that, one way or another, this misery could not last much longer.

When she woke again the sun had just risen and there was a growling, gurgling sound in her ears, a rumbling so loud that she thought her stomach must have exploded. Then she realized that the noise was not coming from her, nor from Vargo, who was still asleep beside her. Allegra sat up – and decided she must be hallucinating. Only a few paces away was Ero. He was riding on a camel.

It was only when the camel belched noisily that she finally began to believe that her eyes were not deceiving her. Her prayers had been answered. As Ero swooped down from his perch, calling softly, a man appeared beside the camel. The bird alighted next to his link, but Vargo did not stir.

'Well, I'll be!' the stranger said, staring down at her. 'You must be Allegra.'

Cat could only nod.

'Your friend there told Vek you'd be here, but I wasn't sure I believed him,' the man went on. 'Seems half mad if you ask me.'

Allegra assumed that 'her friend' was Ero, and when another bird flew into view she realized that this must be Vek. The bird was a golden oriole, its sleek plumage a brilliant yellow – except for the black on its wings and tail, and in the lines between its eyes and bill. He was beautiful, and Cat found herself wondering if Ero was jealous – then laughed, partly at the incongruous nature of that trivial thought and partly from sheer relief. The man grinned in response.

'My name's Ambron Cuero.' He came closer, and his smile

grew concerned. 'Well, missy, I don't know what you've been up to, but it looks to me like you could use a good meal. I'll see what I can do.'

'Thank you,' Cat whispered in a voice made hoarse from joy.

Ambron fetched a leather flask from the camel's saddle bags, and brought it back to her.

'Drink some of this to start with.' He unstoppered the flask and passed it over. 'Not too much, mind. It'll give you some strength.'

Allegra sipped gratefully. The liquid was sweet and aromatic, and she felt a marvellous surge of pleasure course through her body. Ambron smiled when he saw her reaction.

'Get him to drink some too,' he said, pointing at Vargo.

By the time Vargo had been roused and persuaded to drink a little of the nectar, Ambron had already set out the makings of a traveller's meal – which looked like an extravagant feast to Cat.

'Take it slow,' their saviour advised, as they began to eat. 'You don't want to overdo it.'

They did their best to obey him and, while they ate, Ambron talked. He was a prospector, he told them. Didn't come out this way often, but he was glad he had this time, otherwise the hoopoe might never have found him. At this, as if he knew what was being said, Ero called out happily, and they all turned to look at him.

'You've a lot to thank him for,' Ambron said.

'We do,' Cat agreed, her mouth full.

'What were you doing out here, anyway?'

'It's a long story,' she told him.

*I need to ask you some questions, Ero.*

*Are they hard?* the hoopoe asked suspiciously.

*I don't know.* Once Vargo had had some food and was

beginning to feel a little more alert, the realization that his link had returned – and had brought help – had slowly dawned on him. He felt enormous warmth and gratitude towards the bird, but there were things he needed to find out. *Why did you leave us in the ravine?* he asked.

*You went in the holes.*

*No, you left before that*, Vargo said, then reconsidered. Was it possible that Ero could not remember them coming out again after the first trip into the caves?

*I didn't*, Ero said, sounding offended. *I was guarding your packs. Then I got a headache and then* . . . He fell silent, obviously puzzled.

*What gave you the headache?*

*All the noise. And my feet hurt.*

*Your feet?*

*When the noise came, they got hot*, the hoopoe explained.

*What made the noise?*

*Everything*, Ero said doubtfully.

*Did you hear Cat?* Vargo asked, thinking that this must be related to Allegra's killing the fireworm.

*I can't hear her*, his link replied. *I try, but* . . .

*All right. What do you remember after that?*

*Flying for a long time.* Ero paused thoughtfully. *Then I heard you*, he concluded brightly, *so I knew you were out of the holes.*

*How did you find us?*

*I followed the link*, the hoopoe answered, but once again he did not sound very sure.

*Thank you*, Vargo said. *You may have saved our lives.*

Ero puffed out his chest and raised his crest proudly.

*Vek helped*, he said nobly. *But I was clever.*

After Vargo and Cat had eaten as much as Ambron thought wise, they all set off together, heading towards a village called Imbiani. According to the prospector, this was three days' walk away. He had rearranged the camel's load so that they could take turns to ride, and although Allegra insisted that Vargo went first, she was glad when her turn came. They stopped frequently throughout the day, ate little but often, and the two adventurers gradually began to feel human again. At their camp that evening, Cat decided that Vargo looked strong enough to talk. She needed to discuss something that had been worrying her for a while now.

'When we were still on the coast,' she began, 'you said something about evil breeding. Do you remember what that was about?'

Vargo shook his head, then frowned.

'I wasn't thinking straight,' he said, glancing down at his bandaged arm. 'I don't remember much at all. I . . . Something to do with fireworms?'

'Fireworms breeding?' she suggested.

'Or the hatred within them,' he replied.

'It never used to be like that,' Ambron said unexpectedly.

'You've seen fireworms?' Cat asked.

'I've seen a few in my time, but I wasn't talking about my own memories. I'm not that old.' He laughed.

Cat had guessed that the prospector was in his forties.

'In my grandfather's time,' Ambron continued, 'the worms were hardly ever seen, and when they were, they were like snakes – more frightened of people than we were of them.'

'That's certainly changed,' Allegra said ruefully.

'We need to go back in time!' Vargo exclaimed.

'Easier said than done,' Ambron remarked.

'Innocence is guilty,' Vargo announced, as if he had just solved one of the world's great mysteries.

Cat glanced at him sharply – but his eyes remained clear, his bandage was still clean and there was no other sign of his delirium returning. This, it seemed, was just Vargo's ordinary madness.

'Lock it up and throw away the keyhole. When innocence has gone, what is left?'

'Human nature?' Ambron suggested. He seemed to be taking Vargo's peculiar behaviour in his stride, and Cat was grateful for that.

'Nature!' Vargo muttered ecstatically. 'Worms crawl. Birds fly. Fishes swim. Trees grow upwards.' He thrust a forefinger towards the darkening sky. 'Worms fly. Birds swim. Fishes crawl.'

'Trees grow downwards?' Ambron said.

'Yes!' Vargo exclaimed, pointing to the ground.

'Do you know what he's talking about?' Cat asked.

'Everything's out of place, acting against their natures,' the prospector suggested, then shrugged. 'Just a guess.'

'I could do with an interpreter sometimes,' she told him. 'You've got the job.'

'All right.' He grinned.

'Only purple flowers drown,' Vargo intoned gravely. 'We are the rolling people.'

'That, on the other hand, means absolutely nothing,' Ambron said. 'Sorry.'

'You're fired,' Cat told him.

Vargo joined in with their laughter, but Allegra was uneasily aware that his amusement came from his own private store of jokes, the ones that invaded his mind from time to time and left no room for anything else.

The next day passed slowly, much like the day before. Although Vargo was quiet, he appeared rational, even helping set up the night's camp and prepare their evening meal.

'We should be in Imbiani by this time tomorrow,' Ambron said.

'You've been so kind,' Cat told him. ' I'm not sure how we can ever repay you.'

'It can't hurt to help one another, can it?' he replied. 'Besides, from what you've told me, all Tiguafaya owes you two a debt no one can repay. I was glad to do my bit.'

'Gods!' Vargo breathed suddenly, and Cat saw, to her alarm, that his eyes had glazed over. Even so, the madness did not seem to reach his tongue. 'How far are we from Corazoncillo?' he asked.

'Three days, more or less,' Ambron replied. 'Two if we push it.'

'Why?'

'One of the dragon eggs is hatching,' Vargo said.

# CHAPTER TWENTY-FIVE

When he reached the top of the pass, and was told the astonishing news by the lookout posted there, Nino finally knew he had made the right decision.

Ever since he and Tavia had taken that fateful siesta, he had been haunted by the dream that was more than a dream, and had hoped that the experience would be repeated. But although he occasionally sensed flickers of potential within the network of links, none ever came close to the power he had glimpsed. Even so, the knowledge that such power actually existed had been enough to give him a fresh eagerness for the task he'd set himself.

Naturally enough, he discussed what had happened with Eya. The falcon had seen many of the images too, but had no more idea than Nino about what they might mean. He was also noticeably less enthusiastic than his link, and seemed to be wary of the vision and its implications. They both knew that the birds were at the heart of what had happened, but neither of them had any idea what might have triggered that sudden, brief emergence of the complete network.

Nino had also talked to Tavia about his dream, and she

had made him recognize certain facts – which helped him consider his alternatives when deciding what to do next. Although his wife found it difficult to understand his almost ecstatic reaction to the images, she knew him well enough to see that they had had a profound effect upon him.

The first thing she clarified for him was the fact that the dream had not been dependent on his physical location. The network would have found him no matter where he was. Conversely, he was just as likely to repeat the experience in Tinajo as anywhere else. This was welcome news to Nino, who dearly wanted to stay at home for a while. Tavia was obviously delighted to have him there, but put no pressure on him to stay – and he loved her all the more for that.

The second decision they had made together was that Nino should continue to go about his business, as he had intended to do before he'd had the dream. As things stood he couldn't think of anything better to do and – until he did – this was the only course of action that made any sense. Tavia's reasoning had been that if he was meant to do something specific, then someone – the network itself, perhaps – would let him know. As a result Nino did what he'd been planning to do all along – visiting the links in the area and enlisting their help, explaining his still evolving theories as best he could. As part of this programme he called on the winemaker's daughter and her newly linked rook, but they proved to be a disappointment. The girl and her bird were both slow-witted, and failed to grasp any of the concepts he talked about. The whole process was treated by the girl partly as a joke and partly as a rather frightening mistake; she spent half the time giggling and the other half crying or complaining. Nino tried to explain things, then left her to it, hoping that what he'd said might gradually sink in and pay dividends in the future. As it was, the girl had no concept of the privilege she had been granted.

After a few days, Nino began to feel that something was calling him away. Because he longed to stay at home he fought this for as long as he could. But, after several increasingly restless days, he had come to terms with the fact that he was obviously meant to do something. His only problem was that he wasn't sure *what* to do. Once again he turned to his wife for guidance, feeling doubly guilty about making her a part of his decision to leave. But she had seen it coming for a while, and although she would be sad to see him go, she tried not to resent the other obligations in his life. Trying to stop him from going would only make it worse for them both. During the earlier discussions, they'd realized that the various intersections in the spider's web of contacts must have some special significance – otherwise why would they have appeared so clearly? It therefore made sense for Nino to visit one of these places – but although instinct had played a major role in his work so far, it was not telling him anything now. He did not feel drawn to any particular site.

'You'll have to make a rational decision,' Tavia had said, teasing him. 'Do you think you can manage that?'

But even logic hadn't produced a clear answer – although Nino had recognized some of the network's foci. He had been to Corazoncillo Valley not so long ago, but had learnt nothing. What could have changed there? Elva was lost to them now, so there was no point going there. Besides, he was sure that if he had been meant to call upon the oracle he would have known it for a fact. Teguise was a possibility; he had not been to the city for some time, and could at least take the opportunity to exchange news with the others. Of the intersections he did *not* know, the dusty graveyard seemed like a place Vargo had once described, but Nino had no idea where it was; the crooked red crater had obviously been familiar to Eya – but the bird had merely told his link that it was a place for his kind, not humans; and the ancient ravine was a complete mystery.

In the end Nino had decided to head for Teguise, hoping that, at the very least, he might be able to talk to someone else who had been part of the vision. Failing that, he could always discuss the problem with Ico and Andrin. Perhaps together they could decide what he should do next. He said goodbye to Tavia and baby Nino with a heavy heart, and set out across the firelands.

Midway through the second day of his journey, an instinct he could not explain had made him change course. The feeling that he had been going the wrong way had been getting stronger all morning, and he finally turned sharply to the north, almost doubling back on himself, and set his sights on Corazoncillo.

Now, as the sun sank below the ridge at the far end of the valley, he practically ran down the trail towards the village, the weariness of six days' walking forgotten. His arrival was greeted with a mixture of joy and relief, and as he hurried towards the old market square, he exchanged a few words with several locals – overhearing comments that made him feel rather awkward.

'It's the bird-man,' one woman whispered. 'He'll know about dragons.'

'He'll tell us what to do,' her companion said, nodding.

'About time too!' a man called out. 'Have you come from Teguise? Did the President send you?'

'No,' Nino replied. 'But I do work for her.'

'It'll happen soon now then,' someone else said knowingly. 'You'll see.'

The torchlight in the market square gave the scene a slightly macabre air. People were standing all around, watching, and oddly silent. No one had dared venture too close to the clutch of huge eggs at the centre of the open space, but they were nonetheless the focus of everyone's attention. The eleven shells glinted in the flickering light like gigantic black pearls. The mood of the waiting villagers seemed to be a mixture of excitement, hope, fear and foreboding. Above them, Eya wheeled in the darkening sky. He called once, a harsh sound that made several people look up in alarm, then flew out of sight. Although he said nothing to his link, Nino knew he was unhappy, and recalled the peregrine's earlier words. *There are shadows.*

As Nino made his way to the front rank of spectators, he spotted Cabria, one of the village elders who had befriended both him and Vargo on their earlier visits, and made his way to his side. The two men nodded to each other – but before either could speak, there came the sound of a sharp, almost metallic tapping. It lasted only a few moments, but in that time an absolute hush descended on the crowd. After it stopped, some of the onlookers turned to look at Nino.

'Tell me what's happened,' he said quietly. As far as he could see, none of the eggs had moved or looked any different from when he had last seen them.

'It began when some people heard a sort of rustling,' Cabria replied. 'We thought it might be rats, but we couldn't see anything. Then the tapping began, like you just heard, only not so loud.'

'When was that?'

'Two days ago. It took us a while to convince ourselves it was really coming from one of the eggs, but then we realized what must be happening and sent a messenger to Teguise. To be honest, we weren't sure what else to do. Since then all we've done is argue.'

'What about?'

'Will it be friendly? Should we do anything to help it, or leave well alone? That sort of thing.'

'I'm sure it won't harm you,' Nino said, pretending to have more confidence than he actually felt. Who could tell what a dragon was likely to do? 'Are you sure the tapping's only coming from one of the eggs?'

'Yes, that one,' the old man replied, pointing. 'The fourth from the right, near the middle.'

He went on to explain that one of the children – little Rico, who hadn't known any better – had run forward to touch the egg, and said that it was warm.

'I'd like to talk to him,' Nino said.

Cabria nodded.

'The heat's really intense now,' he added, 'as if there's a fire inside. And yesterday evening a crack appeared in the shell. You had to get pretty close to see it, though. Then, about four hours ago, another one opened, running across the first, but there's been nothing since. Can't be too long now though, don't you think?'

'I've no idea,' Nino answered. Only the gods knew when the last dragon had hatched in Tiguafaya, and Nino wasn't sure that any man had *ever* witnessed the birth of such a creature.

'Vargo should be here,' the old man said.

'He'll get here if he can,' Nino assured him. 'He's been travelling in the west.'

They stared at the egg in silence for a few moments.

'This is a bit of history, eh?' Cabria said quietly.

'It certainly is,' Nino agreed. 'I'm going to take a look.'

He walked forward, uncomfortably aware that everyone was watching him, and edged his way between two of the outlying eggs. He did not need to touch them to tell that they were still as cold as they had been on his previous visit, but heat was radiating from the one Cabria had pointed out. It was so hot that Nino half expected to see the shell glowing red, but it was still black and shiny – except for the shadows of the X-shaped crack in its side. Touching it now, as Rico had done earlier, would be out of the question. Gazing at the egg brought Nino no enlightenment, and he was about to return to the others when the tapping began again. Because he was standing so close it sounded very loud, and he instinctively took a step back. He expected to see something happen – the crack widen or a part of the shell fall away – but there was no change. When his heart had stopped pounding, he went back to Cabria. A small, worried-looking boy was standing next to the elder.

'Hello, Rico.'

'Hello.' The child looked as though he expected to be punished, so Nino smiled and spoke softly.

'It's all right. You didn't do anything wrong. All I want to know is, did you feel anything when you touched the egg?'

'Only that it was warm.'

'Nothing else?'

Rico shook his head. 'Was I supposed to?' he asked, a troubled look in his large brown eyes.

'No,' Nino reassured him. 'I was just wondering, that's all.'

Time passed, and nothing happened. Even the tapping had stopped. Night drew on, and people began to drift away to their beds. It might be hours, or even days, before the dragon emerged and, in the meantime, the villagers had their own lives to lead, their own concerns to attend to. A watch was organized and, even though he was loath to leave the scene, Nino eventually went to his own lodgings in the guest house. He left instructions that he was to be woken immediately if there were any significant developments.

In the early morning, before the sun had risen, Nino was called out. He was told that the tapping had begun again,

much louder now, and the fissures were widening noticeably. He threw on some clothes and ran to the square, where
the crowd that had already gathered was keeping a respectful distance.

As Nino joined them, he was just in time to see the
egg split with a sharp crack. A large piece of shell fell out,
releasing a cloud of steam, and a curiously sweet but
unpleasant odour filled the air. The crowd gasped as what
looked like a black beak, but which actually proved to be the
dragon's snout, poked through the hole. After that progress
was slow and cumbersome but constant, with more of the
shell falling away, and more of what looked like a giant lizard
becoming visible. Eventually it was recognizable as a dragon
– with wings, tail, fangs and talons – but the onlookers all
knew, long before it emerged fully, that something was very
wrong. This was not the magnificent creature they had
expected, but a sickly, feeble thing, covered in a thick slime
it was too weak to shake off. It tottered forward, its talons
scrabbling uncertainly on the ground, its eyes still closed.
The heat and vapours that had accompanied its birth soon
dissipated, making the air around seem colder than before.
Although its mouth opened, all that emerged was a thin,
croaking wail – not the bursts of flame everyone had been
expecting.

Like the rest of the onlookers, Nino was appalled by the
sight of this pathetic creature, moved to both pity and
revulsion. Cat had told him that the eggs made her – and
Vargo – feel ill, and now it was easy to see why. Nino felt
sick. Why couldn't I sense this, as she could? he wondered
– then realized, with a sinking feeling, that more and more
of the villagers were glancing at him. They expect me to
know what to do, he thought helplessly. And I haven't got a
clue.

*It's too cold here.* Eya's words came back to him, and he

clutched at the straw they offered.

'It needs warmth!' he shouted. 'Build a fire, a big one. Quickly!'

As the villagers began to rush about, Nino approached the dragon warily, but the creature hissed and flailed at him when he came too close. His presence obviously disturbed, perhaps even frightened the hatchling, so he kept his distance. Once the fire was blazing, the beast edged close to the heat and seemed a little more at ease. Then it grew very still, and Nino didn't hold out much hope. It seemed that conditions for the hatching had been all wrong from the start – and there was nothing they could do about it now.

The day passed slowly. The new-born dragon remained by the fire, which the villagers kept burning, using up a great deal of their own fuel supplies. The creature's scales were dull, and when its eyes flickered open briefly, they were a drab brown, not the burning yellow or hypnotic orange of legend. Every so often its entire body shook, as if in the grip of some strange palsy. Nothing could have been further from the grandeur and majesty of its supposed forebears.

The dragon died in the early evening, before it was even a full day old. With an ugly, rattling sigh, it simply collapsed in a messy heap and did not stir again. Although no one had really expected any other outcome, the mood of the villagers was still sombre and a little angry. So much had been expected, so many hopes pinned on the dragon's return. Some people cried. Most were stony-faced. It was a devastating setback.

Worse still was the suspicion that there were more disasters to come. Nino felt the sidelong glances, heard the whispers. What if they're *all* like that? Why didn't someone stop this happening? What should we do now?

Nino heard all the questions. And knew he had no answers.

# CHAPTER TWENTY-SIX

Even though the sun had only just risen, Ico was already awake when Ysanne came into her bedroom. These early morning visits had become quite frequent lately, especially since Andrin had been away. The little girl was crying and, as always, her tears brought Ico's maternal instincts to the fore.

'What's the matter, sweetheart? Did you have a bad dream?'

'Yes,' Ysanne whispered, as she climbed into her mother's bed. 'No. Tas said it was real.'

'Did she? And how did Tas know that?'

'She saw it too. It was sad.'

'Tas shared your dream?' Ico had never heard of dreams spanning a link.

'It wasn't magic,' Ysanne told her mother quickly. Ever since the experiment that had produced such unpleasant results she had been distinctly wary of anything magical.

'Magic isn't bad,' Ico reassured her. 'You just have to be careful how you use it, that's all.'

'I didn't use any,' the child insisted. 'I didn't.'

'But you and Tas saw something?'

'One of the dragon babies is sick.'

Ico took a few moments to consider this.

'You saw inside the egg?' she asked eventually.

'It's come out,' Ysanne replied.

Ico was stunned. If what her daughter had seen was really true, if one of the dragons had hatched but was ill . . . she couldn't imagine what that meant.

'I'm cold,' the little girl said, snuggling closer.

Ico held her tight, and tried not to feel too pessimistic. She had a feeling it was going to be a very long day.

Her first appointment of the day was with Maciot. She usually looked forward to their time together, knowing she would enjoy his company, and knowing that he was the one person who could be relied upon to remain calm, no matter what was being discussed. She did not always agree with everything he had to say, but his advice was always welcome. Recently, however, all that had changed.

It had been several days since Tao had fallen ill, and during that time Maciot had been understandably preoccupied. Although the mirador was alive, his condition was still the same, in spite of almost constant care. Maciot could not communicate with him yet, and this had left the senator in a kind of limbo. Although Ico had done her best to help her friend cope, trying to convince him that Tao's fighting spirit would eventually win through, Maciot was badly affected by the uncertainty. He often fumbled for words now, where once he had been both fluent and articulate. He wavered over decisions, sometimes found the simplest logic hard to follow, and tended to forget things unless he wrote them down. He was doing his best, but Ico needed more than that. There were various crises brewing all around her, and she needed her chief advisor to be the rock she could always lean on. Right now he was crumbling before her eyes.

'Sorry I'm late,' he mumbled as he hurried into the conference chamber, carrying a sheaf of documents. He was hollow-eyed from lack of sleep.

'It's all right. How's Tao?'

'No change.' He always gave the same answer to her oft-repeated question, and Ico was running out of encouraging responses.

'Don't give up hope,' she said.

'I can't afford to,' he replied. He sounded bitter, and that surprised her. The haunted look in his eyes was still there, but had been joined by anger now. 'Gods!' he exclaimed. 'I've been so stupid.'

'What do you mean?'

'Tao was always going to die before me, even if this hadn't happened.'

'He's not going to die,' Ico said, speaking more in hope than from conviction.

'Maybe,' Maciot admitted. 'But that's not the point. I should have been prepared. It's only since he's been ill that I've realized just how much I depend on him. Not just the companionship of the link, but for my work. So much comes through the birds, and he's the one who passed it all on to me. I'm lost without him.'

'No one can lose a link, even temporarily, and not be affected by it,' Ico pointed out.

'The worst thing is,' he went on, as though she had not spoken, 'I know I've let you down.'

'That's not true,' she lied.

'Isn't it? When you thought Soo was dead, you got on with what you had to do.'

'And so will you,' she told him. 'I need you to be strong, Alegranze.'

He looked up at her. Ico rarely used his first name, and it was an indication of her concern.

'Aren't the other birds helping?' she asked. Several of the Firebrands and their links had been co-opted as inter-mediaries to assist Maciot with his communications.

'It's not the same,' he replied quietly.

'Of course it isn't!' Ico stated forcefully, wanting to lift him out of his dark mood. 'Things change. We have to adapt. When Tao recovers you'll be back to your old ways. Until then, we have to do the best we can with what we've got.'

'I know,' he muttered, then looked up again, a deter-mined expression on his face. 'Right, where shall we start?' He shuffled his papers, dropped some of them, and swore under his breath. When he'd retrieved them from under the table, he managed a rueful smile. 'Sorry about all the self-pity.'

'Don't worry about it. You'll be fine,' she said gently, then became deliberately businesslike. 'Has there been any news from Corazoncillo recently?'

'Not that I'm aware of,' he replied, glancing uncertainly at the documents now spread out over the table. 'Why?'

'Ysanne and Tas had a dream last night, about one of the eggs hatching. I don't want to put too much store by it, but I'd like to know what's going on – if anything.'

'Ysanne *and* Tas?' he queried, obviously surprised.

'Yes.'

'Shall I send a courier?' he asked.

'I think I'll ask Soo,' Ico decided. 'She'll get there and back quicker – and the place means something to her.' I don't know what, she added to herself, but it must be to do with the dragons, and if one of the eggs really has hatched . . .

'Good idea,' Maciot said. He had finally found the piece

of paper he'd been looking for. 'Nino was heading there, wasn't he?'

'Yes, but that was nearly a month ago. He'll probably have moved on by now.'

'This could be good news,' the senator said, brightening as the impact of the dream belatedly sank in. 'If one of the dragons is alive, maybe – didn't Vargo say? – maybe it'll be able to help us. With the fireworms, I mean.'

'It could be bad news too,' Ico replied, hating to dash his hopes, but owing him the truth. 'If the dream was accurate, then the dragon's ill.'

'Oh.' Maciot looked down and pushed some documents about aimlessly.

'We'll just have to wait and see,' Ico concluded. 'Do you have any news from the Empire?'

This was clearly a question that the senator was better prepared to answer.

'Yes,' he replied. He picked out three sheets of paper and scanned their contents. 'Prince Tzarno's apparently gone back to Zepharinn – probably because his brother's due to marry soon. At least that's the rumour. So it may not have anything to do with Madri's visit.'

'I take it we haven't heard from him yet?'

'No.' Their envoy's last message had been a report of his arrival in Uga Stai, and they judged that he was almost certainly in the imperial capital by now. 'The *Goshawk* is due to return to Uga Stai in . . .' Maciot consulted his notes. 'Three day's time.'

'So it could be a while before we get a full report?'

The senator nodded.

'If Tzarno is back in Zepharinn, that surely means they're not about to attack,' Ico reasoned. 'I assume his forces have remained in the south.'

'As far as we can tell, yes,' Maciot replied. 'Anyway, I

don't think they'd opt for a surprise attack. If they're looking at this as a holy war, they'll want to make a lot of noise about it, rally popular support. We ought to get *some* warning.'

'Let's hope so,' Ico said. 'Tzarno might be clever enough to use that against us.'

'What?' He looked puzzled.

'If we assume—' she began impatiently.

'It's all right,' he interrupted her. 'Sorry. I've got it now. I'm not very quick at the moment.'

'I just don't want us getting complacent,' Ico explained, brushing his apology aside. 'Any word on Kantrowe?'

'Not much. But I did get a description of the Prophet from one of my men who saw him speaking at a rally a while back. He said he was very thin, gaunt even.'

'That doesn't sound like Tias.'

'If it *is* him, he must've lost a lot of weight.'

'I doubt he's eaten as well during the last two years,' Ico said dryly. 'Anything else?'

'I don't think so.'

'All right. Let's move on.' She had not been looking forward to this part of the meeting. 'Have we found Martinoy yet?'

'No.' Maciot sounded frustrated. 'There've been several sightings, but . . .' He shrugged helplessly.

The mysterious leader of the supposed fireworm cult still eluded their efforts to locate him. However, a few more unsubstantiated facts had emerged. Rumours that worms were being bred in captivity were becoming more widespread, although the reasons given for this varied wildly. Some people believed that the creatures were being kept as a weapon to use against their enemies, others that they were part of an elaborate sabotage plot mounted by the Empire's spies. Yet another theory was that those breeding the worms were in thrall to the dragons, and would eventually release the spawn to wreak havoc on their human foes. And a few people were saying that the whole thing was a secret government project, aimed at producing untainted creatures to help control the volcanoes. The only explanation that Ico could be sure was untrue was this last one, much as she liked the idea in theory.

Although Ico had advised against using military force to storm the cult's earlier meeting place, she was no longer sure she had done the right thing. There was no proof that anything illegal had gone on inside – and certainly no proof that it was where Tao had been injured – and using soldiers to break into private property was something she was loath to do. She still had the feeling that the cult might eventually be of some use to Vargo in his search, and this had also influenced her decision. The building had seemed very quiet recently, and three days ago one of the chivaree had been able to get inside – but had found nothing out of the ordinary.

'What about other cult members?' Ico asked.

'We've identified several fairly conclusively,' Maciot replied, 'but none of them are talking. They must've taken some sort of vow of silence, and I don't see how to break it.'

'Keep trying.' She could see that her friend was beginning to fidget now, obviously wanting to go and check on his link, so she decided to end the meeting. 'That's it, I think, unless you've got anything else.'

Maciot shook his head. They stood up and walked slowly over to the door.

'Are you coming to the council this afternoon?' she asked. Cucura and Kehoe were due to visit the palace for one of their regular briefings, held ever since the threat of war had been raised.

'I . . . I don't . . .'

'I'll let you know what happens,' she told him, recognizing his reluctance.

'Thank you.'

'Try to get some rest,' Ico advised, putting a hand on his arm.

The council of war turned out to involve little of real interest. Neither Admiral Cucura nor Commander Kehoe had anything significant to report, but they updated the President on the disposition of their forces. This included the implementation of the new scheme to patrol the northern border, which seemed to be going well.

'Within the next few days we should have the entire border covered,' Kehoe informed them. 'Except for the far western end. And not even Tzarno would be mad enough to try invading there.' He grinned at Ico.

She treated him to a tolerant smile.

'How are the Firebrands performing?' She had sensed a slight distrust on the part of the soldiers in earlier reports, but the fact that the plan was working seemed to have allayed any fears.

'They've done well,' the commander replied. 'Though some of them are finding a soldier's life a bit hard.'

'They'll get used to it,' Ico said confidently. 'They lived in caves in the firelands for a long time, remember.'

'As well as keeping watch, we're also mapping out the entire region,' Kehoe added. 'That way we'll be able to identify all possible routes for an invasion force.' His expression made it clear that he still thought a land attack was unlikely.

'Good. I don't suppose you've had any word on the whereabouts of my husband, have you?'

'No, ma'am,' the commander replied, obviously surprised. 'I'd assumed he'd be letting you know directly.'

So had I, Ico thought, but she said nothing.

That evening, after she'd put Ysanne to bed – assuring her that there would be no nasty dreams that night – Ico found herself thinking that Maciot was not the only person indulging in self-pity. Although she was not usually one to feel sorry for herself, she suddenly felt very lonely.

Only the gods knew where Vargo was. He had been away for so long she'd almost forgotten what he looked like – and that made her very sad. They had been such close friends once. Madri and Angel were absent too, but at least she knew where they were, and could reasonably expect them to be back before too long. She hadn't heard from Nino in almost a month. Maciot was there, of course, but he wasn't exactly himself at the moment. And then there was Andrin.

Her husband had already been away for longer than she had expected – ten days so far, she calculated – and the probability was that he'd embarked on some wild-goose chase without bothering to tell anyone. It was the longest they'd been apart since their enforced separation – when she had been abducted by pirates – and at least she'd had an excuse then! She understood, and even approved his occasional need to get away, but she was annoyed and hurt that he had abandoned her for so long at a time like this. All the buttresses of her life seemed to be falling away, and left her feeling uncharacteristically vulnerable.

It was almost enough to make her wish she had a mentor – someone like Famara had been to Vargo – but she had always been too strong-willed and independent to need one – and it was too late now. When she had been very young she had looked up to her father but, as she grew up, it had become obvious to them both that her will was stronger than his. Diano had never been able to match his daughter's fire, and he knew it.

Andrin was the only one who had been able to do that.

# CHAPTER TWENTY-SEVEN

'You can't just walk into the middle of their camp!' Jada exclaimed.

'Why not?' Andrin asked. 'They're not going to know who I am.'

Their day, like Ico's, had begun at first light, when they had left their outpost and climbed to the top of a small peak that overlooked the border.

'Won't your accent give you away?'

'I doubt it. Most armies are drawn from all over the place, and they'll probably just assume I'm from some outlying territory to the west. I could circle round to approach from that direction.'

'But what if they see you cross the border?' Jada persisted. 'There's not much cover down there.' The valley below them was mostly bare earth, with occasional patches of scrub. Although there was nothing to mark the actual border as such, the contrast between the firelands to the south and the increasingly fertile hills that rolled away to the north made the transition fairly plain. 'Perhaps you should wait for dark.'

'No.' Andrin felt too restless to contemplate any further delay. 'I'm going today. Even if they do spot me, we're not at war yet. What would they do?'

'They'll be suspicious,' his companion argued. 'This area is usually completely deserted. We don't need to be at war for them to take a dislike to spies.'

'Me, a spy?' Andrin said innocently. 'I'm just a simple fisherman whose boat got wrecked on the rocks a little further south.'

'I thought you came from the west,' Jada pointed out. 'What were you doing fishing the Inner Seas?'

Andrin shrugged dismissively.

'A man's got to make a living,' he said.

'You'd better decide on a story and stick to it,' Jada advised. 'I still think you're mad. What's the point of using the birds? Haven't they given us enough information?'

'I can talk to people,' Andrin explained. 'Find out what they're thinking as well as what they're doing.'

'And that's worth the risk, is it?'

'I think so.'

Jada shrugged, knowing it was not worth arguing with Andrin when he was in this mood. He had also seen what Andrin was capable of when the need arose. He had saved Jada's life when his magical ice-shield had protected them from the devastating eruption at Tisaloya. Jada had been unconscious for all of their subsequent flight – which was something he regretted bitterly – but he would never forget his miraculous escape.

Now that the patrols had covered most of the border's length, their thoughts had turned to what was happening on the other side. Ayo and Tir, Jada's linked sparrowhawk, had been among the birds who'd made several flights over foreign territory, and the picture that had emerged was not very encouraging. The imperial army had established several camps within a day's march of the eastern end of the border. Two of these were very close, on the shore of the Inner Seas, while the rest were further along the coast, between the boundary and the distant port of Uga Stai. Their location made no sense unless the Empire was contemplating a move against Tiguafaya, either by land or sea, but for the moment there seemed to be no further activity.

The jagged peak on which Andrin and Jada were crouched was some miles inland. The nearest encampments were to their right, only visible as darker patches on the otherwise dull terrain and from the drifting smoke of cooking fires. The birds had noted patrols leaving the camps every so often, heading west, parallel to the border. Detachments had also been seen travelling in other directions, but these were less regular. Ayo had been sent to follow one of these groups that morning, and now returned to his link with some surprising and rather disturbing news. The white eagle descended in a wide spiral and alighted near the two men.

*The soldiers went to see a valley that's been scorched by the shining breath*, he reported.

*You mean they crossed the border?* Andrin asked, frowning.

*No. The valley is beyond four hills that way.* Ayo jabbed his massive bill towards the northwest.

*There's been an eruption on Empire land?* Andrin asked, aghast.

*Yes. The earth is stirring. There are other people going there too*, the eagle added. *With bells.*

Before Andrin had the chance to ask what that meant, Jada spoke, interrupting the silent conversation.

'What's going on?' He'd seen Andrin's changing expressions and could wait no longer.

Andrin told him what Ayo had said. Both men were aware of the implications.

'I have to see this for myself,' Andrin decided.

'Why?'

'To see if it's a trick.'

'You're joking!' Jada exclaimed. 'Why would the Empire go to such lengths? More to the point, *how* could they? You can't just conjure up a volcanic eruption.'

'If there are other people there, I'll be able to mix in, ask questions,' Andrin said, ignoring his companion's objections. He stood up and stared into the distance.

'You're not thinking of going right now?' Jada said.

'Why not?'

'You're not equipped.' They had only taken the barest essentials with them when they had left the outpost.

'I'll be fine.'

'I'll come with you,' Jada offered loyally, although he did not sound enthusiastic.

'No. You've got to go back and tell the others what I'm doing. And get a message to Teguise.' Andrin was guiltily aware that he'd already been away from Ico and Ysanne for a long time.

'When will you come back?' Jada asked. He was obviously worried.

'I don't know. I'll stay until I get the information I need.'

'There are others gathering intelligence. Madri and—'

'Madri's only going to learn what they *want* him to learn,' Andrin cut in. '*This* is where the army is – so this is where we'll get the best information.'

'Are you sure you want to do this?'

'Oh, yes.' Andrin had been itching for some real action for some time, and now that the opportunity had presented itself he had no doubts about what he should do.

'All right.' Jada gave in. 'You'd better not let anyone see you with *him*, though,' he added, indicating the eagle. 'That sort of companion could get you into trouble over there.'

Andrin grinned.

'Point taken,' he said. 'We'll be careful.'

'Good luck.'

Ayo took off suddenly, rising majestically into the sky as Andrin began to walk down the dusty slope towards the border.

It took Andrin most of the morning to reach the hill overlooking the destroyed valley. During that time he had twice seen some soldiers in the distance, but they had paid no attention to him, and he'd continued to walk openly. Far above, Ayo circled lazily, keeping pace with his link.

Judging by its surroundings, the valley had once been a reasonably fertile place. The river that ran into it was still flowing, but had split into many separate streams – which threaded their way through the crevasses and hollows in the dark rock that covered the ground. A little smoke rose from the centre of the collapsed cone, but otherwise the place was silent and dead. Much of the new surface had a dull, glazed look to it – a result of the searing heat of the clouds of shining breath. Andrin had seen the effect often enough, and knew the violence and terror that preceded it. This was indeed the work of a volcano, one that had evidently reduced a green vale to a blackened wasteland in a very short space of time. And it meant that the Empire now had the perfect excuse to act upon the ultimatum Kudrak had delivered to Ico.

'Terrible, isn't it?'

The voice came from just behind him and Andrin swung round, alarmed – and annoyed that he had let someone get so close without being aware of his presence. The man who stood gazing at the devastated valley was not a soldier and, as far as Andrin could see, carried no weapon. He was dressed in threadbare clothes and dusty sandals. The only unusual aspect of his appearance was the twisted headband of orange cloth tied round his forehead.

'Yes, it is,' Andrin replied, wondering why Ayo hadn't warned him of the stranger's approach, but not wanting to look up in case he betrayed his connection to the eagle.

'Was this your home?'

'No. I come from further west,' Andrin improvised. 'But I . . . I knew some of those who lived here. I heard about the fire and came to see for myself.'

'It seems everyone was killed,' the man said. 'At least we haven't been able to find any survivors. Such vengeance is fearsome.'

Vengeance for what? Andrin thought, but held his tongue, wondering if he had already said too much.

'I am called Derim,' the stranger said, with a small polite bow. 'I serve the gods.'

'As do I,' Andrin responded.

When Derim looked at him curiously, he wondered if his response had been a mistake.

'You do not wear the mark of the Prophet,' Derim observed.

'I don't know what you mean,' Andrin replied, deciding to play the role of country bumpkin.

'The orange,' Derim said, touching his headband. 'I am of the Kundahari.'

'Ah. I have heard of such, but I've never seen this style before.'

Derim smiled condescendingly.

'You *are* from the far west. Come, my brothers are about to ring bells for the dead. Will you join us?'

As they set off, Andrin was able to take a surreptitious glance at the sky, but Ayo was nowhere to be seen.

'The eruption happened exactly half a month ago,'

Derim informed him. 'At the last full moon, which makes it a doubly ominous event, don't you think?'

'I wouldn't know.' His companion's earlier mention of the Prophet had reminded Andrin of Kantrowe. The idea that his old enemy might be in the Empire, not only alive but spreading his malign influence, had been eating away at his mind like acid. He wanted to ask about him now, but didn't know how to approach the subject without arousing suspicion. In the event, Derim did it for him.

'The Prophet says that conflict is as inevitable as the turning of the moon.'

'This is the prophet called Kantrowe?'

'You know of him?'

'Only by reputation.'

'He is a great man,' Derim said reverently.

'And he has the ear of Prince Tzarno?'

Derim nodded.

'And all god-fearing men,' he confirmed.

'Do you think there will be war?'

'If the gods decree it. Heresy cannot be allowed to spread. Look what it leads to.' Derim spread his arms wide, indicating the expanse of bare rock ahead of them.

By this time they were approaching a group of men, who were all wearing orange headbands. Some were kneeling, while others stood at the edge of the lava field, staring at the devastated landscape in silence. Several were holding bells, of all types and sizes. When they reached the edge of the group, Derim motioned for Andrin to stand still, then pulled out a tiny bell of his own, which hung on a chain round his neck.

'It is time,' he said, and rang a single chime.

Immediately all the others rang their bells as loudly as they could, producing a cacophony that reminded Andrin of a less violent version of the chivaree's aural assault. After a few moments they all stopped, and the clamour faded into silence.

'We have driven the evil spirits away,' Derim intoned. 'Now let us honour the dead.'

This time, at his signal, the bells were rung in a complicated sequence, each peal taking the place of the one before as it died away. The tune that emerged was slow and sonorous, hardly a work of art, but oddly moving nonetheless. That too eventually came to an end, quietly and with dignity, and for a short time each of the men bent their heads – in prayer, Andrin supposed. He had expected the Kundahari to be raving fanatics, and this apparently genuine display of sentiment and respect had caught him off guard. However, Derim's next words made him reassess the company he had fallen into.

'May the blasphemous sorcery that took these innocent lives be turned back upon its makers!' Derim cried. 'Give us the strength to seek them out, wherever they may be, and to destroy them utterly.'

'Give us the strength,' his followers responded in unison.

'All right, you lot, you've had your fun. Now clear off!'

The newcomer was dressed in the uniform of the imperial army, and behind him stood a dozen soldiers. Their approach had been masked by the music, and once again Ayo had failed to warn his link.

'We are honouring the dead of this place,' Derim said, unperturbed by the interruption. 'And the gods.'

'Well, go and do it somewhere else,' the soldier responded. 'This valley is under military jurisdiction.'

'The gods' jurisdiction encompasses the whole world, Captain.'

'That's as maybe, but I have my orders from General Tzarno. Go and argue with him if you want to. Now move!'

'As you wish.' As Derim began to lead the Kundahari

away, Andrin stood where he was, not sure what to do.

'Are you with them or not?' the captain asked, spotting him.

'No.'

'Got more sense, eh?'

'I just came to see the valley for myself,' Andrin explained. There was clearly no love lost between the Kundahari and the army.

'A mess, isn't it?' the soldier remarked. 'Well, now you've seen it, you'd better go. There's nothing to do here.'

'I used to know someone . . .' Andrin mumbled, wanting to prolong the conversation.

'None of them had a chance. I'm sorry.'

'Someone must be to blame for this.'

'That lot'll have you believe it's the magicians down in Tiguafaya,' the captain said, jerking his thumb towards the retreating Kundahari. 'But that's crap, if you ask me. The fires under the earth are a law unto themselves.'

'You don't think we should go to war, then?'

'Do me a favour, son! What for? There's nothing down there worth having. Tzarno's keen to be a hero, but it's not the generals that die, is it? I mean, look at this lot.' He pointed at the valley. 'How's an army supposed to march over stuff like that? And this is nothing compared to the real firelands south of the border. We'd be crazy to try, but that's what's going to happen if this idiot prophet gets his way.'

'Kantrowe?'

The soldier nodded.

'He's got the Kundahari all riled up over nothing. If it weren't for that bastard we'd all be home in nice clean barracks instead of pissing around down here.'

The open vehemence of the captain's outburst gave Andrin reason for hope. If enough officers in the imperial army felt this way, then war might be averted. However, when the captain spoke again, his words gave Andrin pause for thought.

'Someone should do us all a favour and stick a knife in his scrawny throat.'

I might just do that, Andrin thought. I might just do that.

# CHAPTER TWENTY-EIGHT

In the two days since his audience with the Emperor and his inner council, Madri had heard nothing. Although this did not surprise him in the least, nor did it make the waiting any easier. Such food and drink as his party required had been provided but, apart from that, they had been left entirely to their own devices. They had been free to explore the city and, to a certain extent, the fortress, and the four soldiers had been out and about, gathering what information they could. Madri and Angel had not stirred too far from their lodgings, wanting to be available in the unlikely event of a further meeting being called. They had spent their time talking, reading, and occasionally wandering up to the nearest battlements to look out over the imperial capital. No one took much notice of them on these brief expeditions – other than the few horrified glances provoked by Angel's appearance, something that always hurt Madri more than his friend.

They had been on the ramparts the previous day when Katerin, the Emperor's bride-to-be, had arrived at the fortress, and they had caught a glimpse of her amid a large and colourful entourage as it entered the gates. Even from a distance, it was clear that she was as striking a woman as her reputation indicated, and – even though it was immensely frustrating for Tiguafaya's ambassador – Madri found that he could understand Madar's preoccupation with his forthcoming nuptials.

Later that same day, when they were back in their guest quarters, Angel had suffered a relapse into the gentle madness that, together with his misshapen features, had once turned him into an outcast. Such attacks had been rare in recent years, now that he was no longer forced to live as a wandering hermit, and although Madri was used to dealing with them, it still came as something of a shock

'The apple-taster's needed, needed,' Angel exclaimed suddenly.

Madri knew that his friend sometimes referred to himself as 'the apple-taster'.

'To do what?' he asked, watching Angel closely.

'We sing the ripples in the water, in the mirrors, mirrors.'

That sounded like something Vargo had once said, when he too had been in the grip of his own eccentric madness. A long time ago, Andrin had voiced the opinion that Angel and Vargo were 'allies in insanity'. When the two were together, their conversations were often incomprehensible to anyone else. However, they took great comfort from each other's company, laughing at jokes only they understood. On this occasion, however, Angel was clearly unhappy.

'What's wrong, Tre?' Madri asked. 'Are you all right?'

'Spirits come. Apples rot. Flowers drown, drown. The apple-taster's gone. Too far, too cold, cold.'

After that he had fallen silent, and there was nothing Madri could say to loosen his tongue.

A restless night had followed, and when they woke the next morning, Angel was obviously still troubled. Although the madness seemed to have passed, all he would say was that something was wrong – and he was either unable or unwilling to elaborate.

The morning was still only a few hours old when they received an unexpected visitor. When Madri saw that Kudrak was at the door, he wondered briefly whether the envoy had been chosen as the Emperor's messenger – but soon realized that this was not the case. After the exchange of formal greetings, the real reason for Kudrak's visit became clear.

'I have come to ask if you, and your companion, would care to join me for the celebrations today. There is always much of interest to see as a new circle begins.' Noting the look of surprise on Madri's face, he added, 'We are not uncivilized men, Ambassador. Just because we have our differences of opinion, it doesn't mean we cannot extend each other such courtesies as are within our gift.'

'Thank you,' Madri replied, wondering if this courtesy was genuine or whether Kudrak had an ulterior motive, 'but I should really remain available in case the Emperor wishes to see me.'

'I understand your concern,' Kudrak said, 'but, in truth, there is little chance of any communication from the Imperial Council today. This night will be the first of the new moon, and when a new month begins Zepharinn reaffirms its faith in prayer and procession. Today is not a time for politics or debate. Madar and his betrothed will be completing the pilgrim ring, together with all god-fearing citizens, so you may join us if you wish without fear of neglecting your duties.'

He's a smug bastard, Madri thought, but he actually sounds as though he means it. He obviously wants to demonstrate the piety of his city and its people, but if he's got anything more sinister in mind he's hiding it well.

'It would be a shame to miss such such an opportunity,' Kudrak went on earnestly. 'The circle of the seven temples is worth seeing for its own sake, and when the way is thronged with people, there are few sights that can match it. Leave one of your attendants here, and I will furnish him with the details of our route. That way he'll be able to find you at any time, should the need arise. Not that I think it will,' he added, with a smile.

'All right. Thank you. We accept.' Madri had realized that he was unlikely to hear anything that day, and it might be useful to witness the mass procession and gauge the mood of the people.

'Excellent,' Kudrak said. 'We will begin at the Second Temple. That way, when we complete the ring, we'll be in the right place to see the new hierophant accept the robes of office.'

Perched high above the city, atop one of the tallest towers in the fortress, Prince Tzarno and Castellan Ty were in private conference.

'Not the best timing, eh?' Ty commented.

'That's an understatement,' Tzarno replied. 'As if the new circle didn't represent enough of a delay, my dear brother has to pick this moment to bring his bride to the city. All the council can talk about is the wedding,' he added disgustedly.

'Madar may have got more than he bargained for in Katerin,' the castellan said. 'She has a mind of her own.'

'It's not her *mind* that concerns me,' the younger man replied. 'I just hope she's not too fertile.'

'Even if she is, nine and a half months is a long time.'

'You think Madar will wait until the wedding night? I wouldn't.'

'Perhaps your brother is a more honourable man than you,' Ty remarked mildly.

Tzarno shot him an angry glance, then laughed when he saw the older man's smile.

'You could be right,' he conceded. 'It just complicates matters, that's all.'

'We'll deal with whatever happens,' Ty stated calmly. 'What's Madar been saying to you? Ruhail's been very unhappy about your private meetings.'

'The usual feeble crap. He wants cast-iron assurances that our allies are trustworthy, that *his* people won't be put at any undue risk – and he wants information about Tiguafaya that we can't possibly know until we go there!' The prince threw up his hands in disbelief. 'He's so cautious he makes my skin crawl.'

'Which makes his choice of wife all the more surprising,' the castellan commented thoughtfully.

'It's the one thing he's done recently that I can respect,' Tzarno admitted grudgingly. 'I didn't think he had it in him.'

'But he'll sanction war if we give him enough reason,' Ty said.

'Sooner or later he won't have any choice,' the prince agreed. 'The trouble is, it's looking more and more like later.'

They stood in silence for a while, looking down on Zepharinn. Even from such a great height, the movement of huge crowds of people as they circled the pilgrim ring was clearly visible. It was as if the city were in the grip of a vast, writhing serpent.

'It won't be long before the Kundahari make their presence felt,' Ty said. 'Especially if Kantrowe stirs them up properly. He's down there somewhere, I presume.'

Tzarno nodded.

'He doesn't believe any of it, you know.'

'Any of what?'

'All of it. Heresy. Magic being the cause of eruptions. It's just an excuse. He's obsessed with getting revenge on Tiguafaya, that's all. I doubt he even believes in the gods.'

'Then he's an excellent actor,' Ty commented.

'A lot of fanatics are,' the prince said. 'That's why people follow them.'

'That's also why they're dangerous.'

'I know. Don't worry. I can handle him.' Tzarno paused, considering. 'The eruption in our territory will become common knowledge soon, and then we can get the Kundahari to start a real hue and cry.'

'Why not just get "the Prophet" to announce it?'

'Because Madar has decreed that we're to keep it secret for as long as possible, and because the Prophet is too closely connected to me. I don't want my brother getting the idea that I'm forcing his hand.'

'Even when you are.'

'Exactly.' Tzarno grinned. 'Besides, the Kundahari will have found the valley for themselves by now. I took the precaution of putting the whole area under military guard – which only made them even more determined to see it for themselves. The news should get back here soon enough.'

The veteran nodded.

'How do things stand in the south?'

'Supplies will be our biggest problem, but we have the men in place. We just have to wait until Lamia and Zarzuelo are ready.'

'*Can* we trust these allies?' the castellan asked.

'Don't you start!' Tzarno exclaimed. 'I'll make sure we can. They'll either do their job or they'll die. Either way we gain by it. Tiguafaya can conjure up all the magic they like. I'm going to crush them anyway.'

Taking part in the pilgrim ring, albeit as an observer, had been every bit as astonishing as Kudrak had claimed. Madri and Angel had walked the circle linking each of the major temples among a mass of people who were shouting slogans, singing or muttering prayers almost constantly. The barrage of noise was extraordinary. Around each of the seven holy places the crush had been even greater, and they had been hard put to see much of the buildings, let alone appreciate what was evidently some spectacular architecture.

The fervour of the crowds was almost frightening. Many men were wearing orange headbands, which Madri learnt was the mark of the Kundahari, and their eyes burned with a fierce intensity. Detachments of Seax Guards kept a watchful eye on the proceedings, and accompanied some of the more important people as they made their observances.

Kudrak made a point of acting as their guide, proudly telling them about the various rituals that were taking place, and about the sites of special veneration. However, Madri was less interested in the ambassador's commentary than in listening to the words of the pilgrims themselves, the gossip and opinions which interspersed their formal responses. Most seemed to be in a buoyant mood, laughing and joking when they were not actually chanting or at prayer. Although a few wore the deadly serious expressions of zealots, the rest seemed to be treating the day as one long festival. Food and drink were readily available, musicians played, and women and children mingled with their menfolk. Madri overheard several mentions of the Prophet, including various rumours about when and where he was to speak, but he was never able to catch sight of the man himself. Kudrak was not interested in answering questions about Kantrowe, but the influence he wielded over the hearts and minds of many in the crowd was obvious.

Finally, arriving back where they had begun – at the Second Temple – they were ushered inside by soldiers, joining the privileged few who would witness the day's final ceremony. Under the attentive gaze of his Emperor and his bride-to-be, and many other court dignitaries, Nandi passed over the duties of hierophant, along with the richly embroidered robes of office, to Otric, High Priest of the Third Temple. Whether he did so with a profound sense of relief at the end of an onerous duty, or with regret because Otric would now preside over the marriage of Madar and Katerin, was something the onlookers would never know.

Back at their own lodgings, Madri and Angel were both very tired and, for once, appreciative of the luxurious nature of their accommodations. Even so, Angel – who had been in a miserable mood all day – became even more morose as evening drew in.

'What's the matter, Tre?'

'I don't know. I shouldn't be here.'

'Why not? Where *should* you be?'

'I don't know!' Angel said in exasperation. 'But something's very wrong somewhere.'

Before they had the chance to discuss this further they were interrupted by a page, who brought with him an elaborately sealed letter from Chamberlain Ruhail. Madri read it with a rising sense of futility and rage.

'Bad news?' Angel asked.

'No news at all, really,' Madri replied. 'This is useless! Ruhail says that "due to the unusual circumstances" at the moment, the council are unable to give "the Tiguafayan problem" their full attention until after Madar's wedding.' The ceremony was to take place on the day of the next full moon, half a month away. 'All he's done here is repeat their demands. Oh, and he's invited us to stay for the wedding, as honoured guests.'

'Are we going to?'

'No.' Madri was still fuming at their dismissal, and the

manner in which it had been carried out. 'There's no point, and I can't stand any more hanging around. We'll leave tomorrow. That way the *Goshawk* won't have to be kept waiting for long.' The envoy paused, drawing a deep breath. 'The Empire can find some other way to tell us if they're going to declare war,' he said. 'I want to go home.'

# CHAPTER TWENTY-NINE

Vargo, Cat and Ambron reached the rim of the Corazoncillo valley soon after noon, two and a half days after Vargo's premonition. During that time his mood had veered wildly between an optimistic excitement that made it almost impossible for him to sleep or even keep still, and a doom-laden foreboding that – to Cat's dismay – seemed to grow stronger the closer they came to their destination. Now, as they began the final descent, she found herself shivering, even though the day was hot.

Having been warned of his friends' approach by Eya, Nino left the village in time to intercept them on the trail. Mindful of Allegra's earlier comments about Vargo's fragile state of mind, Nino wanted to be the one to tell them what had happened. It would not lessen the impact of the news, but at least he had some understanding of how it might affect the former musician.

They met halfway down the path and, at a glance, Nino took in his friends' haggard appearance, their worried, expectant faces, and the matching concern on the face of the stranger who was leading the camel. Nino's gaze met

Allegra's, and he knew she had read the awful truth in his eyes.

'Did it hatch?' Vargo asked.

'It did,' Nino replied gravely, not at all surprised that Vargo had foreseen the event. Indeed, the only real surprise was that he had not seen its eventual outcome.

'But?' Vargo said, sensing his friend's unease.

'It died later the same day,' Nino said, knowing there was no way to sugar-coat such appalling news.

Vargo stared up at the sky for a few moments, then closed his eyes and hung his head. Behind him Cat hovered, ready to give him whatever support he needed.

'I'm sorry,' Nino added.

'I did wonder,' Vargo said quietly. 'It didn't feel right.'

'There are still ten more,' Allegra pointed out, knowing even as she spoke that her words would provide scant consolation.

Vargo looked round at her and smiled.

'But do any of them retain their innocence?' he asked.

Later that day, after the newcomers had been told everything that had happened – including how Nino had helped the villagers complete the unpleasant but necessary task of burying the remains of the dead hatchling –they gathered in the main room of the guest hall to discuss the implications of the creature's fate. Vargo was tired now, as well as depressed. He had been to the village square, to try to communicate with the remaining eggs, but had had no more success than on previous occasions. Each of the eggs had been silent and cold, giving no indication when they might hatch.

Nino had asked Cabria, the village elder, to join them and it was he who first overcame the general reluctance to assess the situation.

'Could it be that this is the wrong place for the eggs? The fact that they ended up here was a matter of chance, after all.'

'I doubt it's that simple,' Vargo said wearily.

'I always believed it *wasn't* just chance,' Nino added. 'I thought they were *meant* to come here.' His tone implied that he was no longer sure of this.

'The birds don't like it here,' Ambron remarked. 'They think it's cold.' He had been aware of Vek's uneasiness about the place for a long time.

'No colder than many other places,' Cabria said.

'I don't think it's just a matter of temperature,' Nino commented.

'Perhaps the dragons need to feel the fires *beneath* the earth,' Ambron suggested. 'There haven't been any eruptions near here for quite a while.'

'Lighting the fire did seem to help a little,' Nino said. 'Not enough, of course.'

'We can hardly re-create conditions as they were inside Tisaloya,' Cat pointed out. 'The biggest bonfire in the world wouldn't do that.'

'Should we think about ways of moving the eggs, then?' Cabria suggested.

'The only thing we know that's capable of lifting them is a full-grown dragon!' Nino said. 'They're just too heavy.'

'With enough camels and manpower we might be able to shift them one at a time,' Ambron argued.

'I doubt it. The hatchling weighed a lot, but the liquid surrounding it was so dense it was almost solid – and the shell is incredibly heavy. Frankly, I've no idea how we could do it.'

'And anyway, where would we take them?' Cat asked. 'Tisaloya doesn't exist any more.'

'There must be other caves with similar conditions,' Ambron persisted.

'No, there aren't,' Vargo stated.

The others all looked at him. He had spoken with unusual certainty, and his eyes blazed, in spite of his exhaustion.

'What do you mean?' Allegra asked eventually. 'There are hundreds of cave systems in the firelands.'

'Not like Tisaloya.' Vargo became animated as he sat forward in his chair. 'What if it wasn't the heat or the fumes or the volcanic activity, but something else altogether?'

'What?' Nino asked.

'The fireworms!' Cat exclaimed.

'Exactly,' Vargo said, smiling at her. 'Tisaloya was their breeding ground too. There were thousands of them there, remember?'

'You mean the dragons can only hatch successfully if the worms are there to help them?' Nino hazarded.

Vargo nodded.

'Perhaps the bond between them went even further than we imagined.'

'Gods,' Nino breathed. 'And I thought Angel was the strangest midwife I'd ever meet.'

'I doubt even he could help at a dragon birth,' Vargo added, still smiling. 'But the fireworms might.'

'So what does this mean?' Cabria had been following this development with increasing alarm. 'Do you want to bring fireworms here?'

'Why not?' Vargo replied. 'If we can't take the eggs to the volcanoes, at least we can bring the heat of the volcanoes to *them*!'

While the humans were talking, Eya, Ero and Vek were perched on the roof of the guest hall. They made a strange group. Although the peregrine was much larger than the other two, his plumage appeared drab by comparison – and he seemed to tolerate the company of his more colourful companions only because they too were linked. They were united now by their disquiet at having come to a place they all instinctively distrusted.

'I've been here before,' Vek said. 'My link wanted to see the dragon eggs soon after they were brought here. It's got colder since then, though.'

Ero shivered theatrically. He did not really understand what it was that made the others so uneasy about Corazoncillo, but their feelings had begun to influence his own – and he did not like to be left out of any important discussion.

'That's why the eggs don't hatch properly,' he observed knowledgeably.

'There are shadows here,' Eya said. 'We feel them even if our links do not.'

'Perhaps the hatchlings feel them too,' Vek suggested.

'They are alone,' the falcon went on. 'Their parents abandoned them. How can they thrive?'

Before anyone had a chance to answer his question, they were interrupted by a wordless chattering from far above. All three looked up, but only Eya's peerless eyesight saw the dark streak in the sky.

'Soo comes.'

'Here?' Ero was rather afraid of Ico's sparrowhawk.

'She flies to the eggs,' Eya replied. 'She bears their marks.'

'Should we greet her?' Vek asked. He had never met Soo, and was not aware of her reputation.

'She'll come to us if it is necessary,' Eya said.

All three watched as the newcomer circled round above the distant square, then dipped down out of sight, presumably approaching the eggs. A few moments later she reappeared and flew directly towards their perch. When she alighted, the others were all aware of the fierce light in her eyes, and the dark streaks in her plumage seemed more prominent than ever.

'The hatchling?' she asked.

'It died,' Eya answered. 'It was a weak and feeble thing.'

Soo ruffled her feathers and twitched, glaring about her. Ero tried to make himself as small as possible.

'I kept my part of the bargain,' Soo declared, apparently speaking to no one in particular. 'Why leave us now?'

The other birds glanced at each other, but remained silent.

'Is it so far from the heavens?' Soo asked. 'Or is your eyesight clouded?'

'What's she talking about?' Vek whispered to Eya, but he had no chance to answer.

'Omens!' Soo exclaimed. 'I am sick of omens. I have flown with the dragon spirits. Which of *you* will do so?'

No one volunteered.

'Perhaps Pajarito can help,' Vek suggested timidly, 'if it's omens you're concerned with.'

'Fool!' Soo snapped. 'We go there only when we are called. The sky sings a different song now.'

The oriole flinched, and offered no more advice. Soo turned to Eya.

'Your link is closest to understanding. Tell him—'

The sparrowhawk broke off abruptly as all four birds felt the air stir, an invisible breeze ruffling their feathers and their minds. The door of the guest hall had been opened, and now they heard it close again. Allegra appeared below them, walking slowly away from the building. She took several deep breaths, ran her fingers through her bedraggled hair, then turned around and was about to go back inside when she spotted four pairs of avian eyes fixed upon her. For a moment she stared back, puzzled, but then Ero called softly in greeting and she smiled. Raising a hand, she waved tentatively, before returning to her human companions.

'She was the one who called!' Soo whispered.

'Yes! She drew us all together,' Eya agreed. 'She gave us purpose.'

'The dreaming?' Vek exclaimed. 'I felt that too, but . . . She isn't even linked.'

Soo turned her unnerving gaze upon Ero.

'Were you with her?' she demanded.

'Yes . . . No . . . The noise hurt. I don't know anything.' The hoopoe began hopping from one foot to the other in his agitation. 'My toes burned.'

Soo made a chattering noise of disgust, then unfurled her powerful wings and swooped away from the roof. Her parting words as she rose into the sky were directed at Ero and Eya.

'Tell your links to come back to Teguise. There is much to discuss.'

'Soo's here,' Cat announced as she re-entered the cabin.

'Ico must have got your message,' Nino remarked to Cabria.

'Quick work,' the village elder said approvingly.

'Eya will tell her what's happened,' Nino added. 'The news will get back to Teguise soon enough.'

After that no one seemed to have anything more to say, and the gathering broke up. Their discussion of the implications of the hatchling's death, and the possible ways of preventing a repetition, had gone on for some time. Vargo had almost convinced them that fireworms were the answer, but they were still no further forward. No one knew where to find the elusive creatures. The only thing that had changed was that now they had two reasons to keep on trying.

That evening, as Allegra completed her regular dressing of Vargo's wound, they told Nino about their exploits. When they came to the part about the ravine and, more especially, the episode where Cat had been able to crush the tainted fireworm, Nino realized that several more of the images from his dream had been explained. He told the other two what he had experienced.

'It was as though the whole network – not just the bits I've seen – woke up for a few moments,' he concluded. 'It came alive, and it looks as if you were the ones who caused it.' He was excited now.

'And you all gave me the strength to kill it?' Cat said doubtfully.

'I felt the purpose, the need, but at the time I didn't know what it was. That's what brought us all together.'

'All *that* to kill one fireworm?'

'And to save the two of you.'

'But I didn't *do* anything,' Allegra protested. 'I'm not even linked.'

'You must have done something,' Nino insisted. 'You or Vargo.'

'Don't look at me,' Vargo said. 'I don't remember anything.'

'Well, whoever it was, we have to find out exactly what happened. This could be the key to *everything*. With that sort of power to call on, there's nothing we couldn't do.'

They discussed the possibilities for a long time, but did not reach any firm conclusion. Nino would have continued all night but Vargo was exhausted, and called a halt – at least for the time being.

'Perhaps the network's not ready yet,' he said, yawning. 'All we can do is keep on working. But right now I'm going to bed.'

The next morning, Nino and Cat were up well before Vargo and met over breakfast.

'Here we are again,' she remarked.

'We have to stop meeting like this,' he said, and smiled.

'Why? I rather like it. You're one of the few people who seem to be able to make sense of my life. Which is more than I can!'

'I didn't get far last night.'

'But you tried.'

'You know, I've been thinking,' Nino went on. 'It could have been *where* you were, rather than what you did.'

'In the caves, you mean?' she replied wearily.

'Yes. Vargo knew the place with the dragon fossil was important, and the ravine is obviously one of the intersections of the network.'

'Well, I'm not going back there unless I have to,' Cat stated determinedly.

Nino accepted this in silence, recognizing her need to distance herself from her ordeal.

'So where will you go next?' he asked eventually.

'Teguise. Ero told Vargo that Soo wants us to go back.'

'Eya told me the same thing,' Nino said, nodding contentedly. 'We can travel together.'

'Good.' Allegra smiled. 'To be honest, it's a relief to be returning to the city. At least we're not likely to be attacked by fireworms there.'

# CHAPTER THIRTY

Galan Zarzuelo had taken to spending more and more time on the observation platform of his watchtower. The lookouts posted there had initially taken his presence as a veiled insult, an indication that their leader did not trust them to carry out their duties properly. Now they just assumed – correctly – that he wanted to see the arrival of any ships for himself.

Before Lamia had left to continue her voyage to Uga Stai, she had promised that she would either return or send a message to Zarzuelo 'within a month of this day'. That month was almost over, and if neither Lamia nor her messenger arrived during the next three days, the alliance would be meaningless. After all, if she could not keep this simple promise, what chance was there of her honouring any of the others?

Worse still, if no one came, Zarzuelo would be disgraced, made to look a fool among the brethren. After the decisive vote, the other fleets had left the atoll, each pirate leader giving an undertaking to send at least one ship back twelve days later, to be advised of any further developments. That deadline would expire the day after tomorrow – and representatives of all his rivals would therefore be present when – if – Lamia failed to abide by her oath. After such a humiliation, even the Survivor's own men might well lose faith in him.

Outwardly he remained ebulliently confident, emphasizing the glory that lay ahead, but in his private moments Zarzuelo wondered nervously whether he had bitten off more than he could chew. If any of his men saw the uncertainty underlying his behaviour – especially in his frequent visits to the tower – they had the good sense not to mention it.

Of course, the pirate chief had not been content simply to wait. A number of his own ships had been despatched on various missions – to spy out the coastlines of both Tiguafaya and the Empire, to gather intelligence on the movements and strengths of their respective naval forces, and to keep a discreet eye on the other pirate fleets. Some of these vessels had already returned, but had reported nothing out of the ordinary. So when a fresh sail was spotted, approaching from the northwest, Zarzuelo was keen to know the ship's identity and to hear what her crew had to say.

'It's the *Dawn Song*,' the lookout said, a few minutes later. 'Jon Zophres' ship.'

'I know who it is,' Zarzuelo snapped. 'What's he doing here so early?'

'Perhaps he couldn't resist your hospitality,' Yawl suggested with a grin.

'Bring him to me as soon as they drop anchor,' the Survivor ordered. 'I want him where I can keep an eye on him.'

Lamia could not see the stars beyond the brilliant blue of the morning sky, but she could feel them. Ever since the black fleet had sailed, she had watched the heavens and read the signs written there. As always with such things it was a matter of careful interpretation, and the ambiguity of some of the messages made her feel slightly uneasy. The stars pointed clearly to her continuing mission, to her journeying, and even to the alliance with the pirates. They foretold battles at sea, and victory, but her destiny after that was clouded, with several aspects she did not understand.

On a more mundane level, the stars also told her that the month since her meeting with Zarzuelo was almost over. Her captain assured her that they would reach the atoll in time, but she could not help wondering –with a certain degree of amusement – how their arrival so close to the self-imposed deadline would affect the mood of the pirate leader. Zarzuelo was both proud and vain, mindful of his status and dignity even though he was a barbarian, and having to rely on others – especially strangers who were led by a woman – would not sit easily with him. On the other hand, she was confident of his ability to lead his own forces, driven as he was by an overweening belief in his own importance and the necessities of fate, as well as by the greed that was a universal characteristic of all such men. Lamia despised him, but recognized his usefulness.

Beneath her feet the black wood of the deck shuddered and swayed as the ship ploughed on through the waves. Lamia looked around, checking that the other seven vessels were still keeping pace with her own, and wondered how her fellow anti-mages, the most powerful talents the Amagiana could provide, were faring. For many of them it was their first experience of life at sea, the first journey outside their homeland. For a few it was also the first time outside the cloistered realm of their walled academy, and, for them especially, the vast open spaces of the restless ocean must seem intimidating. However, Lamia had no doubts about their ability to perform their duties admirably when the time came. Each of them was driven not only by an unshakeable belief in the righteousness of their cause, but also by a burning desire to avenge the fate of the Martyr. Lamia was proud to be one of them, and would be prouder still when they returned home in triumph. She recalled Vitrahk's parting words.

'They are yours to command, Emissary. Let your faith guide you.'

'And the stars,' she had replied, as convention demanded.

'Then no harm can befall you,' he had said, completing the ritual exchange. 'Fare you well, my child.'

That had been six days ago. Two more would pass before the fleet reached the pirate islands – which would be their first sight of land since the coastline of their native land had sunk beneath the eastern horizon – and Lamia was eager to begin work. The voyage was becoming tedious and had been entirely uneventful, except for one thing. After their first night at sea, Lamia had woken to find that the huge white birds were back. There were seven of them now, and although they had flown over each of the ships, as if inspecting them, it was always her vessel they returned to. Every morning she looked for them and every morning they were there, gliding effortlessly through the air. No one knew what their presence signified.

'You've no news, then?' Zophres said.

'Not yet,' Zarzuelo replied, trying his best to sound unconcerned. 'Have you?'

'As a matter of fact, I have. The Empire won't be making any move against Tiguafaya just yet.'

'Why not? How do you know this?'

'Madar is getting married, at the next full moon. Nothing will be decided before then, however much Tzarno would like it to be.'

'The full moon's not so long away,' Zarzuelo said, after a

quick mental calculation. 'I doubt it'll cause much delay.'

'I'll let you know.'

'*You'll* let me know?' the Survivor exclaimed. 'I suppose you're in Madar's confidence, then.'

'Of course,' Zophres replied, grinning. 'I've been invited to the wedding.'

The *Dawn Song* left that same afternoon, but another of Zophres' ships arrived two days later, together with Endo, Snake and the other pirate leaders. They had made good on their promise. All that remained was to see whether Lamia would do so as well.

For appearances' sake, Zarzuelo could no longer spend time in the lookout tower, so when the message came that the black fleet had been sighted he was with many of his guests in the feasting hall. He allowed himself only a small smile, not wanting to betray his relief, and suggested that they go up to see the arrival for themselves.

The eight black craft made an impressive, sinister spectacle as they entered Goat Channel in single file, like empty shadows moving across the face of the earth.

'Not much of a fleet,' someone commented.

'Their strength is not in numbers,' Zarzuelo told them. 'We're supplying the sword-arms. They're here to fight magic.'

'Still got their pets, I see,' Snake remarked, indicating the albatrosses.

'The mollymarks haven't done them – or us – any harm so far,' the Survivor pointed out, even though he was not immune to the general superstition, and watched the birds as uneasily as any of the others.

Later that day, a meeting was held in Zarzuelo's cabin on the *Night Wolf*. As before, Lamia was accompanied by two attendants, but this time the pirate chief was flanked by Endo, Snake and a few of the other captains. It made the cabin crowded, and introductions took some time, but eventually they settled down to business.

'Are all your forces here?' Lamia asked via her translator.

'Far from it,' Zarzuelo replied. 'The brethren of the isles do not lie idle. We can gather here within five days once I send out the call to arms. We will have a fleet of fifty-one ships,' he added grandly, 'all with a full complement of fighting men.'

If the Emissary was impressed by the size of the pirate force, she gave no sign of it when this was translated for her. She merely nodded and spoke again in her strange tongue.

'Our captains are not familiar with the waters off the coast of Tiguafaya,' the interpreter said. 'It would be useful to have one of your men join each of our vessels, to assist with navigation.'

'That can be arranged,' Zarzuelo said. He was happy with the idea, even though he was not expecting to get too many volunteers for the job. Having his own pilots on board the foreign craft would mean that he would be more likely to be able to rely upon them when they went into battle.

'Then we are ready,' Lamia decreed. 'We should send a message to Prince Tzarno in Uga Stai.'

'He's not there,' the pirate leader replied, revelling in the opportunity to display his superior intelligence. 'Emperor Madar is to marry at the full moon, and the prince will be in Zepharinn until then. Their forces will not move until after the celebrations.'

The Emissary did not react when this was relayed to her, but she frowned as she and her assistant exchanged further words.

'A message should be sent nonetheless,' she decided

eventually. 'They will thus be aware of our situation whenever they're ready to begin.'

'Agreed. One of your ships would probably receive a more cordial welcome in Uga Stai than one of mine,' Zarzuelo added dryly, to the amusement of his colleagues. 'But I will send a deputy with your crew, to confirm the alliance.'

Lamia nodded at this, and glanced at the other men in the room.

'Chavez,' Zarzuelo said. 'You're volunteered.'

'Aye, Captain,' the deputy responded obediently, though he sounded none too thrilled at the idea.

'The rest of your fleet may be here for some time,' the Survivor went on. 'Do you wish to come ashore?'

'No. Thank you,' the interpreter replied without consulting Lamia.

'Do you need supplies?'

'Our provisions are sufficient for the time being.'

'Then at least join me in a toast to our new venture,' Zarzuelo said, indicating an array of goblets on the cabin table and the flagon next to them.

The interpreter was about to refuse when Lamia put a hand on his arm and spoke softly. He turned back to Zarzuelo and gave a small bow.

'We will drink to the success of our mission.'

'Excellent!'

Measures were poured out and the cups handed round. The innocuous-looking liquid was known to the pirates as grog, a particularly lethal concoction of rum, brandy, wine and spices – with a little lime juice to give it some bite. The brethren were all looking forward to seeing how the foreigners handled it.

'Blood and gold,' Zarzuelo said, raising his goblet in the traditional toast.

'And the death of magic,' Lamia added, via her companion.

The Survivor tossed back his measure in full, swallowing rapidly with evident pleasure. The other buccaneers followed suit, even as they watched the easterners. The two robed men were rather more circumspect, and even though they managed not to choke, their distaste and discomfort were obvious. Several pirates began to grin, but when they looked at Lamia their smiles faded. She had drunk the entire contents of her cup as if it had been no more than water, then held it out for more. Her face was impassive and untroubled as her eyes met Zarzuelo's and, after a few moments, he burst out laughing and poured for them both.

This time they drank as comrades.

# CHAPTER THIRTY-ONE

'He's done *what*?' Ico exclaimed in horror.

'He's gone into the Empire,' Kehoe repeated unhappily. 'He's trying to find out what their army is doing.'

Ico didn't know whether to cry or to scream. She had been waiting for a message from Andrin for so long – and now she was presented with this! The news had not even come from Andrin himself, but had been sent via Jada, then an army courier, and finally Commander Kehoe. Coming on top of everything else that had happened recently, it was a savage blow.

'There's more, I'm afraid.'

'Go on,' Ico said, her heart sinking still further.

'Apparently, Ayo saw the site of a recent eruption well inside Empire territory. Andrin told Jada he wanted to have a look at that for himself.'

Ico was astonished.

'You're sure it was on Empire land?'

'Positive,' the soldier replied. He too was aware of the implications. 'There had been some vague reports of smoke about a month ago, but it was thought to be just a bush fire.'

Ico said nothing for a while, trying to recover her composure.

'When did all this happen?' she asked eventually.

'Andrin crossed the border nine days ago.'

'Nine days! Why wasn't I told before now?' she demanded angrily.

'I'm sorry, ma'am,' Kehoe said awkwardly. 'Jada didn't tell us what was going on for a day or so. I think he was hoping that Andrin would be back almost immediately. And the lines of communication with the north are not the best. The terrain's not easy, even for camels, carrier pigeons aren't reliable in a place like that, and all the linked birds were on patrol along the border. I know that's not good enough, and steps have been taken to rectify the matter. I take full responsibility for the delay,' he added formally, as if expecting a reprimand.

Ico's mind filled with questions she knew Kehoe could not answer.

'It's not your fault, Ardell,' she said at last. 'My husband would never have made a good soldier. Discipline is not one of his strong points. There's no way you could have anticipated this – but I'd appreciate being kept informed on a regular basis from now on.'

'Of course, ma'am. The border posts are all on constant alert, and the moment we learn anything there's a relay of linked birds ready to fly.'

'No one's seen Ayo, I suppose?'

'No. Jada said he went with Andrin.'

Ico felt a surge of anger that she did her best not to reveal. Surely Andrin could have sent her a message via Ayo? Then again, at least this meant that Andrin was not entirely alone in his venture. Although the eagle could not protect him from every one of his rash impulses, he might be able to temper them a little – and provide her husband with some support.

'So he could be anywhere by now?' she concluded.

Kehoe nodded.

'He might even be back in Tiguafaya. Even the birds would take a while to get a message back here.' The hopeful tone in his voice sounded forced.

'I'd like to think so, Commander,' Ico told him resignedly, 'but I rather doubt it.'

After Kehoe left her, Ico fell into a round of morbid speculation. From the report, it seemed likely that the site of the eruption was no more than a day's travel north of the border. Most of the imperial army camps were not much further away, so the fact that Andrin had still not returned implied one of two things. Either he had ventured further afield, or he had been detained against his will. She preferred not to dwell on the second possibility, and told herself that her wilful husband was probably halfway to Uga Stai by now. Probably having the time of his life, she thought bitterly, while I sit here and wait. Ico recognized that a small part of her wished their roles were reversed – or, better still, that the two of them were exploring enemy territory together. They had always worked better as a team.

Kehoe's only piece of good news concerned the apparent inactivity of the imperial army. Having established their bases, they appeared to be doing nothing further. It seemed that no invasion was imminent, even though no firm news had come out of the Empire for some time. They had still not heard from Madri, and their other contacts had reported only vague and often contradictory rumours. If war was coming, it was treading softly and without haste.

Ico's mind returned to Andrin, wondering what fool-hardy scheme he had hatched now. Where are you, my love? she wondered. You idiot. If it had been possible she would have sprouted dragon wings there and then, and flown north to seek him out. But that was not permitted.

Nine days ago, she thought dismally. That had been a particularly fateful day – the day Ysanne and Tas had had their prophetic nightmare, and the day the dragon had been born and died. Even though this had not been entirely unexpected, it was still depressing to have had their worst fears confirmed. The only consolation had come from Soo's telling her that Vargo, Cat and Nino were all on their way back to Teguise. They should arrive soon now, and Ico would at least be able to share her problems with friends.

The day after Soo's return, they had suffered another dreadful setback, when Tao died without ever regaining consciousness. Here again the news had not been unexpected, no matter how hard they had prayed for his recovery, but Maciot had been – and still was – distraught. Although Ico had her own sadness and fears to cope with, she had tried to console her advisor, telling him that he would soon find another link, even though she knew that this idea – however logical it might be – was no help at all. There would be no miraculous reunion for Maciot and Tao, as there had been for her and Soo, and no future link would ever wholly replace the loss of one that had lasted for so long. Maciot was a shell of a man now, devoid of any real feeling or purpose. He had never married, and Tao had been his only true companion for many years. For their bond to have been severed in so cruel and arbitrary a manner seemed horribly unfair.

On the other hand, life had to go on. Even if Ico had been robbed – for a while, at least – of the services of her trusted advisor, there was no escaping her own responsibilities. With Tao gone, they had lost their last real hope of learning more about the fireworm cult. Giavista Martinoy had disappeared. He had not been seen for some time, and the organization he was supposed to lead had also gone very quiet. If there had been any gatherings recently, they had successfully evaded the attentions of both Maciot's network of informers – which was still functioning, if less efficiently – and the chivaree. It was almost as though the cult had actually reverted to being the figment of their imagination Ico had once believed it to be. Even the gossip was dying down. However, Ico did not think they had heard the last of Martinoy and his supposed experiments. Perhaps, she thought hopefully, Vargo will be able to find out what's going on. After all, he had been searching for the fireworms for a long time now, and had surely developed an affinity for their ways – in spite of his lack of success so far.

At least the volcanoes had been relatively quiet recently. Respite from one quarter was welcome. Even so, Ico felt that an eruption would simply be one more aspect of the complete shambles that her life – both personal and professional – had become.

*The dragon spirits touched you*, Soo declared. *Can't you see what's happening?*

Ico sensed her link's repressed anger, but didn't understand the reason for it.

*I don't know what you mean*, she replied helplessly.

*The shapes in the sky are distorted. How can the dreaming go well?*

*What shapes?*

*The ones we form together*, Soo replied impatiently. *The sky's dreaming will be the end of all things.*

*Tell me what I can do*, Ico pleaded, dismayed by the sparrowhawk's fatalism.

*I see only my omens. And I will not be with you for long.*

*What?* Ico cried, thoroughly alarmed now. *What do you mean?*

Soo did not answer, but flew away, leaving Ico to fret. She

was still there, sitting on a stone bench in one of the palace courtyards, when her next visitor found her.

'Ico?'

She looked up, raising her chin from cupped hands.

'Alegranze. Come and sit with me.' Ico forced herself to smile.

Maciot did as he was told, moving stiffly, like an old man. His eyes were filled with a strange, unhealthy light, and were rimmed with red.

'Am I disturbing you?' he asked quietly.

'Only from thoughts I'd rather not have,' she replied, wondering whether he was paying a social call or had something to tell her. Whichever it was, she was determined to wait patiently. Maciot was trying hard to deal with his pain, and she owed him too much to discount his suffering.

'I've more bad news, I'm afraid,' he said.

Ico groaned inwardly, but steeled herself not to let her dread show.

'What it is?'

'One of the chivaree who was working for us has been found dead.'

'Murdered?'

'Not exactly,' Maciot replied heavily. 'He'd been eaten by a fireworm.'

The next day brought Ico some much-needed relief. One of the camel patrols she'd sent out in the hope of speeding her friends' journey returned with three very weary travellers. Vargo, Cat and Nino were all unkempt and dirty from their long days on the road, and were delighted by the prospect of comfortable accommodations in the palace guest rooms. However, they all knew that before they could rest or get themselves cleaned up, they had to bring Ico up to date. For her part, Ico was almost overjoyed to have some old friends

– people she loved and trusted – to share her burdens for a little while. After hugging each of them, she arranged refreshments, summoned Maciot, and led them to one of the larger reception rooms so that they could relax while they exchanged their news. Although she half expected Maciot not to join them, he arrived quickly, doing his best not to let his depression show. Ico was glad he had come, hoping that the meeting might take his mind off his own loss for a while. She had not had time to warn the others, but Maciot's care-worn appearance did not go unnoticed.

'Are you all right?' Cat asked solicitously.

'Tao's dead.' His voice was flat, toneless.

'Oh, gods!' Cat exclaimed, stricken. 'How did that happen?'

'We don't really know,' Ico said, when Maciot did not reply.

'I'm all right.' It was a brave but transparent lie. 'Life goes on. I want to hear your news.'

That was virtually the last contribution Maciot made to the conversation. No one knew what to say to him, and so they took him at his word. Throughout the ensuing discussion he appeared to be listening intently – and even made some notes – but he barely spoke at all, and let Ico ask all the questions.

At her prompting, the travellers began by giving a full account of the birth and death of the dragon, then described Vargo's theories about the eggs and fireworms, and the various impressions that they – and their birds – had received while in Corazoncillo. Vargo and Cat told her of their explorations, concentrating on the extraordinary events in the western ravine. Then Nino took over, relating how the events there had apparently interacted with his own efforts to create a vast network of links. There was much to consider, and Ico had countless questions, but she knew it was her turn to bring them up to date. And so, somewhat reluctantly, she told them about the disastrous visit of Ambassador Kudrak, about the threat of war with the Empire and the subsequent efforts made to try to avert that threat. Not unnaturally, this news came as a considerable shock to her friends. They had grown used to thinking of the volcanoes as the main danger to Tiguafaya, and were horrified to find that the Empire – far from helping them with this problem as they had hoped – was possibly going to pose another, equally deadly threat.

'With any luck we'll hear from Madri soon,' Ico added. 'He may even be on his way home as we speak. Then we'll know what we're facing.'

No one said anything, as they were still trying to come to terms with what they had just learnt, so Ico took a deep breath and continued.

'Of course, Madri's not the only one working in the Empire on our behalf. Andrin has seen fit to set out on an expedition of his own, overland.'

'Alone?' Nino asked incredulously.

'Yes.' She told them of the efforts made to patrol the northern border, and gave the few details Kehoe had been able to pass on about Andrin's disappearance. Although she managed to keep her voice even and calm, she knew when she looked into Vargo's eyes that he had not been fooled. The compassion she saw there reminded her of an earlier time, when the friendship between herself, Andrin and Vargo had been the most important thing in her life. 'The gods know where he is now,' she concluded.

Once again, no one knew how to respond.

'Andrin can look after himself,' Nino said eventually. 'I'm sure he'll be back soon.'

'I'm sure he will,' she said, hoping this was true. 'I just wish . . .' She shrugged, leaving the thought unfinished.

'Right now, there's nothing we can do about the Empire. We just have to wait. In the meantime, we've had some problems here in Teguise.' Ico gave them a report on the rumours surrounding the fireworm cult and its elusive leader, the incident in Ysanne's nursery, and finally the death of the chivaree the day before. She glanced at Maciot every so often, both to check whether he wanted to contribute anything and to see how he was bearing up. There was no proof that Tao's investigation of the cult had led to his death, but she and Maciot had both been assuming that there must be some connection. Although he rarely met her eyes, and said nothing, her friend did not seem unduly distressed.

'The only fact we're sure of is that there's *something* going on – though we don't know what or why – and that there *are* some worms in Teguise. Beyond that it's all guesswork. There's no sign of the creature that killed the chivaree, but the body was left in the open. No one made any attempt to hide it. It was almost as if they wanted us to find him.'

'Sending us a message?' Nino suggested.

'Probably,' Ico agreed. 'But what?'

'Perhaps he got too close to their secret.'

'The attack implies that the worm was tainted,' Vargo said, going straight to the heart of the problem. 'Even if they *are* being bred here, they're not the ones we're looking for.'

'Unless the cult is responsible for corrupting the worms after they're born,' Cat said. 'We don't know what their motives are.'

'It's more likely they're born bad,' Vargo responded. 'There are too many people here in the city, and the influence of everyone's fears would be too strong. I still think we're more likely to find untainted swarms in remote areas.'

'But if we knew *how* it was being done, perhaps we could control the process,' Allegra persisted. 'We could even try it ourselves – shield them from harmful influences, protect them with our own beliefs, if you like.'

'I did wonder if the cult might be a blessing in disguise,' Ico said, trying to ignore Maciot's tortured, incredulous expression. 'Do you think there's any chance they might be able to help you?'

'I doubt it,' Vargo replied.

'There's no proof the worms are being bred here,' Nino pointed out. 'They could be bringing them in from outside.'

'Well, either way, the search for fireworms is our paramount task,' Ico concluded. 'For a number of reasons. We've done everything we can about the Empire for the time being, so I want to devote all our available resources to finding the worms. Unless we solve the problem of the volcanoes, there may not be much of Tiguafaya left for us to defend.'

Later that afternoon, after giving him a chance to bathe and rest for a while, Ico went to see Nino. They talked again about the network and his dream experience – something she could relate to easily enough – then turned to something that had been preying on her mind for a while.

'Would you and Eya talk to Soo for me?' she asked. 'She's been so odd recently. I know everyone's under a lot of pressure, but she's angry all the time, and she won't talk to me – or at least when she does, I can't make sense of it – but I've a feeling it's got something to do with this network of yours.' The words came out in a rush, as if she was ashamed to admit her failure. 'Will you speak to her?'

'I can't promise anything,' he replied, 'but I'll try.'

'And will you talk to Ysanne and Tas?'

'Are they having problems too?'

'I'm not sure. It's just a feeling. Ysanne seems to be scared of magic now, and I think that's my fault. She may be able to tell you what's going on. If she and Tas dreamed together about the dragon eggs, they may have seen more, perhaps even been part of *your* dream.'

'They must have been,' Nino said. 'All the links were.'

Then why didn't *I* feel it? Ico wondered, but kept the thought to herself.

'Of course I'll talk to them,' Nino went on. 'If you think it'll help.'

'They like you. Ysanne often talks about her Uncle Nino.' It was a slight exaggeration, but one she felt justified in making. 'How's your baby?'

'Growing fast,' he replied, with a touch of regret.

'This will all be over one day,' she told him. 'Then you can be with Tavia and your son.'

This time it was Nino's turn to remain silent, his thoughts obviously far away.

'Do you think,' Ico began tentatively, 'that there's any chance you could communicate with Andrin or Ayo through the network?'

'Now, you mean?'

She nodded, unable to hide her anxiety any longer.

'I doubt it,' Nino said ruefully. 'It might be something we could do in the future, but not now. Not yet. If we're right, the whole network only came to life when Vargo and Cat were in grave danger, in a specific place. No one knows how to re-create those conditions. Before that, everything I achieved was just bits and pieces, and the parts that work best are always with the birds who normally fly in flocks. Lines between individuals are harder to integrate. And if Andrin and Ayo are so far away . . . I'm sorry.'

'Will you try anyway?' Ico persisted. 'I really need to know if he's all right.'

'I'll try,' Nino promised.

'I didn't mean to land you with all these extra problems.'

'That's what friends are for. You're not alone in this, Ico. We'll all help in any way we can.'

'Thank you.' She kissed his cheek, taking comfort from his words.

'Can I come in?'

Vargo was lying on the bed in his room, wearing only a towel tied round his waist. At first Ico thought he might be asleep, but he opened his eyes and grinned.

'I'm not dressed for receiving the President.'

'Then pretend it's just me,' she said, walking into the room.

He sat up, watching as she sat in the only chair available.

'I . . .' Ico hesitated. 'I wanted to tell you something else about the fireworm cult.'

'What?' Vargo had the feeling that this wasn't what she'd been going to say.

'I had a dream about it. There were coloured worms, and people in grey robes, and you were in it too.' She chose not to mention that he had been naked. 'You called out to them – "I need your help." So I wondered . . .'

Vargo thought about this. He knew Ico had had prophetic dreams before, but they had always been quite specific. This seemed very vague.

'It's probably nothing,' she ended lamely.

'That's not what you really came to talk about, is it?'

'It could be important,' she began, then faltered. 'No. I suppose not. It's good to see you again, Vargo.' She paused again, aware of his steady gaze. 'How are you?'

'I'm fine. It's wonderful just to feel clean again. How are *you*?'

'Miserable.'

'Why?' he asked, when she didn't go on.

'Oh, everything. I never wanted all this. Sometimes I think

agreeing to run for president was the most stupid thing I've ever done.'

Vargo had expected her to mention Andrin's absence, but she stopped there.

'You've never been one to back away from a fight,' he said.

'I'm still not. It just gets so lonely sometimes.'

'You've plenty of friends, all around you,' he pointed out. 'People who love you.'

'I know. But just lately it seems that the ones who are the most important to me are never here when I need them.'

'I'm here now,' he said softly.

It was dark by the time Allegra returned to the palace. As soon as she had been able to wash the dust of the firelands from her skin, and dress in clean clothes, she had gone to visit her parents, who lived in one of the poorer areas of the city, not far from the docks. They had been delighted to see her, and had listened avidly to her greatly abbreviated version of her travels. She had shared their frugal evening meal, though she was not really hungry, and had answered their questions as best she could. Her mother assumed that she would be sleeping at their home that night, but her father had known better, and had cut short his wife's attempt to dissuade Cat from leaving.

'It's her life, Mother. Let her do what she has to.'

Allegra had gone, promising to return, but feeling guilty nonetheless. Now, as she made her way towards the guest quarters, she could not help thinking of the way Vargo and Ico had looked at each other during the meeting, and wondered whether she should read anything more into those glances.

When she reached Vargo's room, and looked in through the open door, she saw him sitting on a stool, stripped to the waist. Ico was standing behind him, a pair of scissors in her hand. Locks of his brown hair, which had grown quite long, lay on the floor. They were both laughing. It was a perfectly innocent scene, but to Cat there was an intimacy about it which she felt like a dagger in her heart. She was about to slip away when Vargo spotted her.

'Hello, Cat,' he said, grinning happily. 'What do you think?' He ran his fingers through his newly cropped hair.

'You're as handsome as ever,' she replied, forcing herself to smile.

'How are your parents?'

'They're fine.'

'I should be going,' Ico said. Her smile of welcome had been tinged with regret, and there was an uncertainty in her voice that made Cat think she was hoping Vargo would tell her to stay.

He said nothing, however.

'Goodnight,' Ico said quietly, and she and Vargo kissed each other on the cheek. Their eyes met for only an instant, but it was long enough for Cat to imagine all sorts of silent messages passing between them.

When Ico had gone, Allegra stood uncertainly just inside the door, while Vargo knelt on the floor and collected all the hair into a small heap. His bare torso glistened in the lamplight.

'We should get some sleep,' Cat said.

'After what we're used to,' he replied, standing up and brushing off his hands, 'these beds will be so comfortable we'll probably never wake up.'

'Goodnight, then.'

'Goodnight, Cat.'

She turned to go to her own room, only to hesitate when he spoke again.

'Cat?'

'What?' she asked and waited, hoping.

'Nothing,' he said eventually. 'See you in the morning.'

Some hours later, Allegra lay on her own bed, still wide awake. She had begun by feeling sorry for herself, and had gone on to feel angry with Ico for being so perfect, and was now cursing her own cowardice. She had had Vargo to herself for months. Why was it now, when they were back in Teguise, under Ico's roof, that she suddenly saw how foolish she had been? Go and wake him up, she told herself. Tell him how you feel. How else is he supposed to know? It should be obvious, even to him, another part of her brain argued. He isn't a child.

This internal debate went on for some time, going round in ever-decreasing circles, until she knew she'd get no sleep unless she did something about it. Getting out of bed, she wrapped a robe around herself and felt her way over to the door. A lamp burned low in the corridor, and she reached Vargo's room in a few silent steps. The door opened quietly, and she listened while her eyes adjusted to the gloom inside. By the time she was able to see, her ears had already told her all she needed to know.

Vargo's bed was empty.

Cat was woken early the next morning, after what seemed only minutes since she had finally cried herself to sleep. Amid the general bustle of activity outside her room, she was able to gather that Madri's ship had docked at first light, and that he and Angel were on their way to the palace. When she had dressed, and splashed cold water on her face in a vain attempt to stop herself looking quite so wretched, she hurried to the conference room. Ico and Vargo were already there, together with Nino, Maciot, Commander Kehoe and Admiral Cucura. Madri and Angel arrived a moment later, and their grim expressions did nothing to relieve the already tense atmosphere.

'Are we at war?' Ico asked bluntly.

'Not yet,' Madri replied.

As succinctly as possible, the ex-admiral told them the situation as it had been when he left Zepharinn. Then, when they had had a chance to absorb this, he described his meeting with the inner council, what he had observed in the imperial capital, and the rumours he had heard.

'I feel I've let you down,' he concluded. 'I should have waited until they reached a decision, but it was beyond my strength. They won't even begin to discuss it until after the wedding – and only the gods know how long the debate will take.'

'So we're back where we started?' Ico said.

'Pretty much,' he admitted despondently. 'I'm sorry.'

Some further half-hearted discussion followed, and the rest of the morning was spent bringing Madri and Angel up to date on what had taken place while they'd been away. The death of the dragon caused the most impact. Angel was mortified, at one point wailing like a child. Although they calmed him down, his misery remained, and he claimed to have known something was wrong at the time.

'I should have been there. I told you. I was needed there, not in Zepharinn!' He looked at Madri, accusation in his mismatched eyes.

'You couldn't have done anything,' Nino told him.

'We didn't know it was coming, Tre,' Vargo added. 'Nobody did.'

'We'll organize things better next time,' Ico said, wondering what Angel could possibly have done to help the hatchling.

The discussion went on and on, but there was little that Allegra was not already familiar with, and she took no part in the continuing conversation. After a while she stopped listening too, and simply watched Vargo and Ico – noting every glance that passed between them, every word directed to the other, every gesture and expression. She saw telltale signs in all of them – and found herself torn between love and hate. Voices that weren't there began crowing in her head, tormenting her.

At least now I know what it's like, she thought, vaguely aware of a certain irony amid her anguish. I'm going mad.

# CHAPTER THIRTY-TWO

On the same day that Madri returned to Teguise, two different travellers reached Zepharinn after long and arduous journeys.

Orazio Guern moved like a sick animal, stumbling frequently as he dragged himself along, alive only because his will to survive was instinctive. He was painfully thin, weak from hunger and half blind from exhaustion, and his once sturdy clothes were now little more than a collection of soiled rags. He was filthy, and his bare feet – his shoes had been stolen several days earlier – were cut and bruised, encrusted with blood and dirt.

It had taken Orazio almost a month to reach the imperial capital, and for much of that time he had not known where he was or where he was going. He had existed only on the variable charity of those he met along the way, and on his own developing talent as a scavenger – eating whatever he could beg, find or steal, and sleeping wherever he could when darkness came. During his journey he had encountered some kindness, especially when his story about the fire from below the earth had been believed. But more often he had been spurned, called all sorts of names – of which 'madman' was the least hurtful – and learned to keep his distance. Yet he never forgot his purpose, the reason he had been spared when the rest of his family had been killed, and it was his search for retribution that had driven him on. He had eventually begun to hear mentions of the half-mythical city of Zepharinn, the seat of all power, and knew that there, if anywhere, he would find justice. Then he heard another name, whispered with increasing fervour by the people he met, and he began to beg not for alms but for news of the Prophet, the man who was going to save the empire from evil. These whispers had finally led him to Zepharinn.

The citizens took little notice of Orazio – what was one more beggar, after all? – but that suited him. Being noticed rarely seemed to lead to anything good, and often meant only insult or injury. The city was bewildering, a world away from the valley that had been his home. Nothing could have prepared him for the vastness of it all, for the crowds of people, the endless rows of tall buildings, the noise and smells. Every turn revealed new wonders; every step drew him deeper into the mystery. Orazio did not belong here, and he knew it, but the dogged determination that had claimed his soul was close to fulfilment now. He felt the pull of destiny.

Andrin also entered Zepharinn on foot but, in contrast to his fellow traveller, he looked both healthy and presentable. It had taken him much less time to cover the same distance, partly because he was a much more experienced traveller – and partly because he had ridden a good deal of the way.

Stealing the horse had probably been a stupid thing to do, but it had been so easy he'd been unable to resist. The animals had been corralled at the edge of one of the army encampments, surrounded only by a flimsy, temporary fence. It was obvious that the soldiers expected no trouble in that largely uninhabited region, and the sentries on duty had grown careless. All it had taken was for Ayo to swoop down, screaming like a banshee, and a stampede had begun that soon broke through the picket, sending horses galloping in all directions. It had then been a simple matter to separate one out and drive it away from the others, beyond the attentions of the disorganized guards.

When the horse had calmed down – with Ayo keeping his distance now – Andrin had approached cautiously. The mare – whom he had subsequently named Mud, because of the dull colour of her coat – had watched him warily at first, but she was a docile creature, a pack animal rather than a cavalry mount, and he soon won her confidence. She was already wearing a bridle and reins, but no saddle, and Andrin had never ridden a horse before. However, he reckoned that it shouldn't be too difficult; after all, horses moved much more smoothly than camels. In the event he had only fallen off twice before he got the hang of it, and they made their way north at a leisurely but steady pace.

Because the horse was prominently branded with the insignia of the imperial army, Andrin had to be careful of chance encounters. He avoided towns and villages when he could, occasionally leaving Mud tethered some way outside when he needed to go closer. Navigation was comparatively easy. All roads, it seemed, led to Zepharinn, and even if using popular routes meant a greater risk of discovery – and the chance of encountering military patrols – it also meant that Andrin was able to move forward confidently. Food was a bigger problem. He had no money, and nothing to barter with, but, unlike Orazio, he was an expert scavenger. And of course Ayo was able to hunt for his link as well as for himself. Andrin had survived in the firelands; in the increasingly fertile and prosperous land of the Empire he fared well enough.

As it turned out, the risk he had taken with the horse had no unfortunate repercussions, and when they were about a day's walk from the imperial capital, he had set Mud free to wander where she would. He went on alone – apart from the eagle who, as usual, was little more than a white speck far above. Although Andrin had sometimes considered sending Ayo back to Teguise, to tell Ico what he was doing, on each occasion he had decided against it. He rationalized that this was because he needed the bird with him, but though that was partly true, the real reason was that he knew Ico would disapprove of what he was doing. And what exactly *am* I doing? he asked himself as he strode into Zepharinn. His journey had been prompted by a casual remark, and now he was beginning to have his doubts. Even finding Kantrowe – if the Prophet really was Tias Kantrowe – would be difficult enough in this huge, intimidating city which was at least ten times the size of Teguise. And even if he succeeded, and managed to avoid the bodyguards that would surely accompany such a man, would he be able to kill him – even though he was a sworn enemy – in cold blood? Andrin had no scruples about killing if the cause was just, but he was no assassin. The impulse that had brought him to Zepharinn still felt right but, as he turned another corner and found himself staring up at the imposing walls of the Imperial Fortress, he could not help wondering what exactly he was supposed to do now.

Inside the castle walls, preparations for the imperial wedding – now only four days away – were in full swing. Chamberlain Ruhail was being kept busy with matters of protocol, while Treasurer Meos and his staff were dealing with the endless financial repercussions of the decisions being made hourly by Madar and his bride. Katerin was living up to her reputation, and was turning out to be a very demanding mistress. Guests were arriving constantly from all parts of the Empire, as were a succession of merchants, all eager to offer their services and deliver their goods. The provision of food for so many extra mouths, even as the plans for the marriage feast itself were being put into place, was placing the enormous kitchens under considerable strain. The servants grumbled and complained but, like everyone else, they were caught up in the excitement of the great event. The only exception was Prince Tzarno, who held himself aloof from all the bustle and spent many hours alone, brooding. Although his patience was wearing perilously thin, he knew he had little choice but to wait. His moment would come.

The rest of the city was in an almost equal ferment. The Seax Guards, under the command of Castellan Ty, were responsible for the security of all the dignitaries attending the ceremony, and as such they had mapped out the procession routes to and from the Third Temple with great care, anticipating any potential dangers. Hierophant Otric was overseeing the redecoration of his temple, in readiness for the glittering occasion that would mark the mid-point of his month of duty, and was also rehearsing all his acolytes – the musicians and choristers, the pennant carriers and servers – who would be assisting him in the various rites.

Among the general population, a festival mood already existed, anticipating the full-scale celebrations that were to follow. The Kundahari were playing a leading role in the life of the streets, and while some onlookers considered their emphasis on the religious aspects of the forthcoming marriage to be unnecessarily austere, most people tolerated and even approved their presence. At any time of day there was bound to be at least one man, wearing the distinctive orange band around his head, preaching to anyone who would listen. However, few attracted much of a crowd, though the Prophet himself was a different matter. He appeared in public only rarely, and his speeches were much anticipated.

Thus it was that, even though his senses had been dulled by suffering, Orazio was able to learn that the Prophet would be speaking the next day in Geyan Square – and knew what he must do.

Andrin had no such sense of purpose. He too had heard the gossip, and was determined to see the Prophet, but he was not sure what to do after that. Although he told himself that this would change once he knew whether the Prophet really was Tias Kantrowe, he still had no idea what his next move should be.

The fact that he still had no money did not bother Andrin unduly. The great influx of people into the city meant that none of the many hostelries had any free rooms. Countless visitors would be sleeping in less salubrious quarters, and Andrin was happy to join them. In the end he befriended some stable lads and, in return for helping them with their chores, was able to rest in the comparative comfort of a straw-filled loft above the horses' stalls.

Before he fell asleep he thought of his wife and daughter, wondered what they were doing, and asked their forgiveness for having abandoned them for so long. For the first time since he had entered the Empire, Andrin felt homesick.

The Prophet looked round at the men gathered about him. Although he sometimes despised their attitude of almost slavish devotion, such loyalty nonetheless had its uses. The latest news, which had arrived with Derim and his group, had filled them all with righteous indignation. Their eyes shone with fanatic zeal, and the Prophet wondered how long he would be able to keep them under control – indeed, whether he actually wanted to. He and Tzarno had known of the eruption in the south for some time now, but had kept the knowledge to themselves, not wishing to antagonize Madar unnecessarily. However, it was reaching the point where it might soon be common gossip, and the Kundahari could not be kept quiet indefinitely. It was a matter of choosing his moment.

'Will you speak of it this morning?' Derim asked.

'This is a delicate matter. Alienating the secular powers will not advance our cause.' While his followers were trying to work out what he meant by this, the Prophet fixed his unnerving gaze on Derim. 'Besides, when the time is right, I feel it would be better if it came from you, as one who has seen the devastation with his own eyes.'

'Me?' Hundreds of people were expected in Geyan Square within the hour, and Derim had never spoken in front of such a crowd before. 'I am not worthy.' He nervously fingered the tiny bell that hung at his neck.

'You serve the gods, do you not?'

'I do.'

'Then what other strength do you need?'

Derim's reply went unheard as the sounds of a fierce struggle and angry shouting could be heard just outside the open door to the chamber. One of the Kundahari, who had been standing guard, peered in and gestured in apology.

'I am sorry, Prophet. This beggar—'

'I come from the valley that was destroyed!' a voice yelled desperately. 'My family was killed.' A boy was struggling in the grasp of two men. Although he had no hope of matching their strength, that did not stop him from trying.

'Shall we throw him out?' the sentry asked uncertainly.

'No. If what he says is true, then he is in need of our help. Bring him in.'

The ragged creature that appeared before them was a pitiful sight, and most of the Kundahari eyed him with considerable suspicion. All sorts of lunatics had tried to enlist the Prophet's aid for their own mad causes, and this one looked more disreputable than most.

'What's your name?'

'Orazio Guern.'

'Tell me your story, Orazio,' the Prophet said gently. His instincts had already told him that the time for disclosure had come.

'All this I have seen with my own eyes!' Derim concluded dramatically, his words ringing out over the strangely quiet square. He had begun timidly, overawed by the responsibility, but as the story of what he had seen unfolded, and the injustice of the situation made his anger rise, his voice had become louder and more passionate – and the audience, who were waiting impatiently for Kantrowe, began to pay attention to what he was saying. Now, as he finished, the silence was replaced by a muttering, a low growl that grew into a roar of anticipation when the Prophet strode out onto the dais. He eventually managed to quieten them by raising his bony hands and staring ahead with his impassive pale eyes.

'Know then that this is true.' His voice, while still thin and reedy, now cut like a knife, carrying easily to all corners of the arena. 'It is as we feared. The contagion of vile sorcery is spreading, and threatens to condemn us all.' He turned round and beckoned to someone behind him. Orazio shuffled onto the stage, still dressed in filthy rags, his eyes glazed from long torment and sudden fear. The crowd, who had been shouting, grew quiet again, staring at the boy.

'This is Orazio Guern. He is the only one of his community to have survived the eruption. All his family, his friends, his land, his home, are gone for ever. This is the fate that awaits us all! Unless we act.'

The Prophet paused again, waiting for the rumbling of the throng to die down.

'What is it you want, Orazio?'

'Justice,' the boy answered obediently, as loud as he could. Then he broke down in helpless tears, and the Prophet put a consoling hand on his shoulder.

'Justice,' he repeated. 'And retribution. I had not wanted to speak of this at such a time – a time of joy and celebration – but I can hold my peace no longer. Hierophant Otric must take note of this proof of blasphemy. The council must decide to act now, with no further delay. The spectre of war overshadows us all. But war – and justice – must come!'

With that he turned and left the stage, taking Orazio with him, while the crowd erupted in a storm of noise. As he made his way from the square, to the sound of increasingly rabid chanting and the clamorous pealing of bells, the Prophet smiled to himself. There was no way Madar would be able to ignore *this*, wedding or no wedding.

# CHAPTER THIRTY-THREE

'Look at it this way,' Vargo told Ico earnestly. 'You two have been in much worse situations than this, and you've always been all right in the end.'

'I know,' she conceded, 'but sooner or later our luck's going to run out.'

'I don't think luck has anything to do with it. You and Andrin were always meant to be together.' Vargo knew this was true, even though it cost him a great deal to say it aloud – especially after what had happened two nights ago. 'I mean,' he went on hurriedly, 'you were almost burnt at the stake and he rescued you—'

'He had a lot of help,' Ico pointed out. 'Not least from you.'

'Then when he was the Ice Mage, he was trapped inside a lava stream,' Vargo went on, undeterred. 'And you managed to pull him out!'

'Yes, but there's nothing we can do to help each other *this* time. I don't even know where he is.'

'But that's the same as when you were taken by the pirates. Andrin never gave up hope then.' This was very close to a lie, but Vargo wasn't about to admit that. 'Your predicament then was worse than anything he could be involved in now,' he argued, hoping it was true.

'At least he's not pregnant,' Ico said, with a smile.

'Trust me. *Nothing* will keep him from coming back to you and Ysanne,' Vargo declared, even as a tiny, shameful part of his mind wondered what might happen if Andrin *didn't* come back.

'And in any case, I'll always have you,' she said quietly.

'That's very true,' Vargo agreed, his tone deliberately pompous. 'I've always thought you deserved better than that great blond ox. And I have loved you faithfully since we first met.'

Ico laughed, as he had meant her to, but for the first time in her life, she knew that Vargo wasn't joking. The old warmth of their friendship had returned in full measure, combined with a new understanding, and she felt an enormous debt of gratitude towards him. He had restored at least some of her faith in humanity and love, in happiness and fate. She too had spent some time recently wondering about what might have been.

'I've missed you, Vargo,' she said fondly.

'Of course,' he replied. 'I'm a very missable person.'

The moment passed in smiles.

Nino was beginning to be unnerved by Soo's unwaving glare. He had been trying to discover what was going on inside the sparrowhawk's feral brain for some time, with a conspicuous lack of success. It did not help that their conversation had to be relayed via Eya – and that the peregrine was obviously finding the whole process very awkward – but Nino had promised Ico he would try, so he made one last effort.

*Ask Soo if she was part of the network when Vargo and Cat were in the ravine*, he said, then waited through a long exchange between the two birds.

*Yes*, Eya replied eventually.

That's it? Nothing else? Nino thought privately, glancing at his link in surprise. What was all that about then?

*Is that part of the reason she's angry?* he hazarded.

*Soo says anger is irrelevant*, Eya reported a few moments later. *When you join the sky's dreaming, no one will hear anything but the singing.*

*What does she mean?* He was beginning to see why Ico had been so concerned. Soo's pronouncements were taking on an increasingly ominous tone.

*I'm not sure.* After a pause, the peregrine added, *The last song will be lost.*

*Did Soo say that?* Nino asked, confused now.

*Yes.*

*Ask her why she told Ico she wouldn't be with her for long.*

Throughout the entire exchange Soo had kept her eyes fixed upon Nino, not even glancing at Eya, but now she blinked rapidly several times, twitched violently, and then took to the air in a single fluid motion. The interview was evidently over. In retrospect, Nino was surprised it had lasted as long as it did.

*Did she say anything else?* he asked.

*She said ' You have eyes to see. So look.'*

Oh, great, Nino thought. That's very helpful. So what am I supposed to tell Ico?

'The outposts along the border are all on full alert,' Commander Kehoe confirmed. 'As soon as there's any movement from the imperial army, we'll be able to react. The coastal stations are keeping watch too, of course.'

'We've eight ships patrolling the northern waters,' Admiral Cucura added. ' Their navy won't be able to start any major manoeuvres without us knowing.'

'If what Ambassador Madri reported is correct,' Ico said,

'that's not going to happen in the immediate future. It's still three days until the full moon, and their decision won't be made until then. But keep watching.' She paused. 'I don't suppose we've had any word from the pirates.'

'Not directly, no,' Cucura answered. 'In fact, the only thing we *have* learnt is rather worrying. Apparently Jon Zophres has been visiting the Empire quite frequently – and he's also been seen approaching Galan Zarzuelo's base.'

'There's no telling what he's up to,' Kehoe remarked sourly.

'One way and another, the atoll's been pretty busy recently,' the admiral went on. 'Lots of comings and goings, including at least one major gathering. The pirates could be planning something.'

'They've probably got wind that there might be conflict coming,' the commander said. 'They'll be looking forward to some easy pickings in the aftermath.'

'We'll see about that,' Cucura growled.

'You don't think Tzarno might be trying to enlist their aid?' Ico asked. ' With Zophres as a go-between?'

'I don't think the Empire would ever contemplate such an alliance,' the admiral replied. 'They've been fighting the pirates as long as we have.'

'The brethren of the islands are the only true free men,' Kehoe quoted sarcastically. 'It would take something quite extraordinary to make them join anyone's navy.'

Ico nodded.

'You're right.'

'Let's hope so,' Cucura added. 'We don't want Zarzuelo trying to emulate his father, do we.'

The logistical discussion ended soon after that, and when the two military men had left, Ico turned to the fourth member of the group – the now almost habitually silent Maciot.

'So, all we have to decide now is whether it's worth sending another envoy to Zepharinn.'

'Their decision would almost certainly be made before he got there,' the senator pointed out.

'Not necessarily. The debate could take a few days. If you left now, there might still be time to influence them.'

Maciot stared at her, his expression a mixture of astonishment and horror.

'Me?' he gasped eventually.

'I can't think of anyone better qualified,' Ico stated calmly. 'With your connections, you should be able to get there quickly enough. And you know more about the situation than anyone.'

'But . . .' He was still looking utterly bewildered. 'I *can't*.'

'Why not?'

'I . . .' He fell silent, shaking his head.

'I would never belittle your loss, Alegranze. You know that,' Ico said quietly. 'But this may be the last chance we have to talk to the Empire rather than fight them. I know you won't let me down.'

She faced him squarely, not letting him escape her gaze. It was a gamble, perhaps a desperate one, and she knew it. She was convinced that the mission would give him the sense of purpose that Tao's death had destroyed. And if it did not, then the repercussions probably wouldn't be too serious.

'Are you . . . sure about this?' he asked hesitantly.

'Quite sure,' she declared.

A few moments passed in which Maciot seemed to gather himself together, to become something like the dependable figure he had once been.

'All right,' he said at last. 'I'll go and get ready.'

'Uncle Nino, Uncle Nino!' Ysanne had run to him as soon as he'd entered the nursery, and he could not help smiling, seeing in her a miniature version of her mother – in both appearance and character.

'Hello, little one. How are you today?' he asked as he picked her up and swung her around.

'I'm well, thank you,' she replied, solemnly polite, as soon as she had stopped giggling with delight.

'Good.' Nino put her down, then sat on the floor so that he was at her level. 'Is Tas here?'

Ysanne glanced round, obviously talking to her link, and the firecrest appeared from behind a vase on top of one of the cupboards.

'We were playing hide-and-seek,' Ysanne explained. 'Tas is better than me because she's so small.'

'You and Tas do everything together, don't you?'

The girl nodded, and the bird uttered her piercing cry as if she too was agreeing.

'Even when you're asleep?' Nino prompted.

'You mean the dreams?' Ysanne said perceptively.

'That's right,' he said, then noticed that she had said 'dreams' and not ' dream'. 'I know about the one with the dragon egg. Have there been others?'

'Oh, yes, lots,' she replied happily. 'It's because of the singing.'

'What singing?' he asked, remembering his earlier conversation with Soo and feeling more than a little uneasy.

Ysanne's face grew very still then, and Nino saw his own anxieties mirrored in the little girl's eyes. She did not say anything for so long that he was about to prompt her again, but then she suddenly changed the subject.

'Have you seen my new boat?' she asked brightly. 'It has sails and everything.' She turned away and went to fetch her toy. It was a beautifully carved fishing boat which, Nino guessed, had been made by Andrin.

'It's very nice,' he said, admiring it dutifully before

returning to his original purpose. 'Your Mama tells me you're scared of magic. Is that right?'

Once again Ysanne's face was expressionless, and she glanced at Tas.

'It's bad,' she whispered eventually. ' Mama told me so.'

'I'm sure she didn't say that.'

'No,' Ysanne agreed, drawing out the single syllable and sounding confused. 'Not with words. But her face was all scrunched up. That's what told us.' She paused, then added defiantly, 'It's your fault, anyway. You made the singing.'

'*I* did?'

'That's where the magic comes from.'

The network, Nino realized. She's talking about all the links. Could she be in closer contact with it than I am?

'Is the singing there all the time?' he asked tentatively.

'Yes, if you listen very carefully,' Ysanne replied, nodding.

'How . . . how do you hear it?' Nino tried to fight back a small stab of envy, and told himself not to be so stupid.

'Like I hear Tas,' she answered simply.

'And the dreams come the same way?'

'Sometimes. Is that bad?'

'No. No. Definitely not.' Nino smiled to reassure her. 'Will you tell me more about your dreams?'

'Other people's music,' Vargo said reverently.

'Mirrors everywhere,' Angel responded.

The two men had met by chance on one of the palace's upper balconies, and had immediately fallen into the strange, abbreviated form of speech that made most of their conversations unintelligible to anyone else. They were looking at the sky now, watching a few fast-moving clouds racing against the blue. They were both restless, both unsure about what they were supposed to be doing, both prone to moments of hilarity and sadness. And they were both, on occasions, quite mad.

'Newness is a passage,' Vargo said.

Angel nodded.

'Life and death and river banks. I lost my oars.'

'Not your fault. They'll be new again.'

'Cloud hopes,' Angel said gravely.

They stood side by side for a while, still gazing upwards. Then Angel looked around, and seemed to come to his senses. A puzzled expression crossed his twisted face.

'Where's Ero?'

Vargo seemed surprised by the question, then glanced around himself, clearly perplexed. The hoopoe was nowhere to be seen. Vargo had no idea where his link was – and suddenly realized that there was someone else he had not seen in a long time, not since the end of the seemingly interminable meeting with Madri and Angel on the day of their return. And now, all of a sudden, he felt lost, incomplete.

'Where's Cat?' he said.

# CHAPTER THIRTY-FOUR

Finally, after a great deal of discussion and several false starts, Nino was ready. He had tried to duplicate as many of the conditions of his revelatory dream as possible, and had contacted as many of the links as he could – including everyone in Teguise and some in the surrounding districts – asking them to lend their support. Most importantly, he had spent a long time with Ysanne and Tas, trying to learn the secrets of the 'singing' and the ease with which they seemed to 'hear' it. In this respect he and Eya had made some progress, learning to listen in a completely new way. The best way he could describe it was as a sound beyond all other sounds, something that you felt rather than heard. For Ysanne and Tas the process was instinctive; he and Eya had to work on it – and even then they were only occasionally successful.

Now, as the appointed hour approached, Nino knew there was no going back. Only one aspect of the arrangements bothered him, and that was the effective absence of Vargo and Ero. The hoopoe had vanished without trace and Vargo was preoccupied with trying to find him, so their active participation could not be taken for granted. Nino could only hope that the network would include them wherever they were, because he believed that the two of them were probably vital to the attempt. However, there was nothing he could do about that now. If he tried to wait for their return, the efforts of all the others might well be wasted. As it was, he was far from certain of success.

Whatever had caused the network to spring into life before, it had not been the concerted effort he was planning now. It was quite possible that it had been something that could never be deliberately duplicated – but he knew they could not afford to wait for destiny. Even if they did not activate the entire network, there was still a chance that the experiment would help them contact Andrin. This was the primary objective, and if they could achieve that, Nino would be happy. Anything else would be a bonus.

Although he believed that his own physical location was not important to the process, he had nonetheless given some thought as to where he should be. In the end he had chosen Ysanne's nursery, mainly because he wanted a place where the little girl could be as relaxed and comfortable as possible. During their talks over the last two days, he had done much to try and allay her fears about magic. She was bound to be a little nervous, however, and Nino hoped to minimize this by keeping her in familiar territory.

There were five of them in the room as siesta time crept closer, three humans and two birds. Ysanne was stretched out on her bed, and although she seemed quite at ease, the fact that she insisted on clutching her boat to her chest made Nino wonder what was going on inside her pretty little head. The toy was almost certainly a reminder of her father, something she would perhaps be able to use as a talisman when they went in search of him. Tas was perched on the rail above her link's head, and was keeping unusually quiet and still.

Naturally enough, Ico had also insisted on being present, and she was more obviously nervous than her daughter. Nino had rarely seen his friend so agitated, and was concerned that her mood might affect Ysanne's. As president, she had been under a great deal of stress recently but, even so, Nino thought she had been acting strangely the last few days. The experiment clearly meant a great deal to her, and this made him all the more determined to do his best. The fifth member of the group was Eya, who was perched solidly on the back of a chair, apparently unruffled by the prospect before them. Compared to everyone else in the chamber, he was the personification of calm.

'Ready?' Nino asked.

Ysanne, whose eyes were tight shut, nodded and Tas let out a tiny cry.

'I'm ready,' Ico said, her voice trembling. Nino smiled at her reassuringly.

*Ready.* The peregrine's voice sounded quietly in Nino's head.

*Is Soo there?* he asked as he lay down on a blanket on the floor.

*She's still outside*, Eya reported.

Soo had refused to join them inside the nursery – something that Nino was not altogether unhappy about – but had agreed to stay close, well within her link's telepathic range.

'It's time,' Nino said aloud, and the silence in the room took on a more profound quality.

Think of the singing, he told himself, knowing that the others were all doing the same. Let it come to you. Don't rush. Relax. Let your instincts take over.

Time passed slowly, approaching the realm of dreams.

Relax.

He heard it then, a sound that was beautiful and unearthly, a song that contained every emotion he had ever known or imagined – but it was very faint, and seemed to be coming from far, far away. Melodies flickered in and out of existence, and were impossible to follow. The visions came next; some familiar, others strange, all of them brought together by the iridescent spider's web of lines and circles that glimmered and shifted constantly. It too was impossible to grasp, slipping away like the echoes of a dream as soon as he tried to hold onto something tangible. Nino sensed the effort, the reaching out, felt all the links, human and avian, willing the network into being. He recognized many friends, saw their faces and heard their hopes and wishes, their shared concern. Parts of the whole glowed strongly, but elsewhere the darkness was impenetrable, and Nino realized then that they were going to fail. What they had achieved was remarkable in itself, and in other circumstances he would have felt proud of all his colleagues. As it was, having once experienced the full glory that was possible, he knew that by comparison this was only a pale phantom. It was nothing like the power he had glimpsed, and the longer they went on trying the more energy they would waste.

*It's enough. Thank you.* He hoped that all those involved would hear him and know that he was truly grateful for their struggle, even though it had ended in disappointment.

He sat up wearily at the same time as Ysanne.

'Papa wasn't there,' she exclaimed, half indignant, half afraid.

'No, sweetheart,' Ico replied, controlling her voice with difficulty. 'We couldn't reach him.'

Nino felt his heart sink as he saw the tears brimming in his friend's eyes, and could find no words to comfort her.

Outside the window, Soo chattered wordlessly and flew away.

'But you've got to help me find her,' Vargo pleaded.

'Have you ever thought that perhaps she doesn't *want* to be found?' Ico replied. 'It's her life. Perhaps she just needs some time on her own.'

'Then why didn't she tell me where she was going? And why has Ero gone too?'

'Maybe they're together,' she said, thinking that that much was obvious at least.

'But it's been three days!' he protested. 'What if she's in trouble?'

'Look, Vargo, I don't see what I can do. You know she's not at her parents' house.'

He had the good grace to look ashamed. He had not even known where Cat's parents lived, and had had to come to Ico for help in finding out.

'We've already checked all the old Firebrand haunts, as well as anywhere else we can think of,' Ico went on. 'I can hardly ask Kehoe to detail half the city garrison to do a house-to-house search, can I? We do have other things on our minds, you know.'

Vargo looked suddenly crestfallen.

'I'm sorry. It's just . . .' He shrugged helplessly, unable to put his feelings into words. 'I'm sorry.'

Ico watched him with a mixture of fondness and irritation. With Maciot gone, she had hoped that Vargo would be able to fill his role as her chief advisor for a while, but his concern for Allegra – although it was completely understandable – seemed to have robbed him of all perspective. The fact that he had not taken a full part in Nino's experiment still rankled with Ico, and made her faint but very real feelings of resentment towards Allegra rather more obvious. She had been aware of these feelings ever since Cat had become Vargo's constant companion, and had been slightly ashamed of them. Until now.

For his part, Vargo had always sensed a certain amount of tension between the two most important women in his life, although he had never understood the reasons for it. His reunion with Ico after so long had been unexpectedly joyful but now, after only a few days, Cat's absence seemed to have left a gaping hole in his existence. The fact that Ero had gone too only added to his unease.

'Looks as if we've both been left to our own devices, doesn't it?' Ico said.

Allegra was drunk. She had been drunk for as long as she could remember. But although the wine made her head spin and her limbs do things she wasn't expecting, it couldn't stop the voices in her head. She was still miserable, still going mad.

She didn't know quite how she had come to be where she was. Beneath the city's western wall lay an area of dilapidated houses, inhabited by the flotsam and jetsam of human society. Vagrants, thieves, artists and outsiders of all kinds formed the bulk of the ever-shifting population – and Cat had felt an immediate affinity with their alienation, their supposed lack of regard for what was expected of normal citizens. She had simply lost herself, in more ways than one, and had then ended up here – in the crooked hovel that Famara had once called home.

Remarkably, it was much as she remembered it – dark and musty and bare. Only the emptiness was new. The blanket that had hung from the roof in lieu of a door was now no more than a few shreds of cloth, the bed was in tatters, and most of the shelves, where Famara had kept her jars and bottles, were broken. Anything of value was long gone, but no one was in residence. Although there were some signs that the hut had been used recently, it was too poor a dwelling for even the beggars of Teguise to want to stay very long. In her drunken state, Allegra had no such scruples. She had slumped to the floor, and had been there ever since.

Now, with her last bottle almost empty, the reality of her situation was beginning to seep into her sodden brain. The possible dangers for a young woman alone in such a place had not really occurred to her until now. She took another slug of wine to fortify herself, then froze as she sensed movement in the doorway. Moments later, her fear turned to a happy smile as the first of a rowdy gang of sparrows came hopping towards her, chattering inquisitively. She rummaged in her pockets, found the remnants of a stale crust, and fed them the crumbs. The noise level rose as they fought over the food.

'Why can' you be poli'e?' she scolded them half-heartedly, even as she laughed at their antics. They reminded her of Famara's linked clan – and that brought a flood of wonderful memories. Before long all the bread had gone and the sparrows had abandoned her, but she was still glad that they had befriended her, even if only for a little while. It was a few moments after they had gone that she realized she was crying.

The wine had begun to taste sour and she threw the dregs away, then began to make a mental list of her grievances. She railed at Andrin for not being there, at Ico for being there and *still* being perfect, at Soo for making them come back to Teguise, at Famara for being dead, at Vargo for . . .

Her thoughts faltered and spun.

'You knew, di'n't you?' she said aloud. 'Why di'n't you tell 'im? At leas' hint?' She was talking to Famara, as Vargo sometimes did, and she laughed, thinking that this was yet another sign that she was following in his footsteps down the path to madness.

Allegra was angry with all the world, but most of all with herself. And she was tired, so very, very tired.

Curled up on the remnants of Famara's pallet, Cat let herself drift away. Just before she fell asleep she thought she heard the soft call of a hoopoe, as she had done on several occasions during her wandering. When this had first happened she had looked for Ero, thinking hopefully that perhaps Vargo had come to find her. But she had seen neither the bird nor his link – and now she no longer bothered even to look. Or to hope.

Cocooned in her own despair, Cat escaped into dreams of flying.

# CHAPTER THIRTY-FIVE

Concentrate! Andrin told himself. Focus. Imagine what you want, then project it.

A pale wisp of flame blossomed in the straw in front of him. It leapt and shimmered for a few moments, then guttered out, leaving the straw unburnt. He sighed heavily.

You're going to have to do better than that, he thought. There are sources of power all around – and you're the Ice Mage! At least I was once, he amended doubtfully.

Andrin had always doubted his own magical talents, right up until the time when he had demonstrated them in an unthinking but spectacular fashion. Now he was trying to create a simple image from his own memories – the most basic spell known to wizardry – and his efforts so far had been less than impressive. Even so, he was getting tired, and knew that he could not go on for much longer. The imperial wedding was tomorrow, and dawn only a few hours away, and he would need all his strength if he was to have any chance of carrying out his plan.

He was alone that night in the stable loft, and his best hope was that when he tried again the next day, the presence of a large number of people would help his magic grow and become more potent. Experience had taught the Firebrands that the more people who witnessed a magical illusion, the more effective it would be. As far as Andrin understood it, the onlookers' instinctive belief in what their own senses were telling them reinforced the original projection, making it appear more and more substantial so that in the end it was virtually indistinguishable from reality.

That was the theory, at least. And tomorrow Andrin would be putting it to the test.

Andrin had been in a state of shock for some time after he'd seen the famous Prophet for himself. He had realized immediately that this was not Tias Kantrowe, no matter what he chose to call himself, but it was a little while before he'd been able to put a name to the familiar death's-head face. The Prophet was indeed one of those who had fled into exile from Teguise after the fall of the old government, but he had not been the leader of that regime. His real name was Mazo Gadette, a devious and clever opportunist who had once acted as an aide to the man whose identity he had now usurped.

Why had he chosen to change his name? Andrin wondered as he stood watching the performance in Geyan Square. And what had happened to the real Tias Kantrowe?

In the end he had decided that such questions were irrelevant and, in any case, he had been more concerned by the reaction of the crowd to the Prophet's words, and by the appearance of Orazio Guern, the refugee from the devastated southern valley. The onlookers had taken up his demand for war without thinking, swept along by a tidal wave of mass hysteria. It had been a frighteningly powerful demonstration of support, one which took no account of the

realities of war, nor of the consequences both for the people
of the Empire and the distant land of Tiguafaya.

Andrin had had to fight to control his own murderous
rage at such blatant manipulation, and the lies that had been
used to do it, but he had the good sense to realize that
simply killing Gadette would achieve nothing. It would
only create a martyr for the Kundahari to venerate, and
whose influence from beyond the grave would ensure a
terrible revenge. What Andrin had to do was to discredit the
Prophet in the eyes of his followers. The problem was, how
could he do that? He knew Gadette was no religious seer,
but an impostor who served only his own interests, not the
gods. Even his name was false. But Andrin could not simply
get up in public and announce these facts. Even if he
was allowed to speak, who would believe him? In the present
climate, the citizens of Zepharinn were more likely to tear
him limb from limb.

Andrin knew that the Prophet was a fraud. Ironically,
however, he had realized that the only way to convince anyone else of this was to resort to a deception of his own. And
that was when he had conceived his current plan.

Soon after the near-riot in Geyan Square, the imperial
powers that be had bowed to public pressure. A proc-
lamation, signed by First Chamberlain Ruhail himself,
had been posted by the end of the next day. It announced
that, in view of recent developments, the Imperial Council
at the High Court was already in session, preparing their
response to the situation. The necessary decisions would
be taken in due course but, in deference to the solemnity
of the occasion, these would not be announced publicly
until the evening of the full moon – after the marriage of
Emperor Madar and the Lady Katerin of Acubar. While
not meeting the demands of the most belligerent citizens,
this was enough to restore the general atmosphere of good

will, and the festivities were renewed with increased vigour.

Andrin had little doubt about the way the council debate would end, but the manner in which the results were to be conveyed to the people had given him the perfect opportunity to put his own plan into action.

As was only fitting, the day of Emperor Madar's wedding dawned bright and clear, promising fine weather for all those who were to take part in or watch the ceremonies. Even though the wedding was not due to start until noon, the route to be taken by the various processions, from the Imperial Fortress to the Third Temple, was already lined with people. Some had been there all night, wanting to be certain of a glimpse first of Madar himself and then – after a decent interval to ensure that the couple did not see each other before the appropriate moment – of Katerin. The Seax Guards were out in force, together with several other army detachments drafted in for the occasion, but for once the rapport between the soldiers and the general populace was cordial and good-natured. In spite of the recent disturbances, no one was really expecting any trouble. The romance of the day meant that all other issues would be set aside, at least temporarily.

Throughout the morning, as the crowds swelled and the temperature rose, the atmosphere remained cheerful and expectant. This was especially so around the Third Temple, where the spectators had the additional entertainment of watching all the guests arrive. The privilege of a seat within the shrine had been granted to only a few hundred people, and even the lowliest of them – those assigned to the pews near the back – were acutely aware of their elevated status. They were all decked out in their finery and most smiled proudly, acknowledging the admiration of the crowds, as they walked at a dignified pace between the guards who flanked the doors.

Among those who arrived in the middle of the morning was a strikingly handsome man in a flamboyant costume, in which bright red was the dominant colour. Although most of the onlookers did not know who he was, a few recognized him, and his name spread through the crowd in a swirl of whispers and sidelong glances.

'That's Jon Zophres.'

'The invincible one?'

'Not a scratch on him.'

'They say he consorts with pirates and princes.'

'That's right. Jon Zophres.'

'He can consort with me any time!'

If the subject of these comments was aware of the interest he had provoked, especially among the female members of the audience, he gave no sign of it – but when a familiar voice called out to him, he strode over to the cordon that marked the edge of the crowd.

'Well met, Chavez,' he said pleasantly. 'What brings you here?'

The pirate glanced at the robed man who stood next to him.

'I bring a message from the Emissary,' the stranger answered, and his exotic accent made the people near by strain even harder to hear what was being said. 'The black fleet is with our friends.'

'And we can be ready in five days after we receive word,' Chavez added. 'We tried to tell this to . . . our contact here, but he was unavailable.' He and the easterner had already been to the fortress, but had been told that Prince Tzarno was too busy to see them at present. Zophres took the pirate's meaning easily enough.

'I'll tell him,' he said. 'He'll be pleased.'

'What news from here?' Chavez asked.

'Join me in Geyan Square this evening,' Zophres replied. 'You'll learn all you need to know then.'

At last the guests were all in place, and Otric waited only for the principals to arrive. The hierophant was flushed with his own importance, but always mindful of his dignity. Although the preparations had been made with meticulous care, he still feared some mishap – an acolyte who forgot some detail of his duties, a singer who fluffed a line, any discretion against propriety among the guests . . . the list of possible disasters was endless. And then he heard the cheering outside grow louder, and knew that Madar's coach was arriving and that there was no more time to think. The rituals were about to begin.

Katerin's entrance was breathtaking. Even in the shadowed confines of the temple, the rich yellow material of her gown shone like flame, and everyone else there became moths flying in her orbit. After the initial music had been played, and the preliminary rites completed, everyone grew quiet and still, ready for the formal ceremony to begin.

And then came the next surprise, which eclipsed even the bride's entrance. In the past it had always been traditional for the Emperor to repeat the marriage vows for both partners, while his bride remained silent and submissive, a sign of her obedience to the imperial will. Katerin had other ideas, however, and when she spoke up, in a voice that was both clear and confident, the rapidly stifled gasps from the congregation did not bother her at all. Madar's smile as he watched his beloved made it obvious that he approved of this break with time-honoured convention, though others seemed less sure. Only a few people had known in advance about what was going to happen, but the news soon spread from the temple and ran through the waiting throng like wildfire. It was yet another indication that Katerin would be no ordinary Empress.

Prince Tzarno, sitting at the head of the most important dignitaries, did not know what to make of her. Paradoxically, she seemed to be the sort of woman to whom he himself would be attracted, but for the moment he could see her as nothing more than an obstacle. He had long since grown bored with the endless ceremonial, and his restlessness had been further increased by the message from Jon Zophres – relayed to him as he had entered the temple.

At least, Tzarno thought as the rituals dragged on, there won't be long to wait now. He too was looking forward to the events that were to come that night in Geyan Square.

Even as Madar and his new Empress emerged together from the temple, to massive cheers, another crowd was beginning to gather in the city's largest square. The mood here was a little less festive. The promised announcements were not due for several hours yet, but tensions were already running high. Few were in any doubt as to what was coming, but reactions to the prospect varied from elation to a little fear. The Kundahari were heavily represented among the mass of people, and many of those who had gone there simply because it would be their only opportunity to see Madar and Katerin that day were somewhat disconcerted by the grim faces beneath the orange headbands.

By the time darkness fell and the full moon was glowing brighter than all the torches and lamps below, the crush of men and women in the square was immense, and all eyes were focused on the dais where two gilded thrones had been erected. The wedding feast was over now, and the waiting would soon be over too.

A burst of cheering and applause erupted over the hum of conversation as Prince Tzarno led a contingent of court officials onto the stage. Among them First Chamberlain Ruhail, Treasurer Meos and Castellan Ty were easily recognized, as was the jubilant Otric, and each of them acknowledged the reception with varying degrees of humility and disdain. The ovation increased in volume to a huge roar of approval a few moments later, when Madar and Katerin emerged from the shadows, hand in hand. They faced the throng, smiling radiantly, then turned to ascend their thrones.

Once they were seated, the final leading actor in this as yet wordless play appeared. The Prophet walked briskly to the centre of the stage, bowed low to the Emperor and his consort, then turned to face the spectators. He was greeted with renewed cheering, but the noise gradually diminished as he held up both hands for quiet.

Far above, a pale shape, like a flying ghost, dipped towards the square.

The Prophet stared out over the sea of faces with eyes that seemed to be lit from within. He opened his mouth to speak ... and it was at that moment that the dragon swallowed him.

# CHAPTER THIRTY-SIX

Cat struggled painfully back towards consciousness. She had no idea how long she had slept, but the daylight outside the hut was bright enough to hurt her eyes. However, it wasn't the sunlight that had woken her, but the fact that a shadow had fallen across her world. A man stood in the open doorway. In Cat's bleary state he was only a silhouette against the glare, and this gave him an anonymous air of menace.

'What d'you want?' she croaked. Her tongue felt as though it was coated in feathers.

'Come with me,' the man replied. 'I want to show you something.'

The idea of going anywhere was loathsome. Allegra felt horribly sick, and every movement made her already foul headache even worse. The effort of sitting up had almost exhausted her.

'Show me what?'

'Salvation.'

Cat groaned inwardly.

'I think it's too late to save me,' she muttered. 'Go away.'

'It concerns your search.'

That got her attention. She squinted at her visitor, but his features remained indistinct.

'Who are you?'

'Among the keepers of the flame I am called the Seer. My worldly name is Giavista Martinoy.'

Allegra's hangover began to fade rapidly. It had not been cured; it was simply that her brain now had more important things to concentrate on. She had met Martinoy once before, a few years earlier, when she and Vargo had gone to his house to inspect some books of ancient magical lore. He had struck her then as a pleasant but rather nervous and ineffectual person, and she had found it hard to believe that he was now the leader of the fireworm cult. Clearly something had changed. Even so, if he really was who he said he was, then this was the man Maciot had been searching for for over a month – and he had come to her! It was an opportunity she could not afford to miss.

'Are you coming?' he asked. 'You, of all people, might understand.'

Cat forced herself to stand up.

'Understand what?'

'I had my first revelation when I was imprisoned in the Paleton,' Martinoy said, ignoring her question. 'It was some time before I knew what it meant, but since then I've made it my life's work. Come.' He turned away and walked a few paces, before stopping to see whether she was following.

Cat staggered after him, ignoring the protests of her body, and fell into step beside him.

'Where are we going?'

He did not answer, but just strode on purposefully. Allegra had expected him to act like a fugitive, to keep to the back alleys, where he was least likely to be seen, but he marched straight towards and along the main thoroughfare leading across the city to the docks. Although they passed several groups of soldiers, none of them paid either Martinoy or Cat the slightest attention. I thought they were supposed to be looking for him, Allegra mused, and wondered whether she should call out to the guards. She discarded the idea initially because, although Martinoy's arrest would be gratifying – especially for Maciot – it was quite possible that what he was about to show her would be more useful still. Later, she began to wonder whether she could attract the soldiers' attention even if she wanted to. No one she and Martinoy passed in the streets had given any sign of noticing them go by. It was as though they were invisible.

'Why don't they see us?' Allegra asked, curiosity eventually overcoming her fear.

Martinoy smiled for the first time.

'You're more observant than most,' he said. 'They *do* see us. They just choose not to recognize that fact. In a sense, we're not important enough for them to notice.'

'Because of something you're doing?'

'Invisibility was one of the first dreams of wizardry. It's a comparatively simple technique.'

'And if I called out, they'd choose not to hear me either?'

'Exactly,' he replied, looking smug. ' Try, if you like.'

Another soldier was approaching from the other end of the street, and as he drew closer Cat hesitated, then took a deep breath and addressed him.

'Hello, Captain. Captain?'

The soldier glanced round, seemed to look through her, then shrugged and went on his way with a slightly puzzled expression. Cat watched him go, still not quite believing what was happening. She found that she was shivering.

'What if I'd bumped into him?'

'He would have looked around for someone else to blame,' Martinoy replied, 'and then probably decided it had just been a particularly strong gust of wind. The human mind is unusually adept at deceiving itself.'

As you're deceiving me? Allegra wondered. She thought of running away, but didn't have the courage even to try. One way or another, she was his prisoner.

By now they had reached a derelict area near the docks, which had been only partly rebuilt after being ravaged by fire. Cat remembered that Andrin's home had once stood there, but it and many like it were gone for good. Much of the ground was a rubble-strewn wasteland, the domain of rats and wild dogs, and it was to one such space that Martinoy led her.

A rusty metal trap door concealed steps leading down to what had once been someone's cellar. Martinoy went in first. Cat was once again tempted to flee, but she had the feeling she would not get far and – in spite of her growing unease – she wanted to see what was hidden down there. The steep stairway led to a tunnel, which ended in a sturdy, iron-shod door. Martinoy peered through a tiny window made of very thick glass, then unlocked the door with a key that hung from his belt. The blast of air that rushed through was so hot that beads of perspiration instantly covered Cat's skin and she gasped involuntarily, inhaling fetid fumes and almost choking. Martinoy led the way inside and she followed carefully, finding herself on a paved walkway above a large, deep pit. The red glow at the bottom of the pit was the source of the searing heat.

'Behold!'

Cat peered down, and saw the grey shapes amid the fiery coals. The worms were smaller than any she had seen before, but the revulsion she felt was just as strong. No matter how young they were, these fireworms were undoubtedly tainted.

'Once they are fully grown,' the cult leader intoned fervently, 'the dragon spawn will cleanse us. Only the truly righteous will be saved. The rest will burn.' His black eyes were shining now. 'The world will be born anew.'

'You intend to set these creatures free? Here in Teguise?'

'I must,' he replied. ' It will be the last plague, filled with our own hatreds and fears. It will purge us.'

'You're mad!'

He stared at her, his ecstatic expression gradually fading. It was replaced by a burning malevolence.

'You've seen them,' he spat. 'They are born in flame to devour the evil that bred them. Their evil will rid us of our own.'

'No!' Cat exclaimed, fighting back her horror and revulsion. 'If we don't corrupt them, they could help us.'

'And you call *me* mad!' he scoffed. 'There is no dealing with dragon spawn. Inhale their essence. It's the only way you can save yourself.'

'No!' She didn't know what he meant, only that she wanted no part of it. 'Never.'

'Then you will die.'

His hand shot out, like a cobra striking, and dealt her a stinging blow to the side of her head. Caught off guard, Cat fell, sprawling on the walkway, and only just managed to stop herself from toppling over the edge into the furnace below. As it was, when she had gathered her wits again Martinoy was gone. She heard the door open, then clang shut. Even as she scrambled to her feet, she knew it was too late. The key grated in the lock.

It was already dusk, at the end of another long and fruitless day of searching, when Vargo finally came to Famara's old home. He had not been back there in a long time and he was reluctant now, knowing that it would revive many memories, not all of them pleasant. Yet as soon as he saw the empty wine bottles and the dent in the bed where someone had slept recently, he cursed himself for not having tried there sooner. He knew Cat had been there – but now she was gone. He felt like kicking the rickety wooden walls in frustration.

'You might have told me, Famara,' he complained. 'Or at least tell me where she's gone now.'

For once his old mentor gave him no answer, not even within the confines of his own thoughts. He stepped outside again, and was greeted by the first really welcome sight he'd seen for some days.

*What took you so long?* Ero asked huffily. The hoopoe was perched on the wall on the opposite side of the alley.

*Ero!* Vargo exclaimed. *Where have you been?*

*With Cat. You told me to.*

*I . . .?* Vargo began, then dismissed the mystery in favour of a more important question. *Where is she?*

*I still remember*, the bird replied, as if this was something to be proud of. *He tried to make me forget, so I came back here.*

*Who did?* Vargo asked, his confusion increasing.

*The man in the cloak. He didn't want anyone to see him.*

*But you did?* Vargo guessed. *Was Cat with him?*

*Yes.*

*Where did they go?*

*No more talking*, Ero decreed. *I have to follow the trail.* He exploded into the air and flew off.

Vargo ran after him, desperate not to lose his link again. He bumped into people several times as they headed east, but Ero did not wait for him, and he was forced to run on, calling out in apology. Eventually, breathless and bruised from a couple of falls, he came to a patch of waste ground. In the light of the newly risen full moon, it looked quite deserted.

*Are you sure this is the right place?*

Ero did not answer, but alighted next to a square piece of rusty metal.

*Down there?* Vargo asked, as he caught up.

*Yes.*

Vargo yanked open the trap door and almost threw himself down the stairs.

Cat had lost all track of time. The only light in the cavern came from the red glow of the stones. She had investigated the entire length of the walkway but, as she had feared, the only way out was through the locked door. She knew there must be other entrances and exits, for the passage of air, but she could not see them. Despair had overtaken her when she realized that sooner or later either the worms would detect her presence or she would die from the heat. She was already drenched with sweat, her throat was raw, and she felt as if her blood was about to boil. Sinking down to the floor, she sat curled up against the stone wall, and wondered bleakly how she had got into such a stupid mess.

Much later her fevered mind had begun to play tricks on her. The only sounds she had heard since Martinoy had left her were the occasional shifting of hot coals, and the rustling as the basking fireworms adjusted their positions. Now she thought she could hear voices again – and almost welcomed them as old friends. Madness might at least make her end more bearable.

Amidst the babble she picked out a burst of familiar song, and almost smiled. Help me, Ero! she thought. Get me out of here.

Vargo all but ran into the door and tried frantically to open it, but it wouldn't budge. Glancing in through the window, his heart pounded as he saw Cat sitting there, bathed in a red glow.

'Allegra!' he yelled, hammering on the door with his fists. 'Allegra!'

She did not look up, and gave no sign of having heard him. He wrenched at the door again, threw himself against it – but made no impression.

'Cat!' he shouted, peering through the glass again.

What he saw then took his breath away. Before his horrified eyes, Allegra vanished into thin air.

# CHAPTER THIRTY-SEVEN

The dragon had been born from a brief corona of flame, rising up from the dais to engulf the Prophet. It was clear from the start that the creature was not real, but that did not stop its appearance terrifying everyone who saw it. The only thing that prevented wholesale panic was the fact that the dragon's image began to flicker almost immediately, so that its outlines blurred and the glittering scales became translucent. Those closest to the apparition could actually see the Prophet *inside* it, apparently unharmed but obviously afraid. From further away, however, it seemed as though the leader of the Kundahari had *become* the monster, and was controlling it. This impression was strengthened when the Prophet spoke. Whatever he had meant to say earlier had been lost in the general amazement, but now his words rose easily above the tumult.

'This is magic!'

His voice had been transformed as much as his appearance. Where once it had been high-pitched and piercing, it was now a low, resonating growl that seemed to shake the very flagstones of Geyan Square. His tone was a mixture of disbelief and outrage, but few of the onlookers recognized this. All they heard was the word that had become synonymous with evil, that the Prophet himself had so often condemned. Many repeated it in horrified whispers or in snarls of disgust, until their ominous muttering grew to resemble a ritual chant.

'Magic. Magic. Magic!'

There was anger in their voices, and it was directed towards the Prophet. His followers could not understand how he could have betrayed them in such a way, defiling their city with the vile sorcery that he had sworn to stamp out in barbarous lands. Others were merely confused, wondering what the purpose of the mesmerizing spectacle could be, and waiting to see what would happen next. They did not have long to wait.

A huge white bird, which shone against the night sky almost as brightly as the moon, swooped down towards the dragon, screaming his harsh war cry. The crowd did not know what his arrival signified. Was this another magical illusion? Or was the eagle real? Although he looked solid enough, no one had ever before seen a bird of his size and colouring. The eagle did not attack, but circled round above the stage, as if guarding the dragon. Pointing fingers marked out his passage, and another whisper spread rapidly among the astonished spectators.

'His familiar. It's his familiar.'

The mood became ugly as the extent of the deception sank in. Everything that had gone before was changed by one unforgivable fact. The Prophet was a wizard.

Andrin was elated by the success of his plan. The crowd had jumped to exactly the conclusion he had hoped for. When he had first thought of the idea, it had been born of desperation, but it had soon exceeded his wildest imaginings.

The intention had been to bring magic to Geyan Square, and to make everyone believe that the Prophet was responsible. However, when the crucial moment had arrived, Andrin had almost lost his nerve, not really believing he could pull it off. His experiments the previous night had produced such feeble results, and it seemed impossible that the mere presence of the throng could transform them into anything worthwhile. Even so, he knew he had to try. As he began to bring his thoughts into focus, Andrin instinctively reached out to his only ally for support.

*Help me, Ayo.*

He had been amazed and gratified by the surge of power that flowed into him in response to his appeal. Although he and Ayo had always made a formidable team, he had never felt anything like this before. Harnessing his new strength, Andrin wasted no time in putting it to use. He caught the memory he wanted, then shaped and projected it with his mind. It was meant to be the magical flames Ico had created, long ago in Manrique Square in Teguise, but in the next instant the image changed to what she had created next. The serpent she had unwittingly summoned then reappeared now and enveloped Gadette. The illusion was even better for Andrin's purpose than flames that did not burn, and so he had not tried to alter it – but the first murmurings of doubt had begun to sound in his head. It was clear that he was no longer in control of what was happening.

Within the dragon, Gadette was flailing around, obviously aware that he was being surrounded by *something*, but unable to tell what it was. Andrin wondered what a dragon looked like from the inside, and almost laughed. The flickering image kept changing, and he assumed that – like the surge of power – this stemmed from the involvement of a huge number of people. Their minds had magnified his efforts beyond recognition, but the results were somehow vague and faltering. It was as if they had no clear idea of what a dragon actually looked like, and therefore weren't sure what they were supposed to be seeing. Even so, it was undeniably effective, and the Prophet's own utterance had helped condemn himself in the eyes of his followers. Andrin had not expected sound to be affected in this way, so the altered voice had come as a bonus, fitting the plan perfectly – and although he had been one of the first to set off the whispers about magic, the process had needed little help from him to become an almost universal assumption.

By the time Ayo entered the picture and – as they had intended – was mistaken for Gadette's link, the tide of opinion was running strongly against the Prophet. But Andrin was now in the grip of his own misgivings. Once again, he was one of the first to point to the eagle and begin the speculation, but when the simple movement cost him a great deal of effort, he realized that he was growing weak. Too late, he remembered that Ico's efforts had left her exhausted and unconscious, and he tried to withdraw from the spell, hoping it would continue under its own momentum. He managed to distance himself a little, but the magic would not completely release him. Some force greater than his own mind was at work, and Andrin felt himself being sucked down into a whirlpool of darkness.

The decision to allow the Prophet to share the stage with the imperial celebrants had been forced upon Madar by public pressure – and it was something that he now regretted bitterly. The inner council had been unanimous in their agreement, even though several of them – especially Chamberlain Ruhail – had regarded it as an expedient measure at best. Only Tzarno and Ty had been wholehearted in their support, claiming that it would enable their men to maintain order in the city. They had pointed out that, as the

Prophet's influence had been crucial in initiating the debate about Tiguafaya, his presence when the results were announced was necessary to ensure their popular acceptance.

However, as soon as the dragon appeared, all such arguments became invalid. Madar had risen to his feet in fury, but had been unable to make his voice heard above the general clamour. Beside him, Katerin had also risen and he moved towards her protectively, even though she gave no sign of fear. The Emperor's rage intensified at the thought of her possible distress. That anyone should have defiled their wedding day in such a manner was unpardonable, but what confused him even more was what Kantrowe hoped to gain by this appalling exhibition.

He was not alone in these thoughts. Most of the courtiers had retreated hurriedly from the stage in fear and bewilderment. Hierophant Otric was practically foaming at the mouth at this blatant display of blasphemy, while many of the others were almost equally horrified. Only Prince Tzarno and Castellan Ty had stood their ground, the latter drawing his sword and shouting to the Seax Guards who were stationed around the dais to do the same. The faces of both men reflected their own stunned reactions, but neither made any move towards the Prophet. They realized very quickly that this battle was not in their domain. Swords would be no use against such an illusory monster.

'What's he doing?' Ty asked in bewilderment.

'The gods know,' Tzarno hissed.

'Shall I kill him?' The castellan was clearly willing to attack the wizard through the dragon mirage.

'Wait!' the prince cautioned, his forehead creasing in thought, his gaze fixed upon the man he knew as Kantrowe.

Imprisoned within the illusion, the Prophet chose that moment to make his fateful pronouncement.

'This is magic!'

Moments later a white eagle flew down to circle above the stage, and the Prophet's guilt was sealed.

Only two men in Geyan Square were in a position to know what was really happening. One was Andrin, who had begun it all. The other stood beside Chavez and Zophres, to one side of the stage. Lamia's envoy had reacted instantly when the vision first appeared, screaming and clapping his hands to the sides of his head, his eyes wide with pain and horror. At the time, neither of his companions had taken this as anything more than a natural reaction to the shock they had all experienced, but as events unfolded and the easterner's distress did not diminish, they turned to him, taking in the full extent of his reaction. He was shaking now, his whole frame twitching as though every nerve in his body were being assaulted, and his eyes were shifting about wildly.

'Evil, evil,' he mumbled. 'Sorcery.'

'I can see that,' Chavez declared, his own voice shaking. 'What's he doing it for?'

'Your guess is as good as mine,' Zophres growled angrily. 'The man must be mad.'

'Can't fight it,' the envoy breathed, sounding as though he was in agony. 'Too big. Help me . . .'

'You're supposed to be able to stop magic,' Chavez complained.

'Can't. Too big,' the man repeated helplessly.

'Stop him,' the pirate insisted, looking up as the eagle swooped overhead.

'Not him,' the easterner groaned.

'Not him?' Zophres said quickly. 'Who is it, then?'

The envoy looked around, and his own tortured instincts drew him to a blond head within the crowd.

\*

For Andrin, time had begun to buckle and crack. Although in reality only a few moments had passed since he'd set the magic in motion, an age seemed to have gone by. What was more, he had no idea what he should do next. His only intention had been to discredit Gadette, and he appeared to have done that, but the entire process was now beyond his control. In fact, he was not sure whether it had ever been *within* his power to shape the magic he had unleashed. Unknown forces were at work here – he kept seeing fleeting images that made no sense – and he was growing weaker by the moment, both physically and mentally.

An instant later Andrin also began to doubt his own sanity. In the empty space between the still hesitating Ty and the wildly flickering dragon, another figure appeared from out of nowhere. Among all those in Geyan Square, only Andrin was in a position to recognize the newcomer. It was Allegra.

# CHAPTER THIRTY-EIGHT

The inexplicable appearance of an unknown woman stunned everyone in Geyan Square – both those on the stage and in the crowd below. Who was she? Where had she come from? She looked real, unlike the dragon, but certainly did not measure up to anyone's notion of a sorceress. Her face was flushed, her perfectly ordinary clothes were stained with sweat, and she was gazing about her in an obvious state of shock. At the same time, the dragon had begun to leak flames, its features blurring and shifting until it was hardly possible to tell what it was.

For her part, Allegra was petrified, unable even to scream. She didn't know where she was or what was happening, but she knew it wasn't a dream. Her escape from the worm-pit was a miracle, and yet her present predicament – which defied explanation – might well be even worse. She had no idea why these people were gathered here, or what their magic entailed, but she could sense that the air was full of hatred. And then, amidst all the strange faces turned her way, her eyes were drawn to one she knew. Andrin was waving and shouting, but she could not hear him over the tumult of the crowd.

A strong hand grabbed her arm roughly, and twisted it behind her back. She felt a blade, cold and sharp against her neck, as her assailant held her fast.

'No more tricks, witch,' Castellan Ty hissed in her ear. 'Or I cut your throat.'

Andrin was close to breaking point. He was at a complete loss to understand anything that was going on now. His state of mind was not helped by the fact that he kept seeing momentary visions – of other people and places – super-imposed on the real world.

He had not thought it possible that anyone could look any more bewildered than the unfortunate Gadette, but Cat had managed it. The magic that had brought her there was clearly as much of a mystery to her as it was to him. He watched, aghast, as Ty moved, quickly capturing the unresisting girl and holding a knife to her throat. The very fact that the castellan had been able to do this threw the astonished Andrin into even deeper confusion. He had believed Cat's appearance to be another illusion, but that seemed not to be the case. She was obviously very real – and therefore so was the danger of her situation. Andrin called again, pushing his way forward in spite of the crush, and oblivious to the disturbance he was creating. He only knew that he had to help his friend.

*Ayo? Ayo! We must help her. Is there anything you can do?*

At first the eagle did not answer. Ever since the reawakening of his second sight, Ayo had been fighting his own thoughts, trying to decide what was real and what was not. In the end that proved impossible, and so he simply accepted everything, no matter how bizarre it seemed. All that was left for him to do was try his best to carry out the plan he and Andrin had devised together. But so much had changed that that seemed almost superfluous now.

The one thing he knew for certain was that Cat was at the

centre of both his worlds – and this made him feel very uncomfortable. So when his link called to him, Ayo's eventual response was to dive towards the dais. Words were useless now and he screamed, reverting to the wild. Even as his eyes fixed upon his prey, he knew that others were watching through him.

The dream had captured them all, sweeping them away regardless of whether they were awake or not. Lines and circles danced as they had done before; images appeared and slipped away in an instant; the power was there once more – but this time it was being pulled in different directions. The straightforward sense of purpose that had united them all the last time was missing. Their goals were different now, unfocused. Their music was full of discords.

And yet the dream brought them all to the same unfamiliar place, seen from above through the eyes of an eagle who was part of the magic but outside it too, the observer for them all.

*Papa!* Ysanne cried joyously. *Look, Tas, it's* . . . She stopped then, suddenly afraid of the crowd, the dragon, and the strange events on the stage.

*What's happening?* Tas asked.

*I'm flying*, Ysanne replied quietly.

After a few moments, in which the girl and her link circled and dipped in a faraway sky, Ysanne's earlier happiness at the sight of her father all but evaporated.

*I don't like this*, she said. Then, after a long pause, she added, *I feel sick*.

The dream should have been exhilarating, but it was not. Nino sensed the power of his borrowed wings, saw with the clarity of an airborne predator, but all his thoughts were concentrated on the unknown city below him.

Nino's wonder and dread were equally intense. Although he had been longing for the opportunity to move within the network again, he had no idea why it had come now – and the scene below him was nonsensical. Cat and Andrin were at the centre of the magic – that much at least was clear – but how could the two of them be together? And where *were* they? Andrin was supposed to be in the Empire, and Cat was somewhere in Teguise!

He stopped trying to understand it all, and simply watched.

Vargo felt himself being dragged beneath the surface of the mirror. He was already dismayed by Allegra's sudden and terrifying disappearance, and had now been thrust into a strange and alarming dream.

*Cat!* he yelled, seeing her again.

He began running, blindly, knowing only that he had to move. Steps fell away behind him unseen, and he did not stop.

*Cat!* His anguished cry echoed in the void.

Vargo ran as he flew, looking down on the burning dragon, at the milling crowd of people, and seeing only her. She was so near – and yet tantalizingly out of reach.

Other wings kept pace with him, dancing on the air, calling softly, but Vargo had no eyes to see, nor ears to hear.

He ran.

Soo was the only one who saw it all and understood. But she shared her knowledge with no one – not even her link.

Ayo's first attack achieved nothing. Fear was his main weapon against humans, and when that failed there was little he could do. Allegra's captors stood firm, and the eagle's talons were of little use against their swords.

Andrin had reached the edge of the dais. He was staggering now, overburdened in both mind and body, but the stubbornness of old drove him on. Pulling himself up, he stepped unafraid into the fire that surrounded the dragon, provoking gasps of horror and amazement from those near by.

'*He's* the wizard!' a voice cried, rising above the general clamour by sheer force of will. 'He's the source of this evil.'

Andrin turned and spotted his accuser, feeling at once his malice and fear, and knowing its source. An anti-mage, he thought indifferently, then turned back to more important matters. Cat was on the far side of the stage, her eyes wide with terror.

'Let her go!' Andrin yelled, fighting the disorientation that still threatened to overwhelm him.

'You know this sorceress?' Ty replied, not slackening his grip.

Andrin was vaguely aware that soldiers were closing in around him. He knew he had power to call on, but he was incapable of deciding what to do with it.

'She isn't— ' he began, only to be silenced by a rush of cold flame as the dragon flailed ineffectually at him.

'This is Andrin Zonzomas, the Ice Mage.' Mazo Gadette's voice was still transformed, and Andrin's heart sank as he realized that his own magic was now being used against him. 'This sorcery is his, not mine!' the dragon roared. 'It's all trickery!'

This pronouncement quieted the crowd, who were now watching in stunned silence. Madar's voice filled the void.

'Do you deny this?' he called.

Andrin hesitated. Once before, in front of another hostile crowd, he had been inspired, able to spin words like magic spells – but even then he had needed Ico to rescue him. Now he found himself tongue-tied and helpless, and this time there was no one to come to his aid.

'He is the Ice Mage,' Gadette repeated. 'Of Tiguafaya. He is the husband to the sorceress who rules that unholy land.'

Madar waited until the rumble of speculation caused by the Prophet's statement had subsided, then repeated his own question.

'Do you deny this?'

'No!' Andrin shouted, pride getting the better of what was left of his good sense.

A group of soldiers moved purposefully towards him, their swords drawn. Andrin swung round, releasing an uncontrolled burst of illusory flame, and the guards fell back. But when they realized that none of them was burnt they came forward again.

'No more,' Andrin mumbled to himself, glancing at Allegra and shielding his mind from the fragmented visions as best he could. He fell to his knees, beaten now, and hardly heard Ayo's agonized cry of distress.

*No! We can't protect you if . . .* The eagle broke off, knowing it was too late. The network was still there, but his link had cut himself off from it. Ayo made a desperate attempt to ward off the soldiers, but there were just too many of them. He soared upwards again, and watched helplessly with all the others as Andrin was captured.

The dragon vanished, fading as rapidly as it had appeared, and some of the Kundahari went to the aid of the Prophet.

A measure of order was thus restored, and Madar strode forward to face the expectant throng.

'These two,' he began, pointing towards the prisoners, 'have brought sorcery into the heart of Zepharinn. For that there can only be one punishment. They are both condemned to death.'

The crowd cheered their approval, then quietened again

as the Emperor made it clear that he had more to say. Behind him the full moon was still rising into the sky like a banner of doom.

'The council's deliberations are complete,' Madar announced. 'The events we have all witnessed here tonight only serve to emphasize that their decision is not only just, but necessary. As of this moment, we are at war with Tiguafaya.'

# CHAPTER THIRTY-NINE

The edges of reality frayed and shrank from Vargo as he ran. People stared, but he was not even aware of their presence. All that mattered was the dream – and the trail that would lead to its end. Although he was still blind to normal light, the path before him was like the glittering road that a low sun spreads across the ocean. Beside it the full moon was but a pale candle.

Desperation lent him strength. The streets of Teguise rushed past unheeded while he flew above another city. He knew now that something had gone horribly wrong, that the dream had somehow been pulled askew. The conflicting forces that were at work meant that, far from saving Allegra, the magic had plunged her into even greater danger. That was why he was retracing his steps – and hers – by following the trail to a real place of safety. Cat had used the network to save Vargo once, even though neither of them had been aware of it at the time, and now he was determined to do the same for her.

He practically fell through the open doorway of Famara's hut, collapsing onto the remains of the bed while the remote drama continued to unfold before his mind's gaze. The knife at Cat's throat filled him with dread. She could be killed at any moment, and he would never forgive himself if he came too late.

Ero swooped into the room, and dropped to the ground in exhaustion.

*Here?* Vargo asked hurriedly.

*Yes*, the hoopoe replied wearily. *This is where she meant.*

This is where you should be, Cat! Vargo thought. Not there. *Help me, Ero.*

Together they tried to bend the dream to their will, to heal the corruption. For several leaden moments there was no response – and then, without warning, the conflict ended. The opposing force simply withdrew, and Vargo felt his heart sing for joy. Distant words of horror – *No! We can't protect you* – faded into silence, unregarded. The death sentences and the declaration of war were mere words, signifying nothing. Vargo and Ero were preparing for one last monumental effort.

*Now?* Vargo asked.

*Now*, the hoopoe confirmed.


Castellan Ty wished he had reacted more quickly. In one moment he had been holding a helpless prisoner; in the next she was gone. By the time he had felt her fading, and decided to kill her on the spot, she had simply disappeared. In his confusion he had come close to stabbing himself, but all that had really been injured was his pride. No captive had ever slipped through his grasp before, but whatever sorcery had brought her there had snatched her away again – and there was nothing he could do about it. Snarling with rage, Ty retrieved his discarded sword and advanced menacingly upon the second prisoner. He too had been condemned to death by imperial decree, and the castellan was intent on carrying out the execution before magic had a chance to rob him of another victim.

'Wait!' Prince Tzarno put a restraining hand on Ty's arm. 'He's not going anywhere.'

The older man glanced round, trying to control his temper, then looked to Madar for guidance.

'Take him to the fortress,' the Emperor decided. 'There are some questions I want answering before he pays the price for his crimes.'

As an unresisting Andrin was led away, Madar turned to his bride and gestured in apology. She came down to join him.

'I'm sorry for all of this, my love.'

Katerin smiled. 'You've certainly gone to some lengths to make it a memorable wedding day!' she said.

The disappearance of the sorceress was the last of the night's wonders. With her vanishing the final remnant of magic died, and Lamia's envoy collapsed to the ground. Although his attempts to combat the evil had been largely ineffective, the effort had drained him nonetheless. Chavez and Zophres helped him to his feet, but it would be several hours before he was fully recovered.

The Prophet had also been badly shaken by his ordeal, and he allowed himself to be led away by his supporters, ignoring calls from the onlookers for him to speak. The imperial party left too, and when it became clear that nothing more was going to happen, the crowds began to disperse, taking with them excited tales of all they had seen and heard. Soon the whole city would know what had happened in Geyan Square, and the events of that particular full moon would eventually pass into legend.

Above them all, Ayo had returned to the single world,

and knew that what he saw he saw alone. He had never felt more isolated in his life.

It took Allegra several moments to realize where she was – and several more to decide that she was not dead. Blood was trickling from a tiny nick at the front of her throat, but she was otherwise unharmed.

It was dark inside Famara's old home, but she knew she was not alone. Ero lay huddled on the floor, his head drooping forward so that his bill rested on the ground, and his eyes were tight shut. Vargo was curled up on the bed, and he too was obviously fast asleep. Cat did not know what had happened to her, where she had been, or how she had got there, but she was certain that Vargo was responsible for her return. Her legs shook as she stumbled over to the bed and shook his arm gently. He stirred, but did not wake. Cat's legs gave way completely then, and she sank to the floor, overwhelmed by all she had been through. Even in the midst of her confusion, she knew that it had all been real. Wherever he was, Andrin was in terrible trouble – and soon all Tiguafaya would be in danger too. War was coming. And somehow she was at least partly responsible for this disastrous turn of events.

'Vargo?' she whispered, shaking him again. ' Please wake up.'

But there was no response. Vargo, like his link, was deeply unconscious.

Is this my fault too? Allegra wondered bleakly. Oh, my love, what have I done?

It was only then that she remembered the fireworms – and the swarm that was breeding in Teguise.

*What happened, Soo?* Ico asked anxiously. *What's going on?* She had been aware of something, but it had been a distant, vague awareness, as if it had been meant for someone else. *Soo, please.*

*Others will tell you*, the sparrowhawk replied, her voice retreating as she flew away.

Others? Ico thought. Which others? Then she began to run.

The door of the nursery stood open and Ico rushed through, finding Yaisa trying, without success, to console a weeping Ysanne. At the sight of her mother the girl's wailing rose to new heights, and she held out her arms. Ico picked the child up and held her, rocking back and forth and whispering in her ear.

'It's all right, sweetheart. Mama's here.'

Her daughter's crying subsided a little but did not stop. Tas hovered above them, adding her own piercing calls to the noise.

'I'm sorry, my lady,' the maid said worriedly. 'I don't know what happened. One moment she was asleep, and the next she was so upset I couldn't get her to tell me anything.'

'It's all right, Yaisa,' Ico replied. 'I expect it was just a nightmare. I'll see to her.'

Ysanne was snivelling now, and hiccuping occasionally, but when Ico asked her what the matter was, she just shook her head vigorously and clung even tighter to her mother's neck.

'Is she all right?' Nino asked. He was standing in the doorway, flushed and breathless, a haunted look in his eyes.

'Getting better,' Ico replied, 'which is more than I can say for myself.'

'Did you see?' Nino asked quietly.

'No. Soo won't talk to me. It felt as though she was trying to protect me somehow, keep me from whatever was going on.' Ico hesitated, seeing the expression on Nino's face. 'And now you're really worrying me,' she said. 'What's happened?'

# PART TWO

# The Singing

# CHAPTER FORTY

Commander Kehoe swore violently.

'Send the signal to withdraw,' he ordered one of his captains. 'There's nothing here worth defending.'

This was certainly true – if they ignored the fact that each retreat took them closer to Teguise.

From the valley below their vantage point came a discordant pealing of bells, marking another imperial victory, another enemy advance. Although the hateful sound had become all too familiar of late, it still set Kehoe's teeth on edge.

The invaders were doing everything wrong, and yet somehow they were still winning. Tzarno's tactics were those of a madman, but they were working! The Tiguafayan forces should have held all the advantages; they knew the unforgiving terrain, could choose their own defensive positions and thus control – to a certain extent – the time and place of each skirmish; and the Firebrands' birds had provided them with aerial intelligence that the imperial army could not possibly match. Finally, the selective use of magic to delude their foes should have provided them with the decisive edge in many of their encounters. So why, Kehoe thought ruefully, did the whole campaign seem doomed?

The most obvious advantage held by the enemy was their sheer weight of numbers. The Empire had deployed a vast force of men and equipment – although that in itself should have presented them with an almost insoluble logistical problem. Providing food and water for such a huge body of men, especially in the desert-like conditions of the northern firelands, was an undertaking no general in his right mind would want to attempt, but Tzarno's resources had been up to the task. Following behind the soldiers came another army of artisans and slaves, building makeshift roads across the trackless waste for the supply wagons to roll along. As they moved south, these supply lines became stretched and more cumbersome, but they showed no sign of failing yet. Kehoe had the feeling that the imperial soldiers ate better than his own men.

However, it was not just the northerners' numerical superiority that was the difference between the opposing forces. Individually and collectively, the invaders seemed to believe themselves invincible. Such reckless conviction led them to attack positions even when the defenders held the high ground. In doing so they suffered heavy casualties, especially in the first wave, but eventually they almost always succeeded. And when it came to hand-to-hand combat, the discipline of the experienced imperial soldiers – together with the ruthless fanaticism of the auxiliaries who fought beside them – made them more than a match for Kehoe's men, most of whom had not seen any real action before the start of this campaign. Overall, Kehoe estimated that Tzarno had lost almost twice as many men as he had – but while every Tiguafayan death depleted both the size and morale of his forces, the effect upon the imperial army seemed negligible. Nothing appeared to worry them, not even the ominous rumblings from beneath the earth, the tremors that spoke of possible earthquakes and eruptions to come. Such warnings had become quite frequent of late.

Moreover, the imperial army seemed to have found a way to negate the Tiguafayans' most potent weapons. Very often, when the mages accompanying the soldiers had projected the illusions designed to confuse or frighten their enemy, the attackers had just ignored them. At other times, the magic had simply failed to work. Several of the Firebrands and their fellow talents had reported that something was blocking their attempts, and a few actually became ill in the process. Increasingly, their scout birds returned in an incoherent state, unable to report sensibly on what they had seen, and Kehoe had reluctantly reached the conclusion that their opponents had discovered a way to counteract all their magical efforts.

In fact, Tzarno had been one step ahead of them the whole time. It had been almost two months since those in Teguise had heard that war had been declared. Kehoe was not really certain how this had come about – some aspects of magic were beyond his comprehension – but when the reality of the news had been confirmed, he had travelled north as fast as he could. Although he had still not believed that the Empire would risk an overland invasion, reports from the border had been inconclusive – so he had gone to take a look for himself, putting various contingency plans into operation as he went.

At first his assumption that the main assault would come by sea seemed to have been confirmed, when the imperial army had withdrawn from their camps near the border. However, instead of heading for the coastal ports to embark on the expected armada, the soldiers had turned westward, intent on crossing the border further inland. As logic had dictated that a land-based invasion must follow the coastal plain, this manoeuvre bypassed some of the Tiguafayan lines of defence. Kehoe had hastily revised his plans, hoping that his adversary's apparently insane reasoning would lead to Tzarno's own downfall. However, such hopes were soon dashed.

From the start it had been obvious that the prince's intelligence was very good. The routes taken by his army were cleverly chosen, taking advantage of the few oases and springs in the area. The imperial scouting parties spread out ahead like the tentacles of an octopus, testing the land and probing defences. The Tiguafayans' border outposts were no match for the forces arrayed against them, and could only put up token resistance. Later, as the front line moved south and Kehoe was able to bring up reinforcements, the fighting had been much fiercer, but he had still been unable to stem the incoming tide.

One of the few redeeming features of the campaign, as far as Kehoe was concerned, was that the terrain it had been fought over was largely unpopulated. The initial encounters had taken place in uninhabited regions and later, when Tzarno turned eastward – heading towards the coast at last – the evacuation plans were already under way, so that at least the commander did not have to worry about endangering the civilian population. Dozens of villages were now deserted, the refugees streaming south towards Teguise, leaving a bleak and cheerless landscape for the advance of war. As time went by and the situation became increasingly desperate, more and more settlements would become ghost towns.

Not everyone had escaped, however. The imperial army's march towards the ocean had cut off two villages, as well as some units of the Tiguafayan forces, and an enclave now existed between the border, the invaders and the sea. There was nothing Kehoe could do to help them, and he could only hope that the navy would come to their aid before they were wiped out. He also hoped that, in the meantime, the officers in charge would prove worthy of their enforced command. As it was, all he could do was make his own retreat as orderly and productive as possible, harrying the enemy at every opportunity without risking too much. In the commander's mind, it seemed increasingly likely that the final battle would be fought from the walls of Teguise itself.

Prince Tzarno arrived back at his command tent in good spirits, his uniform and light armour tarnished with the dust of the firelands and the blood of his enemies. He was not the sort of general who hid from the action, and this was one of the reasons his men usually fought hard for him – even on ambitious ventures such as this. He chose his moments judiciously, but when he went forward into battle, all those who saw him – and he made certain there were many – could not doubt his courage. His reputation as a warrior was as fearsome as his wolf-toothed snarl.

Castellan Ty looked up from his charts as the prince came in.

'I hear the bells ringing for another success.' Like many of the professional soldiers, Ty found the presence of the Kundahari a source of disgust, but he tolerated them, knowing it was necessary to retain the pretence that this was a 'holy' war.

'Of course,' Tzarno replied, with a vulpine grin. 'We can push on again in the morning.'

'You'd think they'd get tired of that cacophony,' the castellan grumbled.

'It sounds a lot worse to the enemy, believe me,' the prince remarked. 'Silence would be music to their ears. Besides, you know as well as I do that the Kundahari have their uses.'

Ty nodded. Fanaticism had its advantages, not least in situations where common sense might make ordinary soldiers hesitate. The Prophet's followers went forward willingly, heedless of any danger, happy to accept a martyr's death for the righteousness of their cause. In doing so, they created opportunities for others to advance in relative safety. For that, old soldiers like Ty were willing to put up with the noise of their bells.

'What news from the enclave?' Tzarno asked.

'There aren't enough of them to pose a real problem,' the castellan replied. 'We could root them out if you want, but in my opinion it'd be a waste of effort. Sooner or later they'll have to make a run for it, either by land or sea, and we'll be ready for them. If they stay put, they'll starve. Of course, they might surrender,' he added, although he obviously thought this unlikely.

'I think we should discourage that idea,' the prince stated firmly. 'I don't want to waste any resources on prisoners.'

'Understood.'

'Do they have sorcerers with them?'

'It's possible. We're not sure,' Ty admitted, 'but each of our units in the cordon has an anti-mage with them, and they've plenty of the tinctures left.'

'Good. It seems our alliance is paying off,' Tzarno observed with satisfaction.

Before the invasion had begun, it had been necessary to co-ordinate the efforts of the imperial forces on land and at sea. As part of this process, several of Lamia's colleagues had been co-opted by Tzarno for use in his campaign. Although these dour talents had at first been regarded with considerable suspicion by the soldiers, they had since proved their worth. As expected, the Tiguafayans had tried to use sorcery as a weapon, but the anti-mages had been able to block much of it telepathically, even turning some of it back upon its originators. This, together with the easterners' tinctures, which had been dissolved in rum rations and supplied for the entire army to drink on a daily basis, had enabled the soldiers to disregard or dismiss the illusions that had been thrown at them. Tzarno and Ty had publicly drunk the potions themselves – to alleviate any fears their men might have felt – and could vouch for their effectiveness. Confidence flowed in their veins with the fiery spirit.

Other than that, the campaign had been planned in normal military fashion, albeit on an extravagant scale and using daring strategy. Preparation had been vital, and had included several exercises in the devastated valley north of the border, which had enabled both soldiers and artisans to get used to the difficulties of the volcanic terrain. Accurate intelligence had also been vital, and it was here that the work of spies, scouts and raiding parties, as well as the interrogation of a few carefully chosen prisoners, had paid off. So far their advance and their supply lines were working extremely well – and Tzarno could see no reason why that should change. Provided the navy and their allies were playing their part with equal success, there was every likelihood that the prince would be drinking a victory toast in Teguise before the month was out. He smiled at the thought as he poured himself a goblet of wine.

'Where's Kantrowe?' he asked casually.

'The last I heard—' Ty began, but got no further as the tent flap opened and the Prophet himself strode in.

'I'm here, Your Highness. At your service.'

'And what have you been up to while we've been persecuting your holy war?'

The Prophet acknowledged the prince's complicitous grin with a slight tightening of his facial muscles, the closest he ever came to a smile. His pale eyes remained impassive.

'I've been greeting two new arrivals among our camp followers,' he said.

'Really? Anyone I should know about?'

'Madar and Katerin.'

'What!' Tzarno exploded. 'Here?'

The Prophet nodded.

'This is unbelievable!' the prince shouted, colour rising dangerously in his cheeks.

'It seems the Emperor wishes to follow the progress of the war himself. Anyone would think he doesn't trust you.'

'Watch your tongue, Prophet,' Tzarno snarled, 'before I tear it out by the roots.'

'And the Empress is here too?' Ty asked.

'Katerin is not a woman to stand idly by and watch great events proceed without her,' the Prophet commented. 'I have a feeling this visit may be her doing.'

'I should have slit the bitch's throat,' Tzarno muttered.

'You may still get the chance,' Ty said quietly. 'But not just yet.'

Tzarno turned to look at the castellan, his eyes blazing, but said nothing.

'Do you trust your brother?' Katerin wondered innocently.

'What makes you ask that?' Madar replied.

The Emperor and his wife were in one of the tents of the supply camp, some miles to the rear of the fighting. Although their arrival had caused some consternation, and the accommodations were basic, that did not seem to concern Katerin in the least.

'Oh,' she said carelessly, 'it's just that he seemed very keen on this expedition – and if he came home a conquering hero, there would be few who could resist his charms. And if, say, you were to meet with an accident before our first son is born—'

'You think Tzarno would contemplate murder?'

'It's not such an unusual means of securing the succession,' she pointed out.

'You shouldn't concern yourself with such things, my sweet.'

'How can I not? I have as much to lose as you. Besides, one of the reasons you love me is that I meddle in things that shouldn't concern me.' Her smile was impish.

Madar was about to respond when a voice from outside the tent forestalled him.

'Your Highness, may I enter?'

'Come in, Kudrak,' the Emperor called, recognizing the voice – and its deferential tone.

The ambassador came in and bowed formally, his expression troubled.

'I've arranged for some refreshments. They are hardly—'

'No matter,' Madar cut in.

'We're more hungry for news,' Katerin added. 'How is the war progressing?'

'Well, Your Highness,' Kudrak replied, unable to meet her resolute gaze directly. 'No doubt Prince Tzarno will be here soon to give you the details himself.' The ambassador was too old to take an active part in the campaign, but some hasty instinct had driven him to travel as an observer. Although he had often regretted his decision – not being used to the rigours of such an undertaking – it was still a matter of some pride for him to witness the progress of the holy war he had predicted some months earlier.

'No doubt,' Katerin remarked, smiling.

'You will want to rest after your journey,' the ambassador said awkwardly, and began to withdraw.

This time it was Madar who answered for them both.

'Not really. Would you like to take a look around, Katerin?'

'Yes, my lord,' his wife replied eagerly.

Kudrak stood aside and held the tent flap, then followed them into the evening air that was pungent with the smoke of campfires. Katerin looked around at the barren landscape.

'Is this really worth fighting for?' she asked.

'We're fighting for a principle, not just for land,' Madar told her. 'Besides, there are hidden riches even here. And further south the country is more hospitable.'

'They must have been very brave,' the Empress said thoughtfully. 'Those who came here first, the pioneers, when all this was unknown territory.'

Madar nodded, but said nothing.

'Do you still have the talisman with you?' Katerin asked, turning to Kudrak.

For answer, the ambassador led them towards the western edge of the encampment. The white eagle was a sorry sight. Heavy chains were clamped tight around both legs, tethering it to the cart on which it rode. Its feathers were dirty and bedraggled, and its entire posture spoke of dejection and defeat. Standing quite still, hunched up, it gazed towards the western horizon with dulled eyes.

'They say that only an eagle can stare directly at the sun without burning his eyes,' Madar said softly.

This time it was Katerin's turn to remain silent, and the expression on her face was unreadable. They went on their way as the last fierce glare of the sunset faded.

Even then Ayo did not move, did not even blink.

# CHAPTER FORTY-ONE

When the enemy swordsmen finally overwhelmed him, Maciot was almost glad.

Defenceless now, he felt only a sense of relief that the blow which would end his life was only moments away. He hardly noticed the pain of the bloody wounds to his arm, shoulder and side.

The fighting had been fierce and brutal, but the outcome had never really been in doubt. The crew of the *Temerar*, the ship that should have taken Maciot to the Empire, had been weakened by two months on the run in foreign waters. What food and drink they had managed to obtain had been hardly enough to keep body and soul together, and being cut off so far from home for so long had been utterly demoralizing.

Their original mission had been abandoned as they neared Uga Stai – when they'd learnt that a Tiguafayan envoy would not be welcome, because the two lands were already at war. The *Temerar* had been pursued by several vessels, but had escaped under cover of night by fleeing to the east, along the coast of the Empire – with each hour taking them further from home. After that they had survived as best they could, evading the naval patrols and raiding coastal villages for supplies. Already sick at heart, Maciot had fallen prey to bodily illness too – as had most of the crew – and he, along with all the others, had become desperate to get back to Tiguafaya, even if it meant risking an encounter with the imperial navy.

For a while luck had been on their side, but eventually they had been spotted, then overtaken, by a fleet of vessels that seemed to be comprised of pirate ships together with some unknown black craft. It had been one of these that had finally drawn alongside and boarded the *Temerar*. By then she had been partly ablaze, after an attack of fire arrows, and many of her sailors were already dead or wounded. Although the survivors had put up a gallant resistance, their defeat had been inevitable. The decks were soon slippery with blood, and the air was thick with smoke.

Slumped to his knees, head bowed, Maciot waited, wondering why he was still alive. Eventually he looked up and, through a haze of exhaustion, saw that the warriors who had disarmed him had withdrawn. Before him stood a robed woman, whose dead eyes regarded him with unnerving calm. All warmth and light seemed to shrink from her presence. Maciot had only encountered one other person whose whole being seemed to be a negation of life – and that had been Maghdim. He had hoped never to meet his like again.

The woman spoke and, although Maciot could not understand anything of what she said, her tone and gestures indicated that she had some purpose in mind for her newest prisoner. As a few of her men moved towards him, Maciot sank into a black void. As he lost consciousness, his final thought was to hope that he bled to death before he discovered what that purpose was.

'Do we give chase, Cap'n?' the helmsman asked.

Zarzuelo watched the Tiguafayan flotilla as it turned to

flee, his eyes narrowed against the setting sun.

'No. Let them run. They can't hide for ever. We're all headed for the same place, after all. We'll wait until the whole fleet is assembled. Then we take Teguise.'

The Survivor could hear destiny calling. In a few days the real battle would begin, and he would at last step out of his father's long shadow. For now the *Night Wolf* and the ships that accompanied her sailed on steadily, guarding the coastline of northern Tiguafaya so that no aid could reach the enclave. But soon, when the signal was received from Prince Tzarno and the rest of the fleet gathered, the waiting would be over.

Ever since Zophres and Chavez had returned to the atoll from Zepharinn – with the news that war had been declared and that their alliance had been ratified – the pirates' anticipation had been growing. At the time, Lamia had been annoyed by the fact that her envoy had not returned, but when she heard the explanation for his absence, her vexation subsided and she had co-operated fully in all the subsequent arrangements. These included assigning many of her colleagues from the Amagiana to duties on land with Prince Tzarno's army, as well as allowing several more to join the crews of some of the pirate ships – as a precaution against the Tiguafayans' use of sorcery. Although there had not been enough anti-mages to place one aboard every vessel, they were divided as equitably as possible among the various fleets that made up the entire sea-borne force. In return, each of the black ships had received one of the pirates to act as navigators and to interpret signals. There had only been one volunteer for these duties, and the rest had been chosen by drawing lots – a process that had amused the easterners, though they tried not to let their feelings show. With her forces stretched so thinly, Lamia was aware that co-operation with her disparate allies would be vital.

Once the brethren of the isles had responded to Zarzuelo's summons, they had set sail almost at once. Some went to the Empire with the assigned anti-mages, while some – including Zophres – went to rendezvous with the admiral of the imperial navy, to co-ordinate tactics. The rest travelled west towards Tiguafaya, under Zarzuelo's command. Although there had been several minor battles since then, in which honours had been evenly divided, there had not yet been a full-scale encounter. But that, the Survivor thought happily, was about to change. And soon.

'A ration of rum!' he shouted. 'To toast the greatest adventure of our lives!'

With each new report, Admiral Cucura was becoming more worried. It was clear now that the unthinkable had happened at sea as well as on land. Not only were imperial forces advancing over the northern firelands, but they had also formed an unholy alliance with all the pirates of the Inner Seas. How such a situation had come about was beyond Cucura's imaginative powers, but his woes did not end there. There was a further threat – from the ominous black vessels that no one recognized and everybody secretly feared. One way or another, his own fleet was badly outnumbered, and many of his crews lacked the experience that might have held them in good stead. He had been expecting to face cumbersome troop ships, bringing the imperial army south, but many of the enemy's vessels were as fast and as manoeuvrable as his own. And the one real advantage that he had been counting on – a superior knowledge of the coastal waters – had been at least partly negated by the unexpected presence of the pirates. His forces were in a desperate situation and, if the reports that magic was also proving ineffective were true, then he could foresee nothing but defeat. Naturally, he did not reveal these thoughts to any of his men, but many of them were quite capable of reaching the same conclusion on their own.

'Sail ahoy!'

The cry from the crow's nest set Cucura's nerves jangling.

'Friend or foe?' his first mate yelled.

'Friend!' the lookout called back eventually. 'It's the *Dolphin*.'

'Signal for a report as soon as they're in range,' Cucura ordered, then went below to study his charts.

The second officer of the *Dolphin* knocked on the open cabin door and was waved inside.

'The admiral's asking for a report, Captain.'

Madri glanced up at the young seaman, and wondered why he – or any of the other members of the crew – should trust an old man from history.

The *Dolphin* was one of Tiguafaya's new ships. She had set sail on her maiden voyage less than a month ago, and some of the work on her superstructure was still being completed. Madri had accepted the command only because he could not stand to be idle when his country was in peril again, and because – in the rush to commission a modern navy – there were no better candidates available. He harboured no ambitions to set the record straight from thirty years ago. Such thoughts were a dangerous delusion, and he simply wanted to do something useful. So far he had failed even in that.

Although the *Dolphin* was a fine vessel, she was untested in battle, and she was proving difficult to handle when the wind and currents were anything other than ideal. The makeshift crew were learning as they went along, not yet used to the ship or to each other, but they were improving with each day at sea – and Madri had sensed in them the first stirrings of pride that always marked an effective team. For himself, he was only now finding his sea-legs again, and his bones creaked almost as loudly as the rigging. Yet the ocean was in his blood, for all that he had denied it for so long, and he found beauty and solace in its unchanging restlessness. In fact, the ex-admiral's only real regret was that Angel was not with him. Being under sail without Tre at his side felt unnatural, but his old friend had been called away to other duties, impelled by forces only he could understand.

'Captain?' the second officer prompted, when he did not receive any instructions. 'What signal should I send?'

Madri brought his thoughts back to the matter in hand.

'Tell them there's no way through, even for a single ship. The blockade is too strong. The enclave will just have to fend for itself.'

'Aye, sir.'

'And we're all going to be needed to defend Teguise soon enough,' Madri added.

'Is that to go in the report, Captain?'

'No,' the older man replied. 'Cucura's no fool. He'll have worked it out for himself.'

# CHAPTER FORTY-TWO

When Ico entered the Senate chamber, she was taken aback to find it full of people. It took her a few moments to work out why this should have surprised her – a full session had been called, after all – and when she realized that it was because of a recurring image in her dream the night before, understanding brought only unpleasant reflections. With a persistence that was usually absent from dreams, all the images she could remember had been centred on a theme of emptiness. The most understandable – and the saddest – of these had been of her own bed, where Andrin should have been, and was not. The most frightening had been entering the nursery only to find that Ysanne had vanished without trace. And the most bizarre had been watching the seawater rush out of Teguise harbour, until all that was left was a jumbled expanse of mud, sand, slime and capsized boats. Although the Senate chamber had been eerily silent and empty in her dream, now it was anything but. The floor and the upper galleries were full to overflowing. But that gave Ico little comfort. She had had prophetic dreams in the past, and the fact that one of her nocturnal predictions had been proved wrong – for the time being, at least – did not mean that the others were also false. One of them was already true, and even though Ysanne had been perfectly safe that morning, it did not follow that she would always be so. Dreams, Ico knew, could all too easily turn to nightmares.

The first order of business was, as always, the progress of the war. From the beginning of the conflict, Ico had taken it upon herself to keep the senators informed about the military reports that were sent to her daily. She always tried to put as positive a slant on the news as possible, but as the days went by this became much more difficult. Ico would have been quite prepared to lie had she felt it necessary or advantageous, but she saw no point in being anything other than honest. The campaign was going badly, both on land and at sea, and there was no disguising this fact. Indeed, the only encouraging aspect was that casualties had so far been kept at a relatively low level. However, this had been achieved at the cost of giving ground and, sooner or later, a stand would have to be made. The death toll then did not bear thinking about. Try as she might, Ico could see no way out. All offers of peace negotiations had been rebuffed, and the Tiguafayans had been left with no option but to meet force with force.

Ico had often wished that she could cast aside her presidential responsibilities and join the fight herself. Many of the other Firebrands had enlisted and she longed to do the same, to act positively rather than remain passive. Her advisors – those who had remained in Teguise – wouldn't hear of it, though, and the fact that she would have to leave Ysanne behind had been enough to quell any further doubts.

'And that, senators, is all I can tell you at present,' she concluded, looking at the sea of worried faces. 'It's been obvious for some time that the Empire's forces are making a co-ordinated effort to attack Teguise from all sides simultaneously. Unless something changes drastically in the next few days, we may soon find ourselves under siege. All I ask is that we all make what preparations we can. A great deal has already been done – including reinforcing the walls and stockpiling food and other supplies – but if we are to survive this challenge, we must miss no opportunity, however small, to strengthen our position.'

The silence that followed her speech was fearful but expectant. There was much that needed saying, but no one was keen to be the first to speak.

'With the city full of refugees, even the stockpiles won't last long,' one senator commented eventually. 'Wouldn't it be better to evacuate them – and even some of our own women and children – to the south until this is over?'

'The resources of the southern provinces are not great at the best of times,' Ico pointed out. 'We might well be condemning both the refugees and their hosts to starvation. Teguise is their best hope, the most easily defended location, and the best supplied. Our countrymen have been forced to abandon their homes. We owe them that much, at least.'

'So are we to linger here until we all starve?' a young senator asked.

'I pray that it won't come to that,' Ico replied, 'but I don't see any alternative.'

'There is one.'

'Which is?'

'Surrender.'

This suggestion was greeted with a storm of abuse and argument, which only died down when Ico held up her hands for silence.

'I would never condone such a course of action,' she said, 'but Senator Vayland is entitled to express his opinion. Go ahead, Senator.'

The young man rose to his feet, and looked around nervously.

'Would life as part of the Empire be so bad? We might lose much, but at least we'd still be alive. You've all heard what's happening. We can't match their forces. If we try, we condemn ourselves to death. There's no honour in surrender, but there's none in a pointless death either. We should choose to live.'

'You're mad!' a senior guildsman called Gallo cried. 'As far as the Empire's concerned this is a *holy* war. Even if we *do* yield, they'll kill us all as heretics – and if they don't, the best we can hope for is life as slaves. A defeatist like you doesn't deserve to call himself a Tiguafayan!'

This outburst provoked another barrage of noise, most of it in agreement with the speaker, and Vayland sat down again. At least I don't need to call for a vote, Ico thought gratefully.

'There is another important factor to be considered,' she said, when she was able to make herself heard. 'If we let the Empire prevail, we'll lose the chance of restoring stability to the land itself for ever. They refuse to see the truth about the fireworms, and will prevent us from doing anything about them. I still believe that unless we succeed in this quest, the volcanoes will eventually claim all Tiguafaya. The only thing that lives here then will be fire.' She knew that many in the chamber shared her conviction, but there were also others who had doubts.

'We've been looking for untainted worms for almost three years,' another senator pointed out, 'and not found them yet. What chance is there now, in the middle of a war?'

'The search goes on as we speak,' Ico answered.

'With Vargo Shaimian?' someone called from the public gallery. 'The madman?'

'Whatever his state of mind, he's still our best chance,'

Ico replied, as calmly as she could. 'But there are also many others involved.'

'Where is Shaimian now?'

'I don't know exactly,' Ico admitted. 'Somewhere in the west, I believe.'

Vargo and Cat had been gone for a long time now – two more of the people who seemed to have abandoned her – and Ico still did not fully understand what had driven them to leave. Vargo had been insistent, and Cat would never let him go alone, in spite of the fact that she had obviously had many other things on her mind.

'It may be too late anyway,' another senator commented. 'Judging by the number of tremors that have been reported recently.'

'That's no reason to stop trying,' Ico rebuked him.

'I don't know why he had to go west,' one of the elder statesmen grumbled. 'If the gossipmongers are to be believed, there are plenty of worms already here in Teguise!'

'You know better than to pay too much attention to rumour, Pietro,' Ico replied.

'Rumours have to start somewhere,' the old man muttered.

'Yes,' Gallo remarked caustically. 'In weak minds and addled heads,'

Ico spoke up quickly, hoping to prevent the discussion from becoming more acrimonious.

'The guards have done everything they can to hunt down any worms being kept in the city, and they haven't found a single one. Until they do, that's the end of the matter.'

If only it were as simple as that, she thought to herself. After the incident when Cat had apparently been magically transported to Zepharinn and back, Vargo and Ero had remained unconscious for more than two days. When they finally awoke, they had both confirmed Allegra's story about a breeding pit somewhere in one of the derelict areas of the city. However, they – like Cat – had been completely unable to find it again. The 'trail' that had led them all there had vanished, and their memories of it had been wiped away. Even so, their story had initiated an intensive search, which had proved fruitless – something that had only added to Ico's frustration and anguish. She had been half inclined to believe that the whole thing was a figment of their collective imagination – but then Cat had suggested that the underground site might be protected by the same sort of magic veil that allowed Giavista Martinoy to walk the streets of Teguise unseen. That sounded too far-fetched to Ico, but she had recently been forced to accept so many incredible and unpalatable truths that one more hardly seemed to matter. The breeding pit might well exist, but she had no intention of sharing this possibility with the Senate unless it became absolutely necessary. In the meantime, all she could do was ensure – discreetly – that the few talents still in Teguise had dragon's tears crystals with them at all times, so that if the threatened 'plague' ever materialized, there would at least be a slim chance of defending themselves against it.

'It's a pity the worms haven't taken it into their heads to attack the imperial army,' Gallo remarked. 'That'd make them less keen to invade.'

This idea had already occurred to Ico and, although she would never admit it publicly, she had even discussed the possibility of herding any swarms against the enemy, using the controlling techniques the Firebrands had discovered. She had told herself that such barbaric methods would be used only as a last resort, but in the event it had not been possible. Magic rarely seemed to be effective on or near the battlefields, and no fireworms had been sighted for the last two months. Quite what *that* signified no one, least of all Ico, could guess.

'I think we'll have to rely on our own efforts,' she said.

'How is the bird-man doing?' Pietro asked.

'He's making progress,' Ico replied. But too slowly, she added silently. 'The magic he has access to is growing more powerful, but there's still a long way to go.'

In fact, Nino had made several more attempts to activate the network, but on each occasion had only partially succeeded. In spite of these disappointments, Ico had come to regard him as vitally important, and was glad that he was still in Teguise. Nino had often expressed the opinion that he ought to be elsewhere – although he could never say where – and Ico knew that he was also longing to return to his family in Tinajo. But, as the only close ally she had left, she had become increasingly reliant upon his advice.

Maciot had vanished on route to Uga Stai, Madri was at sea, Vargo was long gone, and even Angel was away on a mysterious mission of his own. Kehoe and Cucura were with their respective forces. Soo hardly ever spoke to her nowadays, and Andrin . . . Ico pushed that thought aside. If it had not been for Nino, she would have felt herself to be entirely, unbearably alone. As it was, it was all she could do to prevent herself from sinking into utter despair.

'What's the point of looking for more magic?' Another senator was speaking now, pulling Ico out of her reverie and returning her to the debate. 'It's not working anyway!'

'And there are a lot of people in the city who are opposed to its use in *any* circumstances,' someone else added.

'The power Nino Delgado is pursuing is stronger than anything we've ever known,' Ico argued. 'If he were to succeed, I don't think even the imperial army could stand against us. It's an avenue we have to follow, no matter what people think.'

She was already aware of some unrest. A meeting of the Magicians' Guild the previous day had been disrupted by angry protesters, and all the old misconceptions about magic angering the dragons and the volcanoes were gaining credence once more. Ico's own faith had never faltered, though it had been severely tested in recent months.

When Nino had told her what he had seen when the network had sprung into being for the second time, she had not wanted to believe him. She had hoped that it was some sort of delusion, brought on by her friend's anxiety and exhaustion. However, her fears had changed to a dread certainty when others who had been in the net confirmed Nino's vision, even though none of them – not even Cat herself, who had been at the heart of it all – could explain how it had happened. Ico could still remember Ysanne telling her that 'the singing had got all mixed up' – and no one else had come up with a better explanation. Later, when the declaration of war they had all witnessed had proved to be true, her last hopes had been dashed, and she had been forced to accept all the rest.

Andrin had been condemned to death. That much was certain. He had not escaped as Allegra had. There had been no confirmed reports of the execution being carried out, but neither were there any to say he was still alive. Nor had Ayo returned to bring news, good or bad. More significantly, perhaps, none of Nino's subsequent forays into the network had revealed any hint of Andrin's presence, even though the thoughts of the various participants had all been directed towards trying to find him.

When she was with Ysanne, Ico still maintained the pretence that Papa would be back soon, but privately – in her darkest moments – she had reluctantly decided that Andrin must be dead.

Oh, my love, she thought now, mountains should have split open, oceans boiled and rivers run dry. Stars should have fallen from the sky and the sun grown dark. How could you have died and I not know? My heart should have cracked and my eyes frozen over.

It wasn't meant to end this way.

'Time is running out, even for such magic. Isn't that right, Madam President?'

The voice dragged her back to the present and, blinking back the tears that threatened to betray her, Ico forced herself to answer.

'Which is why,' she said, amazed to find that her voice remained steady, 'we'll fight to the best of our abilities using every conventional means. If an age of darkness is to befall our land, then I for one will not accept it meekly. Nor will our fighting men and women. And nor should any of you!'

Even as she spoke, her thoughts were elsewhere, cradling the emptiness inside her. Until recently she had always been confident in her own path, her destiny. But now fate had cheated her.

It wasn't meant to end this way.

# CHAPTER FORTY-THREE

The dome was almost invisible in the twilight. Only a slight iridescence, like the reflection of a dragonfly's wings, betrayed its presence and warned the visitors not to go any closer.

'Not much of a talisman,' Katerin remarked, peering inside.

'No,' Madar agreed, in a voice devoid of any emotion.

'Is all this really necessary? It doesn't look like there's much to be afraid of here.'

'Perhaps not,' the Emperor replied, 'but where sorcery is concerned it's best not to take any chances.'

The prisoner was curled up behind iron bars. The cage was too cramped for him to have stood upright, even if he'd wanted to, but he seemed to be trying to make himself as small, as inconspicuous, as possible. The manacles around his ankles only emphasized his absolute subservience. His loose-fitting clothes were filthy and torn, and his bare hands and feet were covered in sores. His eyes were closed, and his once handsome face was heavily bruised and marked with scabs and dried blood. He looked unutterably weary;

whatever tortures he had endured had obviously stripped him of all dignity, almost all life.

'Chains, within a cage, within a prison,' Katerin said quietly. 'I could almost feel sorry for him.'

'Don't,' Madar advised. 'He's as good as dead. Come away.'

The Emperor led his wife away, and Kudrak followed gladly. None of them looked back.

Andrin stirred then, and watched them retreat with eyes that could have been no more dull and indifferent if they had been made of stone.

'Well, brother, this is a bit of a surprise.'

'Don't you mean an unexpected pleasure, Prince?' Katerin enquired.

'I'm sorry, Empress,' Tzarno replied, fixing her with a malevolent glare. 'An army on the march has little time for courtly etiquette. What brings you here, Madar?'

'This is the first major enterprise of my reign,' the Emperor replied calmly. 'It's only right that I should take an interest, don't you think?'

'An army can only serve one general.'

'And that's you,' Madar agreed readily enough. 'I've no wish to usurp your authority, merely to observe.'

'Your *mere* presence – and that of the Empress – will be a distraction nonetheless. This isn't a game we're playing here.'

'We're aware of that, Tzarno,' Katerin said.

The prince hated that 'we', hated her for presuming to speak for his brother, but he fought to control his temper. He would have liked to wipe that innocent smile off her pretty face.

'Then see what you need to see, go back to Zepharinn and let me get on with the task in hand,' he growled, aware even as he spoke of how she teased him – and of how attracted he was to her. Lust and rage warred within him.

'You still have your talisman with you, I see,' Madar said mildly, ignoring his brother's outburst.

'I've had no cause to use him yet. That will come later, when we're in sight of the walls of Teguise. I doubt Maravedis will have much stomach for a fight when she sees what's become of her husband.'

Andrin's fate had been a source of grievance between the two brothers ever since his capture. Having publicly given his word that the sorcerer would die, Madar had wanted to execute him as soon as possible, especially as the other prisoner had escaped in such an extraordinary fashion. Tzarno, on the other hand, had been eager to take Andrin with the army, back to Teguise, arguing that his fate would symbolize the defeat of his country – and adding that it represented only a temporary stay of execution. That way, the prince had argued, the Tiguafayan's death would count for much more. Madar had finally agreed, and Andrin had become a human trophy, a target for mockery and stones, to be gawked at and spat upon as the cart bearing his cage rolled south in triumphant procession. Even before that he had had to endure a prolonged and brutal interrogation from Castellan Ty, the effects of which marked him still in both body and mind.

From the moment of his capture, in spite of his apparent helplessness, Andrin had been kept under constant guard. To allay any fears about the further use of sorcery, the easterner who had denounced him had been put to work as soon as the envoy's particular talents became known. The dome that now surrounded the prisoner was the anti-mage's creation, acting as a barrier to magic in either direction. Although Andrin had shown no signs of any unusual powers during his incarceration, his captors thought it better to be safe than sorry.

The only attempt to help the prisoner had come from the white eagle that had been seen in Geyan Square. Soon after Tzarno's convoy had left Zepharinn, the bird had been spotted mirroring their course from above. The prince's men had then kept a special watch for the creature, which they took to be the sorcerer's familiar, and eventually set a trap for it. The eagle's efforts to tear open the cage had been doomed to failure from the start, and when it was ensnared by the nets, the furious struggle had been one-sided. Now the bird was as docile and broken in spirit as its former master.

'How long will it take you to reach Teguise?' Madar asked.

'If all continues to go well – and there are no more distractions – four days, maybe five.' Tzarno paused. 'But I don't want you or the Empress anywhere near. I'll have enough on my plate without worrying about your safety.'

'We'll remain well out of harm's way,' Madar agreed affably.

'You need not concern yourself about us, brother,' Katerin added. 'You won't even know we're here.'

Tzarno longed to retort that he was no brother of hers and that, given half a chance, he would *show* her just how he regarded her, but he managed to keep his anger in check.

'I hope you're right,' he said calmly, and contented himself with the thought that one day he would repay her – in full – for all the aggravation she had caused him.

Ayo heard the voices approaching, recognized the mockery in their tone, and the malice. He didn't know why the soldiers hated him, why they tormented him, but he had long since ceased to care. At first he had fought back, flailed with his beak and flapped his massive wings to ward off their attentions, but that had only made them more determined to prolong their amusement at his expense. Now he did not react at all, no matter what indignities or abuse were heaped upon him. It was easier not to feel, or hear, or think.

Abject failure was not something Ayo had ever had to deal with before. Even when his loyalties had been divided, so that he had thought his heart would break, he'd always been able to act, to choose his own course for better or worse. Now he was helpless and defiled, chained and flightless. He longed for the freedom of the skies, but could not even imagine soaring there as he had once done. He was no better than a caged rat, fed on scraps and offal that strangers threw at him, together with a few stones and their laughter.

His misery was compounded by the fact that his link was also imprisoned, in equally degrading circumstances. Andrin was not so far away, but they could not communicate as they used to do. Although Ayo did not know why this should be so, it only added to his despair.

During his captivity, Ayo's shame and guilt had festered so that they now consumed him. He had failed Andrin in Zepharinn. Before that he had neglected to warn his link when first the Kundahari and then the army patrol had approached him in the devastated valley. Ayo had been distracted at the time, by wayward thoughts of eggs hatching and dragons, but that was no excuse. He could tell himself that no harm had come from those failures, but in his mind they had been omens, presaging the more serious errors that had followed. Andrin's capture and then his own had marked the end of their link. And Ayo was convinced that they would soon face the end of their lives as well.

The soldiers had flung the food at his feet, then left him

alone again, disappointed by the bird's stoical indifference
to their taunts. Although the sun had set some time ago, Ayo
still did not sleep. There was no room left in his world for
sleep, or for any kind of ease. Pajarito had told him to play
his part, to be ready. And in that too he had failed.

Andrin's mind had retreated into itself, into the past.
The present meant no more to him than a foul dream, that
encased his convoluted thoughts and numbed body. Memories were his only reality, the only things that could raise his
senses above the stultifying miasma into which they had
fallen. But even then there was no escape from the darkness.
There was no joy in remembering Ico or Ysanne, only pain
and sorrow for what he had lost. So he dwelt endlessly on
more recent torments – and on one in particular.

Mazo Gadette, the man who now called himself by two
other names – both false – had come to Andrin's cell in the
Imperial Fortress after Ty had finished with him. Although
he had ostensibly come to continue the questioning, in reality
he was there to gloat – and to boast. Andrin had remained
silent while Gadette had told him how, after fleeing from
Teguise, he had met up again with his former master, Tias
Kantrowe, how he had murdered him and usurped his name,
using it to inveigle his way into a position of influence. He
had told his captive audience of his clever manipulation
of religious sentiment, of his hidden contempt for the
Kundahari and their simplistic view of the world. No one
with a real brain actually believed all that nonsense about
heresy and magic, he had said. It was simple politics – and,
for himself, the little matter of revenge.

He had told Andrin all this in the knowledge that his
fellow Tiguafayan could not reveal any of his secrets. No one
would believe him. They would simply assume that he was
either mad or trying to deflect blame from himself. It

had been a virtuoso performance, a far more subtle form of torture than that inflicted by the castellan, and the fact that it still occupied Andrin's thoughts nearly two months later was proof of its effectiveness.

Now that Andrin was without hope, beyond even the possibility of joy or contentment, the bitterness that coursed through his entire being was the only thing that let him know he was still alive.

# CHAPTER FORTY-FOUR

'You can't stay here, Tre,' Cabria said gently. 'We all have to go.'

Angel shook his misshapen head violently.

'I won't lose my oars again, again.'

As was so often the case, the wanderer's words made little sense, but on this occasion their meaning was clear enough.

'There won't be anyone left to help you,' Cabria pointed out. 'No food, no fires. What will you do?'

'There are mirrors,' Angel replied, as if this explained everything. 'New cloud hopes. Soon.'

'This isn't even your home,' the village elder tried again. 'What if the imperial soldiers come? You could be killed.'

'Too cold without me,' Angel stated obstinately. 'I stay.'

Cabria looked around helplessly. The last evacuees were moving off, heading for the western end of the valley. The war had not yet touched Corazoncillo, but a messenger had arrived the day before from Commander Kehoe, telling them that a sizeable detachment of the enemy army might be heading towards them. He recommended that they travel south, because he could not spare any of his own troops to defend them. Many of the men from Corazoncillo and Quemada were already away fighting for their country, but the remaining villagers held a meeting that night and – after some debate – had voted to go. Quite why the invaders were heading their way, when the main force was staying closer to the east coast on route to Teguise, was a mystery. Their best guess was that Prince Tzarno had heard about the dragon eggs and wanted one of his officers to take a look at them, perhaps even lay claim to them. Cabria had the feeling that the eggs were also the reason for Angel's refusal to leave. They were certainly what had drawn him to the valley in the first place.

'There's nothing you can do for them, you know,' he said, indicating the dark shapes that lay around them. 'We've tried.'

'No worms in the apple-taster, taster,' Angel responded. The thought seemed to amuse him.

'They'll hatch in their own time,' Cabria went on. 'The soldiers won't be able to hurt them.'

'Newness is a passage, passage.'

He's quite mad, the elder thought. I can't just leave him here to be killed. He probably doesn't even understand the danger he's in.

'You must come with me, Tre,' he said, making one last effort at persuasion. 'If you don't I'll have to call for help and we'll take you away by force. You don't want that, do you?'

Angel said nothing, but a spark flared into life deep within his strange eyes.

'Please, Tre. Come with me.' Cabria held out his hand in supplication.

Suddenly, the air seemed to spin in front of him, a whirl of light that left him feeling giddy – and in that instant Angel vanished. Bewildered and afraid, the village elder glanced all around, even checked behind the dragon eggs, but Angel was nowhere to be seen.

Cabria searched for a while, becoming ever more certain that he would not find anything, and then – in answer to a call from one of his fellow villagers – he turned away and joined the long column of people who were leaving their homes behind.

Silence descended in the Corazoncillo valley. Nothing stirred but the wind.

Much later that same morning, there was a brief shimmering at the edge of the village square, and Angel stepped back into the light. He stood quite still for a few moments, listening. Then, apparently satisfied, he limped over to the eggs, touching each shell as if to reassure himself that they were all still there. Having done that, he hobbled off to the guest hall, where he had been sleeping, collected a blanket and returned to make a crude bed for himself among the dragons.

Resuming a vigil that had already lasted for several days, Angel seemed content.

# CHAPTER FORTY-FIVE

'You're shivering.'

'I'm cold!' Cat snapped irritably.

'Come closer to the fire.' Vargo put an arm round her shoulders, and was hurt when she stiffened at his touch.

Their clothes were still damp from fording the river. As summer began to fade into autumn, the days were getting colder, and less sunlight reached the bottom of the ravine. Even so, Vargo did not believe that Allegra's trembling was just because of the chill in the afternoon air.

'Better?'

'Not really.'

'What's the matter, Cat?'

'Do you really have to ask that?' she exclaimed. 'The last time we came here we almost died.'

'I know.'

She had expected him to deny it, to make a joke of it, or at least claim that it would not happen this time, so his simple, matter-of-fact agreement caught her off guard. She shivered again.

'I don't know what we're doing here,' she complained.

'This is the only place we can be sure of finding fire-worms again.'

'But what good will that do?'

'This is their oracle, the place where they come to find answers,' he explained. 'I have to try to give them some.'

'How?'

'By talking to the oracle myself.' He did not sound altogether certain. 'I'll know what to do when I get there.'

It was one of those vague, Vargo-ish answers that Allegra was finding more and more aggravating. She had the feeling he was hiding something from her, but that no longer surprised her. She was saddened by this, whereas a few months earlier it would have made her angry.

A lot had changed in that time. Her own extraordinary experiences – being abandoned in the breeding pit, the magic that had transported her first to Zepharinn and then back to Teguise, her memory lapses, and the unknown voices that were still sounding intermittently in her head – all these things had left her feeling unnerved and afraid. There was only one thing she had learnt for certain – and that was that she would never be able to use magic. In everything that had happened, she had no control over the process. Her fond imaginings, after she had killed the fireworm, about finding her own magic, were now exposed as simple foolishness and wishful thinking. Even then she had been in the grip of something far more powerful than she could ever hope to be. Cat was under no illusions any more. The magic had used her.

'Well, I'm not going anywhere until we've had some sleep,' she stated belligerently.

'Agreed,' Vargo replied mildly. 'We'll camp here tonight and set off in the morning.'

*

Allegra had thought long and hard before deciding to leave
Teguise again. Vargo's assumption that she would go with
him had rankled, but in the end she had done so – more out
of habit and loyalty than any genuine desire. Although Vargo
evidently knew where his path was supposed to lead, Cat
was no longer sure they were meant to tread it together.

This time they had taken the direct route to the ravine,
which meant that one of the villages on their way had
been Tinajo. They had carried a message for Tavia from
Nino, and had been welcomed with open-hearted hospitality – even though she must have been disappointed by the
contents of her husband's letter. Two villagers had accompanied them on the next stage of their journey, to Imbiani,
where Ambron had been delighted to see them. By then
news of the war had filtered through even to these remote
settlements, and everyone had dozens of questions, most of
which Vargo and Cat had been quite unable to answer. It had
been a relief to move on, this time with Ambron and Vek for
company. The prospector had been cheerfully insistent at
first, but within a few days the strained atmosphere surrounding his travelling companions had affected his mood
as well. Cat knew that he'd been glad to reach the rim of the
canyon and take his leave. By then not even Ero had been
able to relieve the growing tension in the air.

Now, two days later, they stood at the entrance to the cave
system, alone for what felt like the first time in months.
But their relationship had changed; there was an invisible
barrier between them now, one that neither of them seemed
able to breach. The presence of others on the journey had
inhibited them even further, until Cat's anger and hurt had
turned into immutable resentment. She knew that Vargo
had been at least partially responsible for saving her, even
though he had said nothing to confirm this, and that made
her feel guilty. Her emotions had become so confused, she

didn't know how to begin to unravel them. And whatever Vargo was feeling was hidden behind his purpose – and behind his occasional insanity.

Even by his own standards, Vargo was unusually clumsy during their meal that evening. He dropped food, spilled water on himself and on the fire, and almost choked twice. However, to Cat's relief, he remained sane, even making jokes at his own expense.

'What *is* the matter with you?' Even though their supplies were more than adequate this time, she still found the waste exasperating.

'I don't know,' he replied. 'I'm all feathers and thumbs.'

Allegra was about to ask him what on earth he meant when she was distracted by a soft, almost mournful voice that sounded inside her head. She could make no sense of the random series of words, but that did not make them any less real. Voices. Other. Obey. Skies. And then they slipped from her mind like the afterimages of a dream. I'm not *meant* to understand, Cat thought. Is that what madness is?

'Be careful!' she cried, coming back to the present with a rush. Vargo had shifted position, and in doing so had moved one of his boots into the edge of the fire. The leather was already beginning to smoulder when Cat knocked it aside. 'What are you doing?'

'I'm sorry. I . . .' He shook his head, as if to clear it. 'That *was* water in the flagon, not wine, wasn't it?'

'Yes,' she replied shortly. 'What's got into you?'

Vargo could only shrug. He moved carefully away from the flames, distancing himself from her annoyance at the same time. They sat in silence for a while, Cat staring at the glowing twigs but still aware that Vargo was gazing at her.

'Are *you* all right, Cat?' he said eventually.

'Yes.' She paused. 'No. I don't know!'

Echoes of her voice whispered softly round the ravine.

'What is it?' Vargo asked quietly.

'Not what,' she told him. 'Who.'

'Who, then?'

'Don't pretend you don't know. Ico, of course.'

'What about her?'

'You love her.' It was a statement, not a question, but it was still a few moments before Vargo answered.

'Very much,' he said. 'As a friend.'

'A friend! Is that all?'

'Yes. Cat, I—'

'So did you spend the night with her?' she demanded.

'Yes.'

'I knew it!'

'Just as I've spent many nights with you.'

'But we've never . . .'

'Neither did we.'

'You expect me to believe that?'

'It's the truth.' He was calm now, and rational.

'So what did you do all night?' Cat asked. 'Sing each other lullabies?'

'We talked for a long time,' Vargo replied. 'And yes, I held her in my arms – for comfort, nothing more. Then we went to sleep.'

'In her bed?' she asked, still sceptical.

'Yes. The next thing we knew it was dawn and Madri was back, and . . .'

'You've always loved her, haven't you?' Allegra did not wait for an answer. 'This was your chance, with Andrin away. Why didn't you take it?'

Vargo had asked himself the same question at the time, and several times since, but it was only now that he knew the answer for certain.

'I couldn't,' he said. 'Any more than she could.'

'Scared of what Andrin might do, were you?' Cat asked scornfully.

'That never even entered my head,' Vargo replied truthfully, ashamed to admit it. He had not thought of Andrin at all.

'What stopped you, then?'

'You.'

It was a very long time before Cat was able to speak again, and when at last she did, her voice was no more than a whisper.

'Me?'

'I love you, Cat.'

She looked at him then, saw the earnestness and the fear on his face, and knew that this time the words really were meant for her. Her vision blurred at he went on.

'I've always loved you. I didn't know it for a long time, and I've been stupid, I know. I realized just how stupid that night with Ico, but I haven't been able to do anything about it since.' Vargo paused, remembering Ico telling him that she too had wondered what it would be like if the two of them had been together. However, that night she had also said, 'But it can't be, can it.' That was one part of the story he did not intend to tell Cat. 'Can you forgive me?'

Allegra nodded dumbly.

'Part of me's known all along,' Vargo went on. 'When you went off on your own in Teguise, that part asked Ero to watch out for you. That's why he followed you, why we were able to find you eventually. But I wasn't even aware of asking him.'

'And you brought me back,' she said, finding her voice again. 'From Zepharinn.'

'I had to. I'd've done *anything*. You mean more to me than anyone.'

'Even Ico?'

'It's *you* I really want,' he replied fervently, 'but . . .'

That one small word threatened to hurl Cat down from the cloud on which she was floating.

'But what?' she asked quickly, her voice shaking.

'How can I ask you to . . . to be with me, when so much is happening, when I don't even know if—'

'You don't have to *ask*, you stupid man!' Cat exclaimed. 'I already have all the reasons I need. I've always loved you, Vargo. Everyone knew that. Famara knew it years ago! Why couldn't you see?'

Vargo felt himself blushing.

'There are none so blind . . .' he muttered sheepishly.

'If you don't get over here and kiss me *now*,' Cat stated aggressively, 'I shan't be responsible for the consequences.'

Vargo almost fell over in his haste to obey and their first embrace was awkward, but when their lips finally met, all that was forgotten. For a few moments the rest of the world melted away into absolute irrelevance. When they finally drew apart, Allegra became aware of two noises, both of them seeming new and unfamiliar. The first was her own incredulous laughter. The second was the sound of approaching wingbeats.

'You're too late this time, Ero,' she said, glancing round at the newcomer. She had half expected the hoopoe to interrupt their conversation as soon as it approached anything personal, just as he had done so many times in the past. 'Too late!'

'No wonder I was getting clumsy,' Vargo said – and then Cat noticed that Ero was not alone. Next to him, chirruping softly in greeting was Lao, Vargo's second link. Twice each year, in spring and autumn, there was a short period when both migrants were present, and the conflicting pulls on Vargo's mind tended to confuse him and make him even more eccentric than usual. On this occasion, however, nothing could dent Cat's happiness.

'Hello, Lao,' she said softly.

'All of me is here now,' Vargo whispered.

Allegra knew that he was not just talking about the birds, and was content to wait while the three of them exchanged greetings, in words she could not hear but could almost sense. When she could stand it no longer, she pulled Vargo towards her again.

'Now tell them to go away,' she ordered. 'I don't want anyone watching us tonight.'

Vargo smiled and turned to glance at his links. Lao bowed in dignified fashion and flew away silently. Ero hesitated a little longer, then followed the sandpiper into the night. His last indignant call, *hoo-poo-hoo*, would have made Cat laugh if she had heard it. But by then she had already begun to remove Vargo's clothing, and had other things on her mind.

Allegra woke the next morning with the sunlight, feeling warm and contented. Vargo was still asleep beside her, but in spite of the fact that she had had little rest, she was full of energy. It was only when she looked around and saw the entrance to the cave that the anxieties of the real world began to catch up with her again. Do we really have to go in there? she thought. She would have been quite happy to stay right where she was for days, months.

Then Ero came dancing down towards her. His landing was, as always, somewhat inelegant, and he took a moment to compose himself before waddling over towards the shared bed and fixing her with a disapproving stare.

'What?' Cat asked, laughing.

Vargo stirred at the sound of her voice, and the sudden smile that lit up his face when he felt her next to him made Allegra's heart sing.

A little later, the light-hearted mood had been replaced

by one that was both determined and fearful.

'What are they going to do?' Cat asked, indicating Ero and Lao.

'Wait for us here,' Vargo replied. 'They won't come into the caves.' Almost all birds hated going underground and, although Lao was less afraid than most, this particular journey would be impossible even for him. 'Are you ready?'

Cat nodded.

'What exactly are *we* going to do?' she asked.

'Go to the fossil cave and summon the fireworms.'

'What makes you think they'll be any different from the rest?'

'They won't be. They're all tainted.' For once Vargo sounded very sure of himself.

'Then what's the point?'

'We have to change them,' he told her. 'Heal them.'

'Heal them? How?'

Vargo could not meet her gaze then, and his hesitation unnerved her.

'Tell me, Vargo,' she demanded.

'There's only one way we'll ever be able to convince them that we don't hate them.'

'What way?'

'I have to let them eat me,' Vargo replied.

# CHAPTER FORTY-SIX

Tzarno stared at the scout in disbelief.

'What do you mean, they've gone?'

'Just that, General. The Tiguafayans all disappeared during the night. All their positions, the reserve camp, even the lookout posts in the hills – there's no one left. As far as we can tell, there may not be anyone between us and Teguise!'

The prince took a few moments to consider this un-expected development, then turned to glance at Ty.

'Could be a trap,' the castellan suggested.

'An ambush?' Tzarno muttered doubtfully. 'There have been far better places for them to try that. We're almost out of the firelands now.'

'Perhaps their commander's only just thought of it,' Ty said caustically. 'He's been close to incompetent until now.'

'But where would they be hiding?' the prince wondered. 'The valley ahead isn't even all that steep. Not much chance of setting off a rockslide in farming country.'

'Maybe they know something we don't. Could there be an eruption due?' Ty asked, recalling the latest tremors, which had disturbed everyone's rest the night before.

'I think they've finally decided to hide behind city walls,' Tzarno concluded. 'If this gives us a clear run through to Teguise I'm not going to object, but we don't move until we've checked every possibility.' He turned back to the soldier. 'I want scout parties on all the hills, and as far forward as—' He broke off as the sounds of a hurried arrival came from outside the command tent. 'What's going on out there?'

Another soldier ducked under the flap and saluted his commander. He was out of breath, and his face and uniform were streaked with black stains.

'The valley ahead's on fire, General,' he gasped. 'There's no way to control it.'

'Will the fire reach this camp?' Tzarno asked quickly.

'No, sir. I don't think so. There's too much barren ground between us.'

'All right. Make sure everything's ready to move, just in case. Get all your men to a safe distance. And keep me informed.'

'Yes, General.'

As the messenger departed, Tzarno turned back to the scout.

'None of your men saw this coming?' he asked pointedly.

'No, sir.'

'I still want a full reconnaissance. Just make sure you all stay clear of the path of the fire. Get going!'

'That explains their withdrawal,' Ty remarked as the scout left.

'They're getting desperate.'

'If they'd had any sense, they'd have done this long before now – every time they retreated, in fact. They haven't even been poisoning the wells!' The castellan's voice was thick with contempt.

'How long before the fire burns itself out?'

'If they've done a thorough job, two days. Maybe three.'

'We'll have to go around.'

'But that means going east again, right onto the coastal plain,' the castellan said. 'It's a pretty narrow strip there. Are you happy with that?'

'Provided the navy haven't fouled things up, I don't see a problem,' Tzarno replied. 'We'll be out of the mountains altogether soon, and then we'd have to co-ordinate our advance with the fleet anyway. What's the latest news from there?'

'Nothing decisive yet,' Ty answered. 'But our allies have reportedly got several Tiguafayan ships blockaded in a bay just here.' He pointed to the map laid out before them. 'If they can be destroyed before the final push, it would make life easier for everybody.'

'Get a signal to the fleet. Let them know our situation, and ask when they think they'll be in place.'

Ty nodded. 'In the meantime, we have to get the army over the hills to the east here,' he said. 'The terrain shouldn't be a problem for the infantry or the camels, but the supply wagons are going to find it tough going.'

'The supply camp can stay where it is for the time being,' the prince said, with a satisfied grin. 'We can carry our own rations for a few days, and they can catch up when the fire's burnt itself out.'

'And Madar gets to sit around doing nothing,' Ty remarked.

'I do hope it won't be too boring for him,' Tzarno said.

A kind of horrified fascination had drawn Katerin back to the prisoner's cage. The idea that the pathetic creature inside the dome was actually a sorcerer had taken hold of her always active imagination, and the more she thought about him the more intrigued she became. This was the man who had conjured up the image of a dragon on her wedding day, disrupting the celebrations and almost destroying the Prophet. This was the man whose female accomplice had appeared from nowhere and then vanished into thin air, the man who could speak to eagles and hurl flame from his fingertips. Looking at him now, she found it hard to believe. In his present state, the captive inspired pity, not fear.

'Why did you do it, Andrin?' she wondered aloud. 'What was the point?'

The prisoner did not respond. He did not even bother to look at her.

'You could have just walked away, gone back to your wife, but you had to try to be a hero. All you've done is get yourself locked up in a cage. Was it worth it?'

When there was still no response, the Empress began to feel cheated. He was the only sorcerer she had ever met, and Katerin was not used to being ignored.

'Having an eagle for a familiar can't have been easy,' she probed, trying to find a chink in his armour of indifference. 'Not exactly the most inconspicuous of birds, is he?' She paused. 'You know Tzarno will kill him too, when he executes you. He'll probably set his feathers on fire and let him roast.'

That got a reaction, albeit a small and silent one. Andrin shifted his head a fraction, and opened his tormented eyes. The look he gave her was one of such undiluted malice and contempt that not even Katerin could stand before it. She turned away, feeling more shaken than she would have believed possible, and left Andrin to his despair.

As she fled, she glanced to the south and noticed a vast plume of smoke drifting upwards into the sky.

'This was all part of the old Verier family estates,' Captain Jameos explained. 'Since their disgrace, it's been more or less left to grow wild.'

'It looks pretty much like any other scrubland,' Kehoe commented.

'Only on the surface. Because most of the shafts have been filled in or covered over, and the lichen and cactus have covered the waste tips, no one could tell there was a mine down there.'

'Let's hope it fools Tzarno,' the commander said. 'You're sure he'll come this way?'

'Yes, sir. Going inland again would mean they'd lose several days backtracking. I can't see them wanting to do that, and judging by the smoke . . .' He glanced up, looking over the line of hills to the west, and indicated the grey plumes rising toward the heavens. '. . . Atagua and his lads have done a pretty thorough job on the Ratifia Valley. So this is the only route open. The passage over the ridge is easy enough at the north end.'

'And Tzarno won't suspect anything once he reaches the coastal plain?'

'Not if we work fast,' Jameos replied. 'We've already begun. Come with me, sir, and I'll show you.'

Kehoe followed the junior officer with a heavy heart. Given more men and resources, he would have preferred to face the imperial army in straightforward battle, to test their mettle directly. He had known that to be impossible for some time now, but this scheme was a last desperate throw of the dice, and he knew it. Subterfuge would not normally be his chosen method, but circumstances dictated that he act out of character for once.

Jameos led him to a derelict wooden shed, which – had he not been told its real purpose – Kehoe would have taken for an ancient barn. Inside, the hurriedly repaired remains of winching equipment and several wide black holes in the floor told a different story.

'This is one of the few shafts still open,' the captain told him, 'but once you're down into the workings, the tunnels radiating out from here give access to almost the entire mine. All the land for miles around is literally honeycombed below the surface.'

'Take me down,' Kehoe ordered.

Jameos hesitated.

'Is that wise, Commander?' he ventured. 'The men down there now have had mining experience, and it's dangerous enough even for them. The Verier family used slave labour, so they didn't care if they lost a few men as long as they got their silver. But the place was already unstable when it was abandoned.'

'Take me down, Captain,' Kehoe repeated. 'I can't ask my men to risk their lives down there if I'm not prepared to do the same.'

Jameos nodded, and gave an order to the soldiers manning the pulleys. A few moments later, Kehoe found himself travelling down into the earth, the only light coming from the lamp he had been given. The cage in which he and the captain stood rattled and banged against the sides of the shaft, and the ropes creaked alarmingly. He could only imagine the horrors of a life spent as a slave here.

They passed several tunnels, leading off in various directions, but continued on down until the cage bumped onto a solid floor. Getting out, the two men walked a few paces towards a large cavern, which was already a hive of feverish activity. A dozen more tunnels led off into the darkness. The smells of dust, sweat and oil were overlaid with an unidentifiable, darker odour that made Kehoe want to retch.

'This is the hub,' Jameos explained. 'Everything spreads out from here, so it's the logical place to set the trails and fuses.'

'Are there any other caves this big?'

'Several. Some even bigger. It's one of the reasons this should work. Half the joists and support posts are rotten, so once we've weakened them still further, it shouldn't take much to make the whole thing collapse in on itself.'

'And the fire-trails will be enough to do that?'

'Yes, sir. Rock falls will put some of them out, of course, but there are almost certainly some gas pockets around, and if any of those ignite it'll be a bonus, make the collapse even more violent.' Jameos sounded boyishly enthusiastic. 'With a bit of luck it'll be devastating at ground level. We could bury half the imperial army in just a few moments.'

'How soon can all of this be ready?' Kehoe asked, imagining the carnage.

'A few hours. No more.'

'Then there'll be time for you and your men to get clear.' The rest of the army was already heading south, partly for their own protection and partly in order to convince Tzarno that the retreat to Teguise was genuine.

'A few of us are going to have to stay, sir,' Jameos replied. 'We need to get the timing right or this will all be wasted effort. We'll need lookouts on the surface and a way to get a signal down here.'

'This is where you'll light all the fires'

'Yes. We've designed it so that one man can do the whole thing. That's the one drawback, Commander. Whoever stays down here probably won't get out in time.'

'I'd guessed as much,' Kehoe replied. 'Which is why I'm going to do it myself.'

# CHAPTER FORTY-SEVEN

'Why are you crying, Mama?'

'Because I'm sad, sweetheart,' Ico replied, hurriedly brushing away her tears.

As had happened so often recently, her daughter had come into Ico's bedroom as dawn broke, and on this occasion the little girl's stealthy approach had caught her unawares.

'Why are you sad?'

'Because a lot of bad things are happening.'

'Is it because Papa hasn't come home yet?' Ysanne asked, unsatisfied by this vague answer.

'That's one of the reasons,' Ico admitted.

'But it'll be all right when he *does* come home, won't it.'

'Of course it will.' Ico forced herself to smile, wishing she had her daughter's unquestioning faith.

This simple reassurance seemed to be enough for Ysanne, and she snuggled down into the bedclothes. After a few moments she popped up again.

'Why don't we ask the dragon babies to help?'

'What?'

'With the bad things,' Ysanne explained with exaggerated patience.

It sometimes seemed to Ico as if she were the two-year-old and her daughter the adult.

'Did you dream about them again?' she asked curiously. 'Have you been talking to them?'

'No. They're asleep.'

'*Could* you talk to them, if we went to see them?' Ico said, realizing even as she spoke that such an expedition was quite out of the question.

'I don't think so.' Ysanne replied, after giving the matter serious consideration. 'But they helped us before, didn't they?'

'Yes, little one, they did. But that was very special. Do you remember the story I told you? About the island called Elva?'

'The rackle.'

'That's right, the oracle. Well, no one can go there now.'

'Why?'

'Because there's too much fire and lava in the way. Even the sea all around her is boiling. In any case, I don't think the dragons would listen to me at the moment.'

'They have to!' Ysanne exclaimed indignantly. 'You're the President.'

'That's only for people, not dragons,' Ico explained.

That silenced the little girl for a while. When she spoke next it was in a very small but determined voice that made Ico want to weep.

'I don't want you to be sad, Mama.'

Nor do I, Ico thought. But I don't seem to have much choice in the matter.

Teguise woke to another day of whispers and fearfulness. New rumours seemed to spring up every hour, each more ominous than the last, and the atmosphere in the city was made worse by the knowledge that it might soon become a prison. Preparations were being made for a possible siege, but not in an entirely orderly manner. Certain items were already in short supply, and the hurried introduction of rationing had led to almost as many problems as it had solved. Accusations of hoarding and profiteering were becoming more frequent, and some of the ensuing arguments became violent – necessitating the involvement of the city garrison. This was already undermanned and over-stretched, and the guards did not appreciate being forced into the role of arbitrators in such disputes.

The situation was made even more volatile by the presence of large numbers of refugees. Teguise was so over-crowded now that almost every shelter – including the guest quarters of the Presidential Palace, and most government buildings – had been pressed into service as temporary dormitories. Even then, hundreds of people were being forced to sleep in the open. There were already reports of disease spreading among the close-packed inhabitants of the poorer areas, and with more people arriving every day that could only get worse.

It was only on and around the city walls and in the harbour that some sort of order was being forged out of the chaos. Every available mason, carpenter or other skilled artisan was busy fortifying Teguise, preparing the defences that they, together with the returning army, would later occupy. When war finally arrived – as it looked certain to do any day now – the city would not yield without a struggle.

Nino had become obsessed with his work. He hardly slept at all now, and when he did he dreamt of the network. He spent his waking hours talking to as many links as possible, imploring them to join his quest, and explaining his vision.

The influx of refugees from the north had brought many people who were paired with birds, some of whom had never been contacted before, and this gave added impetus to his efforts. A constant stream of visitors and messengers, both human and avian, was evidence of Nino's continuing attempt to build the spider's web of power – the web he had seen only twice in reality, but which was never far from his thoughts or his imagination. Every time he deliberately tried to activate it, he and his colleagues had got a little closer to success and he knew that, one day, he'd be able to call upon the network, to harness that power. But he feared that that day might come too late to save Tiguafaya. And so he drove himself on, defying exhaustion, and forcing all those around him to do the same. Even Eya's almost legendary stamina had been put to the test.

The only time Nino was able to tear himself away from his work was when Ico needed him. His own concerns paled beside hers and he always listened when she talked, recognizing her need, and gave what advice he could. His own obsession did not blind him to the fact that Ico's world was falling apart, nor to the fact that he was the only person she had left to turn to. He did his best to help her whenever he was able.

There was no way of predicting when she would come to him, but this morning Ico's arrival was even more abrupt than usual, and Nino saw at once that she was in some distress. Excusing himself from his current visitors, he led her to a private chamber and closed the door.

'I don't think I can do this any more, Nino,' she said, without preamble. She spoke quietly, in a neutral tone that he found more unnerving than if she had screamed. 'If it wasn't for Ysanne, I might be tempted to consider Orzola's way out.'

'Don't say that!' Nino cried. 'Don't even think it.'

Orzola was a name from one of Tiguafaya's oldest legends, the girl who had committed suicide after discovering that her lover had been murdered.

'She was talking about Andrin again this morning,' Ico went on, obviously referring to her daughter. 'And I don't know what to tell her. Andrin's dead and —'

'You don't know that,' Nino cut in firmly, wishing he had more to offer than uncertainty.

'Then why hasn't there been a message, some kind of sign?' she asked. 'Where's Ayo? And why haven't you been able to see them in the web?'

These were all questions that Nino could not answer, and Ico did not wait for him to try.

'Sometimes I even wish I knew he *was* dead,' she went on, her voice anguished now. 'At least that would be better than this endless wondering, hoping. I'm so afraid, Nino, and I can't show it to anyone but you.'

He put his arms around her and held her as she cried, knowing that nothing he could say would do any good. He could tell her that the war would be won, that Vargo would find untainted worms, that he would find the secret of the network, that Andrin would come home safe and well . . . but it would all be wishful thinking, and they both knew it.

'Presidents aren't allowed to be afraid, not in public at least,' he told her instead. 'It goes with the job. And no one can say you're not a worthy President of Tiguafaya. No one. And I know you won't let any of us down.'

'How can you say that?' she asked, wiping her eyes. 'Half the time I don't know what I'm doing. I'm afraid to go to sleep because of what my dreams might bring. I'm afraid to wake up because of what the day might have in store. I live in dread of every single moment. What am I suppose to *do*?'

'What we all do,' Nino replied. 'The best we can. No one can ask more than that.'

'But—'

She was interrupted when, after a cursory knock, the door flew open and one of the palace guards almost fell into the room. Nino was about to yell at him when he saw the look on the soldier's face and held his tongue.

'Ma'am, you . . . you'd better come quick,' he stammered. 'Something's happened in the nursery.'

Ico needed no further prompting and she ran ahead of the guard, with Nino following close behind. When they reached her daughter's room, Ysanne was nowhere to be seen. Yaisa was slumped in a chair, white-faced and sobbing, while two other servants were trying to coax her into talking. Meanwhile, two more soldiers were searching the room, even though it was obvious that no one else was there.

'What's happened?' Ico gasped. 'Where's Ysanne?'

Yaisa couldn't bring herself to look at her mistress.

'She's gone.' The maid's voice was unnaturally high-pitched.

'Gone? What do you mean, gone?'

'She grew hundreds of tiny wings and flew away!' Yaisa shrieked, and began to weep again.

'Where?' Ico asked, now utterly bewildered as well as frightened.

Unable to speak any more, Yaisa pointed to the window, where the shutters had been thrown back.

Ico stared at the open space through which – if the hysterical maid was to be believed – her own last reason for living had just flown.

# CHAPTER FORTY-EIGHT

'You bastard!' Cat hissed. 'You utter, heartless bastard!'

The silence had only lasted long enough for her to convince herself that Vargo actually *had* said what she thought
he'd said. The silence had lasted only a few heartbeats, but it
seemed as if an age had passed.

'How could you tell me you love me – make love to
me – and then announce that you're going to kill yourself?'
Allegra's distress was matched by her fury and, for a
moment, Vargo thought she was going to hit him. Ero
and Lao had both taken to the air and were fluttering wildly,
obviously greatly agitated.

'No . . . I . . .' His tongue would not obey him, and his
brain could not find the right words.

'What good would it do?' Cat raged. 'How will letting the
worms eat you help anyone?'

'They'll know the tooth . . . the truth.'

'And you'll be dead!'

'Maybe not.'

'What are you talking about? I've seen what fireworms
do!'

'Not here, not at their oracle. The dragon will help us.'

'The dragon?' Cat exclaimed scornfully. 'It's been dead for thousands of years. *How* is it going to help?'

'We need . . . we need to go back in time. To the . . . to—'

'To the innocence? That never made sense the first time around, Vargo. And it certainly doesn't now.'

'I'm getting the words . . . mixed up. Let me—'

'Let you what? Try to justify your suicide?'

'I'll be in the mirror,' he blurted out. 'That's where they'll eat me.' His desperate need to explain himself was thwarted by his absolute inability to do so in a coherent fashion.

Allegra took a deep breath, trying to calm herself.

'What difference does *that* make?' she asked quietly.

'I don't know,' Vargo admitted.

'You don't know? You're willing to risk your life on something you don't *know*?'

'I have to do this, Cat. This is the only way, the only place – and I'm the only one who can do it.'

That gave Allegra pause for thought, and she remembered Nino's words. 'Vargo's the only one who *knows* what the dragons told him.' But that in itself did not justify what he planned. It was too horrible even to think about.

'I should knock you out and tie you up until you come to your senses,' she growled.

Looking at her, Vargo thought her quite capable of doing just that, but his own conviction did not alter.

'I came so close before, Cat,' he said. 'When you rescued me.'

'I suppose that was a mistake,' she muttered sarcastically. 'Obviously I should have let the worm eat you. Then everything would've been all right.'

'No,' he replied earnestly. 'It would've killed me. But it was after that that I knew. It's different now.'

'You're mad! It'll still kill you.' Then another memory resurfaced, another realization.

'This is what you meant when you said, "Mustn't tell Cat", isn't it? This is your secret. You've known for months!'

'No! I was delirious then. You know my brain doesn't work in normal ways.'

Allegra almost laughed then, but found herself crying instead.

'You're going to do this no matter what I say, aren't you?' she said, sobbing now.

'I have to,' he replied softly, reaching out for her.

'Don't touch me!' she warned him, her tear-filled eyes flashing.

'Cat, please.'

'Well, if you're going to kill yourself, you'll have to do it without me. All this time I've been trying to protect you, and now . . . ' The rest of the sentence was lost in another burst of angry tears.

'I need you with me, Cat. I can't do this alone.'

'Gods!' she screamed. 'You not only want me to accept this madness, you want me to *watch* as well?'

'You were there last time,' he said. 'You were an important part of everything that happened – and everything that will happen. I don't understand it all, but—'

'*You* don't understand?' she exclaimed incredulously.

'Besides,' he added, 'if I go alone, I'll probably get lost on my way out.' He risked a tentative smile. 'You know I've got no sense of erection – direction, I mean.'

'You've got no sense at all,' she commented, but the fury had gone from her voice. She sounded very tired now.

'Will you help me?'

Allegra did not answer for a long time. 'On one condition,' she said eventually. 'That you promise me faithfully, absolutely, that you will not die.'

'I promise,' he replied at once.

'You're a lying shit, Vargo Shaimian,' Cat said resignedly. 'I just hope that one day you take our marriage vows more seriously.'

'I will,' he said.

The only way Allegra could cope with the journey into the caves was to refuse to even think about what might happen when they reached their destination. Instead she concentrated on practical matters, retracing their earlier passage and marking the way with chalk again. At least this time she had plenty of oil for the lamp, so there was no danger of their being plunged into total darkness. Even so, she moved carefully and slowly, trying to prolong their journey – still unable to face what might happen when they got to the cave.

The music crept up on them with equal stealth, beginning as no more than a vibration on the edge of hearing. But after a while they could both hear it clearly – a fluted, ethereal cadence that had no real melody, but whose rhythm was marked out by the mountain's breathing, the stone heartbeat that had led them on before. The sound had an almost hypnotic quality that was both soothing and inviting – until Cat remembered that it was being made by the waters of the Great West Ocean as they pounded through the lower caves, pulsing within the labyrinth below. She could not imagine how anything born of such primeval violence could result in such beauty – and because of that she distrusted the siren song of the tides. And yet she kept going, honouring her own promise, even though she knew Vargo might not be able to fulfil his.

Only once did she falter, when a familiar rock formation told her that the lake was now only a short distance away. Her legs simply stopped working, and she stumbled.

'I can't do this,' she whispered. 'I can't.' She'd loved Vargo for so long, and now that she knew he returned her feelings, the thought of losing him so soon made her feel physically sick.

'You can, my love,' he said, coming up behind her and taking her in his arms. 'And so can I.'

For the first time, Cat realized what Vargo was putting himself through. Until that moment she had only regarded his insane scheme as something that affected her, depriving her of the one person in the world who really mattered. Now she forced herself to look at the situation from Vargo's point of view. He was risking everything, his own life, to follow his path. It had not been fair of him to ask her to help, but he was showing great courage, and the least she owed him was to try to do the same.

'Anyway, where's it written down that it has to be fair?' she muttered.

'What?'

'It doesn't matter. Come on.'

When they reached the fossil cavern a few minutes later, they stood and gazed across the mirror-still water at the dragon.

'What now?' Cat asked, her stomach knotting.

'We have to be over on the other side,' Vargo replied.

Allegra did not bother arguing, or asking why, but set off to traverse the rock wall as she had done before. To her surprise she remembered the route easily, and reached the far ledge without mishap. Vargo followed with equal alacrity, and they walked on round to the ancient remains.

'Touch it with me,' Vargo said softly.

Following his lead, Cat reached up and placed her fingertips on one of the bones that had been transformed into part of the mountain itself. It was cold and surprisingly smooth, but she felt nothing out of the ordinary. Glancing at Vargo, she saw that he had not sensed anything either.

'It's not time yet,' he said, sounding neither pleased nor disappointed.

'So we wait?' Cat asked hopefully.

'No. The dragons will set their own course. We still have to go ahead.'

'Are you absolutely sure about this?' she said, making one final effort to see if he might change his mind.

'Yes, I'm the only one who's absolutely convinced of the fireworms' innocence. Even you've had your doubts, haven't you?'

'Yes,' she conceded, 'but surely there must be another way.'

'No. This is *their* sacred place, like Elva is for us, and Pajarito for the birds. It has to happen here.'

'That's not what I meant.'

'The fireworms gain all their knowledge of the world through what they eat – from fire, from the rock and lava and mud – and from people. They have no other senses. And what they learnt from us is that we hate them and think they're evil – so this is the only way to tell them the truth. To heal them. And ourselves.'

Cat fell silent again, knowing that words were useless now. The music rose up around them in subtle waves, louder than before.

She watched, horror twisting in her throat, as Vargo began to strip off his clothes. He was soon naked, and she could hardly bear to look at his infinitely precious body, with which she had only just become so intimate. The ache in her chest threatened to overwhelm her. How could he contemplate allowing those vile worms to latch onto his exposed skin? The very thought was nauseating. And yet that was exactly what he was going to do – and there was nothing she could do to stop him.

'I love you,' she said quietly, using up her last reserves of will-power.

Vargo put his arms around her and kissed her.

'I love you too,' he whispered, then stepped back.

He stooped to pick up a stone from the floor and turned to face the lake. With deliberate care he tossed the pebble out over the water. Cat watched its seemingly endless flight, wishing helplessly that she could call it back. But then it hit the surface and, with a tiny sound that crashed in Cat's ears like thunder, the mirror shattered.

The gate opened.

# CHAPTER FORTY-NINE

Admiral Cucura was in a quandary. Even with his depleted forces he still controlled the waters around Teguise, but the loss of the ships blockaded in Fyal Bay to the north was a potentially serious problem. If he tried to rescue them, he risked weakening his fleet to such an extent that the city would become vulnerable. On the other hand, if he did nothing and the trapped vessels were destroyed – allowing the enemy ships that formed the blockade to join their main force – then the odds against Tiguafaya's eventual defeat would grow even shorter.

He eventually decided that he could not afford to risk exposing Teguise. The flotilla in Fyal Bay would have to fend for themselves. With any luck, they would at least occupy some of the enemy for some time to come.

The series of coded signals that had been sent back and forth between the various ships in Fyal Bay were evidence of the disagreement among their respective captains. Some thought they should make a concerted effort to break the blockade, even if this meant taking heavy losses. They argued that they were doing nothing useful here, and even if only a few of them got through to help in the coming battle for Teguise, then it would be worth it. Others foresaw only disaster in this course of action, claiming that the enemy position seemed impregnable, and that they would risk losing nearly all of their own ships if they tried to make for the open sea. They believed that simply keeping so many imperial vessels busy was in fact the best contribution they could make to the war effort, and that they should only try to escape if the enemy chose to weaken the blockade first. The flotilla's senior officer was of this latter opinion and so, for the time being at least, they kept their positions – watching but doing nothing.

Aboard the *Dolphin*, Madri – who had taken no active part in the debate – silently cursed the command decisions that had led to their being trapped in the first place, and wondered if he would have done any better. Although the attempt to break through to the enclave had been made with all the right intentions, the result had been to make the situation even worse. He had advised against it from the start, but being proved right gave him no satisfaction.

'New sails in sight!' The call came from the crow's nest, but no one on deck was able to see anything of the new arrivals.

'Where?' Madri shouted.

'To the north, hugging the shoreline.'

They saw them then, a line of small sails, creeping southward.

'Those are fishing boats!' the first officer exclaimed.

'It must be the people from the enclave,' Madri said. 'They made it to the coast and are trying to escape on their own. They can't have expected to see us here.'

'One of the enemy vessels is moving to intercept them,' the first officer reported. 'It's the *Night Wolf*.' Zarzuelo's ship, with its distinctive black sails, was easy to identify.

'It'll be a massacre,' Madri breathed to himself, imagining the defenceless craft faced by a pirate warship. He began shouting orders, and the crewmen reacted instantly. Their main sails were unfurled, immediately catching the fresh offshore breeze.

'But, sir—'

'Not now, Lieutenant. There are probably women and children aboard those boats, and I'm damned if I'll let them be butchered by those sea-scum without doing anything to help. Let's go!'

'Aye, sir!'

The *Dolphin*'s abrupt departure caused some confusion among friends and foe alike. Several of the blockaders turned to follow the *Night Wolf*, suspecting a general attack, and the Tiguafayan commander immediately sensed an opportunity. Within a few minutes what had been an almost stationary position became a bewildering swirl of movement.

The pirates' lack of discipline meant that the blockade became unbalanced and was soon broken, with many of the Tiguafayan ships escaping into open water to the south, while others engaged the imperial navy craft. Most of the enemy vessels heading north turned back when they saw what was happening, and the battle was soon joined in earnest. Only the *Night Wolf* and the *Dolphin* kept their course towards the fishing boats, with the pirate vessel well ahead. However, the wind favoured the *Dolphin* and she gained quickly, running under full sail, her crew eager for their first real action.

By now they could see the boats from the enclave clearly, each crowded with men, women and children. Even getting this far must have been a perilous business, and Madri was filled with admiration for their courage and tenacity. The

*Night Wolf* was still bearing down on them, apparently unaware of the *Dolphin*'s approach, but then the pirate ship suddenly heeled about, turning towards her enemy.

'To starboard, ten points!' Madri shouted to the helmsman and, at long last, felt the true glory of his ship as she obeyed the rudder's command. The manoeuvre turned her almost directly at the *Night Wolf*, the two ships now on a slightly angled collision course. The crew of the *Dolphin* were at battle stations, awaiting the next order – but it never came. Madri waited, praying his nerve would hold.

In the end it was Zarzuelo whose nerve cracked, and the *Night Wolf* turned again, trying to outrun her opponent by swinging across her bows. But he had left it too late. The *Dolphin* held her course, still at full speed, and by then all on board knew what Madri intended.

'Brace yourselves,' he yelled above the rushing of the wind. They should have named her the *Ram*, he thought, not the *Dolphin*. We'll see what she's made of now.

The explosive crash of the first impact was deafening. The *Dolphin*'s bows drove deep into the side of the *Night Wolf*'s hull as huge pieces of wood splintered like twigs. The masts and rigging of both ships shuddered and swayed wildly, and there was a terrible grinding noise as the two craft, still locked together, slewed across the waves. Most of their crewmen were too busy trying to stay upright to think about fighting each other, but some arrows were loosed and a few individual duels sprang up, even as the mutual destruction of the ships continued. The *Night Wolf* was now almost torn in half, and the *Dolphin*'s bows were a crumpled mess. Both were taking on water fast, and it was soon obvious that they were sinking.

Zarzuelo's mistake had been his last. He was unconscious even before he sank beneath the water, having been hit by falling timber. He drowned without fulfilling his grandiose destiny, a victim of the man whose life had been destroyed by the pirate's father – and who had now gained some small measure of retribution for the thirty years he had spent in the wilderness. The Survivor was no more, and his end had been ignominious.

The refugees from the northern enclave, who had watched the terrifying encounter from a distance, now turned their attentions to the search for survivors from the double wreck. They pulled several men from the water, not caring whether they were pirates or Tiguafayans. Their enemies were no longer in any position to cause them harm, and their fellow countrymen were greeted as heroes. The rest of the two fleets were now a considerable distance away and still moving south, so when the evacuees were satisfied that they had rescued all survivors, they went on at their own more cautious pace, in the hope of eventually reaching safety.

One of those they left behind was Jurado Madri. He had died following the oldest and most sacred maxim of the sea; a captain goes down with his ship. His last thought had been that he should never have set sail without Angel, and his last words were to bid farewell to his old comrade from afar. After that he was content, regretting nothing. He had played his part; it was up to others now. In the next world, he was sure that the gods would reunite him with Mallina, his long-lost and much-loved wife. And in the end that was all that mattered.

Commander Kehoe sat at the heart of the old mine, his every sense alert for the signal that would allow him to unleash the destruction prepared by Jameos and his men. Three lamps, each burning low, plus a supply of tapers, were his weapons now. When the time came he would light all the oil-soaked trails and fuses, setting off a chain reaction that would turn the ground above into a vast death-trap. He was under no illusions about the likelihood of his own survival. Even if he managed to climb all the way to the surface, using the rusted metal rods on the side of the shaft, he would be in the centre of an unnatural earthquake, and surrounded by imperial soldiers. One way or another, he did not expect to live much longer.

This thought did not bother him unduly. Life no longer seemed a particularly precious commodity. Too much had gone wrong, and he could see no favourable end to the war, even if his current scheme was a success. He had hated giving the order to burn the Ratifia Valley, which had once been one of the most fertile regions in all of northern Tiguafaya. Now it was a blackened ruin. Even if they were finally victorious, its inhabitants would have nothing to come back to. Their wheat, their banana trees and carefully tended vines, their homes and barns, would all be gone. Kehoe could only hope that the rest of the country would not share their fate.

The means of sending him the signal to ignite the giant tinderbox had been arranged so that it would involve only one other person. One of the Firebrands, called Jada – who seemed to the commander to be no more than a boy – had volunteered to stay at the shaft head while his bird monitored the progress of the imperial army. In order for the trap to be sprung at the best possible moment, he would have to wait until the first units were nearly at the centre of the mined area, with the others following behind. The trails would all take some minutes to burn to the maximum effect, and the whole process would therefore reach its climax when most of their enemies were overhead – assuming all went according to plan.

In the subterranean gloom, Kehoe guessed that it was now late afternoon. He already knew that Tzarno's men had begun to cross the hills, exactly as expected, some time before midday. So he reckoned it wouldn't be too long before the signal came.

Just at that moment he heard the sound of a large stone crashing onto the floor at the bottom of the main shaft, and knew he had been right. He ran over and looked up, hearing Jada's echoing voice coming to him as if from another world.

'Light the fires now. They're almost here!'

'Understood!' Kehoe yelled back. 'Get away while you can.'

'Good luck,' Jada called, and then was gone.

Kehoe turned back, ran to the heart of the labyrinth, and set to work. Moments later, flames leapt up in all directions, running into each of the tunnels that radiated out from the hub. The air was already acrid, and the noise of the various fires was extraordinarily loud, but Kehoe waited a few moments longer, wanting to make sure that none of the fuses went out prematurely. When he was satisfied, he ran to the bottom of the shaft, bent low to avoid the worse of the gathering smoke. He found the first of the rungs and began to climb, but had only gone a few steps when the first explosion shook the earth.

The first rock fall swept him back to the bottom of the shaft, the second ended his life, and those that followed entombed his remains under enough stone to build a small mountain.


'This is too easy,' Tzarno said, looking along the coastal plain. 'Why burn the valley to force us to come this way and then not even bother to defend it?'

'Your guess is as good as mine,' Ty remarked.

The last units of the army were just completing their journey over the hills, and there appeared to be nothing to stop them marching south again. The scouts had reported nothing untoward, just a few abandoned buildings and some unusual lumps and hollows. There were no roads, but the terrain should not present any difficulties. After some of their marches in the firelands, this would seem like a pleasant stroll.

'May I make a suggestion?' The Prophet had joined the two soldiers looking out over the plain, and had been watching the movements of a particular sparrowhawk for some time.

'Go ahead,' the prince said.

'Start off as if the whole army is on the march, then hold all but the first units back.'

'Why?'

'I know this place. It used to be the estate of an old colleague of mine. It was once a good source of silver, and there are shafts and pits all over the place. Some may be booby-trapped. Or there may be men hidden underground, waiting to make a surprise attack.'

'Surely there couldn't be enough to present any real threat,' the castellan said. 'The scouts would have seen signs of any large force.'

'Maybe so,' the Prophet conceded. 'But why take the risk? You said yourself this was too easy.'

'They could be planning to use magic, I suppose,' Tzarno commented thoughtfully. 'We'd better make sure a few of our friends are with the advance party.'

'Good idea.'

'All right,' the prince decided. 'Let's see what happens.'

After explaining exactly what he wanted to all his section commanders, Tzarno returned to the observation post to follow their progress. The advance went exactly as planned, with a large band of the Kundahari in the forefront as usual, followed by the first of the infantry units. When they were under way, the Prophet noted the sparrowhawk dip down to the ground and disappear from sight.

'Tell the rest to hold their positions,' he said urgently.

'They already have instructions to go forward a few paces, and then stop,' Tzarno replied patiently.

'Make sure they go no further.'

'Why? What's going—'

Just at that instant, small billows of smoke began to rise from a hundred different places all over the plain. Moments later, the earth beneath their feet shuddered, and great sections of the land before them began to shake and subside. All but the advance party, who were isolated now, drew back hurriedly. Before long the air was filled with smoke and dust, and great chasms were opening up in the ground. Most of the advance party were caught up in the midst of this chaos – either swallowed up or crushed by the man-made earthquake – and Tzarno realized that had his entire army been hard on their heels, he might well have lost half his force or more. He had no idea how the devastation had been triggered, but he was grateful to have escaped as lightly as he had.

'You are a true prophet, Kantrowe,' he said. 'I didn't think the Tiguafayans had such cunning in them, but I tell you now, they'll pay for this. For every one of my men killed here, I'll kill ten in Teguise.'

# CHAPTER FIFTY

The Seer regarded his followers with satisfaction. They had all answered his summons and had gathered at the breeding pit, which lay below a disused tannery in the artisans' quarter. Of course he could have convinced them that it was anywhere, laying false trails for their minds, but there was no need for subterfuge now. This day would see the culmination of his life's work. He would hide from no one – and no one would be able to hide from his creation.

'We are the keepers of the flame,' he intoned, and the cult members, their sweating faces reflecting the red glow of the fires, obediently echoed his rallying cry.

'The sword of retribution is about to strike.' Martinoy was gripped by an ecstatic fervour that held all his followers in its sway. He was inspired, having dreamt of this moment for a very long time. 'You have inhaled their purifying essence, and they are grown to maturity. The time has come!'

The onlookers shifted on the walkway, held captive by the rhetoric but uncertain about what was to happen next. Martinoy had no such doubts. His eyes were ablaze, shining like beacons in the half-light.

'Accept the terror. Focus your hatred, so that the dragon spawn may cleanse us.' The Seer spread his arms wide in a dramatic gesture as the first of the fireworms took to the air from the sunken pit. 'Greet your salvation!'

As the swarm rose up, a low moan came from the cult members, a mixture of anticipation and fear. Moments later the first of the fireworms struck, moving with incredible speed to attach itself to one of the men. He screamed, his faith turning to pain and horror as his flesh began to burn. The rest of the worms fell upon their willing victims then, and the massacre began. The narrow walkway was soon crowded with the dead and dying, and in their frantic efforts to escape several people fell over the edge into the furnace below. The sweltering air soon reeked like a charnel house, and was filled with terrible cries of agony and terror.

Standing a little apart, the Seer gazed over his flock and watched their cleansing with a joyous smile of approval. It was only when one of the fireworms turned its attentions to him that he felt the slightest tremor of doubt – and then he too gave himself up to salvation.

A few minutes later, Giavista Martinoy and all his followers lay dead, horribly mutilated. But the swarm did not stop there. The sturdy, iron-shod door proved no barrier to their determined progress, and it was soon no more than a collection of smouldering embers. The fireworms left their lair, and went in search of fresh prey.

*Where are we going?* Tas asked.

*I told you, silly,* Ysanne replied impatiently. *To Elva.*

*I can't go there.*

*You don't have to go the last bit. You can watch me,* the little girl said, very much aware of her own importance.

Ysanne had found, to her delight, that *real* flying was easy. She had dreamed and imagined and practised, using her arms as wings, but when she had finally made up her mind the magic had simply been there, waiting for her.

It was Uncle Nino who had given her the idea. He was always telling her about his network, and asking her about the singing. He talked all the time about links and webs and focus points, lots of things Ysanne did not really understand, but one of the things he'd said had been about the special importance of links with birds who were communal, usually living in flocks. Although she saw little of them, Ysanne knew that Tas was part of a firecrest clan, and so she'd begun to wonder whether she could become one of them too.

When she'd decided that something was needed to stop her mother being sad – and the singing had told her what to do – she had simply asked for what she wanted, and she had become not just one firecrest, but an entire flock – a net, Nino would have called it. She was still Ysanne, but now she had a hundred pairs of wings, a hundred pairs of sharp eyes, a hundred tiny beaks. She was as light as air, no longer fat and lumpy but sleek and beautiful – and she could fly!

It had been at the moment of this joyous discovery that Yaisa had come into the room, but Ysanne had hardly noticed the nursemaid, or the scream that had followed her as she skimmed out through the open window. She had been flying to the southwest ever since, so fast that Tas had to fight to keep up.

*I've been called, so I'll be allowed to talk to the dragons.* Although she was not sure how she knew this, she was convinced it was true. It had been one of the things that had enabled her to overcome her distrust of magic. Elva would not have called to her in the singing if going there was a bad thing to do. Besides, she'd talked to the dragon babies once – and that had been a *good* thing. And they'd sent her a dream when the sick one had hatched. Which must mean that they wanted to talk to her. *Elva's an o-racle*, she added, pronouncing the word carefully.

*I know*, Tas replied.

*How come you know all this stuff?* Ysanne asked curiously.

*It's one of the stories we all have to learn.*

*Tell me the story*, the little girl demanded imperiously. *Now.*

*All of it?*

*Yes.*

*There are some big words*, Tas commented doubtfully.

*I don't care. Just tell me.*

They flew on, their plumage shimmering in the afternoon sunlight, while Tas collected her thoughts in order to repeat the tale she had learnt from her mother. She stumbled over a few words, but Ysanne listened avidly nonetheless, and did not interrupt.

*Before time began, when all winged creatures were just shapes waiting to hatch, there were spirits who served the great Sky herself. One of these was Elva. When the dragons were born she fell in love with them and, in defiance of the laws, she became their mistress. She bore them many fledglings, and each clutch of eggs was the beginning of a new clan of birds. But Elva's wan-ton diso ... diso-bedience had angered Sky, the an-cestress of all living things. She cast Elva down into the world and turned her to stone so that she could no longer fly – or mate. Elva became a floating island, between the land, sea and air, but in none of them. All birds are forbidden to visit her, but the dragons have never forgotten her. The sacred isle lies beyond a jewelled lake in a place where a whisper can shake mountains and, for those with the courage to travel beyond the world, she is the voice of the dragons.*

Ysanne was impressed. It was the longest story Tas had ever told her, and the best.

*That's what I need*, she declared. *The voice of the dragons.*

*I don't think you should whisper, though*, the firecrest said nervously. *Mountains aren't meant to shake.*

*All right then*, Ysanne agreed. *I'll shout instead.*

When they finally reached the semicircle of enormous cliffs that curved round a black pebble beach, Tas landed gratefully. She was close to exhaustion, but Ysanne was full of energy still, too excited to even consider resting. In the middle of the beach, cut off from the sea by a whale-backed ridge of shingle, was the lake whose green waters did indeed glitter like jewels. Beyond it lay Elva, a tiny island that was no more than a single outcrop of amber-coloured rock. The tide was in, so the island was cut off from the land for the moment, but that was no impediment to Ysanne. In fact, if the little girl had been travelling on foot, she would never have been able to come as close as she had. A small volcano, a little way inland, was emitting a constant flow of lava that divided into two streams – one of which cascaded down to the ocean on either side of the cove, cutting it off completely. The lava produced constant hissing clouds of steam as it met the seawater, and had hardened into two long promontories, projecting out into the ocean on either side of what was obviously a treacherous channel. This made a seaward approach impossible. The whole arrangement seemed deliberate somehow, as if the dragons meant to protect their privacy at all costs – but Ysanne was immune to such considerations. She was still enchanted by her newfound abilities. There was nowhere she dared not go.

*You stay here*, she said unnecessarily. Tas had no intention of moving. *I told you one day I'd fly like Mama did*, she added proudly. *Now I'm going to talk to the dragons like she did too.*

As Ysanne swooped down towards the oracle, Tas watched her progress with some anxiety. Then the firecrest spotted some large white shapes wheeling within the clouds of steam further out to sea, and her unease intensified. An un-invited thought popped into her mind. *There are ghosts here.*

Far below her link, Ysanne circled the island, selecting her land site. As her 'feet' touched the wind-scoured rock, the flock fell away and she was human again. Her own body felt cumbersome and strange, and she was suddenly very tired.

'Hello?' she called, in as loud a voice as she dared.

There was no response – only the muffled echoes from the cliff face.

'My name is Ysanne. I want to talk to you.'

The silence remained, but she sensed a shift in the air, as if someone were watching her.

'It's about my Mama—' she began, only to break off abruptly.

*You have not been beyond the earth's breathing.*

The voice was so vast, so frightening, that even Ysanne's resilient self-confidence was dented for a moment or two. It had seemed to come from all around – from the rock, the air and the sea – as well as sounding inside her own head. And she didn't understand what it had said.

*Does that matter?* she asked eventually, switching instinc-tively to the voice she used with Tas.

This produced another watchful silence.

*No, it doesn't matter,* the voice answered at last, and Ysanne sensed the amusement behind the words. *But are you worthy?*

*Yes,* Ysanne stated defiantly, without quite being sure what she was claiming.

*What is it that you want?*

She had prepared a long list in her head, but now she couldn't think of any of the things she'd intended to wish for. Instead, her attention was caught by a distant call of distress – and she knew that the dragons heard it too.

*Hey! I was here first!*

They took no notice of her. The intruder had taken all their attention and, for the first time, Ysanne wondered about her own situation. She was trapped – by the sea, the cliffs and the lava stream – and unless she found her wings again, she did not see how she could hope to escape.

*Hello?* she tried again.

There was no response for some time, and when the dragons' spirits eventually spoke again, their words did nothing to calm her fears.

*Help us to dance again.*

Ysanne had no idea what they meant.

# CHAPTER FIFTY-ONE

Allegra gasped as the first of the fireworms appeared, flying low over the lake.

'We have to welcome them, Cat,' Vargo said calmly. 'Help me welcome them.' He took a step forward so that he was standing in the shallow water at the edge of the broken mirror.

Cat wanted to scream, to deny that this was happening – that she had *let* this happen – but Vargo's words and his apparent serenity helped her to remain outwardly quiet. Inside, she was praying. That was as close to a welcome as she could get.

The swarm approached much more slowly than was usual, as if they were unsure of something, and it was only when they were quite close that Allegra even considered that she might be in danger too. She stepped back instinctively, and bumped into the rock wall behind her. If they kill him, it would be best if they kill me too, she thought – and then there was no more time to think, because the leading worms had reached their target.

No matter how many times she had imagined this

happening, or told herself that she was prepared for it, the sight of the vile grey creatures clamping themselves onto Vargo's flesh almost broke her resolve. The horror of that moment was more terrible than anything she'd ever experienced before, and she was only able to stay where she was by locking all her muscles rigid. Her fists were clenched so tight that her nails drew blood from her own palms.

Her vision blurred as Vargo threw back his head, his mouth open in a soundless scream, his eyes wide. His body shuddered and twitched as the fireworms began to devour him, but he did not try to escape, nor to fend them off. Vargo had been mad to try this – and she had been mad to let him. It was obviously going horribly wrong. Cat blinked away the tears that filled her eyes, only to find that she still could not see clearly. Something was happening to the worms. The entire swarm – at least a dozen of them – was attached to Vargo now, and some had burrowed deep, so that only half their length was visible. But they all seemed less substantial somehow. She couldn't see Vargo properly either. His outline had become distorted, as if the lamplight was unable to find him. The entire harrowing scene began to flicker; Cat saw movement where there was only stillness, reflections where there was no light. The fireworms became writhing ghosts, transparent spectres. And then there were *two* Vargos.

As she watched, mesmerized, one of the superimposed figures crumpled and distorted, becoming a grotesque mockery of human form as the worms destroyed him from within. Soon all that was left was a scorched and mutilated corpse that sank beneath the surface of the water. The other figure remained upright, still shivering and evidently in great pain, but otherwise unmarked. The ghostly fireworms – who were almost invisible now – left their victim and flew away again, over the trembling surface of the lake.

Cat began to hear the first faint whisperings of hope. 'I'll be in the mirror,' Vargo had said. 'That's where they'll eat me.' And that, it seemed, was what had happened. What she needed to know now was, what was left of him in the real world?

'Vargo?' she breathed, still paralyzed with fear. 'Vargo?'

He did not react to the sound of her voice, but stood, perfectly still now, his arms outstretched as if in supplication.

'Vargo?' Cat said, louder this time. 'Are you all right?'

His arms came slowly down to his sides then and, as he turned to face her, she saw that there were several dark red blotches on his skin. The expression on his face was unreadable – part shock, part bewilderment, part agony. Cat wanted to rush to him, to take him in her arms and reassure herself that he was real, that he wasn't a ghost. She wanted to tell him that everything would be all right now, that his ordeal was over, but some inexplicable force held her back, still pressed against the rock wall.

'They've taken what they need.'

His voice was weak and raw with pain, but Cat was overjoyed to hear him speak at all.

'Did it work?' she asked.

'Everywhere's the same in the mirror,' he replied. 'It's their network.'

'Come here,' she pleaded urgently, still unable to move.

'I can't.'

As dread welled up inside Cat her legs almost gave way beneath her, and she put out a hand to steady herself. As she caught hold of a smooth projection of rock, voices began to babble in her head.

'Why can't you?'

'I'm still part of the mirror,' Vargo replied, glancing down at his feet. He sounded like a frightened little boy.

Allegra remembered him telling her of another occasion
when he'd been trapped within that other realm. It had
taken Famara's dying effort to rescue him then, but Famara
was long gone.

'I can't move either.'

'You mustn't!' Vargo exclaimed. 'If you do you'll be
trapped as well.'

'Then what are we supposed to do?' Her grip tightened
on the stone outcrop, and she realized she was holding one
of the fossil dragon's talons.

*Ask for their help.*

The alien voice in her head was clear for once, and Cat
knew that this time the message was actually meant for her.
In the past she had assumed that – if the voices were real –
she had simply been overhearing other conversations. But
this was different. Even so, she still had no idea where it
came from. She was wondering *who* she was supposed to ask
when she remembered something else Vargo had told her.
'The dragon will help us.'

Cat glanced down at her hand, which still grasped the
age-old claw.

*If there's anyone there, please help me*, she thought. *I don't
know if I'm doing this right, but—*

*Help us to dance again.*

This was a very different voice. It echoed in Cat's head
like rolling thunder, leaving her stunned and almost
speechless.

*Dance?* she asked. *What do you mean?*

There was no answer, but Cat could feel a sense of
longing, a great weight of tragic history – and she began to
think furiously. Below her the stone heartbeat kept up its
ceaseless rhythm, and suddenly she knew what was needed.
First, a partner . . .

*I will dance with you*, she offered.

Then some music.

'Sing, Vargo! You've got to sing!'

He stared at her in utter amazement.

'I can't. You know—'

'They want you to sing,' she insisted. 'They took your music away and now they're giving it back. They want to dance. So sing!'

Vargo seemed completely nonplussed by this development, as if she had asked him to jump to the moon or make a river run uphill.

'The dragons?' he asked eventually.

'Of course!'

'They danced once,' he murmured.

'And they can again – but we need your music, Vargo. Then we can help each other.'

Hesitantly, as if it were the most unnatural thing in the world, Vargo opened his mouth. The sound that emerged was cracked and hoarse from long disuse, and he stopped, cleared his throat, then tried again. This time the note was pure and strong, and Allegra's heart sang with it. This was the Vargo she had known long ago, whose songs could charm the roughest audience. She smiled through her tears and he smiled back, then closed his eyes and began to sing.

It had no words, but it needed none; it was fluid and graceful, and yet rhythmic as well, so that Cat could imagine being whirled around, dressed in a beautiful ball gown. The music of the caves below them swelled up in unison with his miraculous voice, as though he were conducting some vast, elemental orchestra. It was the music of joy and yearning, of movement and laughter.

Something stirred within the rock behind her, and Cat found that she was able to turn round and look at the fossil. It was not moving – its stillness was part of its essence – but an ancient sadness was being lifted from the dragon-child who had never had the chance to live – or to dance. The spirit that had been locked in stone for so long had been set free. Its centuries-long wait was finally over.

Claw in hand with Allegra, a dragon danced in innocence.

# CHAPTER FIFTY-TWO

Cat jumped as she felt arms encircle her.

'I kept my promise,' Vargo whispered in her ear. 'I didn't die.'

Allegra came out of her trance then, and twisted round to embrace him. She had not even realized that he'd stopped singing, let alone been able to escape from the mirror and come to her. She held him as if she would never let go, while the music of the ocean resounded through the cave. She had so many questions she didn't know where to start – How had he escaped? Was his music back for good? Had the fireworms learnt the truth? – but compared to the simple fact that he was alive and they were together again, none of that really mattered.

Far to the south, on the edge of a different sea, a little girl was also dancing. Ysanne didn't know what she had done or where the music had come from, but the pleasure that was all around her spoke of a deep gratitude.

*What is it that you want?*

This time the voice was more gentle, almost affectionate,

and this time Ysanne knew what to say.

*Help them to understand*, she said.

The dance had stopped, and suddenly the cavern felt much emptier.

'The sea is coming to us,' Vargo said, and something in his tone made Cat look up in alarm.

'What do you mean?'

For answer he took one of her hands in his own, then placed his free hand on the surface of the fossil, motioning for her to do the same. The dance began again.

'We set the innocence free,' he told her. 'We can't let it be locked away again.'

This time, Allegra knew what he meant. The dance had to go on. However, that realization was dwarfed by another, quite separate rush of sensations, a bewildering array of invisible light and emotion that spread out into infinity, connecting her to the sky, to the mountains, to all the wings that had ever taken to the air. It was intoxicating and terrifying at the same time, full of power and dangerous knowledge.

'The birds always knew it was you,' Vargo whispered. 'But they couldn't tell you until you were ready.'

'Ready for what?' Cat asked, still reeling from all the images that threatened to swamp her mind.

'Your linking.'

'You mean there *is* a bird for me?'

'Look. And listen.'

Cat did as she was told and slowly, incredulously, she began to understand.

'The music's getting closer,' Vargo warned, bringing her back from her awe-struck wandering.

'How . . .?' she began, and then, as a new wave of horror washed over her, she saw the truth. The water in the lower caves was rising, bringing the music with it as the ocean storm drove on relentlessly. In a very short time the cavern would be flooded.

'But we've got to dance!' she protested helplessly. Unless the dragon who, like Elva, had been turned to stone, was allowed to stay alive until the eggs hatched, the new-born creatures would be doomed, as the first had been. Unless the channel between that long ago time of innocence and the present remained open, there was no hope for the future. 'We've got to stay here.'

'I don't think we have any choice,' Vargo responded. 'There isn't time for us to get out the way we came, and the mirrors are gone. We can't open the gate again.'

They looked at each other in dismay. They had achieved so much, had only just learnt so many secrets – and now it was all about to be snatched away. That they should be doomed to drown when so much was left unfinished – not least their love for each other – seemed desperately unfair.

'We should be in Corazoncillo,' Vargo went on, his voice full of regret. 'To see them born.'

Cat knew that was true – and then saw how it might be possible.

'The network could take us there!' she exclaimed. 'As it took me to Zepharinn. We don't need the mirror.'

Hope sparked in Vargo's eyes, but then he slowly shook his head.

'Even if it's possible, someone has to stay here. Only one of us could go.'

'No!' Allegra cried, appalled by the idea.

'The music's not enough on its own,' he told her. 'And there's no one else.'

'But they need us in Corazoncillo too, to bring the fire.'

'I know. So which of us is going?'

Cat could not, dared not answer.

'It has to be you, Cat,' Vargo stated earnestly. 'You're the centre of everything, you know that now. You're the one the dragons have to thank for all this. No one else can do it all.'

'I won't leave you,' she breathed, nearly choking.

'You must,' he told her sadly. 'Part of me will always be with you, Cat.'

'I don't want *part* of you!' she cried.

'If you don't go, all this, everything we've done, will have been for nothing.'

'I can't!' she wailed.

*I will take your place in the dance.*

The new voice was sharp, almost intimidating, and it startled Cat badly.

'What's happening?' Vargo asked, seeing her expression change.

'I don't know.'

*You are both needed at the centre of the web. The focus at the focus, and the fuel for the fire,* the voice added mysteriously.

*But you'll drown,* Cat responded hesitantly.

*I will dance for as long as is needed. That is all that matters.*

*Are you sure?* Cat asked, unable to hide her joy at the new hope this brought her.

*Go. I'll be there soon.*

*Thank you.*

She turned to Vargo, saw the confusion on his wonderful face, and felt a surge of happiness so intense she could hardly bear it. They had a chance!

'Someone's coming,' she told him. 'To take our place. We can go. Together.'

'Who is it?' he asked.

'I don't know. Does it matter?'

'Whoever it is is sacrificing their life, Cat. It ought to matter.'

Shame enveloped her, then faded. If it was wrong to be selfish, then she would be wrong.

*My fate was decided long ago*, the voice told her, as if aware of her thoughts. *If you don't go, you gain nothing and all Tiguafaya loses much. The sky sings different songs now, and I keep all my bargains. You must both keep yours.*

*Are you sure this is what you want?* Cat asked.

*Sing the last song for me.*

*We will.*

*Then go*, the voice urged. *There's not much time left, and you have others to attend to as well.*

*Others?* Allegra queried, then found that she knew what their saviour had meant.

*Farewell.*

'It's all right,' Cat told Vargo. 'This is meant to happen. And I don't care whether you believe it or not. I'm not letting anything keep us apart now.'

'Another gift?' He meant on top of those they'd already been given by the dragons; the return of his music and his release from the mirror.

Cat nodded.

'More precious than all the rest,' she agreed. 'Take my hands.'

Ico's day had gone from bad to worse. The frantic search for Ysanne had revealed nothing, either on the ground or in the air. Nino had taken charge, and Eya had organized the birds to scour the skies above Teguise, but they had seen nothing unusual. Most of them weren't even sure what they'd been looking for. Only Yaisa had seen Ysanne, and she had stuck to her bizarre story. Ico had been forced to conclude that either the maid was hallucinating or there was some very powerful magic at work. However, nothing altered the simple fact that her daughter was gone. Ico was almost helpless with despair and, on this occasion, not even Nino's reassuring words could comfort her.

When Tir, Jada's sparrowhawk, arrived with the news of Kehoe's death and the failure of his plan to trap the imperial army, it was just one more shadow upon the dark heart of her misery. She felt some pity for the commander, for the fact that his sacrifice had been in vain, but at that moment the coming war seemed the least of her problems. The battle lines would soon be drawn, both on land and at sea, where Cucura's fleet was positioning itself for the final defence of the waters around Teguise. The war would have to take care of itself.

Just when Ico thought the day couldn't get any worse, Nino came to find her. She could tell from his expression that there was no news of Ysanne.

'What now?' she asked, wanting only to hide herself away.

'There's a swarm of fireworms loose in the city.'

'What! Oh gods,' she groaned. It was bad enough that Teguise was being faced with threats from outside, but now it seemed that the city had to deal with a new horror from within. 'So it was true.'

'The thing is,' Nino went on, 'they haven't attacked anyone.'

'What? So what *are* they doing?'

'Come and see.'

He led her to the main gates of the palace and out into the square beyond. The sight that greeted her there was so extraordinary that, for a few moments, it took her mind off her own worries. The entire swarm of fireworms was airborne in the centre of the square and, under the bewildered gaze of the crowd that had gathered to watch, they were moving in intricate, almost graceful patterns, weaving in and out of each other's paths.

'They're dancing!' Ico gasped.

'Looks like it, doesn't it?' Nino replied.

Ico half expected a naked Vargo to step out from the shadows, as he had done in her dream some months before, but he was nowhere to be seen.

'They're not tainted,' she breathed.

'No, they're not,' Nino agreed. 'The evil's gone. Everyone feels it, but no one knows why.'

'What does it mean?'

'I'm not sure, but it's the first piece of really *good* news we've had for a long time.'

'Do you think they'll be corrupted again when the music stops?'

'What music?' he asked, glancing at her curiously.

'I . . .' She shook her head. That had been in her dream too. This was real.

At that moment the dance ended and the fireworms rose into the sky, circled the square once as if in farewell, then flew off to the northwest.

*Can you follow them, Eya?* Nino asked quickly.

*They are fast*, the peregrine replied, *but so am I.*

*See where they go.* Nino was the only one not watching the fireworms retreat, and that was because he suddenly had other things on his mind. The network was coming to life.

*Help me.* This time Allegra knew who she was talking to, and the response was almost overwhelming. And this time she had a specific purpose in mind.

The lines and circles of the web accepted them. Moments later the cavern was gone, and she and Vargo stood in the ravine, between the river and the cave entrance. Ero and Lao were looking at them in astonishment.

*That's a neat trick*, Ero commented.

*Yes, it is, isn't it*, Cat replied. It felt both wonderfully strange and oddly familiar to be talking directly to the hoopoe. Of all the birds, he had been the one to whom she felt closest, whose moods and actions she sometimes understood, but now – to her amazement – she found that her mind was connected telepathically to *all* the linked birds. Her long-held wish had been granted in far greater measure than she could ever have hoped for. Another gift. She was the fulcrum of the network, the centre of the spider's web. It had been her pleas that had unwittingly brought it to life twice before, and now that the dragons had told her of her unique talent she intended to make the fullest use of it.

*What* is *all this?* Lao asked. He had not been there on those earlier occasions, had not been part of the dream.

*It's a net*, Cat explained. *With all the birds and their links.*

*We're singing*, Ero added helpfully. *But my feet don't hurt this time.*

*But we're not all here*, Lao said thoughtfully. *There are some missing.*

Allegra saw that the sandpiper was right. There were some gaps, some slight but obvious flaws in the pattern. The power of what was already there was awesome enough, yet it was not perfect. She had no idea what that implied – and had no time to think about it now.

*You are new among us*, Lao said to Cat.

*Yes.*

*Welcome home.*

*Thank you*, Allegra replied, her heart swelling.

*Why have you shed your feathers?* Ero asked Vargo suspiciously.

Vargo laughed. After all the amazing events of the day, he had forgotten he was naked.

*It's a long story*, he said, and went to fetch some clothes from his pack.

*There's a storm coming*, Lao stated.

*I know*, Cat replied. *We have to go.*

*Where are we going?* Ero asked.

*I have a job for you two.*

*Together?* Lao queried.

*Yes. We need you both to go to Pajarito. You're being called. If you listen to the net, you'll know*, she added, noting their sudden nervousness. *It's very important.*

*It's a long way from here*, Ero said doubtfully.

*You don't have to fly*, Cat reassured him. *We'll use the net. You can be there in an instant.*

*Oh good*, the hoopoe commented. He had forgotten how frightened he had been the last time he'd visited the oracle, and was only thinking that he would be saved a lot of effort. He puffed out his chest to show that he was ready for any mission, no matter how important.

*What should we do when we get there?* Lao asked more soberly.

*I'm not sure yet*, Cat replied, *but it's one of the most important places in the net. Someone has to be there. Do you hear the calling?*

*It's faint*, the sandpiper said. *The sky voices don't sound certain.*

*I hear it*, Ero stated loyally. *Don't mind Lao. He's always like this. No fun at all.*

The sandpiper chirruped softly in response but said nothing.

*Will you go?* Cat asked.

*Yes*, Ero answered emphatically.

*Yes*, Lao echoed. *Where are* you *going?*

*Vargo and I have to start a little fire*, she replied. *In Corazoncillo.*

# CHAPTER FIFTY-THREE

'Take cover!'

Division Commander Ghose joined his men in throwing himself to the ground, finding what cover they could in the bare terrain. Muttering obscenities to himself, he crawled into the shadow of a jagged outcrop of solidified lava. Although it offered him only a little protection, it was better than nothing.

The expedition had been plagued with bad luck from the start – ever since they'd separated from the main body of the army and headed across country, through the barren heart of the firelands. The maps of this region were hopelessly inadequate, and the instructions they'd been given about how to find Corazoncillo had been vague in the extreme. The commander suspected that some of their information – which had come from prisoners taken early in the campaign – had been deliberately misleading. The few settlements they had come across in the interior had been deserted, several of his men had been injured, supplies were running low, and Vulkhar, the anti-mage assigned to them, was a positive liability. Tzarno had only been able to spare one of the easterners to accompany Ghose and, according to most of his men, that was one too many. Vulkhar had been a weak specimen to begin with, but he'd been taken ill on the journey and had slowed their progress considerably. Derim, the Kundahari who had volunteered to come with them, was the only one of the party who had any time for him. In fact, if it had not been for Derim – whom most of the soldiers considered quite mad – they might well have abandoned Vulkhar to his fate along the way. They had met no opposition, magical or otherwise, so what did they need him for?

Their various misfortunes had led to many dark mutterings within the ranks, and doubts about the purpose of their mission – doubts which Ghose secretly shared. However, General Tzarno had deemed it important, and disobeying the prince was not something Ghose would contemplate lightly. Tzarno believed that the people of Tiguafaya had some ludicrous idea about the dragons being vital to their well-being – and if the eggs he'd been told about actually existed, he wanted to find out everything he could about them, and if possible lay claim to them. And so, for several long days now, Ghose and his division had been wandering, hoping with each new ridge they crested that the valley before them would be the one they were seeking. Morale had already been at an all-time low when the storm had hit them.

The hailstones were still hammering down, some almost as big as Ghose's fist, and every man had taken several blows. What was worse, the storm had sprung up out of nowhere, out of a clear blue sky. The commander knew that the soldiers would take this as another omen, another sign that fate had it in for them. He was wondering what to say to try to appease them when he became aware of an unearthly keening.

Peering up cautiously, his head still covered by his arms, he saw Vulkhar standing in the open, his arms raised and his head flung back, wailing at the sky.

'Get down, you fool,' Ghose muttered. A direct hit on the head by one of the larger hailstones would almost certainly prove fatal.

But Vulkhar came to no harm – somewhat to the disappointment of some of the soldiers – and after a few moments the storm relented. The sky above was a cloudless blue once more, and the sun's rays were hot and bright. As the men who had not been knocked unconscious began to pick themselves up, nursing bruises and glancing over at the easterner, the blanket of ice began to melt, turning the dusty earth beneath their feet to mud.

Ghose and Derim both approached the anti-mage, who was still standing in the same spot – though he had lowered his arms now, and his shoulders slumped wearily.

'What was that all about?' the commander asked.

Although Vulkhar was not proficient in the imperial tongue, he knew enough to convey his message.

'Evil,' he breathed. 'Sky-stones from vile sorcery come. We to magic close.'

Angel looked down from the top of the ridge, and knew he was beaten. The effort of conjuring up the hailstorm had taken most of the weather mage's reserves, and his opponent had been able to prevent it doing any real damage. Now it was only a matter of time before the anti-mage and the soldiers with him found the pass. Once they saw the deserted villages of Quemada and Corazoncillo, they would know they had reached their goal, and Angel feared that they might interfere somehow with the hatching that must come soon now. He began to search his mind for another way to stop them.

His second day alone in the valley was almost at an end and, although he had expected others to come, the imperial soldiers were not the visitors he had anticipated. Turning back, he began to hobble down into the valley, considering various possibilities. When he saw sinuous lines of movement below him he stopped to watch, and eventually realized what was happening. Angel's twisted face contorted into a smile, and he began to run as fast as his crooked limbs would allow.

It took Vargo and Cat a few moments to clear their heads when they arrived in Corazoncillo. The transfer had taken only an instant, and had been quite painless, but they still had to recover from the disorientation of being in one place and then – in the blink of an eye – being somewhere else altogether. When they did, the sight that greeted them was as wonderful as it was bizarre.

They had materialized only a few paces away from the square, but the dragon eggs looked quite different now. Their shiny black shells were almost invisible because the entire clutch was being covered by a grey blanket of fireworms – with more arriving all the time. And in the middle of it all, sitting on top of one of the eggs like a proud mother hen, was Angel. He did not even seem surprised to see them.

'It worked!' Cat exclaimed. She could feel no hatred or fear here, no evil.

Vargo nodded, rendered temporarily speechless. This was what he had envisaged months before – and it had all happened without him having to arrange it. Now that the sickness corrupting the fireworms had been cured, they had come to the aid of their former masters without the need of any human prompting. The dragons' midwives had arrived – and they'd brought the heat of the volcanoes with them.

'They're still going to need the fire for them to hatch,' Cat said.

'I know,' he replied. 'That's why we're here.'

'What's Angel doing?'

'He's come to drive away any evil spirits.'

'What?'

'Do you think all men are good?' Vargo asked.

'No,' Cat replied, puzzled by the question.

'Then why should all dragons be good? Some of their spirits may be evil. We can't judge them by human standards, but perhaps Angel's instincts can tell good from bad. They're coming back to our world, Cat. For their sake and ours, I'd rather he was there at their birth.'

Allegra took some time to absorb this idea, but Vargo had sounded so uncharacteristically rational that she found herself believing him.

'He's worried about something else right now,' she said eventually.

Angel had stood up, and was waving his arms erratically, pointing towards the eastern end of the valley. In the fading light it was hard to make anything out, but finally Cat saw what was agitating the weather mage.

'Imperial soldiers. Quite a lot of them.' She had recognized their uniforms from her brief time in Zepharinn.

'Another Maghdim,' Vargo muttered.

Cat was about to say that Maghdim was dead, but then she realized what he meant.

'We can't let an anti-mage get anywhere near the worms,' she said. 'He might corrupt them. And he might disrupt the hatching.'

'We'll deal with him, don't worry,' Vargo stated determinedly.

'Cloud hopes!' Angel cried suddenly, and Vargo pointed to the sky.

Lightning shredded the air above the eastern pass, painting the entire ridge in a harsh, blue-white light. Where it struck the earth, the bolt split and glittered, producing a shimmering dome that protected some of the soldiers. A second blinding streak of fire followed almost immediately, and this time the dome shattered and flew apart with a crash so loud that the earlier thunder seemed quiet by comparison. Beneath the fury, a few soldiers now lay on the ground, either dead or concussed, while the rest were fleeing for their lives. Angel crowed with glee.

'You did that?' Cat asked in awe.

'*We* did,' Vargo replied. 'Allies in insanity. Maghdim couldn't cope with madness either.'

'But—'

'They won't bother us any more. Come on – we've got work to do.'

Allegra saw that she would get no further explanation, and she knew that time was running out. Far to the west, the storm was still rising.

'If we get the worms to burrow straight down,' she said, 'sooner or later they'll reach the earth-fires.'

'I can't talk to them,' Vargo responded. 'I'm not in the mirror any more. Can you do it through the web?'

'I can try.'

But as soon as she asked the network for help, Cat saw that it was no longer necessary. The fireworms *knew*. Instead of settling on the eggs, two newly arrived swarms dived to the ground and began to dig themselves into the earth. Others followed, and soon the whole valley floor began to vibrate with their excavations.

'We'd better get back,' Vargo reasoned. 'It's going to get hot around here.'

'What about Angel?' Cat asked. Their friend was still at the centre of the clutch, apparently quite unconcerned by the strange events going on all around him.

'He'll do what he must,' Vargo replied evenly.

Allegra glanced at him, but his expression gave nothing

away. The ground trembled suddenly, and a subterranean rumbling announced the progress of the fireworms' search.

'Come on,' Vargo urged.

They turned and ran to the outskirts of the village, then on and up a nearby mound of old lava. A red glow now marked the place they had left – and as they watched, the first small fountain of molten rock cascaded into the air.

Soo had dreamt of Pajarito. She had told and been told all that was necessary, and had even received the oracle's blessing. There had been no need for her to go there. She had another destination in mind.

The sparrowhawk knew she would never see the sky's dreaming, but that loss was nothing new to her. All she wanted now was to keep her bargain, and to protect the ones she loved. That was why she had prevented Ico from seeing too much within the network. Her link would have tried to stop her, so it had been easier to keep the knowledge a secret. Even now, Soo knew that she would be vulnerable if Ico called – and she could not afford to be vulnerable. The bargain had to be kept.

The ravine was behind her now, and she had been swallowed by the darkness of the caves, but she did not slow her pace. The imprint of this journey had been in her mind since the day she had hatched. As she flew – with all the grace of her kind, with the speed of an arrow – the music rose all around her, growing louder all the time.

When Soo finally slowed – extending her legs towards the perch she could not see but knew with every fibre, every feather of her body – the dance resumed, talon to talon.

She had reached the end of her journey.

Angel sensed the spirits watching him. Nothing in all his strange life had ever felt so right.

The disease that had robbed him of all external beauty but left him mad had given him other gifts in exchange. He had never questioned his fate, never wondered why he'd been chosen for the roles he played. That was beyond the reach of his philosophy. But now, in the midst of the fire and flame, with the sound of new life tapping urgently at their shells, he knew his purpose was fulfilled. All ten had chosen, and chosen well.

Angel was content. He bade farewell to the last of his magic, and let the fire take him home.

'Why didn't he get out?' Cat cried. 'He didn't have to die!'

They had watched with growing apprehension as the lava began to bubble to the surface, until it became obvious that no human could survive within the inferno produced by the fireworms. It was very hot where they were – and that was more than two hundred paces away.

'Newness is a passage,' Vargo commented obscurely. 'This was meant to happen.'

The echo of the words she had used earlier – to justify another's sacrifice – silenced Allegra, and she turned back to watch what in her mind had become a funeral pyre. Most of the buildings in the village were burning now. The sky above was dark, but the valley was the colour of the earth's blood.

'Look!' Vargo whispered, pointing above the rooftops.

Cat peered through the smoke and fumes, and saw two bright yellow eyes gazing back at her. As she stared, the dragon rose into the sky, spiralling upwards on powerful wings, its black scales glinting in the firelight that had marked its birth.

'We did it!' Cat exclaimed in disbelief. 'We brought them back!'

# CHAPTER FIFTY-FOUR

As each of the dragons rose into the night sky a little of the fire left Corazoncillo, until the red light that had bathed the valley was reduced to the dull glow of embers, and darkness returned to the upper slopes.

'That's all ten!' Cat said delightedly, as they watched the last of the hatchlings take to the air. The rest had already flown away.

'We've gone back in time,' Vargo commented sagely.

Allegra stared at the final black shadow as it wheeled against the stars.

'Where do you think they're going?' she said.

Ico knew it wasn't a dream, because she hadn't been able to sleep that night. She had not even gone to bed. And yet she couldn't see how it *could* be real.

The cave was dark except for some incandescent shapes that moved in graceful, stately fashion. The air was cool and damp, and full of eerie music.

*That's enough.*

The voice was unusually weary, but nonetheless wholly familiar.

*Soo?*

One of the luminous shapes had become still now, and Ico recognized the sparrowhawk's fierce profile.

*I needed you to understand before I go.*

*Go? Go where?*

Soo ignored the question.

*You are a healer in spirit*, she said. *I could not have done this without your teaching. We can only move on if we recover from the wounds of the past.*

*You're not making any sense*, Ico replied. *Where are you?*

*You would have tried to stop me. I'm sorry.*

The first sparks of understanding flared in Ico's brain – and with them came fear.

*You kept me out of the network?*

*Yes. For love. How else could I abandon you and your fledgling?*

*Do you know where Ysanne is?* Ico asked quickly.

*Elva guards her.*

Ico was stunned into silence for a few moments.

*And Andrin?* she said eventually.

*I cannot see him*, Soo replied sadly.

Ico was quiet again as she absorbed this hammer blow.

*The network is allowing us to talk, but it's fading*, the sparrowhawk went on. *I need to rest now. I have been looking forward to that for a long time. Farewell, Ico. Sing the last song for me.*

*No!* Ico cried, but she already knew it was hopeless.

The music reached a crescendo then, as the water flooded into the cavern, and Ico could only watch helplessly as Soo drowned. She had known the pain of this loss before, but that did not make it any less acute now. This time their link was being severed for ever. This time Soo really was dead.

*Farewell*, Ico whispered softly into the darkness.

The fossil had been the cornerstone of the whole labyrinthine structure. As it crumbled, so did the rock around it, both above and below, making the entire mountain tremble. Huge landslides crashed into the ravine and into the Great Western Ocean, ending the music.

Underneath it all, Soo was flying with the dragons, to the heavens once more. But this time she would not be coming back.

The imperial army was just breaking camp when the dragons came. Most of the soldiers had been awake since dawn, and by the time the sun rose over the sea they were almost ready to continue their march down the coastal strip. Tzarno himself was one of the first to spot the ominous shapes, and when he did so his buoyant mood faltered, became a little less confident.

There were three of them, and they came skimming over the top of the western hills in formation, then dived down, following the contours of the land. To the people of the Empire dragons were messengers of the gods, and although these were much smaller than legend would have them believe, their shape and ferocity were unmistakable. Some of the soldiers threw themselves to the ground in fear, and the surviving Kundahari fell to their knees in prayer, but most of those present simply stared in amazement as the dragons flew towards the camp. A few began to draw their swords, but then thought better of it. No one knew what the creatures' appearance portended, but only a fool would try to match them in combat.

In the end, the dragons came close enough for everyone to see their burning yellow eyes, their iridescent scales and deadly talons, but they chose not to attack. Instead they dipped and whirled, turning somersaults and diving steeply, only to pull up again as they neared the ground. As more than one of the awe-struck onlookers remarked, it was almost as if they were playing.

The dragons' only aggressive act was directed towards the command tent – which was always the first to be set up at any camp and the last to be packed away – and because it was unoccupied at the time, no one came to any harm. Two of the three creatures swooped down and ripped gaping holes in the canvas with their trailing claws, screaming as they did so. The third followed, breathing a sudden stream of orange fire that set the tattered remains alight. Then they all took to the skies again, and flew away to the west.

Tzarno stared at the ruins of his tent and laughed. He was acutely aware that all eyes were upon him, and he had to try to forestall any thoughts that this was an ill omen.

'If that's the worst their dragons can do, we need be afraid of nothing in Tiguafaya!' he exclaimed. 'Prepare to march!'

At the supply camp, the day began in a more leisurely fashion. They had not moved for two days now, and saw no likelihood of doing so today. The blackened wasteland of the Ratifia Valley was still burning in places, and the air there was full of soot and smoke.

Madar, as Tzarno had intended, was growing bored but – having given his word not to interfere in the running of the campaign – there was little he could do about it. He was even beginning to wonder whether he and Katerin might have been better off staying in Zepharinn after all, and was considering the possibility of starting their journey home that day. He was worried about his bride. She had developed what he believed to be an unhealthy fascination for the Tiguafayan sorcerer, and spent much of her time observing the prisoner in his cage, trying – unsuccessfully – to get him to talk. Some of the things Katerin had been saying made her husband nervous. If he had not known better, he would have said that her attitude to magic was not as orthodox as it should be. Although she paid lip service to the belief that magic was an evil heresy, she nonetheless seemed unusually interested in such sorcery and what it might achieve. Only that morning she had casually asked him why he thought the gods were leaving it to the Empire to punish this heresy, rather than doing it themselves. He had not been able to give her a satisfactory answer, feeling blasphemous for even considering it, and had wished that the hierophant had been there to explain it for him.

Madar left his tent and went in search of his wife. He found her, as he had feared, staring thoughtfully at the sorcerer – who was ignoring her as usual. The Emperor suspected that his indifference had become something of a challenge for Katerin.

'Here again?' he chided gently.

'What else is there to do in this place?' she replied, and Madar had to admit that she had a point. An army supply camp in the middle of a foreign wilderness was not exactly brimming over with entertainments.

'Perhaps we should let him out, so he can amuse us with some magic tricks,' he suggested.

For a moment Katerin's eyes widened with excitement, but then she realized that her husband was joking, and her smile grew a little forced.

'We should kill him now,' she said, 'and end this cruelty. The bird too.'

'Tzarno has other plans for them.'

'Your brother is a barbarian.'

'Watch your tongue, wife,' he snapped.

'I'm sorry,' she whispered meekly, her cheeks darkening.

Madar was about to tell her to come away, already regretting the harshness of his rebuke, when Katerin pointed to the sky.

'What's that?'

Madar followed the line of her gaze, and saw a dark shape that grew larger with every moment. It was like no bird he had ever seen, both in its shape and its movement.

'It's a dragon!' Katerin exclaimed.

'Don't be—' Madar began, then stopped when he saw that she was right.

By the time the dragon reached the camp and began to circle high above, everyone was aware of its presence. Even the prisoner had twisted round in his cage so that he could look up.

'It's beautiful,' Katerin breathed.

'I've never seen a messenger of the gods before,' Madar said, equally in awe of the spectacle.

The dragon dived then, plunging out of the sky and heading almost directly towards the Emperor and his wife. Madar took Katerin's arm, but she held her ground, staring upwards, even as several imperial guards rushed forward to protect their charges. However, the dragon had a different target in mind. Shrieking wildly, it plunged through the dome that still surrounded the prisoner, and alighted on top of the cage. The dome collapsed in on itself, accompanied by the agonized wailing of the anti-mage who had created it. Then the dragon ripped the iron cage apart with its talons, and stooped to wrench the captive's chains from their foundations, effectively freeing him. The sorcerer stood up on unsteady legs, his eyes still wide with shock. None of the terrified onlookers was capable of making any move to prevent his escape. Like Madar and Katerin, they just stood and stared in amazement. Even so, the sorcerer seemed unable to move under his own power, and remained in the wreckage of his prison.

The dragon glared round, its yellow eyes blazing in challenge, then with a few swift and powerful wingbeats, it flew to the cart where the eagle was still tethered. A single devastating blow reduced the cart to kindling and the bird launched itself into the air, chains still dangling from its legs. The dragon returned, scooped the sorcerer up in its own talons and followed the eagle into the sky.

Still no one moved, except to follow their line of flight.

'This is a sign!' Katerin declared a few moments later, breaking the intense silence.

Madar shot her a glance, but she was in no mood to remain quiet.

'You said yourself that dragons are the gods' messengers,' she went on. 'They've spoken clearly enough here. If they choose to help the Tiguafayan sorcerer, how can we be prepared to wage war upon his country?'

'You're right,' Madar replied, suddenly decisive. 'We've been misled by false prophets. The war must end.' He turned to one of the senior officers present. 'Send couriers to Prince Tzarno immediately,' he ordered. 'Tell him that all of us here are returning to the Empire, and order him, in my name, to turn back his army.'

'Yes, Your Highness,' the soldier answered, and ran off to do his master's bidding.

'Prepare to break camp!' Madar shouted to the other on-lookers. 'I'll not stay in this forbidden land a moment longer than necessary.'

The soldiers and artisans scurried to obey, and Madar turned back to his wife.

'Thank you, my love,' he said. 'Your instincts, as usual, are matchless.'

Katerin smiled, acknowledging the compliment, then raised expressive eyebrows.

'Tzarno won't obey you, you know,' she said quietly. 'Not now that he's so close to his goal.'

'Then he's a bigger fool than even I take him for,' the Emperor replied.

# CHAPTER FIFTY-FIVE

'Do you think the dragons will help us against the Empire?'
Cat asked.

'I don't know,' Vargo replied. 'Ordinarily I don't think
they'd care about human concerns, but after what you did—'

'*We* did,' she corrected him.

'They may consider us friends,' he finished.

'And they might remember that Andrin and Ico got them
to Corazoncillo in the first place,' Cat suggested hopefully.

Vargo did not comment on the likelihood of the dragons
'remembering' something that had happened before they
were born. He knew what Allegra meant.

'Maybe. But I don't think we should rely on their help,'
he said.

Cat nodded, though she couldn't help looking disappointed.

They were resting in one of the abandoned houses in
Quemada. There was virtually nothing left of Corazoncillo
now, so they had made their way along the valley to the other
village. Reaction to everything that had happened had set in
during the walk and, although the light from the blazing

village and the three-quarter moon had been enough for them to see the path clearly, they had both been stumbling by the time they reached their destination. Cat especially had been close to exhaustion, and they had slept soundly for the rest of the night – even though the ground still shook a little every so often.

Now, as the morning sun rose higher in the sky, they were feeling partly refreshed but still weary, and wondered what they should do next. Allegra's first concern on waking had been to tend to Vargo. The red marks on his skin were still there but, as he said, the wounds were no more than mirror-deep, and they did not seem to be causing him much discomfort. Then they had eaten a frugal meal, and talked.

'There has to be some way we can use the network in the war,' Allegra said.

'Maybe. But you must be careful,' Vargo warned. 'There's a fine line between using and abusing magic.'

'There can't be anything wrong in defending my country from invaders,' she countered.

'Perhaps not, but power is always dangerous. Look what happened to Martinoy.'

'There's no comparison!' Cat objected.

'All I'm saying is you should be *careful*. Whoever created this network—'

'Nino, you mean?'

Vargo shook his head.

'He might have discovered it,' he said, 'but I doubt it's his creation, any more than it's yours.'

'I never said it was mine.'

'I know, but you're the one who brought it to life. You're the one who gave it purpose.'

'So what purpose can it possibly have now, apart from defeating the Empire?' Cat asked.

'I don't know,' Vargo admitted. 'But think about it, Cat.

So far it's been used to save people – us, in fact. That makes it a very personal, healing force. We don't know what would happen if anyone tried to use it more widely to *harm* people, even if they are our enemies.'

'But we can't simply ignore power like this!' she exclaimed. 'Are we supposed to just sit here and do nothing?'

'My guess is we should go back to Teguise,' he replied calmly. 'And discuss it with Ico and Nino.'

That seemed an eminently sensible suggestion – and at least it would be doing *something* – but Cat was still not wholly convinced.

'Now?' she asked doubtfully.

'No time like the present,' Vargo replied, laughing. 'Unless it's the past, of course.'

'Take my hands then,' Cat said, even though a part of her still felt that this was wrong. 'Ready?'

But as soon as she asked for help, she knew it wasn't going to work. It wasn't that the network wasn't there – she could sense it all around her – but it felt uncomfortable somehow, almost as if it resented her intrusion. As this feeling grew stronger, Cat remembered Vargo's earlier warning, and began to regret the attempt. Shaken, she drew back and released her lover's hands.

'I . . . I . . .' she stammered. 'It . . .'

'I saw,' Vargo said gently. 'It seems that purpose is not enough. There has to be *need* as well.'

'Does that mean we're meant to stay here?' Allegra's confidence was draining away now, and she wasn't sure of anything any more.

'Nino always thought this place was important,' Vargo remarked.

'That was because the dragons were here. They've gone now.'

Vargo shrugged.

'Then maybe it was telling us we have to walk,' he said.

'Did I cross the line?' Allegra asked quietly.

He shook his head.

'You mustn't doubt yourself, Cat. You were given the link for a reason, and when the time comes, you'll know what to do.'

She could only hope that he was right.

Later that morning, they went out to inspect their surroundings. A pall of smoke still hung over the place where Corazoncillo had been, but the 'volcano' was hardly active at all now, and had produced only a small cone of hardened lava. Most of the fireworms seemed to have gone, though a few were still in evidence, flying to and fro for no apparent reason.

'Cabria and the others won't thank us for this,' Cat said, looking at the sorry remains of the village.

'They'll understand,' Vargo told her. 'They're resilient people.'

Cat's attention was diverted then, as a new swarm of fireworms appeared on the southern horizon, closely followed by a single bird flying high above them. He was too far away for Cat to recognize him at first, but when he turned to dive towards Quemada, she knew at once who it was. Eya alighted on a nearby railing, drooping with tiredness as he finally allowed himself to rest.

*Hello, Eya.*

The peregrine bobbed his head in greeting but did not speak, and Allegra wondered briefly if the network had taken away her universal link.

*Did Nino send you to find us?* she tried.

*No. I was following the fireworms. They led me here.*

Cat was so glad to hear him that it took a moment for the import of his words to sink in.

*That swarm came from Teguise?* she gasped.

*Yes, but they're no longer tainted. Was that your doing?*

*Vargo's*, she replied. *And the dragons have hatched.*
*I know. I saw some of them at dawn.*
*Where were they going?*
*Somewhere to the south*, Eya replied vaguely.

They exchanged more news while the peregrine slowly recovered from his long flight. Cat was dismayed by the unfavourable progress of the war.

'The Empire could reach Teguise in the next two or three days,' she explained to Vargo. 'We'll never get there in time. What should we do?'

Vargo never got the chance to reply. Just at that moment there was a subterranean rumbling so loud and deep that they felt it in their bones – and moments later the ground beneath them heaved upwards, sending them sprawling, as a violent tremor ran the length of the valley. Then there was a short, deceptive interval of quiet stillness, but they weren't fooled.

'There's an eruption coming,' Vargo said as they picked themselves up.

'Gods, what have we done?' Cat whispered.

Vargo knew exactly what she meant. Until now Corazoncillo had been the most stable location in all the firelands, with no eruptions or tremors for miles around. It seemed that their efforts to help the dragons hatch had made the area vulnerable. The ground began shaking again.

'We did what was needed,' he said firmly.

'Can't the worms do something?' she asked, though she knew she was clutching at straws.

Vargo shook his head.

'It's too late,' he said. 'What we did might have triggered it sooner than expected, but this must have been coming for a long time. It would've been the work of months, even years, to prevent it – and the fireworms have only just been cured. All we—'

The rest of his words were drowned by the first deafening

explosion, which hurled the charred remains of Corazoncillo into the sky on a fountain of glowing lava that grew to be more than two hundred paces high in a matter of moments. The noise of the eruption roared in their ears, and the air grew instantly fetid. The first pebbles of rapidly cooling lava rattled down onto the roofs of Quemada, and the earth beneath their feet continued to vibrate. Smoke and ash spread on the wind and on the boiling currents of the volcano itself, forming a cloud the shape of a mountainous grey tree.

It all happened so quickly that Vargo and Cat had no time to even think of escaping. Eya was also mesmerized by the eruption, and remained rooted to his perch.

A second explosion, more violent than the first, ripped up another section of the valley floor – but this time the clouds of incandescent smoke that followed were not flung into the air but spread out, clinging to the surface of the land like a deadly, glowing avalanche. Vargo and Cat had both seen the silvery clouds that Tiguafayans called 'the shining breath' before, but only from a much greater distance. They knew it moved at incredible speed, and that there was no hope of outrunning it. Not even Eya at his fastest would have been able to do that. They looked at each other, certain now that they were about to die, and trying to frame their last words – while the omnivorous monster scorched its way directly towards them, devouring everything in its path.

And then, incredibly, they found themselves inside the most bizarre structure they had ever seen, a curving tent of living flesh that surrounded them, on all sides. Although the fireworms had not been able to prevent the eruption taking place, they *were* able to protect Vargo and Cat. There were hundreds of them, each worm hovering close to its neighbours, forming the shield. They had arrived so quickly and arranged themselves with such precision that it was impossible to tell how the dome had been built. One moment there was nothing; the next it was complete.

As the shining breath reached them, the worms all seemed to inhale, absorbing the searing heat with their own bodies so that none of the gases and ash passed through the gaps. The air inside remained still and relatively cool, even as the poisonous hurricane raged all around them, incinerating the houses of Quemada.

*You have useful friends*, Eya commented dryly. At the last moment the peregrine had left his perch and joined them, so that he too had been saved.

*That's an understatement*, Cat replied, hardly daring to believe her eyes or ears. Within the shield even the sound of the eruption was muffled.

'We don't know how long they'll be able to hold this,' Vargo said urgently. 'Surely the network will recognize our need now.'

'Maybe.' Although Cat longed to escape, she wasn't sure that asking the network for help was the right thing to do.

'Then get us out of here!' he urged.

'Where to?'

'Anywhere!'

But even as the words were spoken, Cat knew it would be no use. The response to her appeal had been instant and emphatic.

'I can't,' she said. 'This is the centre. We have to be here or nothing else will work.'

'What else *is* there?' Vargo was clearly terrified.

'I don't know yet,' Cat replied. 'But I will when the time comes.'

This time it was Vargo's turn to look doubtful.

The eruption at Corazoncillo was only the first of many, and it set off a chain reaction that spread south and east with terrifying speed. Old craters burst into molten life once more, new ones built themselves from the lava that gushed forth, and the sky grew dark as the northern firelands convulsed and shook. The earth itself seemed to fracture along several lines, each describing an arc of a circle – all of which were centred on Corazoncillo. A new mountain range was raised in a few hours, and because of the strange nature of the faults, the vast lava flows nearly all headed southeast – often merging as valleys joined, then dividing again as they surged round existing peaks.

Directly in the path of the lava was the coastal plain, where both armies – the Tiguafayans in full retreat, Tzarno's forces marching on in defiance of the Emperor's command – were left exposed. Beyond that lay the central lowlands – and Teguise.

Unknown to those on land, Tiguafaya was not the only place experiencing violent upheavals. Far to the east, beyond the opposing fleets, the primeval forces that had created the pirate islands were awakening from their long sleep.

The lookout on Lamia's black ship saw it first, but it took him a few moments to find his voice and alert the others. Even then he did not know how to describe what he was seeing.

'Look astern!' he cried in a terrified wail.

Lamia and all the others on board had anticipated going into battle soon, and were looking forward to crushing the Tiguafayan navy and sailing on to Teguise to complete the job. They were not prepared for the sight that confronted them now as they turned to look east.

A vast new mountain had risen above the surface of the ocean. But this was no ordinary mountain. It was made of water. And it was moving.

# CHAPTER FIFTY-SIX

Ico was standing at the edge of one of the docks when Nino eventually found her. She had come, like hundreds of others, to gaze in awe at Tiguafaya's latest mystery. However, unlike any of the other onlookers, she had seen it before. Although all sailors knew that the sea was a capricious mistress, who always kept a few surprises up her sleeves, this latest phenomenon defied explanation. All the water had drained out of Teguise harbour, leaving only an alien morass of mud and sand, dying fish and upturned boats. The ocean's retreat had first been noticed by those working on the seaward defences, and when the level had fallen well below the lowest tide ever recorded the news had spread rapidly throughout the city. By the time many of the present observers had arrived, Ico included, the entire port had been left high and dry.

The President had received many sidelong glances as she arrived and – even though most of the wharves and jetties were crowded now – she had been left alone, a solitary figure in the midst of many. She was obviously in considerable distress, but no one at the docks knew how to deal with presidential tears. For most it was a shock simply to realize that their highly respected leader was at all vulnerable. It was some time before anyone felt able to approach her, and then it was Nino, who had come in answer to a plea from one of the anxious palace guards. Ico did not move as he walked to her side.

'It's just like my dream,' she said quietly, without looking round. 'There's only the Senate chamber left now.'

Nino had no idea what she was talking about. His own dreams had been very strange lately – and very revealing – but they hadn't included anything about Teguise harbour or the Senate.

'Are you all right?' he asked.

Ico laughed, but it was an ugly sound, choked off halfway through by a sob.

'Soo's dead.'

'I'm sorry.' Nino had glimpsed this in his dream the previous night, and although he had hoped he was mistaken, the news didn't come as a complete surprise.

'She was keeping me out, excluding me,' Ico added. 'That's why I could never be part of your precious network. And now it's killed her.'

Nino was shocked by the venom in his friend's voice. He knew the accusation was unjust, but he also knew how distressing the loss of a link could be, and so understood her bitterness.

'And Ysanne too, I expect,' Ico went on, with tears running down her cheeks.

'What?' He was truly horrified now.

'She's on Elva,' Ico told him. 'How's she going to escape from there?'

Nino had no answer. He could only wonder how Ysanne had reached the oracle in the first place. That was something his network dreams had not revealed.

'Andrin's dead too,' she stated miserably. 'And don't tell me I'm wrong. If he were alive Soo would've seen him in the web – and she couldn't.' Ico paused, then finally turned to look at him. 'So what have I got left?' she asked quietly.

As they were making their way back to the palace, they became aware that the sea was not the only part of the world to be behaving oddly. The northern sky was growing ominously dark. They had just entered Manrique Square when the first tremor hit. It was slight, no more than a distant vibration, but they both knew what it meant. The long-promised eruptions had begun.

'That's all we need,' Ico groaned.

Nino did not reply. He was suddenly lost in another realm, a place he usually only visited in his dreams. The network was springing into life once more, and the world about him – even his own body – became meaningless. He half sat, half fell onto the paving stones.

'Nino?' Ico cried in alarm. 'What's the matter?'

Her friend's eyes were shut, although beneath the lids they were still moving rapidly, as though he were looking deep inside himself. Otherwise he seemed almost lifeless, his muscles limp. Ico knelt beside him, as several of the guards – who had been accompanying them at a discreet distance – came to see if they could be of assistance.

'The singing,' Nino whispered, so faintly that Ico could hardly hear him.

When she realized what he had said, her sense of isolation deepened even more. It was obvious that the network was waking again and now, with Soo gone, she had no link. That meant her exclusion was even more complete than before. The fact that this time she knew why she was left out did not really help. Whatever was happening, Ico had no part to play. It was up to others now.

'Can we help you, ma'am?' one of the soldiers enquired.

'No.' Ico was aware of a group gathering to watch. 'Just keep people back a bit, would you? I don't want anyone to disturb him.'

As the guards spread out around them, Nino roused himself briefly.

'It's Cat,' he mumbled. 'It's always been Cat.'

Then he fell into a trance so deep that Ico wondered if he would ever wake again.

A false night had come to the Corazoncillo Valley, the sun blotted out by a canopy of thick, black smoke. The shining breath had dissipated now, and the worms had slowly broken their protective wall around Vargo and Cat, revealing a scene of utter devastation. Once solid buildings were no more than scattered piles of charcoal. The entire village of Quemada had been flattened and reduced to ash, and yet the two humans and their avian companion had suffered no more than mild discomfort.

The eruption, centred on Corazoncillo, was continuing – but more calmly now, and the fireworms had scattered again, going about their mysterious business. Even so, distant rumblings told of further volcanic activity elsewhere.

'I think we're out of immediate danger,' Vargo said, 'but I don't know how long that'll last. We'd better get out of here.'

Cat shook her head.

'We have to *stay* here,' she said. It was the only thing she was sure of.

For once, Vargo did not argue. He had felt the magic stirring, and he knew that Cat was at its core.

Allegra could feel the power, but knew she needed the help of others to use it. She was feeling lost and helpless, with every emotion – from joy to dread, from sorrow to bewilderment – threatening to unhinge her completely. All the birds were there, their voices clear now, though she could not make out what any individual was saying. I have to make sense of this, she thought desperately. Or we'll get nowhere.

*Eya, do you know what's going on?* she asked, hoping that the physical proximity of the peregrine would help her to hear him above the mounting chaos.

*The sky sings a different song now*, he replied enigmatically.

The network's *here*, Cat told herself. So it stands to reason that we ought to use it. But what is its purpose supposed to be this time? And what do we need?

Nino was flying within the network, with a growing sense of excitement. Here was the power, the majesty he had glimpsed before, but now it was stronger than ever, its overall structure clearer than ever. Most importantly, he had realized – belatedly – that Cat was its focus, the link that tied all the others together. Crucially, she was also at the web's geographical centre – at Corazoncillo. He had always known it was an important place, and now he saw exactly why. It was the heart of the web.

Beyond that, he was aware of all the interlocking pieces of the whole falling into place. This network was different from its previous incarnations, and it took a little time to work out why. The shift had been caused by a change in the most important intersections, the foci. One of them – the ravine that Vargo and Cat had visited – had been destroyed, its purpose fulfilled, and it had been replaced by another which Nino could not see clearly. It didn't seem to be connected to any particular location. However, the other familiar sites were still there, and – more importantly – there were links at all of them, reinforcing the complex pattern. Vargo and Cat were at Corazoncillo, and Nino himself was in

Teguise, but the identities of those at the other places were rather more surprising.

When Ambron had left Vargo and Cat at the rim of the canyon, he had decided not to head home straight away. Instead he travelled on, up the coast, then turned east, exploring some of the remotest parts of the northern firelands. He could not explain the impulse that led him on, but then Vek had taken over. The bird had insisted that they make for a particular circular mountain, which had never even been named in the human tongue. At the top, they found themselves on the rim of a small but deep crater and had climbed down, only to discover that the only things at the bottom were a mass of powdery grey dust and a pile of old bones. At first the prospector had not even realized which ancient creature they had belonged to, but now he knew.

As the network absorbed them, drawing strength from their link, Ambron and Vek were lost in wonder, and resolved to play their part as best they could in the great events that were about to take place. The oriole's fluting call echoed from the walls of the dragon graveyard.

Ysanne had been awake nearly all night, feeling cold and lonely. She missed her mother most of all, but it was doubly frustrating to know that Tas was so close and yet not be able to join her link. No bird was allowed to land on the oracle's island, on pain of death, and Ysanne was beginning to wonder if she herself would ever be able to get off. If she couldn't transform herself into the flock again – and she had tried and failed, several times – then it was going to be very hard. She might be able to scramble down off the rock and reach the shingle when the tide was out, but – young as she was – she knew enough to realize that she could never hope to climb the gigantic cliffs, let alone cross the lava streams beyond. She cried a little as dawn came, feeling sorry for herself, but then she decided that the dragons would come back soon and talk to her. That made her feel better, even though she wasn't sure how they would be able to help her.

With the new day, Ysanne had looked around, noting again how none of the birds came anywhere near Elva, even though the cliffs were home to hundreds of gulls. To take her mind off such things, she began talking to herself, and hopped about to try and keep warm.

Then the singing became louder than she had ever heard it before, restoring some of her earlier confidence. All at once she could sense Tas's presence once more – and could see a lot of very strange things. She wondered about using the magic to make her escape, but one of the voices told her to stay where she was. Ysanne was almost certain that it was a dragon's voice, and so she was happy to do as she was told.

Just as no birds ever went to Elva, so no humans came to the great red mountain of Pajarito, for it was here that the voices of the sky spoke to the winged creatures of the world – and to no one else.

Ero and Lao had arrived in the vast, lopsided crater after a journey that had taken only an instant, their minds in shock. There had been no sense of movement or speed, just a beginning and an end. They had been greeted with faint whispers and sighs, nothing more. The oracle had evinced no surprise at their method of travel, nor had it deigned to speak to the ill-matched pair. Neither of them knew what to do and so, trusting in Cat's parting advice, they had simply waited through the night. Ero had even slept; Lao's more acute sensibilities had kept him awake.

In the morning, the silence was even more profound. Even the wind seemed to be holding its breath. Lao was understandably nervous, but prepared to continue their vigil for as long as necessary. In contrast, Ero's limited supplies of patience were already running low.

'I danced the last time I was here,' he remarked, practising a few small steps. 'They liked that.'

Lao would have preferred to remain quiet, with all his senses attuned to the whispered messages of the ancient tumbled stones, but he knew he would get no peace until he made some response. He refrained from asking who 'they' were, and settled for a simple comment.

'If we need to dance, we'll know.'

'Perhaps we should try now,' the hoopoe said, ever hopeful.

'Not yet,' Lao replied firmly.

The sun was rising now, bringing the varied shades of Pajarito to life.

'I've just thought of something,' Ero said, when he had stopped sulking.

'Really?'

'We can talk to Cat!' the hoopoe exclaimed, as if this amazing fact had only just occurred to him.

'Yes,' Lao replied. 'She's linked to all of us.'

'Why?'

'I don't know. Why is Vargo linked to both of us and not just one?'

This question seemed to puzzle Ero considerably, but then he evidently set it aside and returned to his normal cheerful state.

'I always knew she was special,' he claimed. 'I expect that's why Vargo chose to mate with her. She'll be laying eggs soon.'

'Humans don't—' Lao began, then fell silent as Pajarito growled. The boulder on which they were perched began to shake, and a few smaller rocks shifted and rolled down the steeper slopes of the crater. At the same time, both birds felt the living magic – that Cat had called the net – spring back into being. The oracle vibrated to its strange music.

'*Now* we can dance!' Ero cried delightedly.

Nino watched the endless tracery of lines and circles dancing within his mind, and saw that the structure contained weaknesses as well as strengths. He became aware of gaps, of rents in the delicate fabric, which put an enormous strain on all the rest. There were rogue elements loose within the web that must be controlled before they caused the whole thing to fly apart. That thought was clearly disturbing, and Nino instinctively threw himself into the fight to keep the network from disintegrating. In doing so he plunged deeper into the dream, and found himself calling out to the one person who held all their fates in her hands. He could see Cat, and sense her confusion – but he had no idea whether she heard him or not.

Cat's mind was reeling.

*Stop this!* she pleaded. *I can't cope with everything at once. What am I supposed to do?*

The barrage of noise and images did not relent and she knew that, for once, merely asking for help would not be enough. She had to discover the purpose and the need for herself, and then let all the others know. That resolution gave her strength, and she began to search for clues, sifting through the insubstantial world she had helped to create. As she moved onwards, the infinitely complex patterns wavered and shifted unpredictably, either welcoming her or remaining aloof. She saw familiar faces, both human and avian, as well as many she did not recognize. She visited old haunts and places she'd never seen before – and then she found herself in the sky.

Allegra was flying, looking through another's eyes, so

high that she thought she must be nearly touching the stars. All Tiguafaya lay spread out below her, and she could even see the oceans to either side, and the southern part of the Empire. A vast bank of smoke lay over the northern firelands, but that did not obscure the fact that an enormous deluge of glowing lava was pouring towards the coastal plain – or the fact that another eruption far out to sea to the east had caused waves to spread out in a rapidly expanding circle. From her vantage point, the largest wave looked like no more than a ripple, but Cat knew that for it to be visible at all at this height it must be gigantic.

These two opposing threats left her close to panic. The most densely populated part of Tiguafaya, including Teguise itself, was caught between the dual pincers of the lava and the tidal wave. The scale of the destruction, the loss of life, would be catastrophic, unimaginable – and this was obviously what she was meant to prevent. This was the need. But how was she supposed to do anything about it? Even the power of the network was surely not enough to oppose such elemental furies.

*Your time is short.*

The voice, Cat knew, belonged to the dragon through whose eyes she was looking. It was flying above and beyond the net, and the fact that it had taken her with it must mean something.

*What should I do?* she begged.

*There is only one force that can oppose both the volcanoes and the sea*, the dragon replied. *And there is one among you who has done it before.*

# CHAPTER FIFTY-SEVEN

*Andrin! Andrin, we need you!* Cat was shouting now, pleading. She knew that Andrin was still alive, and so was Ayo, but she had no idea where they were – either inside or outside the net.

*Ayo?* she tried. *Can you hear me?* But there was still no response.

Allegra's flight with the dragon was over, and both the need and the purpose for her magic were clear to her now. The idea that she had envisaged was so outrageous that at first she had hesitated to share it with anyone – only to find that just by thinking of it she had already done so. The network gave their support, but unless she could find Andrin there would be no point in going on. He was uniquely suited to shaping the efforts of all the others.

For a brief moment, Cat was aware of her physical body, of the fact that Vargo was holding her. She had almost forgotten him in the disorientating swirl and clamour of the net.

*Make sense of this for me*, she said. *You're a musician again. You can bring them all together. Then I'll be able to make Andrin hear me.*

*I can only do that if you let me work through you*, Vargo replied. *You're the only one we can all hear.*

*What do I have to do?*

*Let me in*, he told her simply.

Cat obeyed gladly, instinctively. She knew what this entailed, and although a short time ago it might have frightened her, that was no longer true. If this endeavour was to succeed, she could keep no secrets from Vargo. Their trust had to be complete.

Allegra sensed the shapes of his mind – his thoughts and memories, his emotions and his mysteries – and felt them intertwine with her own, becoming one. It was the most intimate, most loving embrace she could ever have imagined.

Almost at once she began to perceive a change in the net. Melody and form emerged out of chaos as all the voices joined Vargo's music. It was beautiful and strangely moving, unlike anything she had ever heard before. There was still an occasional discord or false note, but these were minor irritations compared to the earlier cacophony. The visual images were also being calmed, and Cat felt for the first time that she was part of one great link, a single force that could shift even immovable objects. Vargo's reborn passion had shaped the network.

And in that newly formed, lucid world, Cat renewed her search.

Andrin sat on the hilltop, his mind in a daze. Ayo stood next to him, as silent and bemused as his link.

They had no real idea where they were. After his long incarceration, Andrin had been so amazed to find himself high above the earth, held fast in the talons of a dragon, that he had paid no attention to where he was being taken. And it seemed that Ayo could not help. Andrin was not even sure if the two of them were still able to communicate. Their link had been rendered mute for so long that he wondered whether it had atrophied. Everything Andrin valued had been stripped away when he'd been inside the cage, and he was finding it hard to believe that he really had come back from the dead.

The dragon had left them on this lonely hill, and had flown away without any word of explanation. Where the creature had come from, and why it had chosen to free them, were mysteries that Andrin did not ever expect to solve. His legs had given way as soon as he was on the ground again, and he had not moved since. Looking around, he could see at a glance that they had left the firelands. If he'd had to guess, he would have said that they were somewhere in the central lowlands, to the west of Teguise, but nothing seemed familiar. Now that he had returned to the world, it no longer seemed real. It rejected all his efforts to take his place again. He could not even remember what it was like to feel at home anywhere, to be welcomed.

The dome that had been placed around Andrin by the anti-mage had cramped his mind and his magic, just as the cage had cramped his body. His thoughts were now as stiff and painful as his muscles, and his isolation had weakened him in both body and spirit. It would be some time before either would be able to move freely again.

A part of Andrin still wondered whether he'd wake up soon and find he had been dreaming – and that he was back in chains. He looked down at his ankles, at the manacles that were no longer attached to his prison. He stared at the metal that had cut and bruised his flesh for so long, trying to decide if it was real. Ayo had smaller versions attached to his legs, and these seemed equally bizarre.

Andrin still had enough sense left to know that his thoughts were tangled, but there seemed to be nothing he could do about it. For the moment, the desire to sleep, to simply lie down and rest, was almost irresistible. He couldn't remember the last time he had slept for more than a few minutes, just as he could no longer imagine being without pain.

*The earth is stirring*, Ayo said, turning his head to gaze to the north, and Andrin felt a spasm of relief at this confirmation that their link still existed.

Several huge columns of ash were rising from the mountains, merging to form a dark blanket of cloud, but that too seemed remote and meaningless to Andrin.

*There was safety in slumber*, the eagle added.

*But no more*, Andrin replied, with an unaccountably heavy heart.

The hill began to tremble beneath them, but Andrin stayed where he was, having nowhere to go, nothing to do except wait. Odd snatches of sound carried to them on the wind; strange lights appeared in the corners of their eyes, only to vanish again. Something tugged at Andrin's mind, but he didn't know what it was, and he began to wish for true silence, real stillness. Everything else was irrelevant.

But all that changed when the music began. It grew softly, insistently, creeping into his consciousness until he could no longer ignore it. The sound was alien, yet familiar in many ways, and Andrin recognized the imprint of its principal creator. It was only when he remembered that Vargo had lost his music that he became confused again, but by then he could hear something else. It was a voice, calling his name.

*Andrin? Andrin! At last.* The relief and urgency in her voice were equally obvious. *Can you hear me?*

*I can hear you, Cat.* For a moment he had imagined it to be another's voice, and felt a pang of longing and regret, but Allegra gave him no chance to dwell on the pain of his returning memories.

*We need your help*, she told him. *Teguise and most of Tiguafaya will be destroyed soon unless we do something to stop it. You've got to help us.*

Nino was still fighting, but he allowed himself a little hope now. Cat was in charge, and if her plan seemed desperate, it was the only one they had. Vargo's efforts had made his own struggle that much easier and when – to Nino's surprise and joy – both Andrin and Ayo responded to Allegra's prompting, he had begun to believe that they had a chance of success. Andrin's reunion with the web had been agonizingly slow – clearly the after-effects of his time apart had been hard to overcome – but he and Ayo were there now, a new and vital piece of the net. Everything was ready.

Nino sensed Andrin's first stumbling efforts to follow Cat's instructions and, like all the others, he lent him his own support. He was dismayed when the attempt failed, and was even more horrified when he realized the reason for their failure. Nino had assumed that Andrin and Ayo represented the last focus, the most significant missing piece of the network, but he had been wrong. Although their return had strengthened the overall structure, it had not perfected it. And until that happened, all their efforts would be in vain.

The final, crucial link in the circle was still missing. And Nino had no idea who – or what – it was.

# CHAPTER FIFTY-EIGHT

Maciot knew he was dying when he saw Tao perched on one of the black gunwales. He didn't know whether the mirador was a ghost or one of his hallucinations, but when it became clear that no one else could see the bird, the former senator took his appearance as a sign.

He had been slipping in and out of delirium for three days now, as his wounds failed to heal and his fever worsened. During his rational moments, he found it hard to understand why he had been kept alive this long. Surely it would have made more sense for the crew to throw him overboard and be rid of his contagion. But the woman whose authority was unquestioned on board the ship had apparently decided otherwise. Maciot had learnt that her name was Lamia, though she called herself the Emissary, and that her mission was to rid Tiguafaya of all magic. To this end she seemed prepared to do anything, including killing the entire population if necessary. Her fanaticism was truly frightening, and Maciot had no doubt that she was prepared to back it up with action. She appeared immune to fear.

He had gathered this information partly from the interpreter through whom Lamia spoke to him, and partly from the only other person aboard who spoke his own language. The pirate was called Endo, and Maciot recognized the name from his earlier dealings with Ico. Endo's role on board ship seemed to be as pilot and navigator, and he also acted as a go-between when messages were sent to and from the rest of the massive fleet that was preparing to attack Teguise. However, there was nothing anyone could do about the peril that faced them all now. The mountainous wave was bearing down on them with mind-numbing speed.

Maciot, it seemed, would not be dying alone.

He was looking at Tao again, noting incongruously that the mirador's colouring matched that of the ship, when he heard the faintest echo of some distant music. He shook his head, but the sound remained. And then he began to hear voices too.

*Are you just going to sit there?* Tao enquired sharply.

*Tao?* Maciot was convinced that this was another hallucination.

*You have work to do.*

*But you're dead.* He was close to tears.

*I've been given dispensation,* the mirador replied caustically, *so that I can talk to you. So listen! There's no time to waste.*

Maciot did as he was told and, with typical brevity, Tao relayed his instructions.

*The last singing will involve all the links there have ever been,* he concluded. *That's why I'm here, and why* you *have to act now.*

'Lamia!' Maciot yelled suddenly, startling all those near by. 'I have to talk to you.'

The Emissary said something dismissive in her own unintelligible tongue, and resumed her watch to the east.

'If you listen to me, we can all be saved!' he shouted. 'There *is* a way.'

'What way?' the interpreter asked, after a terse exchange with his mistress.

'Magic!'

The expressions this produced on the faces of both Lamia and the translator told Maciot that he'd made a mistake, but he would not be deterred.

'At least let me explain,' he went on. 'What have you got to lose?'

Lamia made an impatient gesture – and then found a knife at her throat. In their preoccupation, none of the easterners had noticed Endo moving – and now it was too late, even for warriors of their abilities.

'Listen for once, you bitch,' the pirate snarled in her ear. 'Magic saved my life once, and you're not going to deny us this chance now.' He marched her forward until she stood in front of Maciot, who was still sitting on the deck. Tao flew over and landed on her shoulder, though she did not seem to notice.

*She will hear you.*

Maciot was no longer surprised by anything, and simply accepted the bird's assurance.

*You must join us, Lamia,* he began, *not try to hinder us.*

The Emissary's eyes widened in terror and she glanced around, as if searching for the source of the voice inside her head.

*Your talent is just another form of magic,* Maciot went on. *Listen. The network is all around us, waiting to welcome you.*

*How are you doing this?* she asked hesitantly, stumbling over the unfamiliar words but certain of their meaning. Although she was obviously still very afraid, she was none-theless regaining a little of her spirit.

*Through the web*, he replied. *You should be part of it, Lamia. In your heart you know that. You were not always as you are today, I can see that. Your magic was innocent once. It can be again.*

*No! Do not say such things!* she cried. *Sorcery is evil.*

*You've been living a lie*, Maciot went on relentlessly. *Magic is no more evil than any other force of nature. It's the way it's used that matters.*

*You lie!* she responded, sounding desperate now.

*Look above you*, he said, pointing to the sky, where the mollymarks still rode majestically on the wind. *Those are your links. They chose you because of your magic. They honour you. The only thing stopping you from joining them is your own refusal to see the truth. Open your thoughts. One of them will talk to you.*

Lamia looked up, and an expression of pure agony passed across her face. When she looked down again, Maciot saw that her eyes, once so dead, were now full of pain – but very much alive.

*You know I'm right, don't you? Tell the others, and join us. Use your talent for magic. Together we can save all of us, and all of Teguise.*

Endo had pulled back now, seeing that his blade was no longer necessary. No one else had even moved, everyone aware that something extraordinary had been happening.

*Decide!* Maciot demanded forcefully. The giant wave could only be moments away now.

He watched as Lamia tore her mind loose from its moorings, casting herself adrift in a strange and violent ocean that she neither knew nor trusted. It cost her everything she had ever believed in, cast doubt upon her whole life, and left her infinitely vulnerable. It was the bravest thing Maciot had ever seen anyone do.

*We will join you*, she said softly.

*Thank you*, he replied, and felt the network gather its strength.

The last gap in the circle closed.

*You can let go now*, Tao said gently, his voice for once full of warmth and affection. *And come with me.*

Maciot died with a grateful smile on his face.

The singing began.

# CHAPTER FIFTY-NINE

It was a sound the world had never heard before.

It was made up of the songs of every bird that had ever lived, of every type of human voice and all the instruments they had ever devised. It contained all the elements of the sky; the soughing of the wind, the pattering of rain, the soft silences of snow and the rolling drums of thunder. Within its unmeasured boundaries lay the warmth of summer and the chill of winter months, the fire of the sun and the diamond-sharp sparkle of stars. It was filled with the shapes of clouds and the colours of sunset, the movement of shadows and the clarity of dawn. Its rhythms were marked out by the beating of countless wings, and its themes were all the mysteries of dreams. It was the culmination of every beautiful thing that had ever been created and then lost, every love that had flourished and then died. It was truly the last song.

Vargo was lost in the music, as much a part of it as it was part of him. He was inspired, transported as he had never been before, aware that this creation was a product of far more than just his own talent. He wished that Famara could have been there to hear it, to see where her tutelage had led him – and it was then that he sensed the memories of her sparrows in the web. Vargo smiled in the midst of his reverie, and guided his mentor's legacy into the music.

The only other sign of approval he might have wished for came of its own accord. The dragons did not sing, but they were listening, and Vargo sensed their silent praise. It was all the encouragement he needed to put every ounce of his being into the song.

In one world, Cat was clasped in her lover's arms, in a valley where a volcano still erupted and where the sky had turned black. In another, she was seeing her vision take shape. With the network complete, she was aware of everything. Her only task now was to sort out what was truly important from among the myriad images available to her. Even though Nino had done much of the groundwork, and Vargo had been the catalyst, making it possible for her to unite them all, Cat knew that the network was, in a sense, her own creation. That had ceased to matter now. It had become self-sustaining; it was alive, complete, filled with need and purpose, and its progress was irreversible. Cat knew exactly where its music was leading them.

Ambron and Vek had known from the start that they were out of their depth. They were not meant to be part of history, of the great events that shaped the nature of the world, but they knew they had no choice. They lent their strength and whatever rough music they possessed – and found it was enough. They discovered ancient songs in the bones of the dragons, and transferred them to their own hearts and lungs. The crater echoed and buzzed, alive again for the first time in many centuries.

Although Ambron was a large man and sometimes

ponderous in his movements, he found himself moved to dance. His heavy boots raised clouds of dust as he stamped and clapped, while Vek whirled in the air above him, a golden streak against the dreaming sky.

Far to the south, another pair were dancing too, in their very different ways. Ero's flight was almost manic, as he bobbed and weaved in the air. Lao stayed on the ground, moving with grace and dignity, but with just as much joy, singing softly all the time. They had both recognized Vargo's music, and had been delighted. Neither had understood why it had been gone for so long; all they knew was that there, in Pajarito, they had the chance to be part of its re-emergence. It was a chance they had no intention of letting slip by.

Of the two, only Lao realized that the music was a sign that greater events were taking place, and he kept the knowledge to himself. For all his grumbling, the sandpiper loved Ero as a brother, and to see him so ecstatically happy, giving full vent to his greatest passion, was a pleasure in itself. Lao would do nothing to spoil his fun.

Pajarito looked on approvingly, adding its own harmonies to the song. And if there was a hint of sadness in the oracle's tone, that hardly came as a great surprise. All sacred places breed melancholy thoughts.

Ysanne was feeling too pleased with herself to worry about the secrets of *her* oracle. She had added her own small voice to the singing, and had felt it grow into a chorus that was the most wonderful thing she had ever heard. It was so loud that it seemed to shake the rock beneath her feet, almost as though the real Elva of long ago was stirring again.

And Ysanne knew now that the dragons were coming back to talk to her. Best of all, she knew this because she could *see* them.

\*

Nino could not have said which of his emotions – astonishment or relief – was the stronger. He had been shocked by the identity and location of the last focus, but the long-anticipated completion of the network had been a source of both immense satisfaction and sudden hope. He believed that the web had been on the point of breaking apart when Lamia finally joined them – and had it not been for that last-minute reprieve, all would have been lost. Now, with stability established, Allegra's plan could go ahead. All it needed was a starting point. Just as the lava flows were radiating out from Corazoncillo, and the source of the giant wave was the eruption in the eastern sea, so the magic needed a centre too. Andrin would initiate it, while Cat supplied the power, but they were too far away to suit their own purpose. The centre had to be in Teguise.

'Take my hand,' he whispered.

Ico did as she was told, even though she knew she could not be part of his great enterprise. With her other hand, she instinctively clasped her dragon's blood pendant – hoping that her talisman would give her strength.

'What do you want me to do?' she asked.

'Nothing. Just be here. You're the centre, Ico. Andrin won't be able to do it without you.

Ico gasped.

'Andrin? she breathed. 'He's alive?'

'He asked for you,' Nino told her. 'Just listen.'

Andrin's disordered mind was beginning to function once more, and now that he had *his* focus in sight, he could begin again. Any world with Ico in it was worth saving.

Something – he wasn't quite sure what – had changed since he had first tried, and failed, to put the magic to work. The plan that Cat had outlined had seemed perfectly plausible to him, but this time he did not have Angel, the weather mage, to help him. Nor did he have the dragon eggs. He needed another source of power – and the network had given him access to it.

At his command, every dragon's tear crystal in Tiguafaya – including those that still lay undiscovered beneath the ground – began to disintegrate. But instead of them simply cooling the area immediately around them, Andrin gathered the cold to himself and fed it into the net. Then, with Ico as his starting point, he brought a new circle into life – one that grew so that it enclosed first the city and then the land and sea for many miles around. When he was satisfied with the circle's position, Andrin called a halt, and released the cold into its length. The temperature along the entire circumference of the circle dropped instantly – and kept on dropping as more and more heat was leached away, until the air itself was frigid. Andrin was the Ice Mage once again.

The hill where he and Ayo now stood was approximately half a mile inside the circle, and so he was able to observe the results of his handiwork. A huge, bright orange lava flow was heading directly towards them, but when it reached the frozen barrier it faltered, then slowed, then stopped. As it cooled, turning from orange to dull red to black as it solidified, it built up into great banks – which then acted as a barrier to the lava that was still flowing from the mountains. Even then the cold did not relent, and forced the molten rock to go *around* the circle, forming one long curving cliff that smoked and shuddered but did not come any closer. Inside the circle, all was safe.

At sea, the effect was even more dramatic. A huge strip of the ocean froze in an arc, enclosing the waters around Teguise and trapping the opposing fleets. The ships furthest from the city were almost caught in the sudden ice floe, but they managed to escape. However, no one expected their reprieve to be anything other than temporary. The tidal wave that was bearing down on them with such incredible speed was more than three times the height of the tallest mast. It was so vast that it defied description, a genuine mountain of churning, blue-green water and foam that would inundate their puny vessels and sweep them all to oblivion. But what happened next stunned the terrified seamen. Moments after the circle had formed, the wave arrived – but instead of crashing over the ice barrier, it froze instantly in the glacial air, creating a crescent-shaped iceberg so immense that it turned back all the other waves that followed.

Anchored to the shore at either end, the gigantic arc remained motionless, like some glittering, primeval harbour wall. Within its protection, most of the sailors were too amazed to do anything but stare in awe. Even those some miles away from the actual line could see enough to know that their lives had been saved by something incredible. No one had any thoughts of war now.

Aboard the black ship, Lamia had fallen to the deck, weeping uncontrollably. Although her collapse came as an embarrassment to her crew – who had never before seen her betray any real emotion – most of them were still mesmerized, staring up at the mountain range of jagged ice. None of them knew what had happened.

Lamia did. She had glimpsed the truth and seen her life for what it had been. Worse still, she knew that she would eventually have to take that knowledge home with her.

Outside the magic circle, the scene was very different. Although the Tiguafayan forces had reached the protected area, Prince Tzarno and the imperial army had not. They were just leaving the last of the firelands behind, but were still only a few hundred paces from the coast. They had been aware of the eruptions inland for some time, and this had made many of the soldiers nervous. But panic set in when a huge wall of glowing lava surged over the nearest ridge, and they began to run, only to find that there was nowhere to go.

Like all those around him, Tzarno was caught between awe and terror, looking one way and then the other as the two primeval forces raced towards each other. Above the roaring he heard Lamia's words again. 'Those who ride on flame fly high and fast, but their fall can be all the greater.' Tzarno smiled briefly, thinking it ironic that the unheeded warning should have been spoken by a mere woman – and that her remembered voice would be the last he ever heard. The bitch really had been a prophetess.

At the realization that his fate was sealed, the prince grew still, almost oblivious to the fearful chaos around him. Alone within the human frenzy, he became a prophet himself, foreseeing the Empire's ruin under his brother's milksop rule, and found himself hoping that Katerin's influence would grow stronger. At least she had some spirit.

And then Tzarno began to laugh. He was still laughing when the tidal wave crashed into the shore with a noise like the splitting of worlds. An instant later, the earth's fire met the sea.

Trapped between these two raging elements, mere humans stood no chance. The entire army perished in that explosive meeting, thousands of lives extinguished in a few devastating moments. Tzarno and Ty did not live to pursue their dreams of imperial glory, and Mazo Gadette was never to gain his revenge. Instead, like all their followers, they vanished without trace beneath the volcanoes' deluge.

The invaders were not the only ones to suffer, of course, but the number of other casualties was surprisingly small. The northern part of Tiguafaya, where the lava and the waves did the most damage, had already been evacuated – even the refugee boats from the enclave had reached the safety of the circle – and so there were few people left to bear the brunt of the dual assault.

Further south, the land was beyond the range of the lava flows and – as the coastline curved away westward – the tidal wave ran more or less parallel to the shore rather than directly towards it, so the damage it caused was greatly lessened.

Before long, the people of Tiguafaya knew, the eruptions would subside, as they had always done before. Their country would survive.

The singing ended. It was a sound the world had never heard before. And would never hear again.

The silence that replaced it was deeper than anything those involved had ever experienced. The sky's dreaming was over. And only Cat knew the price they had paid for their victory.

# CHAPTER SIXTY

Most people in Teguise were not aware of what had happened until reports began to come back with the returning soldiers and sailors. Although the tales they told were difficult to believe, the consistency of their eye-witness accounts soon convinced most people, while others made pilgrimages to the north or out onto the ocean to see for themselves. Eventually, everyone agreed that Teguise had had a remarkable escape – not only from the forces of nature but also from the imperial army. Residents and refugees celebrated together and, although the joy of the evacuees was tempered by the probability of their having no homes to return to, a new spirit of optimism and fellowship was born in the city.

A few hours after the circle had been completed, Ico had returned to the Presidential Palace with Nino – who was in a state of near collapse after all his efforts – and had seen to it that he was tended to properly. Then a compelling instinct had taken her up onto the roof.

The three dragons approached from the southwest, and

made straight for the centre of the city. Two of them circled above the palace, while the third descended in an elegant spiral, landing only a few paces from where Ico stood. As she watched, the dragon lowered its head almost to the floor.

'Mama!' Ysanne cried, as she slid from the creature's neck and ran towards her mother. 'Mama!'

Ico swept her daughter into her arms, her eyes filling with tears of joy and relief.

'I've been flying!' Ysanne announced triumphantly. 'Way up high!'

Ico was too full of emotion to speak, but she nodded her thanks to the dragon. It bowed its head gravely in acknowledgement, then took off again to join the others. As they flew away to the west, Ysanne waved a small hand in farewell.

It was not until dusk that a single dragon returned to Teguise with another passenger, and by then almost the entire population knew that the creatures had visited the President. Although the second arrival created slightly less of a stir, it meant every bit as much to Ico. She could not tell whether this was the same dragon as before, but it landed in almost exactly the same spot – and once again Ico had been drawn to be there. This time it was Andrin who dismounted and almost fell into her welcoming arms. They held each other for several minutes before speaking, content for the moment to luxuriate in their closeness.

'Don't ever do that to me again,' Ico told him eventually.

'I won't,' he whispered hoarsely. 'I know what it felt like, remember? I'm sorry, my love. I never thought—'

'It's all right now,' she said quickly, reassuring him. She could not bring herself to criticize any of his actions; she was only glad that he was safely home.

'Where's Ysanne?' he asked, suddenly anxious.

'Sleeping. Come and see her.'

'I thought . . .' he began, then shrugged.

'I'm sure she'll tell you all about it when she wakes up,' Ico said, smiling. 'She's missed you terribly. And so have I.'

The next morning Ico woke well before Andrin, and spent a long time simply watching his head on the pillow, her heart full and her mind occupied with little except the pleasures of the moment. Eventually her idyll was ended by Ysanne, and even Andrin's deep sleep was unable to withstand his daughter's determined assault. Their joyful reunion the night before had only been kept reasonably brief by the fact that Ysanne had not been able to keep her eyes open. Now, after a night's rest, she was literally bouncing with energy. Left to himself Andrin would probably have slept for several hours more, but he was soon sitting up in bed, rubbing his eyes and smiling as his daughter regaled him with all the things she thought he ought to know.

Finally, when she had run out of breath, Ysanne looked at her father thoughtfully, her huge brown eyes becoming solemn.

'Where have *you* been, Papa?'

Ico saw a shadow pass over his face. They had spoken only briefly the night before, but Andrin's silence as the blacksmith removed the chains from his ankles had spoken volumes. The scars on his body would heal soon enough; those she saw hidden behind his eyes would take longer. But we have time, she told herself. As much time as we need.

'Oh, I've been to all sorts of places,' Andrin replied, nonchalant for his daughter's sake. 'One day I'll tell you about it.'

'Now! Now!' Ysanne demanded imperiously.

'I'm back now,' he told her laughing. 'That's all that matters.'

'Are you going away again?' the little girl asked, becoming serious again.

'No, little one. Never. Not for as long as that. I promise.'

'Good,' Ysanne said, apparently satisfied. 'Mama cried when you went away.'

Andrin glanced at his wife.

'Well, we'll just have to make sure that doesn't happen again,' he said quietly.

'That's why I went to Elva to ask the dragons to help,' Ysanne explained. 'And they did, didn't they!'

'They certainly did,' Ico agreed. 'Right, young lady, it's time you got dressed.' She would have liked to stay exactly where she was, revelling in the company of her husband and daughter, but there were things she felt she had to do. When she thought she had lost Andrin, Ico had made certain decisions. Now that he was back, she intended to stick by those decisions, and the sooner she got matters under way the better.

'But I haven't told you about my dream yet,' Ysanne protested.

'What dream, sweetheart?'

'We have to go to the west gate. Then we'll see them.'

'Who?'

'I don't know, but we have to go this morning.'

'I'll take her,' Andrin volunteered.

'No, we *all* have to go,' Ysanne insisted. 'That was in the dream.'

She would not be dissuaded and in the end, rather than face hours of her stubborn arguments, Ico agreed. At first, when they reached the gate and climbed to the top of the guard tower, there was nothing to see, but then two people appeared in the distance, walking along the road.

'Does this remind you of something?' Ico said.

Andrin nodded. Almost three years earlier, they had stood at the same place on the wall and watched Vargo and Cat's weary return to the city. Now it was the same pair who were returning, but this time Vargo did not seem to be carrying the weight of the world on his shoulders. If anything, it was Allegra who seemed to grow more reluctant with every step they took towards Teguise.

# CHAPTER SIXTY-ONE

'Do you miss them terribly?' Cat asked.

'Of course.'

Even though Vargo's answer did nothing for her own peace of mind, Allegra was glad he had not lied to her. After their experience within the network, she hated the idea of there being secrets between them. If it was unrealistic to suppose that they could share *everything*, as they had done then, they could at least be completely honest with each other.

During the month since their return to Teguise – when they had been carried by two dragons until they were inside the circle and then, at their own insistence, left to walk the rest of the way – a great deal had changed. However, the one thing that many people still found difficult was the price they'd had to pay for the magic. Cat had known it immediately, and it had become apparent to the rest as time passed. After the last song, all the links had been broken.

'I wish you could have had the chance to say goodbye properly,' she said sadly.

'So do I,' Vargo replied. 'But it was the same for everyone.'

They were sitting on rocks above a beach a few miles

south of Teguise, watching a flock of wading birds wandering about in the shallows. Among them were several curlew sandpipers.

'Is Lao down there?' Cat asked quietly.

'I don't know. You'd think I'd be able to tell even without the link, wouldn't you? But I've no idea.' Vargo's eyes had never left the birds. 'They all look the same.'

The human links had gone into a kind of mourning once they'd realized what had happened, grieving for the loss of their unique partnerships. But as far as anyone could tell, the birds no longer remembered their connections to human partners. Although some of them obviously retained vague and confused feelings about the change, often continuing to visit former haunts, most had simply returned to the wild state, rejoining others of their kind.

'Ero will have migrated south by now, won't he?'

'I expect so. He probably went straight from Pajarito.'

'I miss them too,' Cat said. 'Especially Ero.' For a few glorious hours she had known what it was like to be linked, but that was gone now, and would never be repeated. 'I know I could only talk to him for a little while, but it made me feel closer to him. And you knew him for years.'

To her surprise, Vargo smiled.

'I think I'd recognize *him*,' he said. 'It would be hard for anyone that vain to hide.'

'He *was* beautiful.'

'I've a feeling I'll see him again one day,' Vargo added, 'even if we won't be able to talk. And if not, I'll always be able to remember him the way I last saw him – dancing as if his life depended on it.'

His smile crumpled abruptly then, and he began to cry. Cat held him as the tears ran down his face, glad that he was able to grieve openly for his loss, but sad because she could do nothing to ease his pain.

'I feel so guilty,' she said eventually.

'Don't be stupid,' he responded, wiping his cheeks and looking at her in surprise.

'It's just that I'm the one responsible for you all losing your links. If I hadn't—'

'You *saved* us all!' Vargo cut in. 'Most of us would be *dead* if you hadn't played your part. Teguise would've been destroyed.'

'I know,' she admitted. 'I just wish it could have happened differently. Perhaps there might have been some other way . . .'

'That's what it was all for,' he told her earnestly. 'The purpose of all the magic was fulfilled in the singing. It was why the links had been formed in the first place! It was meant to be, Cat. You must believe that.'

'Do you?' she asked doubtfully.

'Yes,' he stated firmly, and Cat knew that he meant it. 'That's what Soo meant when she told Ico that the sky's dreaming would be "the end of all things". The birds knew it was coming.'

'So why didn't our oracles tell us?' she asked.

'Perhaps they did, and we just weren't listening. Or maybe we wouldn't have had the courage to act if we'd known.'

'The birds were stronger than us?'

'Perhaps. But look at the *positive* things, Cat. We've cured the fireworms, the dragons are back, and the threat of war is over. Don't you think we'd have agreed to give up our links for all that?'

'I suppose so.'

'And speaking personally,' Vargo went on, 'I've gained a lot more than I've lost.'

'Really?'

'I have my music,' he replied. 'And I have you. What more could any sane man want?' He leant forward and kissed her.

'Since when have you been sane?' she asked when they drew apart.

'From the day I first met you.'

'Liar!' she accused, laughing.

'It's true,' he protested. 'I just didn't know it for a while. Now I do.'

Ico looked around the familiar confines of her long-neglected workroom. She had been promising herself some time here and now, on her first day of freedom, she intended to spend an hour or two just pottering. Perhaps she would design some new jewellery, or find replacement stones for those pieces that had once contained dragon's tears and which now held only a residue of pale green dust. Whatever she did, it would be something just for herself, because most of her public responsibilities were over now. A new president had taken office that morning.

Ico had made her decision to resign known in the days following the reuniting of her family, and had not regretted it for a moment. She had had enough of public life, and wanted to concentrate on Andrin and Ysanne, and on a simpler method of earning a living. In due course elections had been held, and the new regime was taking over a country that, while there were still plenty of problems to be solved – especially the repercussions in everyday life of losing the links – was in a much better position than it had been when Ico had become its leader. That was something she could be proud of.

Several things gave her considerable satisfaction. Vargo's explanation of how his faith had converted the fireworms, their newly acquired knowledge spreading instantly to all their kind via the 'mirror', was one of the most important. His assurance that the swarms were now working to mini-mize the effects of the recent eruptions, and towards much greater volcanic stability in the future, was reason enough for optimism. And so was the return of the dragons. Their part in the restoration of her family had been a clear signal of their friendship, and now that they were back – for good, it seemed – it was another sign that Tiguafaya was returning to the way it was meant to be. Whether the creatures really were gods was a question Ico did not think was important, but wherever they were now – and none had been spotted for several days – the mere knowledge of their presence was enough to make her feel secure. At the very least, it meant that the fireworms were unlikely to become tainted again.

The other major advantage Ico had passed on to her successor was the fact that the threat of war was gone, at least for the foreseeable future. It had taken almost a month for the frozen wave to melt enough to allow any ships out of the circle. The thaw had happened slowly – and harmlessly – and eventually the arc had broken up into several separate icebergs. Long before then the first tentative negotiations with the imperial navy had begun. In return for the promise of a peaceful withdrawal when possible, the Tiguafayans had agreed to leave the former invaders to themselves, and had even arranged for supplies to be sent to the stranded enemy vessels. Although a close watch had been kept on their movements, their admiral had been as good as his word, and the local ships had been able to return safely to Teguise harbour – which was full of water again.

Now, at last, the foreigners were all able to go home. In the meantime, Ico had received an envoy, who had braved the difficult journey overland from the Empire. He brought with him a letter from the court at Zepharinn, signed by both the Emperor Madar and the Empress Katerin. In it they revoked the earlier declaration of war, and asked for peace between their countries. The wording of the document was rather strange, including several references to 'messengers of the gods', but its intent was clear. One of Ico's last, and most pleasant, duties as president had been to reply to this letter, agreeing to their proposal. That had been several days ago and now, as she sat at her desk, idly polishing a bracelet, Ico was relieved to know that any further developments would be someone else's responsibility.

She had risen very early the previous day – her last in office – and had gone to the Senate chamber. At that hour it was empty, just as it had been in her dream, and she had sat there for a long time, just thinking of everything that had happened during her presidency. Such solitary contemplation seemed a fitting and symbolic end to her political career.

Another dream had come to her that night, and it stayed clear in her mind even now. Like the others, it had had the feeling of prophecy about it, but it looked much further into the future. In it Ysanne had grown into a beautiful young woman, about the same age as Ico was now. She was a weather mage, working with fireworms, talking to dragons and predicting not only rainfall and wind but also any impending volcanic eruptions. She appeared confident and happy, and Ico had woken feeling the same way herself. She was just thinking about the dream again when, as if on cue, the sounds of a boisterous game spilled into the workroom from the hallway outside.

'Shhh!' Andrin hissed in a stage whisper. 'Mama's trying to work.'

Ysanne giggled, and stifled another scream as her father picked her up and turned her upside down.

Ico smiled and put the bracelet down. It could wait. She went out to join the two people she loved most in the whole world.

That evening, long after Ysanne had been put to bed, Andrin and Ico were strolling in Diano's fragrant garden.

They were holding hands in companionable silence, when Ico noticed a pale shape against the night sky. Looking up, she saw Ayo's unmistakable outline, perched on the edge of the flat roof.

'Look,' she said quietly.

Andrin glanced up – and then, without a word, he left Ico and went inside, climbing up the stairs and out of the trapdoor onto the roof. Ayo turned to look at him, moonlight glinting in his bright eyes. The eagle was one of the last birds to have remained close to their former link, and the situation obviously still confused him. Andrin could only guess at what vague memories remained in the bird's mind, but he knew that the time had come for the break to be made clean.

'I don't know if you can hear me, or understand any of this, Ayo, but you have to go your own way now. I've no right to keep you here.'

Ayo did not move, but seemed to be listening intently.

'Fly south,' Andrin urged. 'To your mate and your fledglings. Our time is over.' That was all he could manage, because the lump in his throat was becoming too big.

Ayo called once then, a harsh cry of the wild, and his great wings lifted him into the air as if the words had somehow granted him release. Andrin watched with a heavy heart for as long as the eagle remained visible, then went down to find consolation in Ico's arms.

Morning found Ayo far to the south, at a place where the mountains flowed down to the sea. He screamed in greeting as he dived towards the emerald waters of the lake, his voice echoing from the serrated cliffs that surrounded it on three sides. But the echoes were the only answer that he was given.

Even as his hopes sank, his mind was distracted by a curious sight. He knew that the coastline had been damaged in places by the tidal wave, but surely it had not been strong enough to have such an effect. Elva was gone!

The small island had simply vanished, as if she had never been. There was no sign of her beneath the foaming waves, no remnants even of the causeway that had once joined her to the shingle beach. Ayo wondered briefly if the Sky had forgiven Elva at last, allowing her to fly free again, but such considerations were meaningless now. The cove was empty.

The momentum of his dive over the lake carried him up and away, until he turned, catching the wind perfectly, and hung in the air, almost motionless. For an instant his ever vigilant yellow eyes were blind – and that was when he heard her answering call. Ara *was* there, after all. She had waited for him. The two white eagles flew to meet each other with a fierce joy in their hearts.

In all, Ayo's life had been a strange journey, but now he had come home at last.

Vargo and Cat had chosen to be married in the derelict hall where the Firebrands had once held their meetings. Ico had tried to persuade them to use a more appropriate location, but they had been adamant and, now that the guests had all gathered there, she had to admit it felt right. The place brought back many memories.

To her delight, she found herself sitting next to Nino, and they had time to talk for a while before the ceremony began. After he had recovered from the singing, Nino had returned to his home in Tinajo. His journey had taken longer than usual, because of the great cliff of frozen lava that now blocked the normal route, and he had had to make a long detour to the south. However, when he finally reached his village and his joyful reunion with Tavia and baby Nino, he had been relieved but not altogether surprised to find that Tinajo's luck had held once again. The lava flows had not come within several miles of the place.

He had happily settled back into his life there, and had only returned to the city to honour his promise to be at Vargo and Cat's wedding. His wife and child had accompanied him on this occasion – much to Ysanne's delight. Since their arrival in the hall, she had spent most of her time playing with the baby.

Relaxing as they waited for the ceremony to begin, Nino and Ico were exchanging details of the work they were doing now.

'It's good to be back to what we do best,' he commented. 'Although there's not much point prospecting for dragon's tears any more.'

'How are you getting on?' Ico asked. She meant without Eya to help him.

'I manage,' Nino replied. 'It's slower without Eya, but there are still plenty of finds to be made if you know where to look.'

'Have you seen him at all?'

'I think so. The first time was when I was on my way home. There was a peregrine circling high above me, but from the way he flew, I think it could have been Eya. We never spoke, of course, but maybe that was his way of saying goodbye. I've seen the same bird since, but never as close.'

The sorrow in his voice was familiar to Ico. She knew that the memory of that wordless farewell must be hard for him to bear. She had known of her own loss earlier than all the others, of course – and Soo's departure had been more final. Since then, Ico had tried to console several ex-Firebrands as best she could.

'You still have your family,' she said.

'I know,' he replied. 'I know how lucky I am. And this is a day for new beginnings, after all.'

And then there was no more time for talking, because the

principals were arriving. Vargo's grooming was – for once in his life – impeccable. His clothes were all new and, instead of the flashes that had once denoted his dual links, he now wore the badge of a full member of the Musicians' Guild. His much-delayed acceptance into their ranks had been a formality once he had proved that his former abilities were intact once more, and his services were already in great demand. He didn't look in the least bit nervous, just carefree and enormously happy. His eyes met Ico's briefly while he was waiting for Allegra to arrive, and in that short, silent exchange they both set aside any lingering regrets about what might have been and sealed their own lasting friendship.

A few moments later, Cat entered the hall. She was wearing a bright yellow gown of striking simplicity and elegance, and Vargo stared at her, stunned by the beauty of his bride. Cat's face was as radiant as her dress, and her eyes were bright with joy and laughter as she walked to her lover's side.

Hours later, when much of the food and wine had been consumed and the musicians had been playing for hours, Cat came to talk to Ico. She was sitting beside Andrin, with Ysanne on her lap. It was already well past the little girl's bedtime, but this was a very special occasion. The new president had graciously offered the great hall of the palace for the wedding feast – and it had turned into quite a party.

'Will you do me a favour?' Allegra asked.

'Of course,' Ico replied. 'Anything.'

'Dance with Vargo.'

Ico hesitated.

'Please,' Cat begged. 'I'm worn out, and he'll probably want to dance for hours yet. He won't ask you himself, but I know how much you meant to him, how much you still do.'

'Not half as much as you do now,' Ico said quietly.

'I know.' Allegra's smile was genuine, and Ico saw that she knew and understood all that had gone before. There was no question now of even any subconscious rivalry between them for Vargo's affections, and this was Cat's way of letting her know.

'Come here, little one,' Andrin said to Ysanne, transferring her to his knee. 'Mama's going to dance.' He glanced up at his wife. 'Go on.'

Ico went.

It was after midnight when Andrin and Ico finally arrived home. Ysanne was already fast asleep in her father's arms as he carried her up to the small bedroom that had been turned into her nursery. However, when Ico came to tuck her in, the little girl woke up and smiled at her mother.

'Cat's pregnant,' she announced sleepily. 'Does that mean she'll have a kitten?'

'No, sweetheart,' Ico replied, smiling back. 'How do you know this?'

'She told me, when you were dancing. It's supposed to be our secret.'

'Then why are you telling me?'

'I think she meant me to really,' Ysanne replied earnestly, and closed her eyes again.

Ico was about to leave her daughter to sleep when she saw a tiny movement out of the corner of her eye. Tas had landed on the windowsill.

'Ysanne?' The little girl opened her eyes again. 'You have to let Tas go now,' Ico told her. 'She's a wild bird, and she needs to be free. It's not fair to keep her as a pet.'

'I'm not making her stay,' Ysanne said defensively. 'I expect she'll go in a little while.'

'All right. As long as you understand.'

Ysanne nodded, and Ico kissed her goodnight before going to join Andrin in her old room. Tas stayed where she was for a few moments, then flew over to join Ysanne on the bed.

*They don't know, do they?* the firecrest asked.

*No,* Ysanne said happily. *Elva said it was to be our secret — and it is!*